THE ANGEL OF TERROR

It all begins with a murder. James Meredith is a very rich man, but he is found guilty of shooting his fiancé's suitor in a crime of passion. Meredith's lawyer, Jack Glover, suspects that the fiancé is the guilty one, and indeed, Jean Briggerland—Meredith's first cousin and bride-to-be—is a true heartless beauty. Jean is after Meredith's fortune, but Glover is one step ahead of her, and finds a new bride for Meredith. Then Meredith, too, is murdered. Now the fortune which Jean thought to inherit belongs to a young newspaper artist named Lydia Beale. Jean and her father are practiced in the art of murder, however, and they are soon making plans for the early death of Lydia. Only the old man named Jaggs, hired by Glover to protect her, stands between her and the beautiful angel of death.

KATE PLUS 10

Kate Westhanger has been raised by her uncle, the Colonel, into a life of crime. For him, there is always the next job, the big payoff, and retirement. Crime is a way of life. For Kate, crimes are a puzzle that need to be solved, with each detail offering its own particular challenge. For Inspector Michael Pretherston, Kate herself is a bit of a puzzle. There is no question but that she's good at what she does. Her latest caper involves a variety of disguises that bring her in contact with two of London's top financiers. Pretherston has no idea what Kate's up to, but he seems to keep running into her, first as personal secretary to Lord Flanborough, and later as a Polish princess. Whatever Kate has planned, it will definitely be the scheme of the century. If only he can figure it out before it's too late.

The Angel of Terror

- - -

Kate Plus 10

Two Novels by
Edgar Wallace

Afterword by Ed Hulse

Stark House Press • Eureka California

ANGEL OF TERROR / KATE PLUS 10

Published by Stark House Press
1315 H Street
Eureka, CA 95501, USA
griffinskye3@sbcglobal.net
www.starkhousepress.com

ANGEL OF TERROR
Originally published in hardback and copyright © by Hodder & Stoughton,
London, 1922, and Small, Maynard & Co., Boston & New York, 1922.

KATE PLUS 10
Originally published in hardback and copyright © by Small, Maynard & Co.,
Boston & New York, 1917, and George Newnes Ltd., London , 1919.

"The Filming of Kate" copyright © 2016 by Ed Hulse

ISBN-13: 978-1-944520-15-1

Book design by Mark Shepard, SHEPGRAPHICS.COM

First Stark House Press Edition: November 2016

FIRST EDITION

The Angel of Terror

By Edgar Wallace

CHAPTER I

Newspaper folk are notoriously "compartmental." Only the faintest echoes of the great news storms reach the reposeful compartment in which the typewriters of the fashion experts tap out their considered verdict on the new pannier skirt.

The leader writer, ignorant of violent commotion elsewhere, may work in the dignified, serene atmosphere of international politics; the literary editor, aloof from mundane reality, finds no other print worth reading than that which relates the protracted sorrows of his heroine, what time the city editor, watch in hand, rolls in frenzy in his chair, whilst dishevelled young men work frantically against time to put into intelligible English a story of crime which will make fashion notes and leaders and maudlin fiction slightly less interesting than the advertisement pages.

In her little room under the skylight, Lydia Beale heard something of the Bulford murder case in very much the same way as she heard something of the League of Nations and the war in Mesopotamia. Art editors, calling in for her drawings, asked her if she had ever done court work, and once she had been summoned hastily to touch up a portrait of James Meredith. She did not remember this incident until, years afterwards, an old colleague reminded her. But if the serenity of the fashion room was not shaken by the story of Bulford's death, there were other cells in the great hive of *The Megaphone* which buzzed continuously day and night.

There was no mystery about the shooting of Felix Bulford. The interest lay in the woman behind the crime—that sad beautiful girl whose reluctant evidence would certainly bring about her fiancé's conviction. Jean Briggerland had been engaged to Meredith, a very rich man approaching middle age. Meredith was jealous of the attention paid to the girl by Felix Bulford, an impecunious young club man, and meeting him near the girl's house, had shot him. Meredith cut a despicable figure both at the inquest and the trial. He had denied the girl's story: swore he was not jealous of Bulford, and did not even know him.

His refutation of his fiancee's evidence was the feature of the trial. The city editor read the first notes of the trial and summoned a reporter.

"Go down to the courts and see if you can get hold of Meredith's lawyer," he said. "Glover is the man you want—he is an American. Rennett, Glover & Simpson have a big American practice in London; it is the first time they have ever appeared in a criminal case I fancy. That ought to make a good story the different methods in criminal procedure in the two countries."

It was a "story" which the reporter was destined to miss. Long before he had reached the courts James Meredith had been sentenced to death—a sentence which was expected to be commuted to one of life imprisonment.

"That's that," said Jack Glover between his teeth, as he came out of court with the eminent King's Counsel who had defended his friend and client, "the little lady wins."

His companion looked sideways at him and smiled.

"Honestly, Glover, do you believe that poor girl could do so dastardly a thing as lie about the man she loves?"

"She loves!" repeated Jack Glover witheringly.

"You Americans are so violent," said the counsel, shaking his head. "Personally I believe that Meredith is a lunatic. I am satisfied that all he told us about the interview he had with the girl was born of a diseased imagination. I was terribly impressed when I saw Jean Briggerland in the box. She—by jove, there is the lady!"

They had reached the entrance of the court. A big car was standing by the curb and one of the attendants was holding open the door for a girl dressed in black. They had a glimpse of a pale sad face of extraordinary beauty, and then she disappeared behind the drawn blinds.

The counsel drew a long sigh.

"Mad!" he said huskily. "He must be mad! If ever I saw a pure soul in a woman's face, it is in hers!"

"You've been in the sun, Sir John—you're getting sentimental," said Jack Glover brutally, and the eminent lawyer choked indignantly.

Jack Glover had a trick of saying rude things to his friends, even when those friends were twenty years his senior, and by every rule of professional etiquette entitled to respectful treatment.

"Really!" said the outraged Sir John. "There are times, Glover, when you are insufferable!"

But by this time Jack Glover was swinging along the Old Bailey, his hands in his pockets, his silk hat on the back of his head.

He found the gray-haired senior member of the firm of Rennett, Glover & Simpson (there had been no Simpson in the firm for ten years) on the point of going home.

Mr. Rennett sat down at the sight of his junior.

"I heard the news by 'phone," he said. "Ellbery says there is no ground for appeal, but I think the recommendation to mercy will save his life—besides it is a *crime passionelle* and they don't hang for homicidal jealousy. I suppose it was the girl's evidence that turned the trick?"

Jack nodded.

"And she looked like an angel just out of the refrigerator," he said despairingly. "Ellbery did his poor best to shake her, but the old fool is half in love with her—I left him raving about her pure soul and her other celestial et ceteras."

Mr. Rennett stroked his beard.

"She's won," he said, but the other turned on him with a snarl.

"Not yet!" he said almost harshly. "She hasn't won till Jimmy Meredith is dead or—"

"Or—?" repeated his partner significantly. "That 'or' won't come off, Jack. He'll get a life sentence for sure. I'd go a long way to help Jimmy; I'd risk my practice and my name."

Jack Glover looked at his partner in astonishment. "I didn't know you were so fond of Jimmy?"

Mr. Rennett got up and began pulling on his gloves. He seemed a little uncomfortable at the sensation he had created.

"His father was my first client," he said apologetically. "That was before your father came over from New York and established the American end of the business."

Jack nodded. He had come from Harvard seven years before to succeed his father and despite his youth he was one of the few Anglo-American lawyers who commanded the respect of the commercial world. It was true that this was the first criminal case in which he had figured.

"And you really would go a long way—Rennett—I mean to help Jim Meredith?"

"All the way," said old Rennett shortly.

Jack Glover began whistling a long, lugubrious tune.

"I'm seeing Jim to-morrow," he said. "By the way, Rennett, did you see that a fellow had been released from prison to a nursing home for a minor operation the other day? There was a question asked in your parliament about it. Is it usual?"

"It can be arranged," said Rennett. "Why?"

"Do you think in a few months' time we could get Jim Meredith into a nursing home for—say an appendix operation?"

"Has he appendicitis?" asked the other in surprise.

"He can fake it," said Jack calmly; "it is the easiest thing in the world to fake."

Rennett looked at the other under his heavy eyebrows. "You're thinking of the 'or'?" he challenged and Jack nodded.

"It can be done—if he's alive," said Rennett after a pause.

"He'll be alive," prophesied his partner; "now the only thing is—where shall I find the girl?"

CHAPTER II

Lydia Beale gathered up the scraps of paper that littered her table, rolled them into a ball and tossed them into the fire.

There was a knock at the door, and she half turned in her chair to meet with a smile her stout landlady, who came in carrying a tray on which stood a large cup of tea and two thick and wholesome slices of bread and jam.

"Finished, Miss Beale?" asked the landlady anxiously.

"For the day, yes," said the girl with a nod, and stood up stretching herself stiffly.

She was slender, a head taller than the dumpy Mrs. Morgan. The dark violet eyes and the delicate spiritual face she owed to her Celtic ancestors; the grace of her movements, no less than the perfect hands that rested on the drawing board, spoke eloquently of breed.

"I'd like to see it, Miss, if I may," said Mrs. Morgan, wiping her hands on her apron in anticipation.

Lydia pulled open a drawer of the table and took out a large sheet of windsor board. She had completed her pencil sketch and Mrs. Morgan gasped appreciatively. It was a picture of a masked man holding a villainous crowd at bay at the point of a pistol.

"That's wonderful, Miss," she said in awe. "I suppose those sort of things happen, too?"

The girl laughed as she put the drawing away.

"They happen in stories which I illustrate, Mrs. Morgan," she said drily. "The real brigands of life come in the shape of lawyers' clerks with writs and summons. It's a relief from those mad fashion plates I draw, anyway. Do you know, Mrs. Morgan, that the sight of a dressmaker's shop window makes me positively ill!"

Mrs. Morgan shook her head sympathetically, and Lydia changed the subject.

"Has anybody been this afternoon?" she asked.

"Only the young man from Spadd & Newton," replied the stout woman with a sigh. "I told 'em you was out but I'm a bad liar."

The girl groaned.

"I wonder if I shall ever get to the end of those debts," she said in despair. "I've enough writs in the drawer to paper the house, Mrs. Morgan."

Three years ago Lydia Beale's father had died and she had lost the best friend and companion that any girl ever had. She knew he was in debt, but had no idea how extensively he was involved. A creditor had seen her the day after the funeral and had made some uncouth reference to the convenience of a death which had automatically cancelled George Beale's obligations. It needed only that to spur the girl to an action which was as foolish as it was generous. She had written to all the people to whom her father owed money and had assumed full responsibility for debts amounting to hundreds of pounds.

It was the Celt in her that drove her to shoulder the burden which she was ill-equipped to carry, but she never regretted her impetuous act.

There were a few creditors who, realizing what had happened, did not bother her, and there were others—

She earned a fairly good salary on the staff of the *Daily Megaphone* which made a feature of fashion, but she would have had to have been the recipient of a cabinet minister's emoluments to have met the demands which flowed in upon her a month after she had accepted her father's obligations.

"Are you going out tonight, Miss?" asked the woman.

Lydia roused herself from her unpleasant thoughts.

"Yes. I'm making some drawings of the dresses in Curfew's new play. I'll be home somewhere around twelve."

Mrs. Morgan was halfway across the room when she turned back.

"One of these days you'll get out of all your troubles, Miss, you see if you don't! I'll bet you'll marry a rich young gentleman."

Lydia, sitting on the edge of the table, laughed.

"You'd lose your money, Mrs. Morgan," she said; "rich young gentlemen only marry poor working girls in the kind of stories I illustrate. If I marry it will probably be a very poor young gentleman who will become an incurable invalid and want nursing. And I shall hate him so much that I can't be happy with him, and pity him so much that I can't run away from him."

Mrs. Morgan sniffed her disagreement.

"There are things that happen—" she began.

"Not to me—not miracles, anyway," said Lydia, still smiling, "and I don't know that I want to get married. I've got to pay all these bills first and by the time they are settled I'll be a gray-haired old lady in a mob cap."

Lydia had finished her tea and was standing somewhat scantily attired in the middle of her bedroom preparing for her theatre engagement, when Mrs. Morgan returned.

"I forgot to tell you, Miss," she said, "there was a gentleman and a lady called."

"A gentleman and a lady? Who were they?"

"I don't know, Miss Beale. I was lying down at the time and the girl answered the door. I gave her strict orders to say that you were out."

"Did they leave any name?"

"No, Miss. They just asked if Miss Beale lived here and could they see her."

"H'm!" said Lydia with a frown. "I wonder what we owe them!"

She dismissed the matter from her mind and thought no more of it until she stopped on her way to the theatre to learn from the office by telephone the number of drawings required.

The chief sub-editor answered her.

"And, by the way," he added, "there was an inquiry for you at the office today—I found a note of it on my desk when I came in tonight. Some old friends of yours who want to see you. Brand told them you were going to do a show at the Erving Theatre tonight, so you'll probably see them."

"Who are they?" she asked puzzled.

She had few friends, old or new.

"I haven't the foggiest idea," was the reply.

At the theatre she saw nobody she knew, though she looked round interestedly, nor was she approached in any of the *entr'actes*.

In the row ahead of her and a little to her right were two people who regarded her curiously as she entered. The man was about fifty, very dark and bald—the skin of his head was almost copper-colored, though he was obviously a European, for the eyes which beamed benevolently upon her through powerful spectacles were blue, but so light a blue that by contrast with the mahogany skin of his clean shaven face, they seemed almost white.

The girl who sat with him was fair, and to Lydia's artistic eye, singularly lovely. Her hair was a mop of fine gold. The color was natural; Lydia was too sophisticated to make any mistake about that. Her features were regular and flawless. The young artist thought she had never seen so perfect a "cupid" mouth in her life. There was something so freshly, fragrantly innocent about the girl that Lydia's heart went out to her, and she could hardly keep her eyes on the stage. The unknown seemed to take almost as much interest in her, for twice Lydia surprised her backward scrutiny. She found herself wondering who she was. The girl was beautifully dressed, and about her neck was a platinum chain that must have hung to her waist—a chain which was broken every few inches by a big emerald.

It required something of an effort of concentration to bring her mind back to the stage and her work. With a book on her knee she sketched the somewhat bizarre costumes which had aroused a mild public interest in the play, and for the moment forgot her entrancing companion. She came through the vestibule at the end of the performance, and drew her worn cloak more closely about her slender shoulders, for the night was raw and a sou'westerly wind blew the big wet snowflakes under the protecting glass awning into the lobby itself. The favored playgoers minced daintily through the slush to their waiting cars, then taxis came into the procession of waiting vehicles, there was a banging of cab doors, a babble of orders to the scurrying attendants until something like order was evolved from the chaos.

"Cab, Miss?"

Lydia shook her head. An omnibus would take her to Fleet Street, but two had passed, packed with passengers, and she was beginning to despair when a particularly handsome taxi pulled up at the curb.

The driver leaned over the shining apron which partially protected him from the weather, and shouted:

"Is Miss Beale there?"

The girl started in surprise, taking a step toward the cab.

"I am Miss Beale," she said.

"Your editor has sent me for you," said the man briskly.

The editor of *The Megaphone* had been guilty of many eccentric acts. He had expressed views on her drawing which she shivered to recall. He had aroused her in the middle of the night to sketch dresses at a fancy dress ball, but never before had he done anything so human as to send a taxi for her. Nevertheless, she would not look at the gift cab too closely, and she stepped into the warm interior.

The windows were veiled with the snow and the sleet which had been falling all the time she had been in the theatre. She saw blurred lights flash past and realized that the taxi was going at a good pace. She rubbed the windows and tried to look out after a while. Then she endeavored to lower one but without success. Suddenly she jumped up and tapped furiously at the window to attract the driver's attention. There was no mistaking the fact that they were crossing a bridge, and it was not necessary to cross a bridge to reach Fleet Street.

If the driver heard he took no notice. The speed of the car increased. She tapped at the window again furiously. She was not afraid, but she was angry. Presently fear came. It was when she tried to open the door and found that it was fastened from the outside that she struck a match to discover that the windows had been screwed tight—the edge of the hole where the screw had gone in was rawly new and the screw's head was bright and shining.

She had no umbrella—she never carried one to the theatre—and nothing more substantial in the shape of a weapon than a fountain pen. She could smash the windows with her foot. She sat back in the seat, and discovered that it was not so easy an operation as she had thought. She hesitated even to make the attempt; and then the panic sense left her and she was her own calm self again. She was not being abducted. These things did not happen in the twentieth century, except in sensational books. She frowned. She had said almost the same thing to somebody that day—to Mrs. Morgan, who had hinted at a romantic marriage. Of course, nothing was wrong. The driver had called her by name. Probably the editor wanted to see her at his home; he lived somewhere in South London she remembered. That would explain everything. And yet her instinct told her that something unusual was happening, that some unpleasant experience was imminent.

She tried to put the thought out of her mind, but it was too vivid, too insistent.

Again she tried the door and then, conscious of a faint reflected glow on the cloth lined roof of the cab, she looked backward through the peephole. She saw two great motor car lamps within a few yards of the cab. A car was following; she glimpsed the outline of it as they ran past a street standard.

They were in one of the roads of the outer suburbs. Looking through the window over the driver's shoulder, she saw trees on one side of the road and a long gray fence. It was whilst she was so looking that the car behind shot suddenly past and ahead, and she saw its tail lights moving away with a pang of hopelessness. Then before she realized what had happened, the big car ahead slowed and swung sideways, blocking the road and the cab came to a jerky stop that flung her against the window. She saw two figures in the dim light of the taxi's head lamps, heard somebody speak and the door was jerked open.

"Will you step out, Miss Beale," said a pleasant voice, and though her legs seemed queerly weak she obliged. The second man was standing by the side of the driver. He wore a long rain coat, the collar of which was turned up to the tip of his nose.

"You may go back to your friends and tell them that Miss Beale is in good hands," he was saying. "You may also burn a candle or two before your favorite saint in thanksgiving that you are alive."

"I don't know what you're talking about," said the driver sulkily. "I'm taking this young lady to her office."

"Since when has the *Daily Megaphone* been published in the ghastly suburbs?" asked the other politely.

He saw the girl and raised his hat.

"Come along, Miss Beale," he said. "I promise you a more comfortable ride—even if I cannot guarantee that the end will be less startling."

CHAPTER III

The man who had opened the door was a short, stoutly built person of middle age. He took the girl's arm gently, and without questioning she accompanied him to the car ahead, the man in the rain coat following. No word was spoken, and Lydia was too bewildered to ask questions until the car was on its way. Then the younger man chuckled.

"Clever, Rennett!" he said. "I tell you those people are superhumanly brilliant!"

"I'm not a great admirer of villainy," said the other gruffly, and the younger man, who was sitting opposite the girl, laughed.

"You must take a detached interest, my dear chap. Personally I admire them. I admit they gave me a fright when I realized that Miss Beale had not called the cab, but that it had been carefully planted for her, but still I can admire them."

"What does it mean?" asked the puzzled girl. "I'm so confused—where are we going now? To the office?"

"I fear you will not get to the office tonight," said the young man calmly, "and it is impossible to explain to you just why you were abducted."

"Abducted?" said the girl incredulously. "Do you mean to say that man—"

"He was carrying you into the country," said the other calmly. "He would probably have travelled all night and have left you stranded in some un-get-at-able place. I don't think he meant any harm—they never take unnecessary risks, and all they wanted was to spirit you away for the night. How they came to know that we had chosen you baffles me," he said. "Can you advance any theory, Rennett?"

"Chosen me?" repeated the startled girl. "Really I feel I'm entitled to some explanation and if you don't mind I would like you to take me back to my office. I have a job to keep," she added grimly.

"Six pounds ten a week, and a few guineas extra for your illustrations," said the man in the rain coat. "Believe me, Miss Beale, you'll never pay off your debts on that salary, not if you live to be a hundred."

She could only gasp.

"You seem to know a great deal about my private affairs," she said when she had recovered her breath.

"A great deal more than you can imagine."

She thought he was an American by his speech—she remembered a Southerner she had met who had that kind of soft voice.

"In the past twelve months you have had thirty-nine judgments recorded against you, and in the previous year, twenty-seven. You are living on exactly thirty shillings a week, and all the rest is going to your father's creditors."

"You're very impertinent!" she said hotly and, as she felt, foolishly.

"I'm very impertinent, really. By the way, my name is Glover—John Glover, of the firm of Rennett, Glover & Simpson. The gentleman at your side is Mr. Charles Rennett, my senior partner. We are a firm of solicitors, but how long we shall remain a firm," he added pointedly, "depends rather upon you."

"Upon me?" said the girl in genuine astonishment. "Well I can't say that I have so much love for lawyers—"

"That I can well understand," murmured Mr. Glover.

"But I certainly do not wish to dissolve your partnership," she went on.

"It is rather more serious than that," said Mr. Rennett, who was sitting by her side. "The fact is, Miss Beale, we are acting in a perfectly illegal manner, and we are going to reveal to you the particulars of an act we contemplate, which, if you pass on the information to the police, will result in our professional ruin. So you see this adventure is infinitely more important to us than at present it is to you. And here we are!" he said, interrupting the girl's question.

The car turned into a narrow drive, and proceeded some distance through an avenue of trees before it pulled up at the pillared porch of a big house.

Bennett helped her to alight and ushered her through the door, which opened almost as they stopped, into a large panelled hall.

"This is the way, let me show you," said the younger man.

He opened a door and she found herself in a big drawing room exquisitely furnished and lit by two silver electroliers suspended from the carved roof.

To her relief an elderly woman rose to greet her.

"This is my wife, Miss Beale," said Rennett. "I need hardly explain that this is also my home."

"So you found the young lady," said the elderly lady, smiling her welcome, "and what does Miss Beale think of your proposition?"

The young man Glover came in at that moment, and divested of his long rain coat and his hat, he proved to be of a type that the universities turn out by the hundred. He was good looking, too, Lydia noticed with feminine inconsequence, and there was something in his eyes that inspired trust. He nodded with a smile to Mrs. Rennett, then turned to the girl.

"Now, Miss Beale, I don't know whether I ought to explain or whether my learned and distinguished friend prefers to save me the trouble."

"Not me," said the elder man hastily. "My dear," he turned to his wife, "I think we'll leave Jack Glover to talk to this young lady."

"Doesn't she know?" asked Mrs. Rennett in surprise, and Lydia could have laughed, although she was feeling far from amused.

The possible loss of her employment, the disquieting adventure of the evening, and now this further mystery all combined to set her nerves on edge.

Glover waited until the door closed on his partner and his wife and seemed inclined to wait a little longer, for he stood with his back to the fire, biting his lips and looking down thoughtfully at the carpet.

"I don't just know how to begin, Miss Beale," he said. "And having seen you, my conscience is beginning to get very very busy! But I might as well start at the beginning. I suppose you have heard of the Bulford murder?"

The girl stared at him.

"The Bulford murder?" she said incredulously, and he nodded.

"Why, of course, everybody has heard of that."

"Then happily it is unnecessary to explain all the circumstances," said Jack Glover, with a little grimace of distaste.

"I only know," interrupted the girl, "that Mr. Bulford was killed by a Mr. Meredith, who was jealous of him, and that Mr. Meredith, when he went into the witness box, behaved disgracefully to his fiancee."

"Exactly," nodded Glover with a twinkle in his eye. "In other words, he repudiated the suggestion that he was jealous, swore that he had already told Miss Briggerland that he could not marry her and he did not even know that Bulford was paying attention to the lady."

"He did that to save his life," said Lydia quietly. "Miss Briggerland swore in the witness box that no such interview had occurred."

Glover nodded.

"What you do not know, Miss Beale," he said gravely, "is that Jean Briggerland was Meredith's cousin, and unless certain things happen, she will inherit the greater part of six hundred thousand pounds from Meredith's estate. Meredith, I might explain, is one of my best friends, and the fact that he is now serving out a life sentence does not make him any less a friend. I am as sure, as I am as sure of your sitting there, that he no more killed Bulford than I did. I believe the whole thing was a plot to secure his death or imprisonment. My partner thinks the same. The truth is that Meredith was engaged to this girl; he discovered certain things about her and her father which are not greatly to their credit. He was never really in love with her, beautiful as she is, and he was trapped into the proposal. When he found out how things were shaping and heard some of the queer stories which were told about Briggerland and his daughter, he broke off the engagement and went that night to tell her so."

The girl had listened in some bewilderment to this recital.

"I don't exactly see what all this has to do with me," she said, and again Jack Glover nodded.

"I can quite understand," he said, "but I will tell you yet another part of the story which is not public property. Meredith's father was an eccentric man who believed in early marriages, and it was a condition of his will that, if Meredith was not married by his thirtieth birthday, the money should go to his sister, her heirs and successors. His sister was Mrs. Briggerland, who is now dead. Her heirs are her husband and Jean Briggerland."

There was a silence. The girl stared thoughtfully into the fire.

"How old is Mr. Meredith?"

"He is thirty next Monday," said Glover quietly, "and it is necessary that he should be married before next Monday."

"In prison?" she asked.

He shook his head.

"If such things are allowed that could have been arranged, but for some reason the Home Secretary refuses to exercise his discretion in this matter, and has resolutely refused to allow such a marriage to take place. He objects on the ground of public policy and I dare say from his point of view he is right. Meredith has a twenty years sentence to serve."

"Then how—" began Lydia.

"Let me tell this story more or less understandably," said Glover with that little smile of his. "Believe me, Miss Beale, I'm not so keen upon the scheme as I was. If by chance," he spoke deliberately, "we could get James Meredith into this house tomorrow morning, would you marry him?"

"Me?" she gasped. "Marry a man I've not seen—a murderer?"

"Not a murderer," he said gently.

"But it is preposterous, impossible!" she protested. "Why me?"

He was silent for a moment.

"When this scheme was mooted we looked round for some one to whom such a marriage would be of advantage," he said, speaking slowly. "It was Rennett's idea that we should search the County Court records of London to discover if there was a girl who was in urgent need of money. There is no surer way of unearthing financial skeletons than by searching County Court records. We found four, only one of whom was eligible, and that was you. Don't interrupt me for a moment, please," he said, raising his hand warningly as she was about to speak. We have made thorough inquiries about you, too thorough in fact, because the Briggerlands have smelt a rat, and have been on our trail for a week. We know that you are not engaged to be married, we know that you have a fairly heavy burden of debts, and we know, too, that you are unencumbered by relations or friends. What we offer you, Miss Beale, and believe me, I feel rather a cad in being the medium through which the offer is made, is five thousand pounds a year for the rest of your life, a sum of twenty thousand pounds down, and the assurance that you will not be troubled by your husband from the moment you are married."

Lydia listened like one in a dream. It did not seem real. She would wake up presently and find Mrs. Morgan with a cup of tea in her hand and a plate of her indigestible cakes. Such things did not happen, she told herself, and yet here was a young man, standing with his back to the fire, explaining, in the most commonplace conversational tone, an offer which belonged strictly to the realm of romance, and not too convincing romance at that.

"You've rather taken my breath away," she said after a while. "All this wants thinking about and if Mr. Meredith is in prison—"

"Mr. Meredith is not in prison," said Glover quietly. "He was released two days ago to go to a nursing home for a slight operation. He escaped from the nursing home last night and at this particular moment is in this house." She could only stare at him open-mouthed, and he went on with the story.

"The Briggerlands know he has escaped; they probably thought he was here, because we have had a police visitation this afternoon, and the interior of the house and grounds have been searched. They know, of course, that Mr. Rennett and I were his legal advisers and we expected them to come. How he escaped their observation is neither here nor there. Now, Miss Beale, what do you say?"

"I don't know what to say," she said, shaking her head helplessly. "I know I'm dreaming, and if I had the moral courage to pinch myself hard, I should wake up. Somehow I don't want to wake, it is so fascinatingly impossible."

He smiled.

"Can I see Mr. Meredith?"

"Not till tomorrow. I might say that we've made every arrangement for your wedding, the license has been secured and at eight o'clock tomorrow morning—marriages before eight or after three are not legal in this country, by the way—a clergyman will attend and the ceremony will be performed."

There was a long silence.

Lydia sat on the edge of the chair, her elbows on her knees, her face in her hands.

Glover looked down at her seriously, pityingly, cursing himself that he was the exponent of his own grotesque scheme. Presently she looked up.

"I think I will," she said a little wearily. "And you were wrong about the number of judgment summonses; there were seventy-five in two years—and I'm so tired of lawyers."

"Thank you," said Jack Glover politely.

CHAPTER IV

All night long she had sat in the little bedroom to which Mrs. Rennett had led her, thinking and thinking and thinking. She could not sleep although she had tried hard, and most of the night she spent pacing up and down from window to door turning over the amazing situation in which she found herself. She had never thought of marriage seriously, and really a marriage such as this presented no terrors and might, had the prelude been a little less exciting, been accepted by her with relief. The prospect of being a wife in name only, even the thought that her husband would be, for the next twenty years, behind prison walls, neither distressed nor horrified her. Somehow she accepted Glover's statement that Meredith was innocent without reservation.

She wondered what Mrs. Morgan would say and what explanation she would give at the office. She was not particularly in love with her work, and it would be no wrench for her to drop it and give herself up to the serious study of art. Five thousand pounds a year! She could live in Italy, study under the best masters, have a car of her own— the possibilities seemed illimitable— and the disadvantages?

She shrugged her shoulders as she answered the question for the twentieth time. What disadvantages were there? She could not marry, but then she did not want to marry. She was not the kind to fall in love, she told herself; she was too independent, too sophisticated, and understood men and their weaknesses only too well.

"The Lord designed me for an old maid," she said to herself.

At seven o'clock in the morning— a gray cheerless morning it was, thought Lydia, looking out of the window— Mrs. Rennett came in with some tea.

"I'm afraid you haven't slept, my dear," she said, with a glance at the bed. "It's very trying for you."

She laid her hand upon the girl's arm and squeezed it gently.

"And it's very trying for all of us," she said, with a whimsical smile. "I expect we shall all get into fearful trouble."

That had occurred to the girl too, remembering the gloomy picture which Glover had painted in the car.

"Won't this be very serious for you, if the authorities find that you have connived at the escape?" she asked.

"Escape, my dear?" Mrs. Rennett's face became a mask. "I have not heard anything of an escape. All that we know is that poor Mr. Meredith, anticipating that the Home Office would allow him to get married, had made arrangements for the marriage at this house. How Mr. Meredith comes here is quite a matter outside our knowledge," said the diplomatic lady, and Lydia laughed in spite of herself.

She spent half an hour making herself presentable for the forthcoming ordeal.

As a church clock struck eight, there came another tap on the door. It was Mrs. Rennett again.

"They are waiting," she said. Her face was a little pale and her lips trembled.

Lydia, however, was calmness itself, as she walked into the drawing room ahead of her hostess.

There were four men, Glover and Rennett she knew. A third man, wearing a clerical collar she guessed was the officiating priest, and all her attention was concentrated upon the fourth. He was a gaunt, unshaven man, his hair cut short, his face and figure wasted, so that the clothes he wore hung on him. Her first feeling was one of revulsion. Her second was an impulse of pity. James Meredith, for she guessed it was he, appeared wretchedly ill. He swung round as she came in and looked at her intently, then walking quickly towards her, he held out his thin hand.

"Miss Beale, isn't it?" he said, "I'm sorry to meet you under such unpleasant circumstances. Glover has explained everything, has he not?"

She nodded.

His deep-set eyes had a magnetic quality that fascinated her.

"You understand the terms? Glover has told you just why this marriage must take place?" he said, lowering his voice. "Believe me, I am deeply grateful to you for falling in with my wishes."

Without preliminary he walked over to where the parson stood.

"We will begin now," he said simply.

The ceremony seemed so unreal to the girl that she did not realize what it portended, not even when a ring (a loosely fitting ring, for Jack Glover had made the wildest guess at the size) was slipped over her finger. She knelt to receive the solemn benediction and then got slowly to her feet and looked at her husband strangely.

"I think I'm going to faint," she said.

It was Jack Glover who caught her and carried her to the sofa. She woke with a confused idea that somebody was trying to hypnotize her, and she opened her eyes to look upon the sombre face of James Meredith.

"Better?" he asked anxiously. "I'm afraid you've had a trying time, and no sleep you said, Mrs. Rennett?"

Mrs. Rennett shook her head.

"Well, you'll sleep tonight better than I shall," he smiled, and then he turned to Rennett, a grave and anxious man, who stood nervously stroking his little beard, watching the bridegroom. "Mr. Rennett," he said, "I must tell you in the presence of witnesses, that I have escaped from a nursing home to which I had been sent by the clemency of the Secretary of State. When I informed you that I had received permission to come to your house this morning to get married, I told you that which was not true."

"I'm sorry to hear that," said Rennett politely. "And of course it is my duty to hand you over to the police, Mr. Meredith."

It was all part of the game. The girl watched the play, knowing that this scene was carefully rehearsed, in order to absolve Rennett and his partner from complicity in the escape.

Rennett had hardly spoken when there was a loud rat-tat at the front door, and Jack Glover hastened into the hall to answer. But it was not the policeman he had expected. It was a girl in a big sable coat, muffled up to her eyes. She pushed past Jack, crossed the hall and walked straight into the drawing room.

Lydia, standing shakily by Mrs. Rennett's side, saw the visitor come in, and then as she unfastened her coat, recognized her with a gasp. It was the beautiful girl she had seen in the stalls of the theatre the night before!

"And what can we do for you?" It was Glover's voice again, bland and bantering.

"I want Meredith," said the girl shortly, and Glover chuckled.

"You have wanted Meredith for a long time, Miss Briggerland," he said, "and you're likely to want. You have arrived just a little too late."

The girl's eyes fell upon the parson.

"Too late," she said slowly; "then he is married?"

She bit her red lips and nodded, then she looked at Lydia and the blue eyes were expressionless.

Meredith had disappeared. Lydia looked round for him in her distress, but he had gone. She wondered if he had gone out to the police, to make his surrender, and she was still wondering when there came the sound of a shot.

It was from the outside of the house, and at the sound Glover ran through the doorway, crossed the hall and flew into the open. It was still snowing and there was no sign of any human being. He raced along a path which ran parallel with the house, turned the corner and dived into a shrubbery. Here the snow had not laid, and he followed the garden path that twisted and turned, through the thick laurel bushes and ended at a roughly built tool house. As he came in sight of the shed he stopped.

A man lay on the ground, his arm extended, his head in a pool of blood, his gray hand clutching a revolver.

Jack uttered an exclamation of horror and ran to the side of the fallen man.

It was James Meredith and he was dead.

CHAPTER V

Jack Glover heard footsteps coming down the path, and turned to meet a man who had detective written largely all over him. Jack turned and looked down again at the body as the man came up.

"Who is this?" asked the officer sharply.

"It is James Meredith," said Jack simply.

"Dead?" said the officer startled. "He has committed suicide!"

Jack did not reply and watched the inspector as he made his brief quick examination of the body. A bullet had entered just below the left temple, and there was a mark of powder near the face.

"A very bad business, Mr. Glover," said the police officer seriously.

"Can you account for this man being here?"

"He came to get married," said Jack listlessly. "I dare say that startles you, but it is the fact. He was married less than ten minutes ago. If you will come up to the house I will explain his presence here."

The detective hesitated, but just then another of his comrades came to the scene, and Jack led the way back to the house through a back door into Rennett's study.

The lawyer was waiting for them and he was alone.

"If I'm not very much mistaken, you're Inspector Colhead of Scotland Yard," said Glover.

"That is my name," nodded the officer. "Between ourselves, Mr. Glover, I don't think I should make any statement which you are not prepared to verify publicly."

Jack noted the significance of the warning with a little smile, and proceeded to tell the story of the wedding.

"I can only tell you," he said in answer to a further inquiry, "that Mr. Meredith came into this house at a quarter to eight this morning, and surrendered himself to my partner. At eight o'clock exactly, as you are well aware, Mr. Rennett telephoned to Scotland Yard to say that Mr. Meredith was here. During the period of his waiting he was married."

"Did a parson happen to be staying here, sir?" asked the police officer sarcastically.

"He happened to be staying here," said Jack calmly, "because I had arranged for him to be here. I knew that if it was humanly possible, Mr. Meredith would come to this house and that his desire was to be married for reasons which my partner will explain."

"Did you help him to escape? That is asking you a leading question," smiled the detective.

Jack shook his head.

"I can answer you with perfect truth that I did not, any more than the Home Secretary helped him when he gave him permission to go to a nursing home."

Soon after the detective returned to the shed and Jack and his partner were left alone.

"Well?" said Rennett, in a shaking voice; "what happened?"

"He's dead," said Jack quietly.

"Suicide?"

Jack looked at him oddly.

"Did Bulford commit suicide?" he asked. "Where is the angel?"

"I left her in the drawing room with Mrs. Rennett and Miss Beale."

"Mrs. Meredith," corrected Jack quietly.

"This complicates matters," said Rennett, "but I think we can get out of our share of the trouble, though it is going to look a little black."

They found the three women in the drawing room. Lydia, looking very white, came to meet them.

"What happened?" she asked, and then she guessed from his face. "He's not dead?" she gasped.

Jack nodded. All the time his eyes were on the other girl. Her beautiful lips were drooped a little. There was a look of pain and sorrow in her eyes that caught his breath.

"Did he shoot himself?" she asked in a low voice.

Jack regarded her coldly.

"The only thing that I am certain about," and Lydia winced at the cruelty in his voice, "is that you did not shoot him, Miss Briggerland."

"How dare you!" flamed Jean Briggerland. The quick flush that came to her cheek was the only other evidence of emotion she betrayed.

"I dare say a lot," said Jack curtly. "You asked me if it is a case of suicide, and I tell you that it is not— it is a case of murder. James Meredith was found with a revolver clutched in his right hand. He was shot through the left temple, and if you'll explain to me how any man, holding a pistol in a normal way, can perform that feat, I will accept your theory of suicide."

There was a dead silence.

"Besides," Jack went on, with a little shrug; "poor Jimmy had no pistol."

Jean Briggerland had dropped her eyes, and stood there with downcast head and compressed lips. Presently she looked up.

"I know how you feel, Mr. Glover," she said gently. "I can well understand, believing such dreadful things about me as you do, that you must hate me."

Her mouth quivered and her voice grew husky with sorrow.

"I loved James Meredith," she said, "and he loved me."

"He loved you well enough to marry somebody else," said Jack Glover, and Lydia was shocked.

"Mr. Glover," she said reproachfully. "Do you think it is right to say these things, with poor Mr. Meredith lying dead?"

He turned slowly toward her and she saw in his humorous eyes a hardness that she had not seen before.

"Miss Briggerland has told us that I hate her," he said in an even voice; "and she spoke nothing but the truth. I hate her perhaps beyond understanding— Mrs. Meredith." He emphasized the words and the girl winced. "And one day, if the Circumstantialists spare me—"

"The Circumstantialists," said Jean Briggerland slowly. "I don't quite understand you."

Jack Glover laughed and it was not a pleasant laugh.

"Perhaps you will," he said shortly. "As to your loving poor Jim— well you know best. I am trying to be polite to you, Miss Briggerland, and not to gloat over the fact that you arrived too late to stop this wedding! And shall I tell you why you arrived too late?" His eyes were hard again. "It was because I had arranged with the vicar of St. Peter's to be here at nine o'clock this morning, well knowing that you and your little army of spies would discover the hour of the wedding and would take care to be here before. And then I secretly sent for an old Oxford friend of mine to be here at eight— he was here last night."

Still she stood regarding him without visible evidence of the anger which Lydia thought would have been justified.

"I had no desire to stop the wedding," said the girl in a low soft voice. "If Jim preferred to be married in this way to somebody who does not know him, and does not love him, as I loved him, I can only accept his choice." She turned to the girl and held out her hand. "I am very sorry that this tragedy has come to you, Mrs. Meredith," she said. "May I wish you a greater happiness than any you have found?"

Lydia was touched by the sincerity, hurt a little by Glover's uncouthness, and could only warmly grip the little hand that was held out to her.

"I'm sorry too," she said, a little unsteadily. "For you more than for— anything else."

The girl lowered her eyes and again her lips quivered, and then without a word she walked out of the room, pulling her sable wrap about her throat.

It was noon before Rennett's car deposited Lydia Meredith at the door of her lodging.

She found Mrs. Morgan in a great state of anxiety, and the stout little woman almost shed tears of joy at the sight of her.

"Oh, Miss, you've no idea how worried I've been," she babbled; "and they've been round here from your newspaper office asking where you are. I thought you had been run over or something, and the *Daily Megaphone* has sent to all the hospitals—"

"I have been run over," said Lydia wearily. "My poor mind has been under the wheels of a dozen motor-buses, and my soul has been in a hundred collisions."

Mrs. Morgan gaped at her. She had no sense of metaphor.

"It's all right, Mrs. Morgan," laughed her lodger over her shoulder as she went up the stairs. "I haven't really you know, only I've had a worrying time— and by the way, my name is Meredith."

Mrs. Morgan collapsed onto a hall chair.

"Meredith, Miss?" she said incredulously. "Why I knew your father—"

"I've been married, that's all," said Lydia grimly. "You told me yesterday that I should be married romantically, but even in the wildest flights of your imagination, Mrs. Morgan, you could never have supposed that I should be married in such a violent, desperate way. I'm going to bed." She paused on the landing and looked down at the dumfounded woman. "If anybody calls for me, I am not at home. Oh, yes, you can tell *The Megaphone* that I came home very late and that I've gone to bed, and I'll call to-morrow to explain."

"But, Miss," stammered the woman, "your husband—"

"My husband is dead," said the girl calmly. She felt a brute, but somehow she could not raise any note of sorrow. "And if that lawyer man comes, will you please tell him that I shall have twenty thousand pounds in the morning," and with that last staggering statement, she went to her room, leaving her landlady speechless.

CHAPTER VI

The police search of the house and grounds at Dulwich Grange, Mr. Rennett's residence, occupied the whole of the morning, and neither Rennett's nor Jack's assistance was invited or offered.

Before luncheon Inspector Colhead came to the study.

"We've had a good look round your place, Mr. Rennett," he said, "and I think we know where the deceased hid himself."

"Indeed?" said Mr. Rennett.

"That hut of yours in the garden is used, I suppose, for a tool house. There are no tools there now, and one of my men discovered that you can pull up the whole of the floor; it works on a hinge and is balanced with counter weights."

Mr. Rennett nodded.

"I believe it was used as a wine cellar by a former tenant of the house," he said coolly. "We have no cellars at the Grange, you know. I do not drink wine, and I've never had occasion to use it."

"That's where he was hidden. We found a blanket and pillows down there and, as you say, it has obviously been a wine cellar, because there is a ventilating shaft leading up into the bushes. We should never have found the trap, but one of my men felt one of the corners of the floor give under his feet."

The two men said nothing.

"Another thing," the detective went on slowly, "is that I'm inclined to agree that Meredith did not commit suicide. We found footmarks, quite fresh, leading round to the back of the hut."

"A big foot or a little foot?" asked Jack quickly.

"It is rather a big foot," said the detective, "and it has rubber heels. We traced it to a gate at the back of your premises, and the gate has been opened recently— probably by Mr. Meredith when he came to the house. It's a queer case, Mr. Rennett."

"What is the pistol?"

"That's new, too," said Colhead. "Belgian make and impossible to trace, I should imagine. You can't keep track of these Belgian weapons. You can buy them in any shop in any town in Ostend or Brussels, and I don't think it is the practice for the sellers to keep any record of the numbers."

"In fact," said Jack quietly, "it is the same kind of pistol that killed Bulford."

Colhead raised his eyebrows.

"So it was, but wasn't it established that that was Mr. Meredith's own weapon?"

Jack shook his head.

"The only thing that was established was that he had seen the body and he picked up the pistol which was lying near the dead man. The shot was fired as he opened the position door of Mr. Briggerland's house. Then he saw the figure on the pavement and picked up the pistol. He was in that position when Miss Briggerland, who testified against him, came out of the house and saw him."

The detective nodded.

"I had nothing to do with the case," he said, "but remember seeing the weapon and it was identical with this. I'll talk to the chief and let you know what he says about the whole affair. You'll have to give evidence at the inquest of course."

When he had gone the two men looked at one another.

"Well, Rennett, do you think we're going to get into hot water, or are we going to perjure our way to safety?"

"There's no need for perjury, not serious perjury," said the other carefully. "By the way, Jack, where was Briggerland the night Bulford was murdered?"

"When Miss Jean Briggerland had recovered from her horror, she went upstairs and aroused her father, who, despite the early hour, was in bed and asleep. When the police came, or rather, when the detective in charge of the case arrived, which must have been some time after the policeman on point duty put in an appearance, Mr. Briggerland was discovered in a picturesque dressing gown and, I presume, no less picturesque pajamas."

"Horrified, too, I suppose," said Rennett drily.

Jack was silent for a long time. Then:

"Rennett," he said, "do you know I am more rattled about this girl than I am about any consequences to ourselves."

"Which girl are you talking about?"

"About Mrs. Meredith. Whilst poor Meredith was alive she was in no particular danger. But do you realize that what were advantages from our point of view, namely the fact that she had no relations in the world, are today a source of considerable peril to this unfortunate lady?"

"I had forgotten that," said Rennett thoughtfully. "What makes matters a little more complicated, is the will which Meredith made this morning before he was married."

Jack whistled.

"Did he make a will?" he said in surprise.

His partner nodded.

"You remember he was here with me for half an hour. Well, he insisted upon writing out a will, and my wife and Bolton, the butler, witnessed it."

"And he has left his money—?"

"To his wife absolutely," replied the other. "The poor old chap was so frantically keen on keeping the money out of the Briggerland exchequer, that he was prepared to intrust the whole of his money to a girl he had not seen."

Jack was serious now.

"And the Briggerlands are her heirs? Do you realize that, Rennett—there's going to be hell!"

Mr. Rennett nodded.

"I thought that, too," he said quietly.

Jack sank down in a seat, his face screwed up into a hideous frown, and the elder man did not interrupt his thoughts. Suddenly Jack's face cleared and he smiled.

"Jaggs!" he said softly.

"Jaggs?" repeated his puzzled partner.

"Jaggs," said Jack nodding, "he's the fellow. We've got to meet strategy with strategy, Rennett, and Jaggs is the boy to do it."

Mr. Rennett looked at him helplessly.

"Could Jaggs get us out of our trouble too?" he asked sarcastically.

"He could even do that," replied Jack.

"Then bring him along, for I have an idea he'll have the time of his life."

CHAPTER VII

Miss Jean Briggerland reached her home in Berkeley Street soon after nine o'clock. She did not ring, but let herself in with a key and went straight to the dining room, where her father sat eating his breakfast, with a newspaper propped up before him.

He was the dark-skinned man whom Lydia had seen at the theatre, and he looked up over his gold-rimmed spectacles as the girl came in.

"You have been out very early," he said.

She did not reply, but slowly divesting herself of her sable coat she threw it onto a chair, took off the toque that graced her shapely head, and flung it after the coat. Then she drew out a chair, and sat down at the table, her chin on her palms, her blue eyes fixed upon her parent.

Nature had so favored her that her face needed no artificial embellishment; the skin was clear and fine of texture, and the cold morning had brought only a faint pink to the beautiful face.

"Well, my dear," Mr. Briggerland looked up and beamed through his, glasses; "so poor Meredith has committed suicide?"

She did not speak, keeping her eyes fixed on him.

"Very sad, very sad," Mr. Briggerland shook his head.

"How did it happen?" she asked quietly.

Mr. Briggerland shrugged his shoulders.

"I suppose at the sight of you he bolted back to his hiding place where— er— he had been located by— er—interested persons during the night, then seeing me by the shed— he committed the rash and fatal act. Somehow I thought he would run back to his dug-out."

"And you were prepared for him?" she said.

He smiled.

"A clear case of suicide, my dear," he said.

"Shot through the left temple, and the pistol was found in his right hand," said the girl.

Mr. Briggerland started.

"Damn it," he said. "Who noticed that?"

"That good looking young lawyer, Glover."

"Did the police notice?"

"I suppose they did when Glover called their attention to the fact," said the girl.

Mr. Briggerland took off his glasses and wiped them.

"It was done in such a hurry— I had to get back through the garden gate to join the police. When I got there, I found they'd been attracted by the shot and had entered the house. Still, nobody would know I was in the garden, and anyway my association with the capture of an escaped convict would not get into the newspapers."

"But a case of suicide would," said the girl. "Though I don't suppose the police will give away the person who informed them that James Meredith would be at Dulwich Grange."

Mr. Briggerland sat back in his chair, his thick lips pursed; and he was not a beautiful sight.

"One can't remember everything," he grumbled.

He rose from his chair, went to the door, and locked it. Then he crossed to a bureau, pulled open a drawer and took out a small revolver. He threw out the cylinder and glanced along the barrel and the chambers to make sure it was not loaded, then clicked it back in position, and standing before a glass, he endeavored, the pistol in his right hand, to bring the muzzle to bear on his left temple. He found this impossible, and signified his annoyance with a grunt. Then he tried the pistol with his thumb on the trigger and his hand clasping the back of the butt. Here he was more successful.

"That's it," he said with satisfaction. "It could have been done that way."

She did not shudder at the dreadful sight, but watched him with the keenest interest, her chin still in the palm of her hand. He might have been explaining a new way of serving a tennis ball, for all the emotion he evoked.

Mr. Briggerland came back to the table, toyed with a piece of toast and buttered it leisurely.

"Everybody is going to Cannes this year," he said, "but I think I shall stick to Monte Carlo. There is a quiet about Monte Carlo which is very restful, especially if one can get a villa on the hill away from the railway. I told Morden yesterday to take the new car across and meet us at Boulogne. He says that the new body is exquisite. There is a microphonic attachment for telephoning to the driver, the electrical heating apparatus is splendid and—"

"Meredith was married."

If she had thrown a bomb at him she could not have produced a more tremendous sensation. He gaped at her and pushed himself back from the table.

"Married?" His voice was a squeak.

She nodded.

"It's a lie," he roared. All his suavity dropped away from him, his face was distorted and puckered with anger and grew a shade darker. "Married, you lying little beast! He couldn't have been married! It was only a few minutes after eight, and the parson didn't come till nine. I'll break your neck if you try to scare me! I've told you about that before—"

He raved on and she listened unmoved.

"He was married at eight o'clock by a man they brought down from Oxford, and who stayed the night in the house," she repeated with great calmness. "There's no sense in lashing yourself into a rage. I've seen the bride and spoken to the clergyman."

From the bullying, raging madman, he became a whimpering, pitiable thing. His chin trembled; the big hands he laid on the table-cloth shook with a fever.

"What are we going to do?" he wailed. "My God, Jean, what are we going to do?"

She rose and went to the sideboard, poured out a stiff dose of brandy from a decanter and brought it across to him without a word. She was used to these tantrums, and to their inevitable ending. She was neither hurt, surprised nor disgusted. This pale, ethereal being was the dominant partner of the combination. Nerves she did not possess; fears she did not know. She had acquired the precise sense of a great surgeon in whom pity was a detached emotion and one which never intruded itself into the operating chamber. She was no more phenomenal than they, save that she did not feel bound by the conventions and laws which govern them as members of an ordered society. It requires no greater nerve to slay than to cure. She had had that matter out with herself, and had settled it to her own satisfaction.

"You will have to put off your trip to Monte Carlo," she said, as he drank the brandy greedily.

"We've lost everything now," he stuttered; "everything."

"This girl has no relations," said the daughter steadily. "Her heirs-at-law are ourselves."

He put down the glass and looked at her, and became almost immediately his old self.

"My dear," he said admiringly, "you are really wonderful. Of course, it was childish of me. Now what do you suggest?"

"Unlock that door," she said in a low voice, "I want to call the maid."

As he walked to the door, she pressed the footbell, and soon after the faded woman who attended her came into the room.

"Hart," she said, "I want you to find my emerald ring, the small one, the little pearl necklet, and the diamond scarf pin. Pack them carefully in a box with cotton wool."

"Yes, madam," said the woman, and went out.

"Now what are you going to do, Jean?" asked her father.

"I am returning them to Mrs. Meredith," said the girl coolly. "They were presents given to me by her husband, and I feel after this tragic ending of my dream that I can no longer bear the sight of them."

"He didn't give you those things, he gave you the chain. Besides, why are you throwing away good money?"

"I know he never gave them to me, and I am not throwing away good money," she said patiently. "Mrs. Meredith will return them, and she will give me an opportunity of throwing a little light upon James Meredith, an opportunity which I very much desire."

Later she went up to her pretty little sitting room on the first floor and wrote a letter.

"*Dear Mrs. Meredith*: I am sending you the few trinkets which James gave to me in happier days. They are all that I have of his, and you, as a woman, will realize that whilst the possession of them brings me many unhappy memories, yet they have been a certain comfort to me. I wish I could dispose of memory as easily as I send these to you (for I feel they are really your property), but more do I wish that I could recall and obliterate the occasion which has made Mr. Glover so bitter an enemy of mine.

"Thinking over the past, I see that I was at fault, but I know that you will sympathize with me when the truth is revealed to you. A young girl, unused to the ways of men, perhaps I attached too much importance to Mr. Glover's attentions and resented them too crudely. In those days I thought it was unpardonable that a man who professed to be poor James' best friend should make love to his fiancee, though I suppose that such things happen and are endured by the modern girl. A man does not readily forgive a woman for making him feel a fool— it is the one unpardonable offense that a girl can commit. Therefore, I do not resent his enmity as much as you might think. Believe me, I feel for you very much in these trying days. Let me say again that I hope your future will be bright."

She blotted the letter, put it in an envelope and addressed it, and taking down a book from one of the well-stocked shelves, drew her chair to the fire and began reading.

Mr. Briggerland came in an hour after, looked over her shoulder at the title, and made a sound of disapproval.

"I can't understand your liking for that kind of book," he said.

The book was one of the two volumes of "Chronicles of Crime," and she looked up with a smile.

"Can't you? It's very easily explained. It is the most encouraging work in my collection. Sit down for a minute."

"A record of vulgar criminals," he growled. "Their infernal last dying speeches, their processions to Tyburn— phaugh!"

She smiled again and looked down at the book. The wide margins were covered with pencilled notes in her writing. "They're a splendid mental exercise," she said. "In every case I have written down how the criminal might have escaped arrest, but they were all so vulgar and so stupid. Really the police of the time deserve no credit for catching them. It is the same with modern criminals."

She went to the shelf and took down two large scrap books, carried them across to the fire and opened one on her knees.

"Vulgar and stupid, every one of them," she repeated, as she turned the leaves rapidly.

"The clever ones get caught at times," said Briggerland gloomily.

"Never," she said, and closed the book with a snap. "In England, in France, in America. and in almost any other civilized country, there are murderers walking about today respected by their fellow citizens. Murderers, of whose crimes the police are ignorant. Look at these." She opened the book again. "Here is the case of Rell, who poisons a troublesome creditor with weed-killer. Everybody in the town knew he bought the weed-killer; everybody knew that he was in debt to this man. What chance had he of escaping? Here's Jewelville— he kills his wife, buries her in the cellar and then calls attention to himself by running away. Here's Mordon, who kills his sister-in-law for the sake of her insurance money, and who also buys the poison in broad daylight and is found with a bottle in his pocket. Such people deserve hanging."

"I wish to heaven you wouldn't talk about hanging," said Briggerland tremulously, "you're inhuman, Jean, by God—"

"I'm an angel," she smiled, "and I have press cuttings to prove it! The *Daily Recorder* had half a column on my appearance in the box at Jim's trial."

He looked over toward the writing table, saw the letter and picked it up.

"So you've written to the lady. Are you sending her the jewels?"

She nodded.

He looked at her quickly.

"You haven't been up to any funny business with them, have you?" he asked suspiciously and she smiled.

"My dear parent," drawled Jean Briggerland, "after my lecture on the stupidity of the average criminal, do you imagine I should do anything so *gauche?*"

CHAPTER VIII

"And now, Mrs. Meredith," said Jack Glover; "what are you going to do?"

He had spent the greater part of the morning with the new heiress, and Lydia had listened, speechless, as he recited a long and meaningless list of securities, of estates, of ground rents, balances and the like, which she had inherited.

"What am I going to do?" she said, shaking her head hopelessly. "I don't know. I haven't the slightest idea, Mr. Glover. It is so bewildering. Do I understand that all this property is mine?"

"Not yet," said Jack with a smile, "but it is so much yours that on the strength of the will we are willing to advance you money to almost any extent. The will has to be proved and probate must be taken, but when these legal formalities are settled, and we have paid the very heavy death duties, you will be entitled to dispose of your fortune as you wish. As a matter of fact," he added, "you could do that now. At any rate, you cannot live here in Brinksome Street, and I have taken the liberty of hiring a furnished flat on your behalf. One of our clients has gone away to the continent and left the flat for me to dispose of. The rent is very low, about twenty guineas a week."

"Twenty guineas a week!" gasped the horrified girl, "why I can't—"
And then she realized that she could.

Twenty guineas a week was nothing to her. This fact, more than anything else, brought her to an understanding of her fortune.

"I suppose I had better move," she said dubiously. "Mrs. Morgan is giving up this house and she asked me whether I had any plans. I think she'd be willing to come as my housekeeper."

"Excellent," nodded Jack. "You'll want a maid as well, and of course, you will have to put up Jaggs for the nights."

"Jaggs?" she said in astonishment.

"Jaggs," repeated Jack solemnly. "You see, Miss—I beg your pardon, Mrs. Meredith, I'm rather concerned about you and I want you to have somebody on whom I can rely sleeping in your flat at night. I dare say you think I am an old woman," he said as he saw her smile, "and that my fears are groundless, but you will agree that your own experience of last week will support the theory that anything may happen in London."

"But really, Mr. Glover, you don't mean that I am in any serious danger—from whom?"

"From a lot of people," he said diplomatically.

"From poor Miss Briggerland?" she challenged, and his eyes narrowed.

"Poor Miss Briggerland," he said softly. "She certainly is poorer than she expected to be."

"Nonsense," scoffed the girl. She was irritated, which was unusual in her. "My dear Mr. Glover, why do you pursue your vendetta against her? Do you think it is playing the game, honestly now? Isn't it a case of wounded vanity on your part?"

He stared at her in astonishment.

"Wounded vanity? Do you mean pique?"

She nodded.

"Why should I be piqued?" he asked slowly.

"You know best," replied Lydia, and then a light dawned on him.

"Have I been making love to Miss Briggerland by any chance?" he asked.

"You know best," she repeated.

"Good Lord!" and then he began to laugh and she thought he would never stop.

"I suppose I made love to her, and she was angry because I dared to commit such an act of treachery to her fiance! Yes, that was it. I made love to her behind poor Jim's back, and she 'ticked me off,' and that's why I'm so annoyed with her?"

"You have a very good memory," said Lydia, with a scornful little smile.

"My memory isn't as good as Miss Briggerland's power of invention," said Jack. "Doesn't it strike you, Mrs. Meredith, that if I had made love to that young lady, I should not be seen here today??

"What do you mean?" she asked.

"I mean," said Jack Glover soberly, "that it would not have been Bulford, but I, who would have been lured from his club by a telephone message and told to wait outside the door in Berkeley Street. It would have been I who would have been shot dead by Miss Briggerland's father from the drawing room window."

The girl looked at him in amazement.

"What a preposterous charge to make!" she said at last indignantly.

"Do you suggest that this girl has connived at a murder?"

"I not only suggest that she connived at it, but I stake my life that she planned it," said Jack carefully.

"But the pistol was found near Mr. Bulford's body," said Lydia almost triumphantly, as she conceived this unanswerable argument.

Jack nodded.

"From Bulford's body to the drawing room window was exactly nine feet. It was possible to pitch the pistol so that it fell near him. Bulford was waiting there by the instructions of Jean Briggerland. We have traced the telephone call that came through to him from the club—it came from the Briggerland's house in Berkeley Street, and the attendant at the club was sure it was a woman's voice. We didn't find that out till after the trial. Poor Meredith was in the hall when the shot was fired. The signal was given when he turned the handle to let himself out. He heard the shot, rushed down the steps and saw the body. Whether he picked up the pistol or not, I do not know. Jean Briggerland swears he had it in his hand, but, of course, Jean Briggerland is a hopeless liar!"

"You can't know what you're saying," said Lydia in a low voice. "It is a dreadful charge to make, dreadful, against a girl whose very face refutes such an accusation."

"Her face is her fortune," snapped Jack, and then penitently, "I'm sorry I'm rude, but somehow the very mention of Jean Briggerland arouses all that is worst in me. Now, you will accept Jaggs, won't you?"

"Who is he?" she asked.

"He is an old army pensioner. A weird bird, as shrewd as the dickens, in spite of his age a pretty powerful old fellow."

"Oh, he's old," she said with some relief.

"He's old, and in some ways, incapacitated. He hasn't the use of his right arm, and he's a bit groggy in one of his ankles as the result of a Boer bullet."

She laughed in spite of herself.

"He doesn't sound a very attractive kind of guardian. He's a perfectly clean old bird, though I confess he doesn't look it, and he won't bother you or your servants. You can give him a room where he can sit, and you can give him a bit of bread and cheese, and a glass of beer, and he'll not bother you."

Lydia was amused now. It was absurd that Jack Glover should imagine she needed a guardian at all, but if he insisted, as he did, it would be better to have somebody as harmless as the unattractive Jaggs.

"What at time will he come?"

"At about ten o'clock every night, and he'll leave you at seven in the morning. Unless you wish, you need never see him," said Jack.

"How did you come to know him?" she asked curiously.

"I know everybody," said the boastful young man; "you mustn't forget that I am a lawyer and have to meet very queer people."

He gathered up his papers and put them into his little bag.

"And now what are your plans for today?" he demanded.

She resented the self-imposed guardianship which he had undertaken, yet she could not forget what she owed him.

By some extraordinary means he had kept her out of the Meredith case and she had not been called as a witness at the inquest. Incidentally, in as mysterious a way, he had managed to whitewash his partner and himself, and although the Law Society were holding an inquiry of their own (this the girl did not know) it seemed likely that he would escape the consequences of an act which was a flagrant breach of the law.

"I am going to Mrs. Cole-Mortimer's to tea," she said.

"Mrs. Cole-Mortimer?" he said quickly. "How do you come to know that lady?"

"Really, Mr. Glover, you are almost impertinent," she smiled in spite of her annoyance. "She came to call on me two or three days after that dreadful morning. She knew Mr. Meredith and was an old friend of the family's."

"As a matter of fact," said Jack icily, "she did not know Meredith, except to say 'how do you do' to him, and she was certainly not a friend of the family. She is, however, a friend of Jean Briggerland."

"Jean Briggerland!" said the exasperated girl. "Can't you forget her? You are like the man in Dickens' books— she's your King Charles' head! Really, for a respectable and a responsible lawyer, you're simply eaten up with prejudices. Of course, she was a friend of Mr. Meredith's. Why, she brought me a photograph of him taken when he was at Eton."

"Supplied by Jean Briggerland," said the unperturbed Jack calmly, "and if she'd brought you a pair of socks he wore when he was a baby I suppose you would have accepted those too."

"Now you are being really abominable," said the girl, "and I've got a lot to do."

He paused at the door.

"Don't forget you can move into Cavendish Mansions tomorrow. I'll send the key round, and the day you move in, Jaggs will turn up for duty bright and smiling. He doesn't talk a great deal—"

"I don't suppose you ever give the poor man a chance," she said cuttingly.

CHAPTER IX

Mrs. Cole-Mortimer was a representative of a numerous class of women who live so close to the border-line which separates good society from society which is not quite as good that the members of either set thought she was in the other. She had a small house where she gave big parties, and nobody quite knew how this widow of an Indian colonel made both ends meet. It was the fact that her menage was an expensive one to maintain. She had a car, she entertained in London in the season, and disappeared from the metropolis when it was the correct thing to disappear, a season of exile which comes between the Goodwood Race Meeting in the south and the Doncaster Race Meeting in the north.

Lydia had been surprised to receive a visit from this elegant lady, and had readily accepted the story of her friendship with James Meredith. Mrs. Cole-Mortimer's invitation she had welcomed. She needed some distraction, something which would smooth out the ravelled threads of life which were now even more tangled than she had ever expected they could be.

Mr. Rennett had handed to her a thousand pounds the day after the wedding, and when she had recovered from the shock of possessing such a large sum, she hired a taxicab and indulged herself in a wild orgy of shopping.

The relief she experienced, when he informed her he was taking charge of her affairs and settling the debts which had worried her for three years, was so great that she felt as though a heavy weight had been lifted from her heart.

It was in one of her new frocks that Lydia, feeling more confident than usual, made her call. She had expected to find a crowd at the house in Hyde Park Crescent, and she was surprised when she was ushered into the drawing room to find only four people present.

Mrs. Cole-Mortimer was a chirpy, pale little woman of forty-something. It would be ungallant to say how much that "something" represented. She came toward Lydia with outstretched hands.

"My dear," she said with extravagant pleasure, "I am glad you were able to come. You know Miss Briggerland and Mr. Briggerland?"

Lydia looked up at the tall figure of the man she had seen in the stalls the night before her wedding and recognized him instantly.

"Mr. Marcus Stepney, I don't think you have met."

Lydia bowed to a smart looking man of thirty, immaculately attired.

He was very handsome, she thought, in a dark way, but he was just a little too "new" to please her. She did not like fashion plate men, and although the most captious of critics could not have found fault with his correct attire, he gave her the impression of being over-dressed.

Lydia had not expected to meet Miss Briggerland and her father, although she had a dim recollection that Mrs. Cole-Mortimer had mentioned her name. Then in a flash she recalled the suspicions of Jack Glover, which she had covered with ridicule. The association made her feel a little uncomfortable, and Jean Briggerland, whose intuition was a little short of uncanny, must have read the doubt in her face.

"Mrs. Meredith expected to see us, didn't she, Margaret?" she said, addressing the twittering hostess. "Surely you told her we were great friends?"

"Of course I did, my dear. Knowing your dear cousin and his dear father, it was not remarkable that I should know the whole of the family," and she smiled wisely from one to the other.

Of course! How absurd she was, thought Lydia. She had almost forgotten, and probably Jack Glover had forgotten too, that the Briggerlands and the Merediths were related.

She found herself talking in a corner of the room with the girl, and fell to studying her face anew. A closer inspection merely consolidated her earlier judgment. She smiled inwardly as she remembered Jack Glover's ridiculous warning. It was like killing a butterfly with a steam hammer, to loose so much vengeance against this frail piece of china.

"And how do you feel now that you're very rich?" asked Jean kindly.

"I haven't realized it yet," smiled Lydia.

Jean nodded.

"I suppose you have yet to settle with the lawyers. Who are they? Oh, yes, of course Mr. Glover was poor Jim's solicitor." She sighed. "I dislike lawyers," she said with a shiver; "they are so heavily paternal! They feel that they and they only are qualified to direct your life and your actions. I suppose it is second nature with them. Then, of course, they make an awful lot of money out of commissions and fees, though I'm sure Jack Glover wouldn't worry about that. He's really a nice boy," she said earnestly, "and I don't think you could have a better friend."

Lydia glowed at the generosity of this girl whom the man had so maligned.

"He has been very good to me," she said, "although, of course, he is a little fussy."

Jean's lips twitched with amusement.

"Has he warned you against me?" she asked solemnly. "Has he told you what a terrible ogre I am?" And then without waiting for a reply: "I sometimes think poor Jack is just a little—well, I wouldn't say mad, but a little queer. His dislikes are so violent. He positively loathes Margaret, though why I have never been able to understand."

"He doesn't hate me," laughed Lydia, and Jean looked at her strangely.

"No, I suppose not," she said. "I can't imagine anybody hating you, Lydia. May I call you by your Christian name?"

"I wish you would," said Lydia warmly.

"I can't imagine anybody hating you," repeated the girl "And of course Jack wouldn't hate you because you're his client— a very rich and attractive client too, my dear." She tapped the girl's cheek and Lydia, for some reason, felt foolish.

But as though unconscious of the embarrassment she had caused, Jean went on.

"I don't really blame him, either. I've a shrewd suspicion that all these warnings against me and against other possible enemies will furnish a very excellent excuse for seeing you every day and acting as personal bodyguard!"

Lydia shook her head.

"That part of it he has relegated already," she said, giving smile for smile. "He has appointed Mr. Jaggs as my bodyguard."

"Mr. Jaggs?" The tone was even, the note of inquiry was not strained.

"He's an old gentleman in whom Mr. Glover is interested, an old army pensioner. Beyond the fact that he hasn't the use of his right arm, and limps with his left leg, and that he likes beer and cheese, he seems an admirable watch dog," said Lydia humorously.

"Jaggs?" repeated the girl. "I wonder where I've heard that name before. Is he a detective?"

"No, I don't think so. But Mr. Glover thinks I ought to have some sort of man sleeping in my new flat and Jaggs was duly engaged."

Soon after this Mr. Marcus Stepney came over and Lydia found him rather uninteresting. Less boring was Briggerland, for he had a fund of stories and experiences to relate, and he had, too, one of those soft soothing voices that are so rare in men.

It was dark when she came out with Mr. and Miss Briggerland, and she felt that the afternoon had not been unprofitably spent.

For she had a clearer conception of the girl's character, and was getting Jack Glover's interest into better perspective. The mercenary part of it made her just a little sick. There was something so mysterious, so ugly in his outlook on life, and there might be not a little self-interest in his care for her.

She stood on the step of the house talking to the girl whilst Mr. Briggerland lit a cigarette with a patent lighter. Hyde Park Crescent was deserted save for a man who stood near the railings which protected the area of Mrs. Cole-Mortimer's house. He was apparently tying his shoe laces.

They went down on the sidewalk and Mr. Briggerland looked for his car.

"I'd like to take you home. My chauffeur promised to be here at four o'clock. These men are most untrustworthy."

From the other end of the Crescent appeared the lights of a car. At first Lydia thought it might be Mr. Briggerland's, and she was going to make her excuses, for she wanted to go home alone. The car was coming too, at a tremendous pace. She watched it as it came furiously toward her and she did not notice that Mr. Briggerland and his daughter had left her standing alone on the sidewalk and had withdrawn a few paces.

Suddenly the car made a swerve, mounted the sidewalk and dashed upon her. It seemed that nothing could save her, and she stood fascinated with horror, waiting for death.

Then an arm gripped her waist, a powerful arm that lifted her from her feet and flung her back against the railings, as the car flashed past, the mudguard missing her by an inch. The machine pulled up with a jerk and the white-faced girl saw Briggerland and Jean running toward her.

"I should never have forgiven myself if anything had happened. I think my chauffeur must be drunk," said Briggerland, in an agitated voice.

She had no words. She could only nod and then she remembered her preserver, and she turned to meet the solemn eyes of a bent old man whose pointed white beard and bristling white eyebrows gave him a hawk-like appearance. His right hand was thrust into his pocket. He was touching his battered hat with the other.

"Beg pardon, Miss," he said raucously, "name of Jaggs! And I have reported for dooty!"

CHAPTER X

Jack Glover listened gravely to the story which the girl told. He had called at her lodgings on the following morning to secure her signature to some documents, and breathlessly and a little shamefacedly, she told him what had happened.

"Of course it was an accident," she insisted; "in fact, Mr. and Miss Briggerland were almost knocked down by the car. But you don't know how thankful I am your Mr. Jaggs was on the spot."

"Where is he now?" asked Jack.

"I don't know," replied the girl. "He just limped away without another word and I did not see him again, though I thought I caught a glimpse of him as I came into this house last night. How did he come to be on the spot?" she asked curiously.

"That is easily explained," replied Jack. "I told the old boy not to let you out of his sight from sundown to sunup."

"Then you think I'm safe during the day," she rallied him.

He nodded.

"I don't know whether to laugh at you or to be very angry," she said, shaking her head reprovingly. "Of course it was an accident!"

"I disagree with you," said Jack. "Did you catch a glimpse of the chauffeur?"

"No," she said in surprise. "I didn't think of looking at him."

He nodded.

"If you had, you would probably have seen an old friend, namely the gentleman who carried you off from the Erving Theatre," he said quietly.

It was difficult for Lydia to analyze her own feelings. She knew that Jack Glover was wrong, monstrously wrong. She was perfectly confident that his fantastic theory had no foundation, and yet she could not get away from his sincerity. Remembering Jean's description of him as "a little queer," she tried to fit that description into her knowledge of him, only to admit to herself that he had been exceptionally normal as far as she was concerned. The suggestion that his object was mercenary, and that he looked upon her as a profitable match for himself, she dismissed without consideration.

"Anyway, I like your Mr. Jaggs," she said.

"Better than you like me, I gather from your tone," smiled Jack. "He's not a bad old boy."

"He is a very strong old boy," she said. "He lifted me as though I were a feather— I don't know now how I escaped. The steering gear went wrong," she explained unnecessarily.

"Dear me," said Jack politely, "and it went right again in time to enable the chauffeur to keep clear of Briggerland and his angel daughter!"

She gave a gesture of despair.

"You're hopeless," she said. "These things happened in the dark ages; men and women do not assassinate one another in the twentieth century."

"Who told you that?" he demanded. "Human nature hasn't changed for two thousand years. The instinct to kill is as strong as ever or wars would be impossible. If any man or woman could commit one cold-blooded murder there is no reason why he or she should not commit a hundred. In England, America and France fifty cold-blooded murders are detected every year. Twice that number are undetected. It does not make the crime more impossible because the criminal is good looking."

"You're hopeless," she said again, and Jack made no further attempt to convince her.

On the Thursday of that week she exchanged her lodgings for a handsome flat in Cavendish Place and Mrs. Morgan had promised to join her a week later, when she had settled up her own business affairs.

Lydia was fortunate enough to get two maids from one of the Agencies, one of whom was to sleep on the premises. The flat was not illimitable and she regretted that she had promised to place a room at the disposal of the aged Mr. Jaggs. If he was awake all night, as she presumed he would be, and slept in the day, he might have been accommodated in the kitchen, and she hinted as much to Jack. To her surprise the lawyer had turned down that idea.

"You don't want your servants to know that you have a watchman."

"What do you imagine they will think he is?" she asked scornfully. "How can I have an old gentleman in the flat without explaining why he is there?"

"Your explanation could be that he did the boots."

"It wouldn't take him all night to do the boots. Of course, I'm too grateful to him to want him to do anything."

Mr. Jaggs reported again for duty that night. He came at half-past nine, a shabby looking old man, and Lydia, who had not yet got used to her new magnificence came out into the hall to meet him.

He was certainly not a prepossessing object, and Lydia discovered that, in addition to his other misfortunes, he had a slight squint.

"I hadn't an opportunity of thanking you the other day, Mr. Jaggs," she said. "I think you saved my life."

"That's all right, Miss," he said in his hoarse voice. "Dooty is dooty!"

She thought he was looking past her till she realized that his curious slanting line of vision was part of his infirmity.

"I'll show you to your room," she said hastily.

She led the way down the corridor, opened the door of a small room which had been prepared for him and switched on the light.

"Too much light for me, Miss," said the old man, shaking his head. "I like to sit in the dark and listen, that's what I like, to sit in the dark and listen."

"But you can't sit in the dark; you'll want to read, won't you?"

"Can't read, Miss," said Jaggs cheerfully. "Can't write either. I don't know that I'm any worse off."

Reluctantly she switched out the light.

"But you won't be able to see your food."

"I can feel for that, Miss," he said with a hoarse chuckle. "Don't you worry about me. I'll just sit here and have a big think."

If she was uncomfortable before, she was really embarrassed now. The very sight of the door behind which old Jaggs sat having his "big think" was an irritation to her. She could not sleep for a long time that night for thinking of him sitting in the darkness, and "listening" as he put it, and had firmly resolved on ending a condition of affairs which was particularly distasteful to her, when she fell asleep.

She woke when the maid brought her tea, to learn that Jaggs had gone.

The maid, too, had her views on the "old gentleman." She hadn't slept all night for the thought of him, she said, though probably this was an exaggeration.

The arrangement must end, thought Lydia, and she called at Jack Glover's office that afternoon to tell him so. Jack listened without comment until she had finished.

"I'm sorry he is worrying you, but you'll get used to him in time, and I should be obliged if you kept him for a month. You would relieve me of a lot of anxiety."

At first she was determined to have her way, but he was so persistent, so pleading, that eventually she surrendered.

Lucy, the new maid, however, was not so easily convinced.

"I don't like it, Miss," she said; "he's just like an old tramp and I'm sure we shall be murdered in our beds."

"How cheerful you are, Lucy," laughed Lydia. "Of course, there is no danger from Mr. Jaggs and he really was very useful to me."

The girl grumbled and assented a little sulkily, and Lydia had a feeling that she was going to lose a good servant. In this she was not mistaken.

Old Jaggs called at half-past nine that night and was admitted by the maid, who stalked in front of him and opened his door.

"There's your room," she snapped, "and I'd rather have your room than your company."

"Would you, Miss?" wheezed Jaggs, and Lydia, attracted by the sound of voices, came to the door and listened with some amusement.

"Lord bless me life, it ain't a bad room either. Put the light out, my dear, I don't like light. I like 'em dark, like them little cells in Holloway prison, where you were took two years ago for robbing your missus."

Lydia's smile left her face. She heard the girl gasp.

"You old liar!" she hissed.

"Lucy Jones you call yourself— you used to be Mary Welch in them days," chuckled old Jaggs.

"I'm not going to be insulted," almost screamed Lucy, though there was a note of fear in her strident voice. "I'm going to leave tonight."

"No, you ain't, my dear," said old Jaggs complacently. "You're going to sleep here tonight, and you're going to leave in the morning. If you try to get out of that door before I let you, you'll be pinched."

"They've got nothing against me," the girl was betrayed into saying.

"False characters, my dear. Pretending to come from the Agency when you didn't. That's another crime. Lord bless your heart, I've got enough against you to put you in jail for a year."

Lydia came forward.

"What is this you're saying about my maid?"

"Good evening, Ma'am."

The old man knuckled his forehead.

"I'm just having an argument with your young lady."

"Do you say she is a thief?"

"Of course she is, Miss," said Jaggs scornfully. "You ask her!"

But Lucy had gone into her room, slammed the door and locked it.

The next morning when Lydia woke, the flat was empty save for herself. But she had hardly finished dressing when there came a knock at the door, and a trim, fresh-looking country girl, with an expansive smile and a look of good cheer that warmed Lydia's heart, appeared.

"You're the lady that wants a maid, ma'am, aren't you?"

"Yes," said Lydia in surprise. "But who sent you?"

"I was telegraphed for yesterday, ma'am, from the Country."

"Come in," said Lydia helplessly.

"Isn't it right?" asked the girl a little disappointedly. "They sent me my fare. I came up by the first train."

"It is quite all right," said Lydia, "only I'm wondering who is running this flat, me or Mr. Jaggs?"

CHAPTER XI

Jean Briggerland had spent a very busy afternoon. There had been a string of callers at the handsome house in Berkeley Street.

Mr. Briggerland was of a philanthropic bent, and had instituted a club in the East End of London which was intended to raise the moral tone of Limehouse, Wapping, Poplar and the adjacent districts. It was started without ostentation with a man named Faire as general manager. Mr. Faire had had in his lifetime several hectic contests with the police, in which he had been invariably the loser. And it was in his role as a reformed character that he undertook the management of this social uplift club.

Well-meaning police officials had warned Mr. Briggerland that Faire had a bad character. Mr. Briggerland listened, was grateful for the warning, but explained that Faire had come under the influence of the new uplift movement, and from henceforward he would be an exemplary citizen. Later, the police had occasion to extend their warning to its founder. The club was being used by known criminal characters; men who had already been in jail and were qualifying for a return visit.

Again Mr. Briggerland pointed to the object of the institution which was to bring bad men into the society of good men and women, and to arouse in them a desire for better things. He quoted a famous text with great effect. But still the police were unconvinced.

It was the practice of Miss Jean Briggerland to receive selected members of the club and to entertain them at tea in Berkeley Street. Her friends thought it was very "sweet" and very "daring" and wondered whether she wasn't afraid of catching some kind of disease peculiar to the East End of London. But Jean did not worry about such things. On this afternoon, after the last of her callers had gone, she went down to the little morning room where such entertainments occurred and found two men, who rose awkwardly as she entered.

The gentle influence of the club had not made them look anything but what they were. "Jailbird" was written all over them.

"I'm very glad you men have come," said Jean sweetly, "Mr. Hoggins—"

"That's me, Miss," said one, with a grin.

"And Mr. Talmot."

The second man showed his teeth.

"I'm always glad to see members of the club," said Jean busy with the teapot; "especially men who have had so bad a time as you have. You have only just come out of prison, haven't you, Mr. Hoggins?" she asked innocently.

Hoggins went red and coughed.

"Yes, Miss," he said huskily, and added inconsequently, "I didn't do it!"

"I'm sure you were innocent," she said with a smile of sympathy, "and really if you were guilty I don't think you men are so much to blame. Look what a bad time you have! What disadvantages you suffer, whilst here in the West End people are wasting money that really ought to go to your wives and children."

"That's right," said Mr. Hoggins.

"There's a girl I know who is tremendously rich," Jean prattled on. "She lives at 84 Cavendish Mansions, just on the top floor, and of course she's very foolish to sleep with her windows open, especially as people could get down from the roof— there is a fire escape there. She always has a lot of jewelry— keeps it under her pillow I think, and there is generally a few hundred pounds scattered about the bedroom. Now that is what I call putting temptation in the way of the weak."

She lifted her blue eyes, saw the glitter in the man's eyes and went on.

"I've told her lots of times that there is danger, but she only laughs. There is an old man who sleeps in the house— quite a feeble old man who has only the use of one arm. Of course, if she cried out, I suppose he would come to her rescue, but then a real burglar wouldn't let her cry out, would he?" she asked.

The two men looked at one another.

"No," breathed one.

"Especially as they could get clean away if they were clever," said Jean, "and it isn't likely that they would leave her in a condition to betray them, is it?"

Mr. Hoggins cleared his throat.

"It's not very likely, Miss," he said.

Jean shrugged her shoulders.

"Women do these things, and then they blame the poor man to whom a thousand pounds would be a fortune, because he comes and takes it. Personally I should not like to live at 84 Cavendish Mansions."

"Eighty-four Cavendish Mansions," murmured Mr. Hoggins absent-mindedly.

His last sentence had been one of ten years penal servitude. His next sentence would be for life. Nobody knew this better than Jean Briggerland as she went on to talk of the club and of the wonderful work which it was doing.

She dismissed her visitors and went back to her sitting room. As she turned to go up the stairway her maid intercepted her.

"Mary is in your room, Miss," she said in a low voice.

Jean frowned but made no reply.

The woman who stood awkwardly in the center of the room awaiting the girl greeted her with an apologetic smile.

"I'm sorry, Miss," she said, "but I lost my job this morning. That old man spotted me. He's a split— a detective."

Jean Briggerland regarded her with an unmoved face save that her beautiful mouth took on the pathetic little droop which had excited the pity of a judge and an army of lawyers.

"When did this happen?" she asked.

"Last night, Miss. He came and I got a bit cheeky to him and he turned on me, the old devil, and told me my real name and that I'd got the job by forging recommendations."

Jean sat down slowly in the padded Venetian chair before her writing table.

"Jaggs?" she asked.

"Yes, Miss."

"And why didn't you come here at once?"

"I thought I might be followed, Miss."

The girl bit her lip and nodded.

"You did quite right," she said, and then after a moment's reflection. "We shall be in Paris next week. You had better go by the night train and wait for us at the flat."

She gave the maid some money and after she had gone, sat for an hour before the fire looking into its red depths.

She rose at last a little stiffly, pulled the heavy silken curtains across the windows and switched on the light and there was a smile on her face that was very beautiful to see. For in that hour came an inspiration.

She sought her father in his study and told him her plan and he blanched and shivered with the very horror of it.

CHAPTER XII

Mr. Briggerland, it seemed, had some other object in life than the regeneration of the criminal classes. He was a sociologist— a loose title which covers a great deal of inquisitive investigation into other people's affairs. Moreover, he had published a book on the subject. His name was on the title page and the book had been reviewed to his credit; though in truth he did no more than suggest the title, the work in question having been carried out by a writer on the subject who, for a consideration, had allowed Mr. Briggerland to adopt the child of his brain.

On a morning when pale yellow sunlight brightened his dining room, Mr. Briggerland put down his newspaper and looked across the table at his daughter. He had a club in the East End of London and his manager had telephoned that morning, sending a somewhat unhappy report.

"Do you remember that man Talmot, my dear?" he asked.

She nodded, and looked up quickly.

"Yes, what about him?"

"He's in a hospital," said Mr. Briggerland. "I fear that he and Hoggins were engaged in some nefarious plan and that in making an attempt to enter— as of course they had no right to enter— a block of flats in Cavendish Place, poor Talmot slipped and fell from the fourth floor window sill, breaking his leg. Hoggins had to carry him to a hospital."

The girl reached for bacon from the hot plate.

"He should have broken his neck," she said calmly. "I suppose now the police are making tender inquiries?"

"No, no," Mr. Briggerland hastened to assure her. "Nobody knows anything about it, not even the— er— fortunate occupant of the flat they were evidently trying to burgle. I only learned of it because the manager of the club, who gets information of this character, thought I would be interested."

"Anyway, I'm glad they didn't succeed," said Jean after a while. "The possibility of their trying rather worried me. The Hoggins type was such a bungler that it was almost certain they would fail."

It was a curious fact that whilst her father made the most guarded references to all their exploits and clothed them with garments of euphemism, his daughter never attempted any such disguise. The psychologist would find in Mr. Briggerland's reticence the embryo of a once dominant rectitude, no trace of which remained in his daughter's moral equipment.

"I have been trying to place this man Jaggs," she went on with a little puzzled frown, "and he completely baffles me. He arrives every night in a taxicab, sometimes from St. Pancras, sometimes from Euston, sometimes from London Bridge station."

"Do you think he is a detective?"

"I don't know," she said thoughtfully. "If he is, he has been imported from the provinces. He is not a Scotland Yard man. He may, of course, be an old police pensioner, and I have been trying to trace him from that source."

"It should not be difficult to find out all about him," said Mr. Briggerland easily. "A man with his afflictions should be pretty well known."

He looked at his watch.

"My appointment at Norwood is at eleven o'clock," he said. He made a little grimace of disgust.

"Would you rather I went?" asked the girl.

Mr. Briggerland would much rather that she had undertaken the disagreeable experience which lay before him, but he dare not confess as much.

"You, my dear? Of course not! I would not allow you to have such an experience. No, no, I don't mind it a bit."

Nevertheless, he tossed down two long glasses of brandy before he left.

His car set him down before the iron gates of a squat and ugly stucco building, surrounded by high walls, and the uniformed attendants, having examined his credentials, admitted him.

He had to wait a little while before a second attendant arrived to conduct him to the medical superintendent, an elderly man who did not seem overwhelmed with joy at the honor Mr. Briggerland was paying him.

"I'm sorry I shan't be able to show you round, Mr. Briggarland," he said. "I have an engagement in town, but my assistant, Dr. Carew, will conduct you over the asylum and give you all the information you require. This, of course, as you know, is a private institution. I should have thought you would get more material for your book in one of the big public asylums. The people who are sent to Norwood, you know, are not the mild cases, and you will see some rather terrible sights. You are prepared for that?"

Mr. Briggerland nodded. He was prepared to the extent of two full noggins of brandy. Moreover, he was well aware that Norwood was the asylum to which the more dangerous of lunatics were transferred.

Dr. Carew proved to be a young and enthusiastic alienist whose heart and soul were in his work.

"I suppose you are prepared to see jumpy things," he said with a smile, as he conducted Mr. Briggerland along a stone-vaulted corridor.

He opened a steel gate, the bars of which were encased with thick layers of rubber, crossed a grassy plot (there were no stone-flagged paths at Norwood) and entered one of the three buildings which constituted the asylum proper.

It was a harrowing, heart breaking, and to some extent, a disappointing experience for Mr. Briggerland. True, his heart did not break, because it was made of infrangible material and his disappointment was counterbalanced by a certain vague relief.

At the end of two hours' inspection they were standing out on the big playing fields, watching the less violent of the patients wandering aimlessly about. Except one, they were unattended by keepers, but in the case of this one man, two stalwart uniformed men walked on either side of him.

"Who is he?" asked Briggerland.

"That is rather a sad case," said the alienist cheerfully. He had pointed out many "sad cases" in the same bright manner. "He's a doctor and a genuine homicide. Luckily they detected him before he did any mischief or he would have been in Broadmoor."

"Aren't you ever afraid of these men escaping?" asked Mr. Briggerland.

"You asked that before," said the doctor in surprise. "No. You see, an insane asylum is not like a prison; to make a good get-away from prison you have to have outside assistance. Nobody wants to help a lunatic escape, otherwise it would be easier than getting out of prison, because we have no patrols in the grounds, the wards can be opened from the outside without a key and the night patrol who visits the wards every half hour has no time for any other observation. Would you like to talk to Dr. Thun?"

Mr. Briggerland hesitated only for a second.

"Yes," he said huskily.

There was nothing in the appearance of the patient to suggest that he was in any way dangerous. A fair, bearded man, with pale blue eyes, he held out his hand impulsively to the visitor, and after a momentary hesitation, Mr. Briggerland took it and found his hand in a grip like a vice. The two attendants exchanged glances with the asylum doctor and strolled off.

"I think you can talk to him without fear," said the doctor in a low voice, not so low, however, that the patient did not hear it, for he laughed.

"Without fear, favor or prejudice, eh? Yes, that was how they swore the officers at my court martial."

"The doctor was the general who was responsible for the losses at Caperetto," explained Dr. Carew. "That was where the Italians lost so heavily."

Thun nodded.

"Of course, I was perfectly innocent," he explained to Briggerland seriously and taking the visitor's arm he strolled across the field, the doctor and the two attendants following at a distance. Mr. Briggerland breathed a little more quickly as he felt the strength of the patient's biceps.

"My conviction," said Dr. Thun seriously, "was due to the fact that women were sitting on the court martial, which is, of course, against all regulations."

"Certainly," murmured Mr. Briggerland.

"Keeping me here," Thun went on, "is part of the plot of the Italian government. Naturally, they do not wish me to get at my enemies, who I have every reason to believe are in London."

Mr. Briggerland drew a long breath.

"They are in London," he said a little hoarsely. "I happen to know where they are."

"Really?" said the other easily, and then a cloud passed over his face and he shook his head.

"They are safe from my vengeance," he said, a little sadly. "As long as they keep me in this place pretending that I am mad, there is no possible chance for me."

The visitor looked round and saw that the three men who were following were out of earshot.

"Suppose I came tomorrow night," he said, lowering his voice, "and helped you to get away? What is your ward?"

"No. 6," said the other in the same tone. His eyes were blazing.

"Do you think you will remember?" asked Briggerland.

Thun nodded.

"You will come tomorrow night—No. 6, the first cubicle on the left," he whispered. "You will not fail me? If I thought you'd fail me—" his eyes lit up again.

"I shall not fail you," said Mr. Briggerland hastily. "When the clock strikes twelve you may expect me."

"You must be Marshal Foch," murmured Thun, and then, with all a madman's cunning, changed the conversation as the doctor and attendants, who had noticed his excitement, drew nearer. "Believe me, Mr. Briggerland," he went on airily, "the strategy of the Allies was at fault until I took up the command of the army—"

Ten minutes later Mr. Briggerland was in his car driving homeward, a little breathless, more than a little terrified at the unpleasant task he had set himself; jubilant, too, at his amazing success.

Jean had said he might have to visit a dozen asylums before he found his opportunity and the right man, and he had succeeded at the first attempt. Yet he shuddered at the picture he conjured— that climb over the high wall (he had already located the ward, for he had followed the general and the attendants and had seen him safely put away), the midnight association with a madman—

He burst in upon Jean with his news.

"At the first attempt, my dear, what do you think of at?" His dark face glowed with almost childish pride, and she looked at him with a half smile.

"I thought you would," she said quietly. "That's the rough work done, at any rate."

"The rough work!" he said indignantly.

She nodded.

"Half the difficulty is going to be to cover up your visit to the asylum, because this man is certain to mention your name, and it will not all be dismissed as the imagination of a madman. Now I think I will make my promised call upon Mrs. Meredith."

CHAPTER XIII

There was one thing which rather puzzled and almost piqued Lydia Meredith, and that was the failure of Jean Briggerland's prophecy to materialize. Jean had said half jestingly that Jack Glover would be a frequent visitor at the flat; in point of fact, he did not come at all. Even when she visited the offices of Rennett, Glover & Simpson, it was Mr. Rennett who attended to her, and Jack was invisible. Mr. Rennett sometimes explained that he was at the courts, for Jack did all the court work, sometimes that he had gone home.

She caught a glimpse of him once as she was driving past the Law Courts in the Strand. He was standing on the pavement talking to a be-wigged counsel, so possibly Mr. Rennett had not stated more than the truth when he said that the young man's time was mostly occupied by the processes of litigation.

She was curious enough to look through the telephone directory to discover where he lived. There were about fifty Glovers, and ten of these were John Glovers, and she was enough of a woman to call up six of the most likely only to discover that her Mr. Glover was not amongst them. She did not know till later that his full name was Bertram John Glover, or she might have found his address without difficulty.

Mrs. Morgan had now arrived, to Lydia's infinite relief, and had taken control of the household affairs. The new maid was as perfect as a new maid could be, and but for the nightly intrusion of the taciturn Jaggs, to whom, for some reason, Mrs. Morgan took a liking, the current of her domestic life ran smoothly.

She was already becoming accustomed to the possession of wealth. The habit of being rich is one of the easiest acquired, and she found herself negotiating for a little house in Curzon Street and a more pretentious establishment in Somerset, with a sang-froid which astonished and frightened her.

The purchase and arrival of her first car, and the engagement of her chauffeur had been a thrilling experience. It was incredible, too, that her new bankers should, without hesitation, deliver to her enormous sums of money at the mere affixing of her signature to an oblong slip of paper.

She had even got over the panic feeling which came to her on her first few visits to the bank. On these earlier occasions she had felt rather like an inexpert forger, who was endeavoring to get money by false pretense, and it was both a relief and a wonder to her, when the nonchalant cashier thrust thick wads of banknotes under the grille, without so much as sending for a policeman.

"It's a lovely flat," said Jean Briggerland looking round the pink drawing room approvingly, "but of course, my dear, this is one that was already furnished for you. I'm dying to see what you will make of your own home when you get one."

She had telephoned that morning to Lydia saying that she was paying a call, asking if it was convenient, and the two girls were alone.

"It is a nice flat, and I shall be sorry to leave it," agreed Lydia. "It is so extraordinarily quiet. I sleep like a top. There is no noise to disturb one, except that there was rather an unpleasant happening the other morning."

"What was that?" asked Jean stirring her tea.

"I don't know really what happened," said Lydia. "I heard an awful groaning very early in the morning and I got up and looked out of the window. There were two men in the courtyard. One, I think, had hurt himself very badly. I never discovered what happened."

"They must have been workmen, I should think," said Jean, "or else they were drunk. Personally, I have never liked taking furnished flats," she went on. "One always breaks things, and there's such a big bill to pay at the end. And then I always lose the keys. One usually has two or three. You should be very careful about that, my dear; they make an enormous charge for lost keys," she prattled on.

"I think the house agent gave me three," said Lydia. She walked to her little secretaire, opened it and pulled out a drawer.

"Yes, three," she said, "there is one here, one I carry and Mrs. Morgan has one."

"Have you seen Jack Glover lately?"

Jean never pursued an inquiry too far, by so much as one syllable.

"No, I haven't seen him," smiled Lydia. "You weren't a good prophet."

"I expect he is busy," said the girl carelessly. "I think I could like Jack awfully—if he hadn't such a passion for ordering people about. How careless of me!" She had tipped over her tea cup and its contents were running across the little tea table. She pulled out her handkerchief quickly and tried to stop the flow.

"Oh, please, please don't spoil your beautiful handkerchief," said Lydia, rising hurriedly; "I will get a duster."

She ran out of the room and was back almost immediately, to find Jean standing with her back to the secretaire examining the ruins of her late handkerchief with a smile.

"Let me put your handkerchief in water, or it will be stained," said Lydia putting out her hand.

"I would rather do it myself," laughed Jean Briggerland and pushed the handkerchief into her bag.

There were many reasons why Lydia should not handle that flimsy piece of cambric and lace, the most important of which was the key which Jean had taken from the secretaire in Lydia's absence, and had rolled inside the tea-stained handkerchief.

A few days later Mr. Bertram John Glover interviewed a high official at Scotland Yard, and the interview was not a particularly satisfactory one to the lawyer. It might have been worse, had not the police commissioner been a friend of Jack's partner.

The official listened patiently whilst the lawyer, with professional skill, marshalled all his facts, attaching to them the suspicions which had matured to convictions.

"I have sat in this chair for twenty-five years," said the head of the C. I. D., "and I have heard stories which beat the best and the worst of detective stories hollow. I have listened to cranks, amateur detectives, crooks, parsons and expert fictionists, but never in my experience have I ever heard anything quite so improbable as your theory. It happens that I have met Briggerland and I've met his daughter too, and a more beautiful girl I don't think it has been my pleasure to meet."

Jack groaned.

"Aren't you feeling well?" asked the chief unpleasantly.

"I'm all right, sir," said Jack, "only I'm so tired of hearing about Jean Briggerland's beauty. It doesn't seem a very good argument to oppose to the facts—"

"Facts!" said the other scornfully. "What facts have you given us?"

"The fact of the Briggerlands' history," said Jack desperately. "Briggerland was broke when he married Miss Meredith under the impression that he would get a fortune with his wife. He has lived by his wits all his life, and until this girl was about fifteen, they were existing in a state of poverty. They lived in a tiny house in Ealing, the rent of which was always in arrears, and then Briggerland became acquainted with a rich Australian of middle age who was crazy about his daughter. The rich Australian died suddenly."

"From an overdose of veronal," said the chief. "It was established at the inquest—I got all the documents out after I received your letter—that he was in the habit of taking veronal. You suggest he was murdered. If he was, for what? He left the girl about six thousand pounds."

"Briggerland thought she was going to get it all," said Jack.

"That is conjecture," interrupted the chief. "Go on."

"Briggerland moved up west," Jack went on, "and when the girl was seventeen she made the acquaintance of a man named Gunnesbury, who went just as mad about her. Gunnesbury was a midland merchant with a wife and family. He was so infatuated with her that he collected all the loose money he could lay his hands on—some twenty-five thousand pounds—and bolted to the continent. The girl was supposed to have gone on ahead, and he was to join her at Calais. He never reached Calais. The theory was that he jumped overboard. His body was found and brought into Dover, but there was none of the money in his possession that he had drawn from the Midland Bank."

"That is a theory, too," said the chief shaking his head. "The identity of the girl was never established. It was known that she was a friend of Gunnesbury's, but there was proof that she was in London on the night of his death. It was a clear case of suicide."

"A year later," Jack went on, "she forced a meeting with Meredith, her cousin. His father had just died—Jim had come back from Central Africa to put things in order. He was not a woman's man, and was a grave, retiring sort of fellow, who had no other interest in life than his shooting. The story of Meredith you know."

"And is that all?" asked the chief politely.

"All the facts I can gather. There must be other cases which are beyond the power of the investigator to unearth."

"And what do you expect me to do?"

Jack smiled.

"I don't expect you to do anything," he said frankly. "You are not exactly supporting my views with enthusiasm."

The chief rose, a signal that the interview was at an end.

"I'd like to help you if you had any real need for help," he said. "But when you come to me and tell me that Miss Briggerland, a girl whose innocence shows in her face, is a heartless criminal and murderess, and a conspirator—why Mr. Glover, what do you expect me to say?"

"I expect you to give adequate protection to Mrs. Meredith," said Jack sharply. "I expect you, sir, to remember that I've warned you that Mrs. Meredith may die one of those accidental deaths in which Mr. and Miss Briggerland specialize. I'm going to put my warning in black and white, and if anything happens to Lydia Meredith, there is going to be serious trouble on the Thames Embankment."

The chief touched a bell and a constable came in. "Show Mr. Glover the way out," he said stiffly.

Jack had calmed down considerably by the time he reached the Thames Embankment and was inclined to be annoyed with himself for losing his temper.

He stopped a newsboy, took a paper from his hand and, hailing a cab, drove to his office.

There was little in the early edition save the sporting news, but on the front page a paragraph arrested his eye.

"DANGEROUS LUNATIC AT LARGE

"The Medical Superintendent at Norwood Asylum reports that Dr. Algernon John Thun, an inmate of the asylum, escaped last night and is believed to be at large in the neighborhood. Search parties have been organized, but no trace of the man has been found. He is known to have homicidal tendencies, a fact which renders his immediate recapture a very urgent necessity."

There followed a description of the wanted man. Jack turned to another part of the paper and dismissed the paragraph from his mind.

His partner, however, was to bring the matter up at lunch. Norwood Asylum was near Dulwich and Mr. Rennett was pardonably concerned.

"The womenfolk at my house are scared to death," he said at lunch. "They won't go out at night and they keep all the doors locked. How did your interview with the commissioner go on?"

"We parted the worst of friends," said Jack, "and, Rennett, the next man who talks to me about Jean Briggerland's beautiful face is going to be killed dead through it, even though I have to take a leaf from her book and employ the grisly Jaggs to do it."

CHAPTER XIV

That night the "grisly Jaggs" was later than usual. Lydia heard him shuffling along the passage and presently the door of his room closed with a click. She was sitting at the piano and had stopped playing at the sound of his knock, and when Mrs. Morgan came in to announce his arrival, she closed the piano and swung round on the music stool, a look of determination on her delicate face.

"He's come, Miss."

"And for the last time," said Lydia ominously. "Mrs. Morgan, I can't stand that weird old gentleman any longer. He has got on my nerves so that I could scream when I think of him."

"He's not a bad old gentleman," excused Mrs. Morgan.

"I'm not so worried about his moral character, and I dare say that it is perfectly blameless," said Lydia determinedly, "but I have written a note to Mr. Glover to tell him that I really must dispense with his services."

"What's he here for, Miss?" asked Mrs. Morgan.

Her curiosity had been aroused, but this was the time she had given it expression.

"He's here because—" Lydia hesitated, "well, because Mr. Glover thinks I ought to have a man in the house to look after me."

"Why, Miss?" asked the startled woman.

"You'd better ask Mr. Glover that question," said Lydia grimly.

She was beginning to chafe under the sense of restraint. She was being "schoolmarmed" she thought. No girl likes the ostentatious protection of the big brother or the headmistress. The soul of the schoolgirl yearns to break from the "crocodile" in which she is marched to church and to school, and this sensation of being marshalled and ordered about, and of living her life according to a third person's programme, and that third person a man, irked her horribly.

Old Jaggs was the outward, visible sign of Jack Glover's unwarranted authority and slowly there was creeping into her mind a suspicion that Jean Briggerland might not have been mistaken when she spoke of Jack's penchant for "ordering people about."

Life was growing bigger for her. She had broken down the barriers which had confined her to a narrow promenade between office and home. The hours which she had had to devote to work were now entirely free and she could sketch or paint whenever the fancy took her—which was not very often, though she promised herself a period of hard work when once she was settled down.

Toward the good looking young lawyer her point of view had shifted. She hardly knew herself how she regarded him. He irritated, and yet in some indefinable way, pleased her. His sincerity—? She did not doubt his sincerity. She admitted to herself that she wished he would call a little more frequently than he did. He might have persuaded her that Jaggs was a necessary evil, but he hadn't even taken the trouble to come. Therefore, but this she did not admit, Jaggs must go.

"I don't think the old gentleman's quite right in his head, you know, sometimes," said Mrs. Morgan.

"Why ever not, Mrs. Morgan?" asked the girl in surprise.

"I often hear him sniggering to himself as I go past his door. I suppose he stays in his room all night, Miss?"

"He doesn't," said the girl emphatically, "and that's why he's going. I heard him in the passage at two o'clock this morning; I'm getting into such a state of nerves that the slightest sound awakens me. He had his boots off and was creeping about in his stockings, and when I went out and switched the light on he bolted back to his room. I can't have that sort of thing going on, and I won't! It's altogether too creepy!"

Mrs. Morgan agreed.

Lydia had not been out in the evening for several days, she remembered as she began to undress for the night. The weather had been unpleasant, and to stay in the warm, comfortable flat was no great hardship. Even if she had gone out, Jaggs would have accompanied her, she thought ironically.

And then she had a little twinge of conscience, remembering that Jaggs' presence on a memorable afternoon had saved her from destruction.

She wondered for the twentieth time what was old Jaggs' history and where Jack had found him. Once she had been tempted to ask Jaggs himself, but the old man had fenced with the question and had talked vaguely of having worked in the country and she was as wise as she had been before.

But she must get rid of old Jaggs, she thought as she switched off the light and kicked out the innumerable water bottles, with which Mrs. Morgan in mistaken kindness, had encumbered the bed—old Jaggs must go—he was a nuisance—

She woke with a start from a dreamless sleep. The clock in the hall was striking three. She realized this subconsciously. Her eyes were fixed on the window which was open at the bottom. Mrs. Morgan had pulled it down at the top, but now it was wide open, and her heart began to thump, thump, rapidly. Jaggs! He was her first thought. She would never have believed that she could have thought of that old man with such a warm glow of thankfulness. There was nothing to be seen. The storm of the early night had passed over and a faint light came into the room from the waning moon. And then she saw the curtains move and opened her mouth to scream, but fear had paralyzed her voice, and she lay staring at the hangings incapable of movement or sound. As she watched the curtain she saw it move again and a shape appeared faintly against the gloomy background.

The spell was broken. She swung herself out of the opposite side of the bed, and raced to the door, but the man was before her. Before she could scream, a big hand gripped her throat and flung her back against the rail of the bed.

Horrified she stared into the cruel face that leered down at her, and felt the grip tighten. And then as she looked into the face she saw a sudden grimace, and sensed the terror in his eyes. The hand relaxed; he bubbled something thickly and fell sideways against the bed. And now she saw. A man had come through the doorway, a tall man with a fair beard and eyes that danced with insane joy.

He came slowly toward her, wiping on his cuff the long-handled knife that had sent her assailant to the floor.

He was mad. She knew it instinctively and remembered in a hazy, confused way, a paragraph she had read about an escaped lunatic. She tried to dash past him to the open door, but he caught her in the crook of his left arm and pressed her to him, towering head and shoulders over her.

"You have no right to sit on a court martial, madam," he said with uncanny politeness, and at that moment the light in the room was switched on and Jaggs appeared in the doorway, his bearded lips parted in an ugly grin, a long barreled pistol in his left hand.

"Drop your knife," he said, "or I'll drop you."

The mad doctor turned his head slowly and frowned at the intruder.

"Good morning, General," he said calmly. "You came in time," and he threw the knife onto the ground. "We will try her according to regulations!"

CHAPTER XV

A TRAGIC AFFAIR IN THE WEST END

Mad Doctor Wounds a Burglar in a Society
Woman's Bedroom

"There was an extraordinary and tragic sequel to the escape of Dr. Thun from Norwood Asylum, particulars of which appeared in our early edition of yesterday. This morning at four o'clock, in answer to a telephone call, Detective Sergeant Miller, accompanied by another officer, went to 84 Cavendish Mansions, a flat occupied by Mrs. Meredith, and there found and took into custody, Dr. Algernon Thun who had escaped from Norwood Asylum. In the room was also found a man named Hoggins, a person well known to the police. It appears that Hoggins had effected an entrance into Mrs. Meredith's flat, descending from the roof by means of a rope, making his way into the premises through the window of Mrs. Meredith's bedroom. Whilst there he was detected by Mrs. Meredith, who would undoubtedly have been murdered, had not Dr. Thun, who, in some mysterious manner, had gained admission to the flat, intervened. In the struggle that followed the doctor, who is suffering from the delusion of persecution, severely wounded the man, who is not expected to live. He then turned his attention to the lady. Happily an old man who works at the flat, who was sleeping on the premises at the time, was roused by the sound of the struggle, and succeeded in releasing the lady from the maniacal grasp of the intruder. The wounded burglar was removed to the hospital and the lunatic was taken to the police station and was afterwards sent under a strong guard to the asylum from whence he had escaped. He made a rambling statement to the police to the effect that General Foch had assisted his escape and had directed him to the home of his persecutors."

Jean Briggerland put down the paper and laughed.

"It is nothing to snigger about," growled Briggerland savagely.

"If I didn't laugh I should do something more emotional," said the girl coolly. "To think that that fool should go back and make the attempt single handed. I never imagined that."

"Faire tells me that he's not expected to live," said Mr. Briggerland. He rubbed his bald head irritably. "I wonder if that lunatic is going to talk?"

"What does it matter if he does?" said the girl impatiently.

"You said the other day—" he began.

"The other day it mattered, my dear father. Today nothing matters very much. I think we have got well out of it. I ignored all the lessons which my text book teaches when I entrusted work to other hands. Jaggs," she said softly.

"Eh?" said the father.

"I'm repeating a well beloved name," she smiled and rose, folding her napkin. "I am going for a long run in the country. Would you like to come? Morden is very enthusiastic about the new car, the bill for which, by the way, came in this morning. Have we any money?"

"A few thousands," said her father, rubbing his chin. "Jean, we shall have to sell something unless things brighten."

Jean's lips twitched, but she said nothing.

On her way to the open road she called at Cavendish Mansions and was neither surprised nor discomfited to discover that Jack Glover was there.

"My dear," she said warmly clasping both the girl's hands in hers, "I was so shocked when I read the news! How terrible it must have been for you."

Lydia was looking pale, and there were dark shadows under her eyes, but she treated the matter cheerfully.

"I've just been trying to explain to Mr. Glover what happened. Unfortunately, the wonderful Jaggs is not here. He knows more about it than I, for I collapsed in the most feminine way."

"How did he get in—I mean this madman?" asked the girl.

"Through the door."

It was Jack who answered.

"It is the last way in the world a lunatic would enter a flat, isn't it? He came in with a key and he was brought here by somebody who struck a match to make sure it was the right number."

"He might have struck the match himself," said Jean, "but you're so clever that you would not say a thing like that unless you had proof."

"We found two matches in the hall outside," said Jack, "and when Dr. Thun was searched no matches were found on him, and I have since learned that, like most homicidal lunatics, he had a horror of fire in any form. The doctor to whom I have been talking is absolutely sure that he would not have struck the match himself. Oh, by the way, Miss Briggerland, your father met this unfortunate man. I understand he paid a visit to the asylum a few days ago?"

"Yes, he did," she answered without hesitation. "He was talking about him this morning. You see, father has been making a tour of the asylums. He is writing a book about such things. Father was horrified when he heard the man had escaped, because the doctor told him that he was a particularly dangerous lunatic. But who would have imagined he would have turned up here."

Her big sad eyes were fixed on Jack as she shook her head in wonder.

"If one had read that in a book one would never have believed it, would one?"

"And the man Hoggins," said Jack, who did not share her wonder. "He was by way of being an acquaintance of yours, a member of your father's club, wasn't he?"

She knit her brows.

"I don't remember the name, but if he is a very bad character," she said with a little smile, "I should say distinctly that he was a member of father's club! Poor daddy, I don't think he will ever regenerate the East End."

"I don't think he will," agreed Jack heartily. "The question is, whether the East End will ever regenerate him."

A slow smile dawned on her face.

"How unkind!" she said, mockery in her eyes now. "I wonder why you dislike him so. He is so very harmless, really. My dear," she turned to the girl with a gesture of helplessness. "I am afraid that even in this affair Mr. Glover is seeing my sinister influence!"

"You're the most un-sinister person I have ever met, Jean," laughed Lydia, "and Mr. Glover doesn't really think all these horrid things."

"Doesn't he?" said Jean softly and Jack saw that she was shaking with laughter.

There was a certain deadly humor in the situation which tickled him too and he grinned.

"I wish to heaven you'd get married and settle down, Miss Briggerland," he said incautiously.

It was her chance. She shook her head, the lips drooped, the eyes again grew moist with the pain she could call to them at will.

"I wish I could," she said in a tone a little above a whisper, "but Jack, I could never marry you, never!"

She left Jack Glover bereft of speech, totally incapable of arousing so much as a moan.

Lydia, returning from escorting her visitor to the door, saw his embarrassment and checked his impulsive explanation a little coldly.

"I—I believed you when you said it wasn't true, Mr. Glover," she said, and there was a reproach in her too for which she hated herself afterwards.

CHAPTER XVI

Lydia had promised to go to the theatre that night with Mrs. Cole-Mortimer, and she was glad of the excuse to leave her tragic home.

Mrs. Cole-Mortimer, who was not lavish in the matter of entertainments that cost money, had a box, and although Lydia had seen the piece before (it was in fact the very play she had attended to sketch dresses on the night of her adventure) it was a relief to sit in silence, which her hostess, with singular discretion, did not attempt to disturb.

It was during the last act that Mrs. Cole-Mortimer gave her an invitation which she accepted joyfully.

"I've got a house at Cap Martin," said Mrs. Cole-Mortimer. "It is only a tiny place, but I think you would rather like it. I hate going to the Riviera alone, so if you care to come as my guest, I shall be most happy to chaperon you. They are bringing my yacht down to Monaco, so we ought to have a really good time."

Lydia accepted the yacht and the house as she had accepted the invitation, without question. That the yacht had been chartered that morning and the house hired by telegram on the previous day, she could not be expected to guess. For all she knew, Mrs. Cole-Mortimer might be a very wealthy woman, and in her wildest dreams she did not imagine that Jean Briggerland had provided the money for both.

It had not been a delicate negotiation, because Mrs. Cole-Mortimer had the skin of a pachyderm.

Years later Lydia discovered that the woman lived on borrowed money, money which never could and never would be repaid and which the borrower had no intention of refunding.

A hint dropped by Jean that there was somebody on the Riviera whom she desired to meet, without her father's knowledge, accompanied by the plain statement that she would pay all expenses, was quite sufficient for Mrs. Cole-Mortimer, and she had fallen in with her patron's views as readily as she had agreed to pose as a friend of Meredith's. To do her justice, she had the faculty of believing in her own invention, and she was quite satisfied that James Meredith had been a great personal friend of hers, just as she would believe that the house on the Riviera and the little steam yacht had been procured out of her own purse.

It was harder for her, however, to explain the great system which she was going to work in Monte Carlo and which was to make everybody's fortune.

Lydia, who was no gambler, and only mildly interested in games of chance, displayed so little evidence of interest in the scheme, that Mrs. Cole-Mortimer groaned her despair, not knowing that she was expected to do no more than to stir the soil for the crop which Jean Briggerland would plant and reap.

They went on to supper at one of the clubs, and Lydia thought with amusement of poor old Jaggs, who apparently took his job very seriously indeed.

Again her angle of vision had shifted, and her respect for the old man had overcome any annoyance his uncouth presence brought to her.

As she alighted at the door of the club she looked round, half expecting to see him. The club entrance was up a side street off Leicester Square, an ill-lit thoroughfare which favored Mr. Jaggs' retiring methods, but there was no sign of him, and she did not wait in the drizzling night to make any closer inspection.

Mrs. Cole-Mortimer had not disguised the possibility of Jean Briggerland being at the club, and they found her with a gay party of young people, sitting in one of the recesses. Jean made a place for the girl by her side and introduced her to half a dozen people whose names Lydia did not catch, and never afterwards remembered.

Mr. Marcus Stepney, however, that sleek, dark man, who bowed over her hand and seemed as though he were going to kiss it, she had met before, and her second impression of him was even less favorable than the first.

"Do you dance?" asked Jean.

A jazz band was playing an infectious two-step. At the girl's nod Jean beckoned one of her party, a tall, handsome boy who throughout the subsequent dance babbled into Lydia's ear an incessant paean in praise of Jean Briggerland.

Lydia was amused.

"Of course she is very beautiful," she said in answer to the interminable repetition of his question. "I think she's lovely."

"That's what I say," said the young man, whom she discovered was Lord Stoker. "The most amazingly beautiful creature on the earth, I think."

"Of course, you're awfully good looking, too," he blundered, and Lydia laughed aloud.

"But she's got enemies," said the young man viciously, "and if I ever meet that infernal cad, Glover, he'll be sorry."

The smile left Lydia's face.

"Mr. Glover is a friend of mine," she said a little quickly.

"Sorry," he mumbled, "but—"

"Does Miss Briggerland say he is so very bad?"

"Of course not. She never says a word against him really." His lordship hastened to exonerate his idol. "She just says she doesn't know how long she's going to stand his persecutions. It breaks one's heart to see how sad this—your friend makes her."

Lydia was a very thoughtful girl for the rest of the evening; she was beginning in a hazy way to see things which she had not seen before. Of course, Jean never said anything against Jack Glover. And yet she had succeeded in arousing this youth to fury against the lawyer, and Lydia realized, with a sense of amazement, that Jean had also made her feel bad about Jack. And yet she had said nothing but sweet things.

When she got back to the flat that night she found that Mr. Jaggs had not been there all the evening. He came in a few minutes after her, wrapped up in an old army coat, and from his appearance she gathered that he had been standing out in the rain and sleet the whole of the evening

"Why Jaggs," she said impulsively, "wherever have you been?"

"Just dodging round, Miss," he grunted. "Having a look at the little ducks in the pond."

"You've been outside the theatre, and you've been waiting outside Niro's Club," she said accusingly.

"Don't know it, Miss," he said. "One theayter is as much like another one to me."

"You must take your things off and let Mrs. Morgan dry your clothes," she insisted, but he would not hear of this, compromising only with stripping his sodden great coat.

He disappeared into his dark room, there to ruminate upon such matters as appeared of interest to him. A bed had been placed for him, but only once had he slept on it.

After the flat grew still and the last click of the switch told that the last light had been extinguished, he opened the door softly, and carrying a chair in his hand, he placed this gently with its back to the front door, and there he sat and dozed throughout the night. When Lydia woke the next morning he was gone as usual.

CHAPTER XVII

Lydia had plenty to occupy her days. The house in Curzon Street had been bought and she had been a round of furnishers, paper hangers and fitters of all varieties.

The trip to the Riviera came at the right moment. She could leave Mrs. Morgan in charge and come back to her new home, which was to be ready in two months.

Amongst other things, the problem of the watchful Mr. Jaggs would be settled automatically.

She spoke to him that night when he came.

"By the way, Mr. Jaggs, I am going to the south of France next week."

"A pretty place by all accounts," volunteered Mr. Jaggs.

"A lovely place— by all accounts," repeated Lydia with a smile. "And you're going to have a holiday, Mr. Jaggs. By the way, what am I to pay you?"

"The gentleman pays me, Miss," said Mr. Jaggs with a sniff. "The lawyer gentleman."

"Well, he must continue paying you whilst I am away," said the girl. "I am very grateful to you and I want to give you a little present before I go. Is there anything you would like, Mr. Jaggs?"

Mr. Jaggs rubbed his beard, scratched his head and thought he would like a pipe.

"Though bless you, Miss, I don't want any present."

"You shall have the best pipe I can buy," said the girl. "It seems very inadequate."

"I'd rather have a briar, Miss," said old Jaggs mistakenly.

He was on duty until the morning she left, and although she rose early he had gone. She was disappointed, for she had not given him the handsome case of pipes she had bought and she wanted to thank him. She felt she had acted rather meanly towards him. She owed her life to him twice.

"Didn't you see him go?" she asked Mrs. Morgan.

"No, Miss," the stout housekeeper shook her head. "I was up at six and he'd gone then, but he'd left his chair in the passage— I've got an idea that's where he slept Miss, if he slept at all."

"Poor old man," said the girl gently. "I haven't been very kind to him, have I? And I do owe him such a lot."

"Maybe he'll turn up again," said Mrs. Morgan, hopefully. She had the mother feeling for the old, which is one of the beauties of her class, and she regretted Lydia's absence probably as much because it would entail the disappearance of old Jaggs as for the loss of her mistress. But old Jaggs did not turn up. Lydia hoped to see him at the station, hovering on the outskirts of the crowd in his furtive way, but she was disappointed.

She left by the eleven o'clock train, joining Mrs. Cole-Mortimer in the station. That lady had arranged to spend a day in Paris, and the girl was not sorry, after a somewhat bad crossing of the English Channel, that she had not to continue her journey through the night.

The south of France was to be a revelation to her. She had no conception of the extraordinary change of climate and vegetation that could be experienced in one country.

She passed from a drizzly, bedraggled Paris into a land of sunshine and gentle breezes; from the bare, sullen lands of the Champagne, into a country where flowers grew by the side of the railway, and that in February; to a semi-tropic land, fragrant with flowers, to white beaches by a blue, lazy sea and a sky over all unflecked by clouds.

It took her breath away, the beauty of it; and the sense and genial warmth of it. The trees laden with lemons, the wisteria on the walls, the white dust on the road, and the glory of the golden mimosa that scented the air with its rare and lovely perfume,

They left the train at Nice and drove along the Grande Corniche. Mrs. Cole-Mortimer had a call to make in Monte Carlo and the girl sat back in the car and drank in the beauty of this delicious spot, whilst her hostess interviewed the house agent.

Surely the place must be kept under glass. It looked so fresh and clean and free from stain.

The Casino disappointed her—it was a place of piaster and stucco, and did not seem built for permanent use.

They drove back part of the way they had come, on to the peninsula of Cap Martin and she had a glimpse of beautiful villas between the pines and queer little roads that led into mysterious dells. Presently the car drew up before a good looking house (even Mrs. Cole-Mortimer was surprised into an expression of her satisfaction at the sight of it.)

Lydia, who thought this was Mrs. Cole-Mortimer's own demesne, was delighted.

"You are lucky to have a beautiful house like this, Mrs. Cole-Mortimer," she said. "It must be heavenly living here."

The habit of wealth had not been so well acquired that she could realize that she also could have a beautiful house if she wished—she thought of that later. Nor did she expect to find Jean Briggerland there, and Mr. Briggerland too, sitting on a big cane chair on the verandah overlooking the sea and smoking a cigar of peace.

Mrs. Cole-Mortimer had been very careful to avoid all mention of Jean on the journey.

"Didn't I tell you they would be here?" she said in careless amazement. "Why, of course, dear. Jean left two days before we did. It makes such a nice little party. Do you play bridge?"

Lydia did not play bridge but was willing to be taught.

She spent the remaining hour of daylight exploring the grounds which led down to the road which fringed the sea.

She could look across at the lights already beginning to twinkle at Monte Carlo, to the white yachts lying off Monaco, and farther along the coast to a little cluster of lights that stood for Beaulieu.

"It is glorious," she said, drawing a long breath.

Mrs. Cole-Mortimer, who had accompanied her in her stroll, purred, the purr of the pleased patron whose protegee has been thankful for favors received.

Dinner was a gay meal, for Jean was in her brightest mood. She had a keen sense of fun and her sly little sallies, sometimes aimed at her father, sometimes at Lydia's expense, but more often directed at people in the social world, whose names were household words, kept Lydia in a constant gurgle of laughter.

Mrs. Cole-Mortimer alone was nervous and ill at ease. She had learned unpleasant news and was not sure whether she should tell the company or keep her secret to herself. In such dilemma, weak people take the most sensational course, and presently she dropped her bombshell.

"Celeste says that the gardener's little boy has malignant small pox," she almost wailed.

Jean was telling a funny story to the girl who sat by her, and did not pause for so much as a second in her narrative. The effect on Mr. Briggerland was, however, wholly satisfactory to Mrs. Cole-Mortimer. He pushed back his chair and blinked at his "hostess."

"Small pox?" he said in horror, "here—in Cap Martin? Good God, did you hear that, Jean?"

"Did I hear what?" she asked lazily, "about the gardener's little boy? Oh yes. There has been quite an epidemic on the Italian Riviera, in fact they closed the frontier last week."

"But— but here!" spluttered Briggerland.

Lydia could only look at him in open-eyed amazement. The big man's terror was pitiably apparent. The copper skin had turned a dirty gray, his lower lip was trembling like a frightened child's.

"Why not here?" said Jean coolly, "there is nothing to be scared about. Have you been vaccinated recently?" she turned to the girl, and Lydia shook her head.

"Not since I was a baby—and then I believe the operation was not a success."

"Anyway, the child is isolated in the cottage and they are taking him to Nice tonight," said Jean, "Poor little fellow! Even his own mother has deserted him. Are you going to the Casino?" she asked.

"I don't know," replied Lydia. "I'm very tired but I should love to go."

"Take her, father—and you go, Margaret. By the time you return the infection will be removed."

"Won't you come too?" asked Lydia.

"No, I'll stay at home tonight. I turned my ankle today and it is rather stiff. Father!"

This time her voice was sharp, menacing almost, thought Lydia, and Mr. Briggerland made an heroic attempt to recover his self-possession.

"Cer—certainly my dear—I shall be delighted—er—delighted."

He saw her alone whilst Lydia was changing in her lovely big dressing room, overlooking the sea.

"Why didn't you tell me there was small pox in Cap Martin?" he demanded fretfully.

"Because I didn't know till Margaret relieved her mind at our expense," said his daughter coolly. "I had to say something. Besides, I'd heard one of the maids say that somebody's mother had deserted him—I fitted it in. What a funk you are, father!"

"I hate the very thought of disease," he growled. "Why aren't you coming with us—there is nothing the matter with your ankle?"

"Because I prefer to stay at home."

He looked at her suspiciously.

"Jean," he said in a milder voice, "hadn't we better let up on the girl for a bit—until that lunatic doctor affair has blown over?"

She reached out and took a gold case from his waistcoat pocket, extracted a cigarette and replaced the case before she spoke.

"We can't afford to 'let up' as you call it, for a single hour. Do you realize that any day her lawyer may persuade her to make a will leaving her money to a—a home for cats, or something equally untouchable? If there was no Jack Glover we could afford to wait months. And I'm less troubled about him than I am about the man Jaggs. Father, you will be glad to learn that I am almost afraid of that freakish old man."

"Neither of them are here—" he began.

"Exactly," said Jean, "neither are here—Lydia had a telegram from him just before dinner asking if he could come to see her next week."

At this moment Lydia returned and Jean Briggerland eyed her critically.

"My dear, you look lovely," she said, and kissed her.

Mr. Briggerland's nose wrinkled, as it always did when his daughter shocked him.

CHAPTER XVIII

Jean Briggerland waited until she heard the sound of the departing car sink to a faint hum, then she went up to her room, opened the bureau and took out a long and tightly fitting dust coat that she wore when she was motoring. She had seen a large bottle of peroxide in Mrs. Cole-Mortimer's room. It probably contributed to the dazzling glories of Mrs. Cole-Mortimer's hair, but it was also a powerful germicide. She soaked a big silk handkerchief in a basin of water, to which she added a generous quantity of the drug, and squeezing the handkerchief nearly dry, she knotted it loosely about her neck. A rubber bathing cap she pulled down over her head, and smiled at her queer reflection in the glass. Then she found a pair of kid gloves and drew them on.

She turned out the light and went softly down the carpeted stairs. The servants were at their dinner, and she opened the front door and crossed the lawn into a belt of trees, beyond which she knew, for she had been in the house two days, was the gardener's cottage.

A dim light burned in one of the two rooms and the Window was un-curtained. She saw the bed and its tiny occupant, but nobody else was in the room. The maid had said that the mother had deserted the little sufferer, but this was not quite true. The doctor had ordered the mother into isolation and had sent a nurse from the infection hospital to take her place. That lady, at the moment, was waiting at the end of the avenue for the ambulance to arrive.

Jean opened the door and stepped in, pulling up the saturated handkerchief until it covered nose and mouth. The place was deserted, and, without a moment's hesitation, she lifted the child, wrapped a blanket about it and crossed the lawn again. She went quietly up the stairs straight to Lydia's room. There was enough light from the dressing room to see the bed, and unwrapping the blanket she pulled back the covers and laid him gently in the bed. The child was unconscious. The hideous marks of the disease had developed with remarkable rapidity and he made no sound.

She sat down in a chair, waiting. Her almost inhuman calm was not ruffled by so much as a second's apprehension. She had provided for every contingency and was ready with a complete explanation, whatever happened.

Half an hour passed, and then rising, she wrapped the child in the blanket and carried him back to the cottage. She heard the purr of the motor and footsteps as she flitted back through the trees.

First she went to Lydia's room and straightened the bed, spraying the room with the faint perfume which she found on the dressing table; then she went back again into the garden, stripped off the dust coat, cap and handkerchief, rolling them into a bundle, which she thrust through the bars of an open window which she knew ventilated a cellar. Last of all she stripped her gloves and sent them after the bundle.

She heard the voices of the nurse and attendant as they carried the child to the ambulance.

"Poor little kid," she murmured, "I hope he gets better." And, strangely enough, she meant it.

It had been a thrilling evening for Lydia, and she returned to the house at Cap Martin very tired, but very happy. She was seeing a new world, a world the like of which had never been revealed to her, and though she could have slept, and her head did nod in the car, she roused herself to talk it all over again with the sympathetic Jean.

Mrs. Cole-Mortimer retired early. Mr. Briggerland had gone up to bed the moment he returned and Lydia would have been glad to have ended her conversation, since her head reeled with weariness, but Jean was very talkative, until—

"My dear, if I don't go to bed I shall sleep on the table," smiled Lydia, rising and suppressing a yawn.

"I'm so sorry," said the penitent Jean.

She accompanied the girl upstairs, her arm about her waist, and left her at the door of her dressing room.

A maid had laid out her night things on a big settee (a little to Lydia's surprise) and she undressed quickly.

She opened the door of her bedroom, her hand was on a switch, when she was conscious of a faint and not unpleasant odor. It was a clean, pungent smell. "Disinfectant" said her brain mechanically. She turned on the light wondering where it came from. And then as she crossed the room she came in sight of her bed and stopped, for it was saturated with water— water that dropped from the hanging coverlet, and made little pools on the floor. From the head of the bed to the foot there was not one dry place. Whosoever had done the work was thorough. Blankets, sheets, pillows were soddened, and from the soaked mass came a faint acrid aroma which she recognized, even before she saw on the floor an empty bottle labelled "Peroxide of Hydrogen."

She could only stand and stare. It was too late to arouse the household and she remembered that there was a very comfortable settee in the dressing room with a rug and a pillow, and she went back.

A few minutes later she was fast asleep. Not so Miss Briggerland, who was sitting up in bed, a cigarette between her lips, a heavy volume on her knees, reading:

"Such malignant cases are almost without exception rapidly fatal, sometimes so early that no sign of the characteristic symptoms appears at all," she read and dropping the book on the floor, extinguished her cigarette on an alabaster tray, and settled herself to sleep. She was dozing when she remembered that she had forgotten to say her prayers.

"Oh damn!" said Jean, getting out reluctantly to kneel on the cold floor by the side of the bed.

CHAPTER XIX

Her maid woke Jean Briggerland at eight o'clock the next morning.

"Oh, Miss," she said, as she drew up the table for the chocolate, "have you heard about Mrs. Meredith?"

Jean blinked open her eyes, slipped into her dressing jacket and sat up with a yawn.

"Have I heard about Mrs. Meredith? Many times," she said.

"But what somebody did last night, Miss."

Jean was wide awake now.

"What has happened to Mrs. Meredith?" she asked. "Why, Miss, somebody played a practical joke on her. Her bed's sopping."

"Sopping?" frowned the girl.

"Yes, Miss," the woman nodded. "They must have poured buckets of water over it, and used up all Mrs. Cole-Mortimer's peroxide, what she uses for keeping her hands nice."

Jean swung out of her bed and sat looking down at her tiny white feet.

"Where did Mrs. Meredith sleep? Why didn't she wake us up?"

"She slept in the dressing room, Miss. I don't suppose the young lady liked making a fuss."

"Who did it?"

"I don't know who did it. It's a silly kind of practical joke, and I know none of the maids would have dared, not the French ones."

Jean put her feet into her slippers, exchanged her jacket for a gown, and went on a tour of inspection.

Lydia was dressing in her room, and the sound of her fresh young voice, as she carolled out of sheer love of life, came to the girl before she turned into the room.

One glance at the bed was sufficient. It was still wet and the empty peroxide bottle told its own story.

Jean glanced at it thoughtfully as she crossed into the dressing room.

"Whatever happened last night, Lydia?"

Lydia turned at the voice.

"Oh, the bed you mean," she made a little face. "Heaven knows. It occurred to me this morning that some person, out of mistaken kindness, had started to disinfect the room— it was only this morning that I recalled the little boy who was ill— and had overdone it."

"They've certainly overdone it," said Jean grimly. "I wonder what poor Mrs. Cole-Mortimer will say. You haven't the slightest idea—"

"Not the slightest idea," said Lydia, answering the unspoken question.

"I'll see Mrs. Cole-Mortimer and get her to change your bed— there's another room you could have," suggested Jean.

She went back to her own apartment, bathed and dressed leisurely.

She found her father in the garden reading the *Nicoise*, under the shade of a bush, for the sun was not warm, but at that hour, blinding.

"I've changed my plans," she said without preliminary.

He looked up over his glasses.

"I didn't know you had any," he said with heavy humor.

"I intended going back to London and taking you with me," she said unexpectedly.

"Back to London?" he said incredulously. "I thought you were staying on for a month."

"I probably shall now," she said, pulling up a basket chair and sitting by his side. "Give me a cigarette."

"You're smoking a lot lately," he said as he handed his case to her.

"I know I am."

"Have your nerves gone wrong?"

She looked at him out of the corner of her eye and her lips curled.

"It wouldn't be remarkable if I inherited a little of your yellow streak," she said coolly, and he growled something under his breath. "No, my nerves are all right, but a cigarette helps me to think."

"A yellow streak, have I?" Mr. Briggerland was annoyed, "And I've been out since five o'clock this morning—" he stopped.

"Doing— what?" she asked curiously.

"Never mind," he said, with a lofty gesture.

Thus they sat, busy with their own thoughts, for a quarter of an hour.

"Jean."

"Yes," she said without turning her head.

"Don't you think we'd better give this up and get back to London? Lord Stoker is pretty keen on you."

"I'm not pretty keen on him," she said decidedly. "He has his regimental pay and £500 a year, two estates, mortgaged, no brains and a title— what is the use of his title to me? As much use as a coat of paint! Beside which, I am essentially democratic."

He chuckled, and there was another silence.

"Do you think the lawyer is keen on the girl?

"Jack Glover?"

Mr. Briggerland nodded.

"I imagine he is," said Jean thoughtfully. "I like Jack— he's clever. He has all the moral qualities which one admires so much in the abstract.

I could love Jack myself."

"Could he love you?" bantered her father.

"He couldn't," she said shortly. "Jack would be a happy man if he saw me stand in Jim Meredith's place in the Old Bailey. No, I have no illusion about Jack's affections."

"He's after Lydia's money I suppose," said Mr. Briggerland, stroking his bald head.

"Don't be a fool," was the calm reply, "That kind of man doesn't worry about a girl's money. I wish Lydia was dead," she added without malice. "It would make things so easy and smooth."

Her father swallowed something.

"You shock me sometimes, Jean," he said, a statement which amused her.

"You're such a half and half man," she said with a note of contempt in her voice. "You were quite willing to benefit by Jim Meredith's death; you killed him as cold-bloodedly as you killed poor little Bulford, and yet you must whine and snivel whenever your deeds are put into plain language. What does it matter if Lydia dies now or in fifty years time?" she asked. "It would be different if she were immortal. You people attach so much importance to human life— the ancients and the Japanese, amongst the modern, are the only people who have the matter in true perspective. It is no more cruel to kill a human being than it is to cut the throat of a pig to provide you with bacon. There's hardly a dish at your table which doesn't represent willful murder, and yet you never think of it, but because the man animal can talk and dresses himself or herself in queer animal and vegetable fabrics, and decorates the body with bits of metal and pieces of glittering quartz, you give its life a value which you deny to the cattle within your gates! Killing is a matter of expediency, permissible if you call it war, terrible if you call it murder. To me it is just killing. If you are caught in the act of killing they kill you, and people say it is right to do so. The sacredness of human life is a slogan invented by cowards who fear death— as you do."

"Don't you, Jean?" he asked in a hushed voice.

"I fear life without money," she said quietly. "I fear long days of work for a callous, leering employer, and strap-hanging in a crowded tube on my way home to one miserable room and the cold mutton of yesterday. I fear getting up and making my own bed, and washing my own handkerchiefs and blouses, and renovating last year's hats to make them look like this year's. I fear a poor husband and a procession of children, and doing the housework with an incompetent maid, or maybe without any at all. Those are the things I fear, Mr. Briggerland."

She dusted the ash from her dress and got up.

"I haven't forgotten the life we lived at Ealing," she said significantly.

She looked across the bay to Monte Carlo glittering in the morning sunlight, to the green-capped head of Cap-d'Ail, Beaulieu, a jewel set in gray stone and shook her head.

"'It is written'" she quoted sombrely and left him in the midst of the question he was asking. She strolled back to the house and joined Lydia who was looking radiantly beautiful in a new dress of silver gray charmeuse.

CHAPTER XX

"Have you solved the mystery of the submerged bed?" smiled Jean. Lydia laughed.

"I'm not probing too deeply into the matter," she said. "Poor Mrs. Cole-Mortimer was terribly upset."

"She would be," said Jean. "It was her own eiderdown!"

This was the first hint Lydia had received that the house was rented furnished.

They drove into Nice that morning, and Lydia, remembering Jack Glover's remarks, looked closely at the chauffeur, and was startled to see a resemblance between him and the man who had driven the taxi-cab on the night she had been carried off from the theatre. It is true that the taxi driver had a moustache and that this man was clean shaven and, moreover, had tiny side whiskers, but there was a resemblance.

"Have you had your driver long?" she asked as they were running through Monte Carlo, along the sea road.

"Morden? Yes, we have had him six or seven years," said Jean carelessly. "He drives us when we are on the continent, you know. He speaks French perfectly and is an excellent driver. Father has tried to persuade him to come to England, but he hates London— he was telling me the other day that he hadn't been there for ten years."

That disposed of the resemblance, thought Lydia, and yet— she could remember his voice, she thought, and when they alighted on the Promenade des Anglaise she spoke to him. He replied in French, and it is impossible to detect points of resemblance in a voice that speaks one language and the same voice when it speaks another.

The promenade was crowded with saunterers. A band was playing by the jetty and although the wind was colder than it had been at Cap Martin, the sun was warm enough to necessitate the opening of a parasol.

It was a race week, and the two girls lunched at the Negrito. They were in the midst of their meal when a man came toward them, and Lydia recognized Mr. Marcus Stepney. This dark, suave man, was no favorite of hers, though why she could not have explained. His manners were always perfect, and towards her, deferential.

As usual, he was dressed with the precision of a fashion plate. Mr. Marcus Stepney was a man, a considerable portion of whose time was taken up every morning by the choice of cravats and socks and shirts. Though Lydia did not know this, his smartness, plus a certain dexterity with cards, was his stock in trade. No breath of scandal had touched him, he moved in a good set and was always at the right place at the proper season.

When Aix was full he was certain to be found at the Palace, in the Deauville week you would find him at the Casino punting mildly at the baccarat table. And after the rooms were closed, and even the Sports Club at Monte Carlo had shut its doors, there was always a little game to be had in the hotels and in Marcus Stepney's private sitting room.

And it cannot be denied that Mr. Stepney was lucky. He won sufficient at these out-of-hour games to support him nobly through the trials and vicissitudes which the public tables inflict upon their votaries.

"Going to the races," he said, "how very fortunate! Will you come along with me? I can give you three good winners."

"I have no money to gamble," said Jean, "I am a poor woman. Lydia, who is rolling in wealth, can afford to take your tips, Marcus."

Marcus looked at Lydia with a speculative eye.

"If you haven't any money with you, don't worry. I have plenty and you can pay me afterwards. I could make you a million francs today."

"Thank you," said Jean coolly, "but Mrs. Meredith does not bet so heavily."

Her tone was a clear intimation to the man of wits that he was impinging upon somebody else's preserves and he grinned amiably.

Nevertheless, it was a profitable afternoon for Lydia. She came back to Cap Martin twenty thousand francs richer than she had been when she started off.

"Lydia's had a lot of luck she tells me," said Mr. Briggarland.

"Yes. She won about five hundred pounds," said his daughter, "Marcus was laying ground bait. She did not know what horses he had backed until after the race was run, when he invariably appeared with a few *mille* notes and Lydia's pleasure was pathetic. Of course she didn't win anything, The twenty thousand francs was a sprat— he's coming tonight to see how the whales are blowing!"

Mr. Marcus Stepney arrived punctually, and, to Mr. Briggerland's disgust, was dressed for dinner, a fact which necessitated the older man's hurried retreat and reappearance in conventional evening wear.

Marcus Stepney's behavior at dinner was faultless. He devoted himself in the main to Mrs. Cole-Mortimer, and Jean, who apparently never looked at him and yet observed his every movement, knew that he was merely waiting his opportunity.

It came when the dinner was over and the party adjourned to the big stoop facing the sea. The night was chilly and Mr. Stepney found wraps and furs for the ladies, and so manoeuvred the arrangement of the chairs, that Lydia and he were detached from the remainder of the party, not by any great distance, but sufficient, as the experienced Marcus knew, to remove a murmured conversation from the sharpest eavesdropper.

Jean, who was carrying on a three-cornered conversation with her father and Mrs. Cole, did not stir, until she saw, by the light of a shaded lamp in the roof, the dark head of Mr. Marcus Stepney droop more confidently towards his companion. Then she rose and strolled across.

Marcus did not curse her because he did not express his inmost thoughts aloud.

He gave her his chair and pulled another forward.

"Does Miss Briggerland know?" asked Lydia.

"No," said Mr. Stepney pleasantly.

"May I tell her?"

"Of course."

"Mr. Stepney has been telling me about a wonderful racing coup to be made tomorrow. Isn't it rather thrilling, Jean! He says it will be quite possible for me to make five million francs without any risk at all."

"Except the risk of a million, I suppose," smiled Jean. "Well, are you going to do it?"

Lydia shook her head.

"I haven't a million francs in France, for one thing," she said, "and I wouldn't risk it if I had."

And Jean smiled again at the discomfiture which Mr. Marcus Stepney strove manfully to hide.

Later she took his arm and led him into the garden.

"Marcus," she said when they were out of range of the house, "I think you are several kinds of a fool."

"Why?" asked the other, who was not in the best humor.

"It was so crude," she said scornfully, "so cheap and confidence-trickish. A miserable million francs— twenty thousand pounds. Apart from the fact that your name would be mud in London if it were known that you had robbed a girl—"

"There's no question of robbery," he said hotly, "I tell you Valdau is a certainty for the Prix."

"It would not be a certainty if her money were on," said Jean drily. "It would finish an artistic second and you would be full of apologies and poor Lydia would be a million francs to the bad. No, Marcus, that is cheap."

"I'm nearly broke," he said shortly.

He made no disguise of his profession, nor of his nefarious plan.

Between the two there was a queer kind of camaraderie. Though he may not have been privy to the more tremendous of her crimes, yet he seemed to accept her as one of those who lived on the frontiers of illegality.

"I was thinking about you, as you sat there telling her the story," said Jean thoughtfully. "Marcus, why don't you marry her?"

He stopped in his stride and looked down at the girl.

"Marry her, Jean are you mad? She wouldn't marry me."

"Why not?" she asked. "Of course she'd marry you, you silly fool, if you went the right way about it."

He was silent.

"She is worth six hundred thousand pounds, and I happen to know that she has nearly two hundred thousand pounds in cash on deposit at the bank," said Jean.

"Why do you want me to marry her?" he asked significantly, "Is there a rake-off for you?"

"A big rake-off," she said, "The two hundred thousand on deposit should be easily get-at-able, Marcus, and she'd even give you more—"

"Why?" he asked.

"To agree to a separation," she said coolly. "I know you. No woman could live very long with you and preserve her reason."

He chuckled.

"And I'm to hand it all over to you?"

"Oh, no," she corrected. "I'm not greedy. It is my experience that the greedy people get into bad trouble. The man or woman who 'wants it all' usually gets the dressing-case the 'all' was kept in. No, I'd like to take a half."

He sat down on a garden seat and she followed his example.

"What is there to be?" he asked. "An agreement between you and I? Something signed and sealed and delivered, eh?"

Her sad eyes caught his and held them.

"I trust you, Marcus," she said softly. "If I help you in this— and I will if you will do all that I tell you to do— I will trust you to give me my share.”

Mr. Marcus Stepney fingered his collar a little importantly.

“I’ve never let a pal down in my life,” he said, with a cough. “I’m as straight as they make ‘em, to people who play the game with me.”

“And you are wise, so far as I am concerned,” said the gentle Jean. “For if you double-crossed me, I should hand the police the name and address of your other wife who is still living.”

His jaw dropped.

“Wha-what?” he stammered.

“Let us join the ladies,” mocked Jean as she rose and put her arm in his.

It pleased her immensely to feel this big man trembling.

CHAPTER XXI

It seemed to Lydia that she had been abroad for years, though in reality she had been three days in Cap Martin, when Mr. Marcus Stepney became a regular caller.

Even the most objectionable people improve on acquaintance, and give the lie to first impressions.

Mr. Stepney never bored her. He had an inexhaustible store of anecdotes and reminiscences, none of which was in the slightest degree offensive. He was something of a sportsman too, and he called by arrangement the next morning, after his introduction to the Cap Martin household, and conducting her to a sheltered cove, containing two bathing huts, he introduced her to the exhilarating Mediterranean.

Sea bathing is not permitted in Monte Carlo until May and the water was much colder than Lydia had expected. They swam out to a floating platform when Mr. Briggerland and Jean put in an appearance. Jean had come straight from the house in her bathing gown over which she wore a light wrap. Lydia watched her with amazement for the girl was an expert swimmer. She could dive from almost any height and could remain under water an alarming time.

“I never thought you had so much energy and strength in your little body,” said Lydia, as Jean, with a shriek of enjoyment, drew herself on the raft and wiped the water from her eyes.

“There’s a man up there looking at us through glasses,” said Briggerland suddenly. “I saw the flash of the sun on them.”

He pointed to the rising ground beyond the seashore, but they could see nothing.

Presently there was a glitter of light amongst the green and Lydia pointed.

"I thought that sort of thing was never done except in comic newspapers," she said, but Jean did not smile. Her eyes were focussed on the point where the unseen observer lay or sat, and she shaded her eyes.

"Some visitor from Monte Carlo, I expect. People at Cap Martin are much too respectable to do anything so vulgar."

Mr. Briggerland, at a glance from his daughter, slipped into the water and with strong, heavy strokes, made his way to the shore.

"Father is going to investigate," said Jean, "and the water really is the warmest place," and with that she fell sideways into the blue sea like a seal, dived down into its depths and presently Lydia saw her walking along the white floor of the ocean, her little hands keeping up an almost imperceptible motion. Presently she shot up again, shook her head and looked round, only to dive again.

In the meantime, though Lydia, who was fascinated by the manoeuvre of the girl, did not notice the fact, Mr. Briggerland had reached the shore, pulled on a pair of rubber shoes and with his mackintosh buttoned over his bathing dress, had begun to climb through the underbrush towards the spot where the glasses had glistened. When Lydia looked up he had disappeared.

"Where is your father?" she asked the girl.

"He went into the bushes." Mr. Stepney volunteered the information. "I suppose he's looking for the Paul Pry."

Mr. Stepney had been unusually glum and silent, for he was piqued by the tactless appearance of the Briggerlands.

"Come into the water, Marcus," said Jean peremptorily, as she put her foot against the edge of the raft, and pushed herself backward, "I want to see Mrs. Meredith dive."

"Me?" said Lydia in surprise. "Good heavens, no! After watching you I don't intend making an exhibition of myself."

"I want to show you the proper way to dive," said Jean. "Stand up on the edge of the raft."

Lydia obeyed.

"Straight up," said Jean. "Now put both your arms out wide. Now—"

There was a sharp crack from the shore; something whistled past Lydia's head, struck an upright post, splintering the edge and with a whine went ricochetting into the sea.

Lydia's face went white.

"What—what was that?" she gasped. She had hardly spoken before there was another shot. This time the bullet must have gone very high and immediately afterwards came a yell of pain from the shore.

Jean did not wait. She struck out for the beach swimming furiously. It was not the shot, but the cry which had alarmed her, and without waiting to put on coat or sandals, she ran up the little road where her father had gone, following the path through the undergrowth. Presently she came to a grassy plot, in the center of which two tall pines grew side by side, and lying against one of the trees was the huddled figure of Briggerland. She turned him over. He was breathing heavily and was unconscious. An ugly wound gaped at the back of his head and his mackintosh and bathing dress were smothered with blood.

She looked round quickly for his assailant, but there was nobody in sight and nothing to indicate the presence of a third person but two shining brass cartridges which lay on the grass.

CHAPTER XXII

Lydia Meredith only remembered swooning twice in her life, and both these occasions had happened within a few weeks.

She never felt quite so unprepared to carry on, as she did when, with an effort, she threw herself into the water at Marcus Stepney's side and swam slowly toward the shore.

She dare not let her mind dwell upon the narrowness of her escape. Whoever had fired that shot had done so deliberately and with the intention of killing her. She had felt the wind of the bullet in her face.

"What do you suppose it was?" asked Marcus Stepney as he assisted her up the beach. "Do you think it was soldiers practising?"

She shook her head.

"Oh," said Mr. Stepney thoughtfully, and then: "If you don't mind I'll run up and see what has happened."

He wrapped himself in the dressing gown he had brought with him and followed Jean's trail, coming up with her as Mr. Briggerland opened his eyes and stared round.

"Help me to hold him, Marcus," said Jean.

"Wait a moment," said Mr. Stepney, feeling in his pocket and producing a silk handkerchief, "bandage him with that."

She shook her head.

"He's lost all the blood he's going to lose," she said quietly, "and I don't think there's a fracture. I felt the skull very carefully with my finger."

Mr. Stepney shivered.

"Hullo," said Briggerland drowsily, "Gee, he gave me a whack!"

"Who did it?" asked the girl.

Mr. Briggerland shook his head and winced with the pain of it.

"I don't know," he moaned. "Help me up, Stepney."

With the man's assistance he rose unsteadily to his feet.

"What happened?" asked Stepney.

"Don't ask him any questions now," said the girl sharply. "Help him back to the house."

A doctor was summoned and stitched the wound. He gave an encouraging report and was not too inquisitive as to how the injury had occurred. Foreign visitors get extraordinary things in the regions of Monte Carlo, and medical men lose nothing by their discretion.

It was not until that afternoon, propped up with pillows in a chair, the center of a sympathetic audience, that Mr. Briggerland told his story,

"I had a feeling that something was wrong," he said, "and I went up to investigate. I heard a shot fired, almost within a few yards of me, and dashing through the bushes, I saw the fellow taking aim for the second time, and seized him. You remember the second shot went high."

"What sort of a man was he?" asked Stepney.

"He was an Italian, I should think," answered Mr. Briggerland. "At any rate, he caught me an awful whack with the back of his rifle, and I knew no more until Jean found me."

"Do you think he was firing at me?" asked Lydia in horror.

"I am certain of it," said Briggerland. "I realized it the moment I saw the fellow."

"How am I to thank you?" said the girl impulsively. "Really it was wonderful of you to tackle an armed man with your bare hands."

Mr. Briggerland closed his eyes and sighed.

"It was nothing," he said modestly.

Before dinner he and his daughter were left alone for the first time since the accident.

"What happened?" she asked.

"It was going to be a little surprise for you," he said. "A little scheme of my own, my dear; you're always calling me a funk, and I wanted to prove—"

"What happened?" she asked tersely.

"Well, I went out yesterday morning and fixed it all. I bought the rifle, an old English rifle, at Amiens from a peasant. I thought it might come in handy, especially as the man threw in a packet of ammunition. Yesterday morning, lying awake before daybreak, I thought it out. I went up to the hill—the land belongs to an empty house, by the way—and I located the spot, put the rifle where I could find it easily and fixed a pair of glass goggles onto one of the bushes, where the sun would catch it. The whole scheme was not without its merit as a piece of strategy, my dear," he said complacently.

"And then—?" she said.

"I thought we'd go bathing yesterday but we didn't, but today—it was a long time before anybody spotted the glasses, but once I had the excuse for going ashore and investigating, the rest was easy."

She nodded.

"So that was why you asked me to keep her on the raft and make her stand up?"

He nodded.

"Well—" she demanded.

"I went up to the spot, got the rifle and took aim. I've always been a pretty good shot—"

"You didn't advertise it today," she said, sardonically. "Then I suppose somebody hit you on the head?"

He nodded and made a grimace, but any movement of his injured cranium was excessively painful.

"Who was it?" she asked.

He shrugged his shoulders.

"Don't ask fool questions," he said petulantly. "I know nothing. I didn't even feel the blow. I just remember taking aim, and then everything went dark."

"And how would you have explained it all, supposing you had succeeded?"

"That was easy," he said. "I should have said that I went in search of the man we had seen, I heard a shot and rushed forward and found nothing but the rifle."

She was silent, pinching her lips absently.

"And you took the risk of some peasant or visitor seeing you—took the risk of bringing the police to the spot and turning what might have easily been a case of accidental death, into an obvious case of wilful murder. I think you called yourself a strategist?" she asked politely.

"I did my best," he growled.

"Well, don't do it again, father," she said, "Your foolhardiness appalls me, and heaven knows, I never expected that I should be in a position to call you foolhardy."

And with this she left him, to bask in the hero-worship which the approaching Mrs. Cole-Mortimer would lavish upon him.

The "accident" kept them at home that night, and Lydia was not sorry.

A settee is not a very comfortable sleeping place, and she was ready for a real bed that night. Mr. Stepney found her yawning surreptitiously and went home early in disgust.

The night was warmer than the morning had been. The *Fohn* wind was blowing and she found her room with its radiator a little oppressive. She opened the long French windows, and stepped out onto the balcony. The last quarter of the moon was high in the sky, and though the light was faint, it gave shadows to trees and an eerie illumination to the lawn.

She leaned her arms on the rail and looked across the sea to the lights of Monte Carlo glistening in the purple night. Her eyes wandered idly to the grounds and she started. She could have sworn she had seen a figure moving in the shadow of the tree, nor was she mistaken.

Presently it left the tree belt, and stepped cautiously across the lawn, halting now and again to look around. She thought at first that it was Marcus Stepney who had returned, but something about the walk of the man seemed familiar. Presently he stopped directly under the balcony and looked up and she uttered an exclamation, as the faintlight revealed the iron gray hair and the grisly eyebrows of the intruder.

"All right, Miss," he said in a hoarse whisper, "it's only old Jaggs."

"What are you doing?" she answered in the same tone.

"Just lookin' round," he said, "just lookin' round," and limped again into the darkness.

CHAPTER XXIII

So old Jaggs was in Monte Carlo! Whatever was he doing, and how was he getting on with these people who spoke nothing but French, she wondered! She had something to think about before she went to sleep.

She opened her eyes singularly awake as the dawn was coming up over the gray sea. She looked at her watch; it was a quarter to six. Why she had wakened so thoroughly she could not tell, but remembered with a little shiver another occasion she had wakened, this time before the dawn, to face death in a most terrifying shape.

She got up out of bed, put on a heavy coat and opened the wire doors that led to the balcony. The morning was colder than she imagined, and she was glad to retreat to the neighborhood of the warm radiator.

The fresh, clean hours of the dawn, when the mind is clear, and there is neither sound nor movement to distract the thoughts, are favorable to sane thinking.

Lydia reviewed the past few weeks in her life, and realized, for the first time, the miracle which had happened. It was like a legend of old—the slave had been lifted from the king's anteroom—the struggling artist was now a rich woman. She twiddled the gold ring on her hand absent-mindedly—and she was married—and a widow! She had an uncomfortable feeling; that, in spite of her riches, she had not yet found her niche. She was an odd quantity as yet. The Cole-Mortimers and the Briggerlands did not belong to her ideal world, and she could find no place where she fitted.

She tried, in this state of mind, so favorable to the consideration of such a problem, to analyze Jack Glover's antagonism toward Jean Briggerland and her father.

It seemed unnatural that a healthy young man should maintain so bitter a feud with a girl whose beauty was almost of a transcendent quality and all because she had rejected him.

Jack Glover was a college man, a man with a keen sense of honor. She could not imagine him being guilty of a mean action. And such men did not pursue vendettas without good reason. If they were rejected by a woman, they accepted their conge with a good grace, and it was almost unthinkable that Jack should have no other reason for his hatred. Yet she could not bring herself even to consider the possibility that the reason was the one he had advanced. She came again to the dead end of conjecture. She could believe in Jack's judgment up to a point—beyond that she could not go.

She had her bath, dressed, and was in the garden when the eastern horizon was golden with the light of the rising sun. Nobody was about, the most energetic of the servants had not yet risen, and she strolled through the avenue to the main road. As she stood there looking up and down a man came out from the trees that fringed the road and began walking rapidly in the direction of Monte Carlo.

"Mr. Jaggs!" she called.

He took no notice, but seemed to increase his limping pace, and after a moment's hesitation, she went flying down the road after him. He turned at the sound of her footsteps and in his furtive way drew into the shadow of a bush. He looked more than usually grimy; on his hands were an odd pair of gloves and a soft slouch hat that had seen better days covering his head.

"Good morning, Miss," he wheezed.

"Why were you running away, Mr. Jaggs?" she asked, a little out of breath.

"Not runnin' away, Miss," he said, glancing at her sharply from under his heavy white eyebrows. "Just havin' a look round!"

"Do you spend all your nights looking round?" she smiled at him.

"Yes, Miss."

At that moment a cyclist gendarme came into view. He slowed down as he approached the two and dismounted.

"Good morning, Madame;" he said politely, and then looking at the man, "is this man in your employ? I have seen him coming out of your house every morning?"

"Oh yes," said Lydia hastily, "he's my—"

She was at a loss to describe him, but old Jaggs saved her the trouble.

"I'm madame's courier," he said, and to Lydia's amazement, he spoke in perfect French, "I am also the watchman of the house."

"Yes, yes," said Lydia, after she had recovered from her surprise. "M'sieur is the watchman, also."

"*Bien*, Madame," said the gendarme. "Forgive my asking, but we have so many strangers here."

They watched the gendarme out of sight. Then old Jaggs chuckled.

"Pretty good French, Miss, wasn't it?" he said and without another word, turned and limped in the trail of the police.

She looked after him in bewilderment. So he spent every night in the grounds, or somewhere about the house? The knowledge gave her a queer sense of comfort and safety.

When she went back to the villa she found the servants were up. Jean did not put in an appearance until breakfast, and Lydia had an opportunity of talking to the French housekeeper whom Mrs. Cole-Mortimer had engaged when she took the villa. From her she learned a bit of news, which she passed on to Jean almost as soon as she put in an appearance.

"The gardener's little boy is going to get well, Jean." Jean nodded.

"I know," she said. "I telephoned to the hospital yesterday."

It was so unlike her conception of the girl that Lydia stared.

"The mother is in isolation," Lydia went on, "and Madame Souviet says that the poor woman has no money and no friends. I thought of going down to the hospital today to see if I could do anything for her."

"You'd better not, my dear," warned Mrs. Cole-Mortimer nervously. "Let us be thankful we've got the little brat out of the neighborhood without our catching the disease. One doesn't want to seek trouble. Keep away from the hospital."

"Rubbish!" said Jean briskly. "If Lydia wants to go, there is no reason why she shouldn't. The isolation people are never allowed to come into contact with visitors, so there is really no danger."

"I agree with Mrs. Cole-Mortimer," grumbled Briggerland. "It is very foolish to ask for trouble. You take my advice, my dear, and keep away.”

“I had a talk with a gendarme this morning,” said Lydia to change the subject. “When he stopped and got off his bicycle I thought he was going to speak about the shooting, I suppose it was reported to the police?”

“Er—yes,” said Mr. Briggerland, not looking up from his plate, “of course. Have you been in to Monte Carlo?”

Lydia shook her head.

“No, I couldn’t sleep and I was taking a walk along the road when he passed,” she said nothing about Mr. Jaggs. “The police at Monaco are very sociable.”

Mr. Briggerland sniffed.

“Very,” he said.

“Have they any theories?” she asked. In her innocence she was persisting in a subject which was wholly distasteful to Mr. Briggerland. “About the shooting I mean?”

“Yes, they have theories, but my dear, I should advise you not to discuss the matter with the police. The fact is,” invented Mr. Briggerland, “I told them that you were unaware of the fact that you had been shot at, and if you discussed it with the police, you would make me look rather foolish.”

When Lydia and Mrs. Cole-Mortimer had gone, Jean seized an opportunity which the absence of the maid offered.

“I hope you are beginning to see how perfectly insane your scheme was,” she said. “You have to support your act with a whole series of bungling lies. Possibly Marcus, like a fool, has mentioned it in Monte Carlo, and we shall have the detectives out here asking why you have not reported the matter.”

“If I were as clever as you—” he growled.

“You’re not,” said Jean, rolling her napkin. “You’re the most unclever man I know.”

CHAPTER XXIV

Lydia went up to her bedroom to put away her clothes and found the maid making the bed.

“Oh, Madame,” said the girl, “I forgot to speak to you about a matter—I hope madame will not be angry.”

“I’m hardly likely to be angry on a morning like this,” said Lydia.

“It is because of this matter,” said the girl. She groped in her pocket and brought out a small shining object, and Lydia took it from her hand.

"This matter" was a tiny silver cross so small that a five-franc piece would have covered it easily. It was brightly polished and apparently had seen service.

"When we took your bed, after the atrocious and mysterious happening," said the maid rapidly, "this was found in the sheets. It was not thought that it could possibly be madame's, because it was so poor, until this morning when it was suggested that it might be a souvenir that madame values."

"You found it in the sheets?" asked Lydia in surprise.

"Yes, Madame."

"It doesn't belong to me," said Lydia. "Perhaps it belongs to Madame Cole-Mortimer—I will show it to her."

Mrs. Cole-Mortimer was a devout Catholic and it might easily be some cherished keepsake of hers.

The girl carried the cross to the window; an "X" bad been scrawled by some sharp-pointed instrument at the junction of the bars. There was no other mark to identify the trinket.

She put the cross in her bag, and when she saw Mrs. Cole-Mortimer again she forgot to ask her about it.

The car drove her into Nice alone. Jean did not feel inclined to make the journey and Lydia rather enjoyed the solitude.

The isolation hospital was at the top of the hill and she found some difficulty in obtaining admission at this hour. The arrival of the chief medical officer, however, saved her from making the journey in vain. The report he gave about the child was very satisfactory; the mother was in the isolation ward.

"Can she be seen?"

"Yes, Madame," said the urbane Frenchman in charge. "You understand, you will not be able to get near her? It will be rather like interviewing a prisoner, for she will be behind one set of bars and you behind another."

Lydia was taken to a room which was, she imagined, very much like a room in which prisoners interviewed their distressed relations. There were not exactly bars, but two large mesh nets of steel separated the visitor from the patient under observation. After a time a nun brought in the gardener's wife, a tall, gaunt woman, who was a native of Marseilles, and spoke the confusing patois of that city, with great rapidity. It was some time before Lydia could accustom her ear to the queer dialect.

Her boy was getting well, she said, but she herself was in terrible trouble. She had no money for the extra food she required. Her husband who was away in Paris when the child had been taken, had not troubled to write to her. It was terrible being in a place amongst other fever cases, and she was certain that her days were numbered.

Lydia pushed a five hundred franc note through the grating to the nun, to settle her material needs.

"And oh, Madame," wailed the gardener's wife, "my poor little boy has lost the gift of the Reverend Mother of San Surplice! His own cross which has been blessed by his holiness the Pope! It is because I left his cross in his little shirt that he is getting better, but now it is lost and I am sure these thieving doctors have taken it."

"A cross?" said Lydia. "What sort of a cross?"

"It was a silver cross, Madame; the value in money was nothing—it was priceless. Little Xavier—"

"Xavier?" repeated Lydia, remembering the "X" on the trinket that had been found in her bed. "Wait a moment, Madame," She opened her bag and took out the tiny silver symbol and at the sight of it the woman burst into a volley of joyful thanks.

"It is the same, the same, Madame! It has a small 'X' which the Reverend Mother scratched with her own blessed scissors!"

Lydia pushed the cross through the net and the nun handed it to the woman.

"It is the same, it is the same!" she cried. "Oh, thank you, Madame! Now my heart is glad—"

Lydia came out of the hospital and walked through the gardens by the doctor's side. But she was not listening to what he was saying—her mind was fully occupied with the mystery of the silver cross.

It was little Xavier's—it had been tucked inside his bed when he lay, as his mother thought, dying—and it had been found in her bed! Then little Xavier had been in her bed! Her foot was on the step of the car when it came to her, the meaning of that drenched couch and the empty bottle of peroxide. Xavier had been put there, and somebody who knew that the bed was infected had so soaked it with water that she could not sleep in it. But who? Old Jaggs!

She got into the car slowly, and went back to Cap Martin along the Grande Corniche.

Who had put the child there? He could not have walked from the cottage; that was impossible.

She was halfway home when she noticed a parcel lying on the floor of the car, and she let down the front window and spoke to the chauffeur. It was not Morden but a man whom she had hired with the car.

"It came from the hospital, Madame," he said. "The porter asked me if I came from Villa Casa. It was something sent to the hospital to be disinfected. There was a charge of seven francs for the service, Madame, and this I paid."

She nodded.

She picked up the parcel—it was addressed to "Mademoiselle Jean Briggerland" and bore the label of the hospital.

Lydia sat back in the car with her eyes closed, tired of turning of turning over this problem, yet determined to get to the bottom of the mystery.

Jean was out when she got back and she carried the parcel to her own room. She was trying to keep out of her mind the very possibility that such a hideous crime could have been conceived as that which all the evidence indicated had been attempted. Very resolutely she refused to believe that such a thing could have happened. There must be some explanation for the presence of the cross in her bed. Possibly it had been found after the wet sheets had been taken to the servants' part of the house.

She rang the bell and the maid, who had given her the trinket, came.

"Tell me," said Lydia, "where was this cross found?"

"In your bed, Mademoiselle."

"But where? Was it before the clothing was removed from this room or after?"

"It was before, Madame," said the maid. "When the sheets were turned back we found it lying exactly in the middle of the bed."

Lydia's heart sank.

"Thank you, that will do," she said. "I have found the owner of the cross and have restored it."

Should she tell Jean? Her first impulse was to take the girl into her confidence, and reveal the state of her mind. Her second thought was to seek out old Jaggs, but where could he be found? He evidently lived somewhere in Monte Carlo, but his name was hardly likely to be in the visitor's list. She was still undecided when Marcus Stepney called to take her to lunch at the Cafe de Paris.

The whole thing was so amazingly improbable. It belonged to a world of unreality, but then, she told herself, she also was living in an unreal world, and had been so for weeks.

CHAPTER XXV

Mr. Stepney had become more bearable. A week ago she would have shrunk from taking luncheon with him, but now such a prospect had no terrors. His views of things and people were more generous than she had expected. She had anticipated his attitude would be a little cynical, but to her surprise he oozed loving kindness. Had she known Mr. Marcus Stepney as well as Jean knew him, she would have realized that he adapted his mental attitude to his audience. He was a man whose stock in trade was a knowledge of human nature, and the ability to please. He would no more have attempted to shock or frighten her than a first-class salesman would shock or annoy a possible customer.

He had goods to sell, and it was his business to see that they satisfied the buyer. In this case the goods were represented by sixty-nine inches of good looking, well dressed man and it was rather important that he should present the best face of the article to the purchaser. It was almost as important that the sale should be a quick one. Mr. Stepney lived from week to week. What might happen next year seldom interested him, therefore his courting must be rapid.

He told the story of his life at lunch, a story liable to move a tender-hearted woman to at least a sympathetic interest. The story of his life varied also with the audience. In this case, it was designed for one who, he knew, had had a hard struggle, whose father had been heavily in debt, and who had tasted some of the bitterness of defeat. Jean had given him a very precise story of the girl's career, and Mr. Marcus Stepney adapted it for his own purpose.

"Why, your life has almost run parallel with mine," said Lydia.

"I hope it may continue," said Mr. Stepney not without a touch of sadness in his voice. "I am a very lonely man—I have no friends except the acquaintances one can pick up at night clubs, and the places where the smart people go in the season, and there is an artificiality about society friends which rather depresses me."

"I feel that, too," said the sympathetic Lydia.

"If I could only settle down!" he said, shaking his head. "A little house in the country, a few horses, a few cows, a woman who understood me—"

A false move this.

"And a few pet chickens to follow you about?" she laughed. "No, it doesn't quite sound like you, Mr. Stepney."

He lowered his eyes.

"I am sorry you think that," he said. "All the world thinks that I'm a gadabout, an idler, with no interest in existence, except the pleasure I can extract."

"And a jolly good existence, too," said Lydia briskly. She had detected a note of sentiment creeping into the conversation, and had slain it with the most effective weapon in woman's armory.

"And now tell me all about the great Moorish Pretender who is staying at your hotel—I caught a glimpse of him on the promenade—and there was a lot about him in the paper."

Mr. Stepney sighed and related all that he knew of the redoubtable Muley Hafiz on the way to the rooms. Muley Hafiz was being lionized in France just then, to the annoyance of the Spanish authorities who had put a price on his head.

Lydia showed much more interest in the Moorish Pretender than she did in the pretender who walked by her side.

He was not in the best of tempers when he brought her back to the Villa Casa and Jean, who entertained him whilst Lydia was changing, saw that his first advances had not met with a very encouraging result.

"There will be no wedding bells, Jean," he said.

"You take a rebuff very easily," said the girl, but he shook his head.

"My dear Jean, I know women as well as I know the back of my hand, and I tell you that there's nothing doing with this girl. I'm not a fool."

She looked at him earnestly.

"No, you're not a fool," she said at last. "You're hardly likely to make a mistake about that sort of thing. I'm afraid you'll have to do something romantic."

"What do you mean?" he asked.

"You'll have to run away with her; and like the knights of old, carry off the lady of your choice."

"The knights of old didn't have to go before a judge and jury and serve seven years at Dartmoor for their sins," he said unpleasantly.

She was sitting on a low chair overlooking the sea, whittling a twig with a silver-handled knife she had taken from her bag— a favorite occupation of hers in moments of cogitation.

"All the ladies of old didn't go to the police," she said. "Some of them were quite happy with their powerful lords, especially delicate-minded ladies who shrank from advertising their misfortune to the readers of the Sunday press. I think most women like to be wooed in the cave-man fashion, Marcus."

"Is that the kind of treatment you'd like, Jean?"

There was a new note in his voice. Had she looked at him she would have seen a strange light in his eyes.

"I'm merely advancing a theory," she said, "a theory which has been supported throughout the ages."

"I'd let her go and her money, too," he said. He was speaking quickly, almost incoherently. "There's only woman in the world for me, Jean, and I've told you before. I'd give my life and soul for her."

He bent over, and caught her arm in his big hand.

"You believe in the cave-man method, do you?" he breathed. "It is the kind of treatment you'd like, eh, Jean?"

She did not attempt to release her arm.

"Keep your hand to yourself, Marcus, please," she said quietly.

"You'd like it, wouldn't you, Jean? My God, I'd sacrifice my soul for you, you little devil!"

"Be sensible," she said. It was not her words or her firm tone that made him draw back. Twice and deliberately, she drew the edge of her little knife across the back of his hand, and he leaped away with a howl of pain.

"You—you beast," he stammered, and she looked at him with her sly smile.

"There must have been cave women, too, Marcus," she said coolly, as she rose. "They had their methods— give me your handkerchief, I want to wipe this knife."

His face was gray now. He was looking at her like a man bereft of his senses.

He did not move when she took his handkerchief from his pocket, wiped the knife, closed and slipped it into her bag, before she replaced the handkerchief tidily. And all the time he stood there with his hand streaming with blood, incapable of movement. It was not until she had disappeared round the corner of the house that he pulled out the hand-kerchief, and wrapped it about his hand.

"A devil," he whimpered, almost in tears, "a devil!"

CHAPTER XXVI

Jean Briggerland discovered a new arrival on her return to the house.

Jack Glover had come unexpectedly from London, so Lydia told her, and Jack himself met her with extraordinary geniality.

"You lucky people to be in this paradise!" he said. "It is raining like the dickens in London and miserable beyond description. And you're looking brown and beautiful, Miss Briggerland."

"The spirit of the warm south has got into your blood, Mr. Glover," she said sarcastically. "A course at the Riviera would make you almost human."

"And what would make you human?" asked Jack blandly.

"I hope you people aren't going to quarrel as soon as you meet," said Lydia.

Jean was struck by the change in the girl. There was a color in her cheeks, and a new and more joyous note in her voice, which was unmistakable to so keen a student as Jean Briggerland.

"I never quarrel with Jack," she said. She assumed a proprietorial air toward Jack Glover, which unaccountably annoyed Lydia. "He invents the quarrels and carries them out himself. How long are you staying?"

"Two days," said Jack, "then I'm due back in town.

"Have you brought your Mr. Jaggs with you?" asked Jean innocently,

"Isn't he here?" asked Jack in surprise, "I sent him along a week ago."

"Here?" repeated Jean slowly, "Oh, he's here, is he? Of course," she nodded. Certain things were clear to her now. The unknown drencher of beds, the stranger who had appeared from nowhere and had left her father senseless, were no longer mysteries.

"Oh, Jean," it was Lydia who spoke. "I'm awfully remiss, I didn't give you the parcel I brought back from the hospital,"

"From what hospital?" said Jean. "What parcel was that?"

"Something you had sent to be sterilized. I'll get it." She came back in a minute or two with the parcel which she had found in the car.

"Oh yes," said Jean carelessly, "I remember. It is a rug that I lent to the gardener's wife when her little boy was taken ill."

She handed the packet to the maid.

"Take it to my room," she said.

She waited just long enough to find an excuse for leaving the party and went upstairs. The parcel was on her bed. She tore off the wrapping—inside, starched white and clean, was the dust coat she had worn the night she had carried Xavier from the cottage to Lydia's bed. The rubber cap was there, discolored from the effects of the disinfectant, and the gloves and the silk handkerchief, neatly washed and pressed. She looked at them thoughtfully.

She put the articles away in a drawer, went down the servants' stairs and through a heavy open door into the cellar. Light was admitted by two barred windows, through one of which she had thrust her bundle that night and she could see every corner of the cellar, which was empty—as she had expected. The clothing she had thrown down had been gathered by some mysterious agent, who had forwarded it to the hospital in her name.

She came slowly up the stairs, fastened the open door behind her and walked out into the garden to think.

"Jaggs!" she said aloud, and her voice was as soft as silk. "I think, Mr. Jaggs, you ought to be in Heaven."

CHAPTER XXVII

"Who were the haughty individuals interviewing Jean in the saloon?" asked Jack Glover, as Lydia's car panted and groaned on the stiff ascent to La Turbie.

Lydia was concerned and he had already noted her seriousness.

"Poor Jean is rather worried," she said. "It appears that she had a love affair with a man three or four years ago, and recently he has been bombarding her with threatening letters."

"Poor soul," said Jack drily, "but I should imagine she could have dealt with that matter without calling in the police. I suppose they were detectives. Has she had a letter recently?"

"She had one this morning— posted in Monte Carlo last night."

"By the way, Jean went into Monte Carlo last night, didn't she?" asked Jack.

She looked at him reproachfully.

"We all went into Monte Carlo," she said severely. "Now, please don't be horrid, Mr. Glover, you aren't suggesting that Jean wrote this awful letter to herself, are you?"

"Was it an awful letter?" asked Jack.

"A terrible letter, threatening to kill her. Do you know that Mr. Briggerland thinks that the person who nearly killed me was really shooting at Jean."

"You don't say," said Jack politely. "I haven't heard about people shooting at you— but it sounds rather alarming.

She told him the story and he offered no comment.

"Go on with your thrilling story of Jean's mortal enemy. Who is he?"

"She doesn't know his name," said Lydia. "She met him in Egypt— an elderly man who positively dogged her footsteps wherever she went and made himself a nuisance."

"Doesn't know his name, eh?" said Jack with a sniff. "Well, that's convenient."

"I think you're almost spiteful," said Lydia hotly. "Poor girl, she was so distressed this morning; I have never seen her so upset."

"And are the police going to keep guard and follow her wherever she goes? And is that impossible person, Mr. Marcus Stepney, also in the vendetta? I saw him wandering about this morning, like a wounded hero, with his arm in a sling."

"He hurt his hand gathering wild flowers for me on the—"

But Jack's outburst of laughter checked her, and she glared at him.

"I think you're boorish," she snapped angrily. "I'm sorry I came out with you."

"And I'm sorry I've been such a fool," apologized the penitent Jack, "but the vision of the immaculate Mr. Stepney gathering wild flowers in a top hat and a morning suit certainly did appeal to me as being comic!"

"He doesn't wear a top hat or a morning suit in Monte Carlo," she said, furious at his banter. "Let us talk about somebody else than my friends."

"I haven't started to talk about your friends yet," he said, "And please don't try to tell your chauffeur to turn round— the road is too narrow, and he'd have the car over the cliff before you knew where you were, if he were stupid enough to try. I'm sorry, deeply sorry, Mrs. Meredith, but I think that Jean was right when she said that the southern air had got into my blood. I'm a little hysterical— yes, put it down to that. It runs in the family," he babbled on. "I have an aunt who faints at the sight of strawberries, and an uncle who swoons whenever a cat walks into the room."

"I hope you don't visit him very much," she said coldly.

"Two points to you," said Jack, "but I must warn Jaggs in case he is mistaken for the elderly Lothario. Obviously, Jean is preparing the way for an unpleasant end to poor old Jaggs."

"Why do you think these things about Jean?" she asked as they were running into La Turbie.

"Because I have a criminal mind," he replied promptly. "I have the same type of mind as Jean Briggerland's, wedded to a wholesome respect for the law and a healthy sense of right and wrong. Some people couldn't be happy if they owned a cent that had been earned dishonestly; other people are happy so long as they have the money—so long as it is real money. I belong to the former category. Jean— well I don't know what would make Jean happy."

"And what would make you happy— Jean?" she asked.

He did not answer this question until they were sitting on the stoop of the National where a light luncheon was awaiting them.

"Jean?" he said, as though the question had just been asked, "No, I don't want Jean. She is wonderful, really Mrs. Meredith, wonderful! I find myself thinking about her at odd moments and the more I think the more I am amazed. Lucretia Borgia was a child in arms compared with Jean— poor old Lucretia has been maligned anyway. There was a woman in the sixteenth century rather like her, and another girl in the early days of New England who used to denounce witches for the pleasure of seeing them burn, but I can't think of an exact parallel, because Jean gets no pleasure out of hurting people any more than you will get out of cutting that cantaloup. It has just got to be cut and the fact that you are finally destroying the life of the melon doesn't worry you."

"Have cantaloups life?" she paused, knife in hand, eyeing the fruit with a frown. "No, I don't think I want it. So Jean is a murderess at heart?"

She asked the question in solemn mockery, but Jack was not smiling.

"Oh yes—in intention at any rate. I don't know whether she has ever killed anybody, but she has certainly planned murders."

Lydia sighed and sat back in her chair patiently.

"Do you still suggest that she harbors designs against my young life?"

"I not only suggest it, but I state positively that there have been four attempts on your life in the past fortnight," he said calmly.

"Let us have this out," she said recklessly. "Number one?"

"The nearly-a-fatal accident in Berkeley Street," said Jack.

"Will you explain by what miracle the car arrived at the psychological moment?" she asked.

"That's easy," he said with a smile. "Old man Briggerland lit his cigar standing on the steps of the house. That light was a brilliant one, Jaggs tells me. It was the signal for the car to come on. The next attempt was made with the assistance of a lunatic doctor who was helped to escape by Briggerland and brought to your house by him. In some way he got hold of a key—probably Jean manoeuvred it—did she ever talk to you about keys?"

"No," said the girl, "she—" she stopped suddenly, remembering that Jean had discussed keys with her.

"Are you sure she didn't?" asked Jack, watching her.

"I think she may have done," said the girl defiantly, "what was the third attempt?"

"The third attempt," said Jack slowly, "was to infect your bed with a malignant fever."

"Jean did it?" said the girl incredulously. "Oh, no, that would be impossible."

"The child was in your bed. Jaggs saw it and threw two buckets of water over the bed so that you should not sleep in it."

She was silent.

"And I suppose the next attempt was the shooting?"

He nodded.

"Now do you believe?" he asked.

She shook her head.

"No, I don't believe," she said quietly. "I think you have worked up a very strong case against poor Jean and I am sure you think you're justified."

"You are quite right there," he said. He lifted a pair of field glasses which he had put on the table and surveyed the road from the sea. "Mrs. Meredith, I want you to do something and tell Jean Briggerland when you have done it."

"What is that?" she asked.

"I want you to make a will. I don't care where you leave your property so long as it is not to somebody you love."

She shivered.

"I don't like making wills. It's so gruesome."

"It will be more gruesome for you if you don't," he said significantly. "The Briggerlands are your heirs-at-law."

She looked at him quickly.

"So that is what you are aiming at? You think that all these plots are designed to put me out of the way so that they can enjoy my money?"

He nodded and she looked at him wonderingly.

"If you weren't a hard-headed lawyer, I should think you were a writer of romantic fiction," she said. "But if it will please you I will make a will. I haven't the slightest idea whom I could leave the money to. I've got rather a lot of money, haven't I?"

"You have exactly £160,000 in hard cash. I want to talk to you about that," said Jack. "It is lying at your bankers, in your current account. It represents property which has been sold or was in process of being sold when you inherited the money and anybody who can get your signature and can satisfy the bankers that they are bona fide payees, can draw every cent you have of ready money. I might say in passing that we are prepared for that contingency and any large check will be referred to me or to my partner."

He raised his field glasses for a second time and looked steadily down along the hill road up which they had come. "Are you expecting anybody?" she asked.

"I'm expecting Jean," he said grimly.

"But we left her—"

"The fact that we left her talking to the police doesn't mean that she will not be coming up here, to watch us. Jean doesn't like me, you know, and she will be scared to death of this tete-a-tete."

The conversation had been arrested by the arrival of the soup and now there was a further interruption whilst the table was being cleared. When the maitre d'hotel had gone the girl asked:

"What am I to do with the money? Reinvest it?"

"Exactly," said Jack, "but the most important thing is to make your will."

He looked along the deserted verandah. They were the only guests present who had come early. From the verandah two curtained doors led into the salon of the hotel and it struck him that one of these had not been ajar when he looked at it before, and it was the door opposite to the table where they were sitting.

He noted this idly without attaching any great importance to the fact.

"Suppose somebody were to present a check to the bank in my name?" she asked. "What would happen?"

"If it were for a large sum? The manager would call us up and one of us would probably go round to your bank. It is only a block from our office. If Rennett or I said it was all right the check would be honored. You may be sure that I should make very drastic inquiries as to the origin of the signature."

And then she saw him stiffen and his eyes go to the door. He waited a second, then rising noiselessly, crossed the wooden floor of the verandah quickly and pushed open the door, to find himself face to face with the smiling Jean Briggerland.

CHAPTER XXVIII

"However did you get here?" asked Lydia in surprise.

"I went into Nice," said the girl carelessly. "The detectives were going there and I gave them a lift."

"I see," said Jack, "so you came into Turbie by the back road? I wondered why I hadn't seen your car."

"You expected me, did you?" she smiled, as she sat down at the table and selected a peach from its cotton-wool bed. "I only arrived a second ago; in fact I was opening the door when you almost knocked my head off. What a violent man you are, Jack! I shall have to put you into my story."

Glover had recovered his self-possession by now.

"So you are adding to your other crimes by turning novelist, are you?" he said good-humoredly. "What is the book, Miss Briggerland?"

"It is going to be called 'Suspected'," she said coolly. "And it will be the Story of a Hurt Soul."

"Oh, I see, a humorous story," said Jack wilfully dense. "I didn't know you were going to write a biography."

"But do tell me about this; it is very thrilling, Jean," said Lydia, "and it is the first I've heard of it."

Jean was skinning the peach and was smiling as at an amusing thought.

"I've been two years making up my mind to write it," she said, "and I'm going to dedicate it to Jack. I started work on it three or four days ago. Look at my wrist!" She held out her beautiful hand for the girl's inspection.

"It is a very pretty wrist," laughed Lydia, "but why did you want me to see it?"

"If you had a professional eye," said the girl, resuming her occupation, "you would have noticed the swelling, the result of writers' cramp."

"The yarn about your elderly admirer ought to provide a good chapter," said Jack, "and isn't there a phrase 'A chapter of accidents'—*that* ought to go in."

She did not raise her eyes.

"Don't discourage me," she said, a little sadly, "I have to make money somehow."

How much had she heard? Jack was wondering all the time, and he groaned inwardly when he saw how little effect his warning had upon the girl he was striving to protect. Women are natural actresses, but Lydia was not acting now. She was genuinely fond of Jean and he could see that she had accepted his warnings as the ravings of a diseased imagination. He confirmed this view when, after a morning of sight-seeing and the exploration of the spot where, two thousand years before, the Emperor Augustine had erected his lofty "trophy," they returned to the villa. There are some omissions which are marked and when Lydia allowed him to depart without pressing him to stay to dinner he realized that he had lost the trick.

"When are you going back to London?" she asked.

"Tomorrow morning," said Jack. "I don't think I shall come here again before I go."

She did not reply immediately. She was a little penitent at her lack of hospitality, but Jack had annoyed her and the more convincing he had become, the greater had been the irritation he had caused. One question he had to ask but he hesitated.

"About that will—" he began, but her look of weariness stopped him.

It was a very annoyed young man that drove back to the Hotel de Paris.

He had hardly gone before Lydia regretted her brusqueness. She liked Jack Glover more than she was prepared to admit, and though he had only been in Cap Martin for two days she felt a little sense of desolation at his going. Very resolutely she refused even to consider his extraordinary views about Jean. And yet—

Jean left her alone and watched her strolling aimlessly about the garden, guessing the little storm which had developed in her breast, Lydia went to bed early that night, another significant sign Jean noted, and was not sorry, because she wanted to have her father to herself.

Mr. Briggerland listened moodily whilst Jean related all that she had learned, for she had been in the saloon at the National for a good quarter of an hour before Jack had discovered her.

"I thought he would want her to make a will," she said, "and, of course, although she has rejected the idea now, it will grow on her. I think we have the best part of a week."

"I suppose you have everything cut and dried as usual," growled Mr. Briggerland. "What is your plan?"

"I have three," said Jean thoughtfully, "and two are particularly appealing to me because they do not involve the employment of any third person."

"Had you one which brought in somebody else?" asked Briggerland in surprise, "I thought a clever girl like you—"

"Don't waste your sarcasm on me," said Jean quietly. "The third person whom I considered was Marcus Stepney," and she told him the gist of her conversation with the gambler. Mr. Briggerland was not impressed.

"A thief like Marcus will get out of paying," he said, "and if he can stall you long enough to get the money you may whistle for your share. Besides, a fellow like that isn't really afraid of a charge of bigamy."

Jean, curled up in a big armchair, looked up under her eyelashes at her father and laughed.

"I had no intention of letting Marcus marry Lydia," she said coolly, "but I had to dangle something in front of his eyes, because he may serve me in quite another way."

"How did he get those two slashes on his hand?" asked Mr. Briggerland suddenly.

"Ask him," she said. "Marcus is getting a little troublesome. I thought he had learned his lesson and had realized that I am not built for matrimony, especially for a hectic attachment to a man who gains his livelihood by cheating at cards."

"Now, now, my dear," said her father.

"Please don't be shocked," she mocked him. "You know as well as I do how Marcus lives."

"The boy is very fond of you."

"The boy is between thirty and thirty-six," she said tersely. "And he's not the kind of boy that I am particularly fond of. He is useful and may be more useful yet."

She rose, stretched her arms and yawned.

"I'm going up to my room to work on my story. You are watching for Mr. Jaggs?"

"Work on what?" he said.

"The story I am writing and which I think will create a sensation," she said calmly.

"What's this?" asked Briggerland suspiciously. "A story? I didn't know you were writing that kind of stuff."

"There are lots of important things that you know nothing about, parent," she said, and left him a little dazed.

For once Jean was not deceiving him. A writing table had been put in her room and a thick pad of paper awaited her attention. She got into her kimono and with a little sigh sat down at the table and began to write. It was half-past two when she gathered up the sheets and read them over with a smile which was half contempt. She was on the point of getting into bed when she remembered that her father was keeping watch below. She put on her slippers and went downstairs and tapped gently at the door of the darkened dining room.

Almost immediately it was opened.

"What did you want to tap for?" he grumbled. "You gave me a start."

"I preferred tapping to being shot," she answered. "Have you heard anything or seen anybody?"

The French windows of the dining room were open, her father was wearing his coat and on his arm she saw, by the reflected starlight from outside, he carried a shotgun.

"Nothing," he said. "The old man hasn't come tonight."

She nodded.

"Somehow I didn't think he would," she said.

"I don't see how I can shoot him without making a fuss."

"Don't be silly," said Jean lightly. "Aren't the police well aware that an elderly gentleman has threatened my life, and would it be remarkable if seeing an ancient man prowl about this house you shot him on sight?"

She bit her lips thoughtfully.

"Yes, I think you can go to bed," she said. "He will not be here tonight.

Tomorrow night, yes."

She went up to her room, said her prayers and went to bed and was asleep immediately.

Lydia had forgotten about Jean's story until she saw her writing industriously at a small table which had been placed on the lawn. It was February but the wind and the sun were warm and Lydia thought she had never seen a more beautiful picture than the girl presented, sitting there in a garden spangled with gay flowers, heavy with the scent of February roses, a dainty figure of a girl, almost ethereal in her loveliness.

"Am I interrupting you?"

"Not a bit," said Jean, putting down her pen and rubbing her wrist. "Isn't it annoying, I've got to quite an exciting part, and my wrist is giving me hell."

She used the word so naturally that Lydia forgot to be shocked.

"Can I do anything for you?"

Jean shook her head.

"I don't exactly see what you can do," she said, "unless you could— but, no, I would not ask you to do that!"

"What is it?" asked Lydia.

Jean puckered her brows in thought.

"I suppose you could do it," she said, "but I'd hate to ask you. You see, dear, I've got a chapter to finish and it really ought to go off to London today. I am very keen on getting an opinion from a literary friend of mine—but, no, I won't ask you."

"What is it?" smiled Lydia. "I'm sure you're not going to ask the impossible."

"The thought occurred to me that perhaps you might write as I dictated. It would only be two or three pages," said the girl apologetically. "I'm so full of the story at this moment that it would be a shame if I allowed the divine fire of inspiration—that's the term, isn't it—to go out."

"Of course I'll do it," said Lydia. "I can't write shorthand, but that doesn't matter does it?"

"No, longhand will be quick enough for me. My thoughts aren't so fast," said the girl.

"What is it all about?"

"It is about a girl," said Jean, "who has stolen a lot of money—"

"How thrilling!" smiled Lydia.

"And she's got away to America. She is living a very full and joyous life, but the thought of her sin is haunting her and she decides to disappear and let people think she has drowned herself. She is really going into a convent. I've got to the point where she is saying farewell to her friend.

Do you feel capable of being harrowed?"

"I never felt fitter for the job in my life," said Lydia, and, sitting down in the chair the girl had vacated, she took up the pencil which the other had left.

Jean strolled up and down the lawn in an agony of mental composition and presently she came back and began slowly to dictate.

Word by word Lydia wrote down the thrilling story of the girl's remorse and presently came to the moment when the heroine was inditing a letter to her friend.

"Take a fresh page," said Jean as Lydia paused halfway down one sheet. "I shall want to write something in there myself when my hand gets better. Now begin:

"'My dear friend'."

Lydia wrote down the words and slowly the girl dictated.

"'I do not know how I can write you this letter. I intended to tell you when I saw you the other day how miserable I was. Your suspicion hurt me less than your ignorance of the one vital event in my life which has now made living a burden. My money has brought no joy to me. I have met a man I love but with whom I know a union is impossible. We are determined to die together—farewell—'"

"You said she was going away," interrupted Lydia.

"I know," Jean nodded. "Only she wants to give the impression—"

"I see, I see," said Lydia. "Go on."

"'Forgive me for the act I am committing, which you may think is the act of a coward and try to think as well of me as you possibly can. Your friend—' I don't know whether to make her sign her name or put her initials," said Jean, pursing her lips.

"What is her name?"

"Laura Martin. Just put the initials L. M."

"They're mine also," smiled Lydia. "What else?"

"I don't think I'll do any more," said Jean, "I'm not a good dictator, am I? Though you're a wonderful amanuensis."

She collected the papers tidily, put them in a little portfolio and tucked them under her arm.

"Let us gamble the afternoon away," said Jean. "I want distraction."

"But your story? Haven't you to send it off?"

"I'm going to wrestle with it in secret, even if it breaks my wrist," said Jean brightly.

She took the portfolio up to her room, locked the door and sorted over the pages. The page which held the farewell letter she put carefully aside. The remainder, including all that part of the story she had written on the previous night, she made into a bundle and when Lydia had gone off with Marcus Stepney to swim, she carried the paper to a remote corner of the grounds and burnt it sheet by sheet. Again she examined the "letter," folded it and locked it in a drawer.

Lydia, returning from her swim, was met by Jean halfway up the hill.

"By the way, my dear, I wish you would give me Jack Glover's London address," she said as they went into the house, "Write it here. Here is a pencil." She pulled out an envelope from a stationery rack and Lydia in all innocence wrote as she requested.

The envelope Jean carried upstairs, put into it the letter signed "L. M." and sealed it down. Lydia Meredith was nearer to death at that moment than she had been on the afternoon when Morden, the chauffeur, brought his big Fiat onto the pavement of Berkeley Street.

CHAPTER XXIX

It was in the evening of the next day that Lydia received a wire from Jack Glover. It was addressed from London and announced his arrival.

"Doesn't it make you feel nice, Lydia," said Jean when she saw the telegram, "to have a man in London looking after your interests— a sort of guardian angel— and another guardian angel prowling round your demesne at Cap Martin?"

"You mean Jaggs? Have you seen him?"

"No, I have not seen him," said the girl softly. "I should rather like to see him. Do you know where he is staying at Monte Carlo?"

Lydia shook her head.

"I hope I shall see him before I go," said Jean. "He must be a very interesting old gentleman."

It was Mr. Briggerland who first caught a glimpse of Lydia's watchman. Mr. Briggerland had spent the greater part of the day sleeping. He was unusually wakeful at one o'clock in the morning and sat on the verandah in a fur-lined overcoat; his gun lay across his knees. He had seen many mysterious shapes flitting across the lawn, only to discover on investigation that they were no more than the shadows which the moving treetops cast.

At two o'clock he saw a shape emerge from the tree-belt and move stealthily in the shadow of the bushes toward the house. He did not fire because there was a chance that it might have been one of the detectives who had promised to keep an eye upon the Villa Casa in view of the murderous threats which Jean had received.

Noiselessly he rose and stepped in his rubber shoes to the darker end of the stoop. It was old Jaggs. There was no mistaking him—a bent man who limped cautiously across the lawn and was making for the back of the house. Mr. Briggerland cocked his gun and took aim—

Both girls heard the shot and Lydia, springing out of bed, ran onto the balcony.

"It's all right, Mrs. Meredith," said Briggerland's voice. "It was a burglar I think."

"You haven't hurt him?" she cried, remembering old Jaggs' nocturnal habits.

"If I have, he's got away," said Briggerland. "He must have seen me and dropped."

Jean flew downstairs in her dressing gown and joined her father on the lawn.

"Did you get him?" she asked in a low voice.

"I could have sworn I shot him," said her father in the same tone, "but the old devil must have dropped."

He heard the quick catch of her breath and turned apprehensively.

"Now, don't make a fuss about it, Jean, I couldn't help it."

"You couldn't help it!" she almost snarled. "You had him under your gun and you let him go. Do you think he'll ever come again, you fool?"

"Now look here, I'm not going to—" began Mr. Briggerland, but she snatched the gun from his hand, looked swiftly at the lock and ran across the lawn toward the trees.

Somebody was hiding. She sensed that and all her nerves were alert. Presently she saw a crouching figure and lifted the gun, but before she could fire it was wrested from her hand.

She opened her lips to cry out for help but a hand closed over her mouth, and swung her round so that her back was toward her assailant and then in a flash his arm came round her neck, the flex of the elbow against her throat.

"Say one of them prayers of yours," said a voice in her ear, and the arm tightened.

She struggled furiously but the man held her as though she were a child.

"You're going to die," whispered the voice. "How do you like the sensation?"

The arm tightened on her neck. She was suffocating, dying she thought, and her heart was filled with a wild, mad longing for life and a terror undreamed of. She could faintly hear her father's voice calling her and then consciousness departed.

When Jean came to herself she was in Lydia Meredith's arms. She opened her eyes and saw the pathetic face of her father looming from the background. Her hand went up to her throat.

"Hullo, people—how did I get here?" she asked as she struggled into a sitting position.

"I came in search of you and found you lying on the ground," quavered Mr. Briggerland.

"Did you see the man?" she asked,

"No. What happened to you, darling?"

"Nothing," she said with that composure which she could command. "I must have fainted. It was rather ridiculous of me, wasn't it?" she smiled.

She got unsteadily to her feet and again she felt her throat. Lydia noticed the action.

"Did he hurt you?" she asked anxiously. "It couldn't have been Jaggs."

"Oh, no," smiled Jean, "it couldn't have been Jaggs. I think I'll go to bed."

She did not expect to sleep. For the first time in her extraordinary life fear had come to her, and she had shivered on the very edge of the abyss. She felt the shudder she could not repress and shook herself impatiently. Then she extinguished the light and went to the window and looked out. Somewhere there in the darkness she knew her enemy was hidden and again that sense of apprehension swept over her.

"I'm losing my nerve," she murmured.

It was extraordinary to Lydia Meredith that the girl showed no sign of her night's adventure when she came in to breakfast on the following morning. She looked bright. Her eyes were clear and her delicate irony as pointed as though she had slept the clock round.

Lydia did not swim that day and Mr. Stepney had his journey out to Cap Martin in vain. Nor was she inclined to go back with him to Monte Carlo to the Casino in the afternoon and Mr. Stepney began to realize that he was wasting valuable time.

Jean found her scribbling in the garden and Lydia made no secret of the task she was undertaking,

"Making your will? What a grisly idea?" she said as she put down the cup of tea she had carried out to the girl.

"Isn't it," said Lydia with a grimace, "It is the most worrying business too, Jean. There is nobody I want to leave money to except you and Mr. Glover."

"For heaven's sake don't leave me any or Jack will think I am conspiring to bring about your untimely end," said Jean. "Why make a will at all?"

There was no need for her to ask that, but she was curious to discover what reply the girl would make, and to her surprise Lydia fenced with the question.

"It is done in all the best circles," she said good humoredly. "And Jean, I'm not interested in a single public institution! I don't know by title the name of any home for dogs and I shouldn't be at all anxious to leave my money to one even if I did."

"Then you'd better leave it to Jack Glover," said the girl, "or to the Lifeboat Institution."

Lydia threw down her pencil in disgust.

"Fancy making one's will on a beautiful day like this, and giving instructions as to where one should be buried. Brrr! Jean," she asked suddenly, "was it Mr. Jaggs you saw in the wood?"

Jean shook her head.

"I saw nobody," she said. "I went in to look for the burglar; the excitement must have been too much for me, and I fainted."

But Lydia was not satisfied.

"I can't understand Mr. Jaggs myself," she said, but Jean interrupted her with a cry.

Lydia looked up and saw her eyes shining and her lips parting in a smile.

"Of course," she said softly. "He used to sleep at your flat, didn't he?"

"Yes, why?" asked the girl in surprise.

"What a fool I am, what a perfect fool!" said Jean, startled out of her accustomed self-possession.

"I don't quite know where your folly comes in, but perhaps you will tell me," but Jean was laughing softly.

"Go on and make your will," she said mockingly. "And when you've finished we'll go into the Rooms and chase the lucky numbers. Poor dear Mrs. Cole-Mortimer is feeling a little neglected, too; we ought to do something for her."

The day and night passed without any untoward event. In the evening Jean had an interview with her French chauffeur and afterwards disappeared into her room. Lydia, tapping at her door to bid her good-night, received no answer.

Day was breaking when old Jaggs came out from the trees in his furtive way and glancing up and down the road made his halting way toward Monte Carlo. The only object in sight was a donkey laden with market produce led by a bare-legged boy who was going in the same direction as he.

A little more than a mile along the road he turned sharply to the right and began climbing a steep and narrow bridle path which joined the mountain road, halfway up to La Turbie. The boy with the donkey turned off to the main road and continued the steep climb toward the Grande Corniche. There were many houses built on the edge of the road and practically on the edge of precipices, for the windows facing the sea often looked sheer down for two hundred feet. At first these dwellings appeared in clusters, then as the road climbed higher, they occurred at rare intervals.

The boy leading the donkey kept his eye upon the valley below and from time to time caught a glimpse of the old man who had now left the bridle path and was picking his way up the rough hillside. He was making for a dilapidated house which stood at one of the hairpin bends of the road and the donkey boy, shading his eyes from the glare of the rising sun, saw him disappear into what must have been the cellar of the house, since the door through which he went was a good twenty feet beneath the level of the road. The donkey boy continued his climb, tugging at his burdened beast and presently he came up to the house. Smoke was rising from one of the chimneys and he halted at the door, tied the rope he held to a rickety gatepost and knocked gently.

A bright-faced peasant woman came to the open door and shook her head at the sight of the wares with which the donkey was laden.

"We want none of your truck, my boy," she said; "I have my own garden. You are not a Monogasque."

"No, signora," replied the boy flashing his teeth with a smile. "I am from San Remo, but I have come to live in Monte Carlo to sell vegetables for my uncle and he told me I should find a lodging here."

She looked at him dubiously.

"I have one room which you could have, boy," she said, "though I do not like Italians. You must pay me a franc a night and your donkey can go into the shed of my brother-in-law up the hill."

She led the way down a flight of ancient stairs and showed him a tiny room overlooking the valley.

"I have one other man who lives here," she said, "an old one who sleeps all day and goes out all night. But he is a very respectable man," she added in defence of her client.

"Where does he sleep?" asked the boy.

"There!" The woman pointed to a room on the opposite side of the narrow landing. "He has just come in; I can hear him." She listened.

"Will madame get me change for this?" the boy produced a fifty franc note and the woman's eyebrows rose.

"Such wealth!" she said good-naturedly. "I did not think that a little boy like you could have such money."

She hustled upstairs to her own room, leaving the boy alone. He waited until her heavy footsteps sounded overhead and then gently he tried the door of the other lodger. Mr. Jaggs had not yet bolted the door and the spy pushed it open and looked. What he saw satisfied him, for he pulled the door tight again and as the footfall of old Jaggs came nearer the door, the donkey boy flew upstairs with extraordinary rapidity.

"I will come later, Madame," he said when he had received the change. "I must take my donkey into Monte Carlo."

She watched the boy and his beast go down the road and went back to the task of preparing her lodger's breakfast.

To Monte Carlo the cabbage seller did not go. Instead, he turned back the way he had come and a hundred yards from the gate of Villa Casa, Morden, the chauffeur, appeared and took the rope from his hand.

"Did you find what you wanted, Mademoiselle?" he asked.

Jean nodded. She got into the house through the servants' entrance and up to her room without observation. She pulled off the black wig and applied herself to removing the stains from her face. It had been a good morning's work.

"You must keep Mrs. Meredith fully occupied today," she waylaid her father on the stairs to give him these instructions.

For her it was a busy morning. First she went to the Hotel de Paris and on the pretext of writing a letter in the lounge secured two or three sheets of the hotel paper and an envelope. Next she hired a typewriter and carried it with her back to the house. She was working for an hour before she had the letter finished. The signature took her some time. She had to ransack Lydia's writing case before she found a letter from Jack Glover—Lydia's signature was easy in comparison.

This, and a check drawn from the back of Lydia Meredith's check book completed her equipment.

That afternoon Morden, the chauffeur, motored into Nice and by nine o'clock that night an aeroplane deposited him in Paris. He was in London the following morning, a bearer of an urgent letter to Mr. Rennett, the lawyer, which, however, he did not present in person.

Morden knew a French girl in London and she it was who carried the letter to Charles Rennett—a letter that made him scratch his head many times before he took a sheet of paper and addressing the manager of Lydia's bank wrote:

"This check is in order. Please honor."

CHAPTER XXX

"Desperate diseases," said Jean Briggerland, "call for desperate reme-dies."

Mr. Briggerland looked up from his book.

"What was that tale you were telling Lydia this morning?" he asked, "about Glover's gambling. He was only here a day, wasn't he?"

"He was here long enough to lose a lot of money," said Jean. "Of course he didn't gamble, so he did not lose. It was just a little seed-sow-ing on my part—one never knows how useful the right word may be in the right season."

"Did you tell Lydia that he was losing heavily?" he asked quickly.

"Am I a fool? Of course not! I merely said that youth would be served and if you have the gambling instinct in you, why it didn't matter what position you held in society or what your responsibilities were, you must indulge your passion."

Mr. Briggerland stroked his chin. There were times when Jean's schemes got very far beyond him and he hated the mental exercise of catching up. The only thing he knew was that every post from London bore urgent demands for money and that the future held possibilities which he did not care to contemplate. He was in the unfortunate posi-tion of having numerous pensioners to support, men and women who had served him in various ways and whose approval, but what was more important, whose loyalty depended largely upon the regularity of their payments.

"I shall gamble or do something desperate," he said with a frown; "un-less you can bring off a coup that will produce twenty thousand pounds of ready money we are going to get into all kinds of trouble, Jean."

"Do you think I don't know that?" she asked contemptuously. "It is because of this urgent need of money that I have taken a step which I hate."

He listened in amazement whilst she told him what she had done to relieve her pressing needs.

"We are getting deeper and deeper into Morden's hands," he said shak-ing his head. "That is what scares me at times."

"You needn't worry about Morden," she smiled. Her smile was a lit-tle hard. "Morden and I are going to be married."

She was examining the toe of her shoe attentively as she spoke and Mr. Briggerland leaped to his feet.

"What!" he squeaked. "Marry a chauffeur? A fellow I picked out of the gutter? You're mad! The fellow is a rascal who has earned the guillotine time and time again."

"Who hasn't?" she asked looking up.

"It is incredible! Its madness!" he said, "I had no idea—" he stopped for want of breath.

Morden was becoming troublesome. She had known that better than her father.

"It was after the 'accident' that didn't happen that he began to get a little tiresome," she said. "You say we are getting deeper and deeper into his hands? Well, he hinted as much and I did not like it. When he began to get a little loving I accepted that way out as an easy alternative to a very unpleasant exposure. Whether he would have betrayed us, I don't know; probably he would."

Mr. Briggerland's face was dark.

"When is this interesting event to take place?"

"My marriage? In two months, I think. When is Easter? That class of person always wants to be married at Easter. I asked him to keep our secret and not to mention it to you and I should not have spoken now if you had not referred to the obligation we were under."

"In two months?" Mr. Briggerland nodded. "Let me know when you want this to end, Jean," he said.

"It will end almost immediately. Please do not trouble," said Jean, "and there is one other thing, father. If you see Mr. Jaggs in the garden tonight, I beg of you do not attempt to shoot him. He is a very useful man."

Her father sank back in his chair.

"You're beyond me," he said helplessly.

Morden occupied two rooms above the garage which was conveniently situated for Jean's purpose. He arrived late the next night and a light in his window, which was visible from the girl's room, told her all she wanted to know.

Mr. Morden was a good looking man by certain standards. His hair was dark and glossily brushed. His normal pallor of countenance gave him the interesting appearance which men of his kind did not greatly dislike and he had a figure which was admired in a dozen servants' halls and a manner which passed amongst housemaids for "gentlemanly" and amongst gentlemen as "superior." He heard the foot of the girl on the stairs and opened the door.

"You have brought it?" she said without a preliminary word.

She had thrown a dark cloak over her evening dress and the man's eyes feasted on her.

"Yes, I have brought it—Jean," he said.

She put her finger to her lips.

"Be careful, Francois," she cautioned in a low voice.

Although the man spoke English as well as he spoke French it was in the latter language that the conversation was carried on. He went to a grip which lay on the bed, opened it and took out five thick packages of thousand franc notes.

"There are a thousand in each, Mademoiselle. Five million francs. I changed part of the money in Paris and part in London."

"The woman—there is no danger from her?"

"Oh, no, Mademoiselle," he smiled complacently. "She is not likely to betray me and she does not know my name or where I am living. She is a girl I met at a dance at the Swiss Waiters' Club," he explained. "She is not a good character. I think the French police wish to find her, but she is very clever."

"What did you tell her?" asked Jean.

"That I was working a coup with Vaud and Montheron. These are two notorious men in Paris whom she knew. I gave her five thousand francs for her work."

"There was no trouble?"

"None whatever, Mademoiselle. I watched her and saw she carried the letter to the bank. As soon as the money was changed I left Croydon by air for Paris and came on from Paris to Marseilles by aeroplane."

"You did well, Francois," she said and patted his hand.

He would have seized hers, but she drew back.

"You have promised, Francois," she said with dignity, "and a French gentleman keeps his word."

Francois bowed.

He was not a French gentleman but he was anxious that this girl should think he was and to that end had told her stories of his birth which had apparently impressed her.

"Now will you do something more for me?"

"I will do anything in the world, Jean," he cried passionately, and again a restraining hand fell on his shoulder.

"Then sit down and write; your French is so much better than mine."

"What shall I write?" he asked. She had never called upon him for proof of his scholarship and he was childishly eager to reveal to the woman he loved attainments of which she had no knowledge.

"Write: 'Dear Mademoiselle.' He obeyed. "'I have returned from London and have confessed to Madame Meredith that I have forged her name and have drawn £100,000 from her bank—'"

"Why do I write this, Jean?" he asked in surprise.

"I will tell you one day—go on Francois," she continued her dictation.

"'And now I have learned that Madame Meredith loves me! There is only one end to this—that which you see—'"

"Do you intend passing suspicion to somebody else?" he asked, evidently fogged, "but why should I say—?"

She stopped his mouth with her hand.

"How wonderful you are, Jean," he said admiringly as he blotted the paper and handed it to her. "So that if this matter is traced to you—" she looked into his eyes and smiled.

"There will be trouble for somebody," she said softly as she put the paper in her pocket.

Suddenly before she could realize what was happening he had her in his arms, his lips pressed against hers.

"Jean, Jean!" he muttered. "You adorable woman!"

Gently she pressed him back and she was still smiling, though her eyes were like granite.

"Gently, Francois," she said, "you must have patience!"

She slipped through the door and closed it behind her and even in her then state of mind she did not slam it, nor did she hurry down the stairs, but went out, taking her time and was back in the house without her absence having been noticed. Her face, reflected in her long mirror, was serene in its repose but within her a devil was alive, hungry for destruction. No man had roused the love of Jean Briggerland, but at least one had succeeded in bringing to life a consuming hate which for the time being absorbed her.

From the moment she drew her wet handkerchief across her red lips and flung the dainty thing, as though it were contaminated, through the open window, Francois Morden was a dead man.

CHAPTER XXXI

A letter from Jack Glover arrived the next morning. He had had an easy journey, was glad to have had the opportunity of seeing Lydia and hoped she would think over the will. Lydia was not thinking of wills but of an excuse to get back to London. Of a sudden the loveliness of Monte Carlo had palled upon her and she had almost forgotten the circumstances which had made the change of scene and climate so welcome.

"Go back to London my dear?" said Mrs. Cole-Mortimer shocked, "What a—a rash notion! Why it is *freezing* in town and foggy and—and

I really can't let you go back!"

Mrs. Cole-Mortimer was agitated at the very thought. Her own good time on the Riviera depended upon Lydia staying. Jean had made that point very clear. She herself, she explained to her discomfited hostess, was ready to go back at once and the prolongation of Mrs. Cole-Mortimer's stay depended upon Lydia's plans. A startling switch of cause and effect, for Mrs. Cole-Mortimer had understood that Jean's will controlled the plans of the party.

Lydia might have insisted, had she really known the reason for her sudden longing for the grimy metropolis. But she could not even convince herself that the charms of Monte Carlo were contingent upon the presence there of a man who had aroused her furious indignation and with whom she had spent most of the time quarrelling. She mentioned her unrest to Jean, and Jean as usual seemed to understand.

"The Riviera is rather like Turkish Delight—very sweet, but unsatisfying," she said. "Stay another week and then if you feel that way we'll all go home together."

"This means breaking up your holiday," said Lydia in self-reproach.

"Not a bit," denied the girl; "perhaps I shall feel as you do in a week's time."

A week! Jean thought that much might happen in a week. In truth events began to move quickly from that night but in a way she had not anticipated.

Mr. Briggerland, who had been reading the newspaper through the conversation, looked up.

"They are making a great fuss over this Moor in Nice," he said, "but if I remember rightly, Nice invariably has some weird lion to adore."

"Muley Hafiz," said Lydia. "Yes, I saw him the day I went to lunch with Mr. Stepney, a fine looking man."

"I'm not greatly interested in natives," said Jean carelessly. "What is he, a negro?"

"Oh, no, he's fairer than—" Lydia was about to say "your father," but thought it discreet to find another comparison. "He's fairer than most of the people in the south of France," she said, "but then all very highly bred Moors are, aren't they?"

Jean shook her head.

"Ethnology means nothing to me," she said humorously. "I've got my idea of Moors from Shakespeare, and I thought they were mostly black. What is he, then? I haven't read the papers."

"He is the Pretender to the Moorish throne," said Lydia, "and there has been a lot of trouble in the French Senate about him. France supports his claims, and the Spaniards have offered a reward for his body, dead or alive, and that has brought about a strained relationship between Spain and France."

Jean regarded her with an amused smile.

"Fancy taking an interest in international politics. I suppose that is due to your working on a newspaper, Lydia."

Jean discovered that she was to take a greater interest in Muley Hafiz than she could have thought was possible. She had to go into Monte Carlo to do some shopping. Mentone was nearer, but she preferred the drive into the principality.

The Rooms had no great call for her, and whilst Morden went to a garage to have a faulty cylinder examined, she strolled on to the terrace of the Casino, down the broad steps towards the sea. The bathing huts were closed at this season, but the little road down to the beach is secluded and had been a favorite walk of hers in earlier visits.

Near the huts she passed a group of dark looking men in long white *jellabs*, and wondered which of these was the famous Muley. One, she noticed, with a particularly negro type of face, wore on his flowing robe the scarlet ribbon of the Legion of Honor. Somehow or other he did not seem interesting enough to be Muley, she thought as she went onto a strip of the beach.

A man was standing on the seashore, a tall, commanding man, gazing out, it seemed, across the sunlit ocean as though he were in search of something. He could not have heard her footfall because she was walking on the sand and yet he must have realized her presence, for he turned and she almost stopped at the sight of his face. He might have been a European; his complexion was fair, though his eyebrows and eyes were jet black, as also were the tiny beard and moustache he wore. Beneath the conventional *jellab* he wore a dark green jacket, and she had a glimpse of glittering decorations before he pulled over his cloak so that they were hidden. But it was his eyes which held her. They were large and as black as night, and they were set in a face of such strength and dignity that Jean knew instinctively that she was looking upon the Moorish Pretender.

They stood for a second staring at one another and then the Moor stepped aside.

"Pardon," he said in French, "I am afraid I startled you."

Jean was breathing a little quicker. She could not remember in her life any man who had created so immediate and favorable an impression. She forgot her contempt for native people, forgot his race, his religion (and religion was a big thing to Jean) forgot everything except that behind those eyes she recognized something which was kin to her.

"You are English, of course," he said in that language.

"Scottish," smiled Jean.

"It is almost the same, isn't it?" He spoke without any trace of an accent, without an error of grammar, and his voice was the voice of a college man.

He had left the way open for her to pass on, but she lingered.

"You are Muley Hafiz, aren't you?" she asked, and he turned his head. "I've read a great deal about you," she added, though in truth she had read nothing.

He laughed, showing two rows of perfect white teeth. It was only by contrast with their whiteness that she noticed the golden brown of his complexion.

"I am of international interest," he said lightly and glanced round toward his attendants.

She thought he was going and would have moved on, but he stopped her.

"You are the first English-speaking person I have talked to since I've been in France," he said, "except the American Ambassador." He smiled as at a pleasant recollection.

"You talk almost like an Englishman yourself."

"I was at Oxford," he said, "My brother was at Harvard, my father, the brother of the late Sultan, was a very progressive man and believed in the western education for his children. Won't you sit down?" he asked, pointing to the sand.

She hesitated a second and then sank to the ground, and crossing his legs he sat by her side.

"I was in France for four years," he went on, evidently anxious to hold her in conversation, "so I speak both languages fairly well. Do you speak Arabic?" He asked the question solemnly, but his eyes were bright with laughter.

"Not very well," she answered gravely. "Are you staying very long?" It was a conventional question and she was unprepared for the reply.

"I leave tonight," he said, "though very few people know it. You have surprised a state secret," he smiled again.

And then he began to talk of Morocco and its history, and with extraordinary ease he traced the story of the families which had ruled that troubled state.

He touched lightly on his own share in the rebellion which had almost brought about a European war.

"My uncle seized the throne, you know," he said taking up a handful of sand and tossing it up in the air. "He defeated my father and killed him, and then we caught his two sons."

"What happened to them?" asked Jean curiously.

"Oh, we killed them," he said carelessly. "I had them hanged in front of my tent. You're shocked?"

She shook her head.

"Do you believe in killing your enemies?"

She nodded.

"Why not? It is the only logical thing to do."

"My brother joined forces with the present Sultan, and if I ever catch him I shall hang him, too," he smiled.

"And if he catches you?" she asked.

"Why, he'll hang me," he laughed. "That is the rule of the game."

"How strange!" she said, half to herself.

"Do you think so? I suppose from the European standpoint—"

"No, no," she stopped him. "I wasn't thinking of that. You are logical and you do the logical thing. That is how I would treat my enemies."

"If you had any," he suggested.

She nodded.

"If I had any," she repeated with a hard little smile. "Will you tell me this—do I call you Mr. Muley or Lord Muley?"

"You may call me Wazeer, if you're so hard up for a title," he said, and the little idiom sounded queer from him.

"Well, Wazeer, will you tell me, suppose somebody had something that you wanted very badly and they wouldn't give it to you, and you had the power to destroy them, what would you do?"

"I should certainly destroy them," said Muley Hafiz. "It is unnecessary to ask. 'The common rule, the simple plan'," he quoted.

Her eyes were fixed on his face, and she was frowning, though this she did not know.

"I am glad I met you this afternoon," she said. "It must be wonderful living in that atmosphere, the atmosphere of might and power, where men and women aren't governed by the finicking rules which vitiate the western world."

He laughed.

"When you are tired of your western civilization," he said as he rose and helped her to her feet (his hands were long and delicate, and she grew breathless at the touch of them), "you must come along to my little city in the hills where the law is the sword of Muley Hafiz."

She looked at him for a moment.

"I almost wish I could," she said and held out her hand.

He took it in the European fashion and bowed over it. She seemed so tiny a thing by the side of him, her head did not reach his shoulder.

"Good-bye," she said hurriedly, and turning, walked back the way she had come and he stood watching her until she was out of sight.

CHAPTER XXXII

"Jean!"

She looked round to meet the scowling gaze of Marcus Stepney.

"I must say you're the limit," he said violently. "There are lots of things I imagine you'd do, but to stand there in broad daylight talking to a nigger—"

"If I stand in broad daylight and talk to a card-sharper, Marcus, I think I'm just low enough to do almost anything."

"A damned Moorish nigger," he spluttered, and her eyes narrowed.

"Walk up the road with me, and if you possibly can, keep your voice down to the level which gentlemen usually employ when talking to women," she said.

She was in better condition than he, and he was a little out of breath by the time they reached the Cafe de Paris, which was crowded at that hour with the afternoon tea people.

He found a quiet corner, and by this time his anger, and a little of his courage, had evaporated.

"I've only your interest at heart, Jean," he said almost pleadingly, "but you don't want people in our set to know you've been hobnobbing with this infernal Moor."

"When you say 'our set,' to which set are you referring?" she asked unpleasantly. "Because if it is the set I believe you mean, they can't think too badly of me for my liking. It would be a degradation to me to be admired by your set, Marcus."

"Oh come now," he began feebly.

"I thought I had made it clear to you and I hoped you would carry the marks to your dying day," there was malice in her voice, and he winced, "that I do not allow you to dominate my life or to censor my actions. The 'nigger' you referred to was more of a gentleman than you can ever be, Marcus, because he has breed, which the Lord didn't give to you."

The waiter brought the tea at that moment and the conversation passed to unimportant topics till he had gone.

"I'm rather rattled," he apologized. "I lost six thousand *louis* last night."

"Then you have six thousand reasons why you should keep on good terms with me," said Jean smiling cheerfully.

"That cave-man stuff?" he asked, and shook his head. "She'd raise Cain."

Jean was laughing inside herself, but she did not show her merriment.

"You can but try," she said, "I've already told you how it can be done."

"I'll try tomorrow," he said after a thought. "By heavens, I'll try tomorrow!"

It was on the tip of her tongue to say "not tomorrow," but she checked herself.

Morden came round with the car to pick her up soon after. Morden! Her little chin jerked up with a gesture of annoyance, which she seldom permitted herself. And yet she felt unusually cheered. Her meeting with the Moor was a milestone in her life from which memory she could draw both encouragement and comfort.

"You met Muley?" said Lydia. "How thrilling! What is he like, Jean? Was he a blackamoor?"

"No, he wasn't a blackamoor," said the girl quietly. "He was an unusually intelligent man."

"H'm," grunted her father. "How did you come to meet him, my dear?"

"I picked him up on the beach," said Jean coolly, "as any flapper would pick up any nut."

Mr. Briggerland choked.

"I hate to hear you talking like that, Jean. Who introduced him?"

"I told you," she said complacently. "I introduced myself. I talked to him on the beach and he talked to me, and we sat down and played with the sand and discussed each other's lives."

"But how enterprising of you, Jean," said the admiring Lydia.

Mr. Briggerland was going to say something but thought better of it.

There was a concert at the theatre that night and the whole party went. They had a box and the interval had come before Lydia saw somebody ushered into a box on the other side of the house with such evidence of deference that she would have known who he was even if she had not seen the scarlet fez and the white robe.

"It is your Muley," she whispered.

Jean looked round.

Muley Hafiz was looking across at her; his eyes immediately sought the girl's, and he bowed slightly.

"What the devil is he bowing at?" grumbled Mr. Briggerland. "You didn't take any notice of him, did you Jean?"

"I bowed to him," said his daughter, not troubling to look round. "Don't be silly, father; anyway, if he weren't nice, it would be quite the right thing to do. I'm the most distinguished woman in the house because I know Muley Hafiz, and he has bowed to me! Don't you realize the social value of a lion's recognition?"

Lydia could not see him distinctly. She had an impression of a white face, two large black spaces where his eyes were and a black beard. He sat all the time in the shadow of a curtain.

Jean looked round to see if Marcus Stepney was present, hoping that he had witnessed the exchange of courtesies, but Marcus at that moment was watching little bundles of twelve thousand franc notes raked across to the croupier's end of the table—which is the business end of Monte Carlo.

Jean was the last to leave the car when it set them down at the Villa Casa. Morden called her respectfully.

"Excuse me, Mademoiselle," he said, "I wish you would come to the garage and see the new tires that have arrived. I don't like them."

It was a code which she had agreed he should use when he wanted her.

"Very good, Morden, I will come to the garage later," she said carelessly.

"What does Morden want you for?" asked her father with a frown.

"You heard him. He doesn't approve of some new tires that have been bought for the car," she said coolly. "And don't ask me questions. I've got a headache and I'm dying for a cup of chocolate."

"If that fellow gives you any trouble he'll be sorry," said Briggerland. "And let me tell you this, Jean, that marriage idea of yours—"

She only looked at him, but he knew the look and wilted.

"I don't want to interfere with your private affairs," he mumbled, "but the very thought of it gets me crazy."

The garage was a brick building erected by the side of the carriage drive, built much nearer the house than is usually the case.

Jean waited a reasonable time before she slipped away. Morden was waiting for her before the open doors of the garage. The place was in darkness; she did not see him standing in the entrance until she was within a few paces of the man.

"Come up to my room," he said briskly.

"What do you want?" she asked.

"I want to speak to you and this is not the place."

"This is the only place where I am prepared to speak to you at the moment, Francois," she said reproachfully. "Don't you realize that my father is within hearing, and at any moment Madame Meredith may come out? How would I explain my presence in your room?"

He did not answer for the moment, then:

"Jean, I am worried," he said in a troubled voice. "I cannot understand your plans—they are too clever for me, and I have known men and women of great attainment. The great Bersac—"

"The great Bersac is dead," she said coldly. "He was a man of such great attainments that he came to the knife. Besides, it is not necessary that you should understand my plans, Francois."

She knew quite well what was troubling him, but she waited.

"I cannot understand the letter which I wrote for you," said Morden. "The letter in which I say Madame Meredith loved me. I have thought this matter out Jean, and it seems to me that I am compromised."

She laughed softly.

"Poor Francois," she said mockingly. "With whom could you be compromised but with your future wife? If I desire you to write that letter, what else matters?"

Again he was silent.

"I cannot speak here," he said almost roughly. "You must come to my room."

She hesitated. There was something in his voice she did not like.

"Very well," she said and followed him up the steep stairs.

CHAPTER XXXIII

"Now explain." His words were a command, his tone peremptory.

Jean, who knew men, and read them without error, realized that this was not a moment to temporize.

"I will explain to you, Francois, but I do not like the way you speak," she said. "It is not you I wish to compromise, but Madame Meredith."

"In this letter I wrote for you I said I was going away. I confessed to you that I had forged a check for five million francs. That is a very serious document, Mademoiselle, to be in the possession of anybody but myself." He looked at her straight in the eyes and she met his gaze unflinchingly.

"The thing will be made very clear to you tomorrow, Francois," she said softly; "and really there is no reason to worry. I wish to end this unhappy state of affairs."

"With me?" he asked quickly.

"No, with Madame Meredith," she answered. "I, too, am tired of waiting for marriage and I intend asking my father's permission for the wedding to take place next week. Indeed, Francois," she lowered her eyes modestly, "I have already written to the British Consul at Nice, asking him to arrange for the ceremony to be performed."

The sallow face of the chauffeur flushed a dull red. "Do you mean that?" he said eagerly. "Jean, you are not deceiving me?"

She shook her head.

"No, Francois," she said in that low plaintive voice of hers, "I could not deceive you in a matter so important to myself."

He stood watching her, his breast heaving, his burning eyes devouring her, then:

"You will give me back that letter I wrote, Jean?" he said.

"I will give it to you tomorrow."

"Tonight," he said, and took both her hands in his. "I am sure I am right. It is too dangerous a letter to be in existence, Jean, dangerous for you and for me—you will let me have it tonight?"

She hesitated.

"It is in my room," she said, an unnecessary statement, and, in the circumstances, a dangerous one, for his eyes dropped to the bag that hung at her wrist.

"It is there," he said. "Jean darling, do as I ask," he pleaded. "You know, every time I think of that letter I go cold. I was a madman when I wrote it."

"I have not got it here," she said steadily. She tried to draw back, but she was too late. He gripped her wrists and pulled the bag roughly from her hand.

"Forgive me, but I know I am right," he began, and then like a fury she flew at him, wrenched the bag from his hand, and by the very violence of her attack, flung him backward.

He stared at her and the color faded from his face, leaving it a dead white.

"What is this you are trying to do?" he glowered at her.

"I will see you in the morning, Francois," she said and turned.

Before she could reach the head of the stairs his arm was round her and he had dragged her back.

"My friend," he said between his teeth, "there is something in this matter which is bad for me."

"Let me go," she breathed and struck at his face.

For a full minute they struggled, and then the door opened and Mr. Briggerland came in, and at the sight of his livid face, Morden released his hold.

"You swine!" hissed the big man. His fist shot out and Morden went down with a crash to the ground. For a moment he was stunned, and then with a snarl he turned over on his side and whipped a revolver from his hip pocket. Before he could fire, the girl had gripped the pistol and wrenched it from his hand.

"Get up," said Briggerland sternly. "Now explain to me, my friend, what you mean by this disgraceful attack upon mademoiselle."

The man rose and dusted himself mechanically and there was that in his face which boded no good to Mr. Briggerland.

Before he could speak Jean intervened.

"Father," she said quietly, "you have no right to strike Francois."

"Francois," spluttered Briggerland, his dark face purple with rage.

"Francois," she repeated calmly. "It is right that you should know that Francois and I will be married next week."

Mr. Briggerland's jaw dropped.

"What?" he almost shrieked.

She nodded.

"We are going to be married next week," she said; "and the little scene you witnessed has nothing whatever to do with you."

The effect of these words on Morden was magical. The malignant frown which had distorted his face cleared away. He looked from Jean to Briggerland as though it were impossible to believe the evidence of his ears.

"Francois and I love each other," Jean went on in her even voice. "We have quarreled tonight on a matter which has nothing to do with anybody save ourselves."

"You're going to marry him next week?" said Mr. Briggerland dully. "By God, you'll do nothing of the sort!"

She raised her hand.

"It is too late for you to interfere, father," she said quietly. "Francois and I shall go our way and face our own fate. I'm sorry you disapprove because you have always been a very loving father to me."

That was the first hint that Mr. Briggerland had received that there might be some other explanation for her words, and he became calmer.

"Very well," he said, "I can only tell you that I strongly disapprove of the action you have taken and that I shall do nothing whatever to further your reckless scheme. But I must insist upon your coming back to the house now. I cannot have my daughter talked about."

She nodded.

"I will see you tomorrow morning early, Francois," she said, "Perhaps you will drive me into Nice before breakfast. I have some purchases to make."

He bowed and reached out his hand for the revolver which she had taken from him.

She looked at the ornate weapon, its silver plated metal parts, the graceful ivory handle.

"I'm not going to trust you with this tonight," she said with her rare smile. "Good night, Francois."

He took her hand and kissed it.

"Good night, Jean," he said in a tremulous voice. For a moment their eyes met, and then she turned as though she dared not trust herself and followed her father down the stairs.

They were halfway to the house when she laid her hand on Briggerland's arm.

"Keep this," she said. It was Francois' revolver. "It is probably loaded and I thought I saw some silver initials inlaid in the ivory handle. If I know Francois Morden, they are his."

"What do you want me to do with it?" he said as he slipped the weapon in his pocket.

She laughed.

"On your way to bed, come into my room," she said. "I've quite a lot to tell you," and she sailed into the drawing room to interrupt Mrs. Cole-Mortimer, who was teaching a weary Lydia the elements of bezique.

"Where have you been, Jean?" asked Lydia, putting down her cards.

"I have been arranging a novel experience for you, but I'm not so sure that it will be as interesting as it might—it all depends upon the state of your young heart," said Jean, pulling up a chair.

"My young heart is very healthy," laughed Lydia. "What is the interesting experience?"

"Are you in love?" challenged Jean, searching in a big chintz bag where she kept her handiwork, for a piece of unfinished sewing. (Jean's domesticity was always a source of wonder to Lydia.)

"In love— good heavens, no."

"So much the better," nodded Jean. "That sounds as though the experience will be fascinating,"

She waited until she had threaded the fine needle before she explained.

"If you really are not in love and you sit on the Lovers' Chair, the name of your future husband will come to you. If you're in love, of course, that complicates matters a little."

"But suppose I don't want to know the name of my future husband?"

"Then you're inhuman," said Jean.

"Where is this magical chair?"

"It is on the San Remo road beyond the frontier station. You've been there, haven't you, Margaret?"

"Once," sad Mrs. Cole-Mortimer, who had not been east of Cap Martin, but whose rule it was never to admit that she had missed anything worth seeing.

"In a wild, eerie spot," Jean went on, "and miles from any human habitation."

"Are you going to take me?"

Jean shook her head.

"That would ruin the spell," she said solemnly. "No, my dear, if you want that thrill and, seriously it is worth while, because the scenery is the most beautiful of any along the coast, you must go alone."

Lydia nodded.

"I'll try it. Is it too far to walk?" she asked.

"Much too far," said Jean. "Morden will drive you out. He knows the road very well and you ought not to take anybody but an experienced driver. I have a *permis* for the car to pass the frontier; you will probably meet father in San Remo— he is taking a motor-cycle trip, aren't you, daddy?"

Mr. Briggerland drew a long breath and nodded. He was beginning to understand.

CHAPTER XXXIV

There was lying in Monaco harbor a long white boat with a stumpy mast, which delighted in the name of "Jungle Queen." It was the property of an impecunious English nobleman who made a respectable income from letting the vessel on hire. Mrs. Cole-Mortimer had seemed surprised at the reasonable fee demanded for two months' use until she had seen the boat the day after her arrival at Cap Martin.

She had pictured a large and commodious yacht; she found a reasonably sized motor launch with a whale-deck cabin. The description in the agent's catalogue that the "Jungle Queen" would "sleep four" was probably based on the experience of a party of young roisterers who had once hired the vessel. Supposing that the "four" were reasonably drunk or heavily drugged, it was possible for them to sleep on board the "Jungle Queen." Normally two persons would have found it difficult, though by lying diagonally across the "cabin" one small-sized man could have slumbered without discomfort.

The "Jungle Queen" had been a disappointment to Jean also. Her busy brain had conceived an excellent way of solving her principal problem, but a glance at the "Jungle Queen" told her that the money she had spent on hiring the launch—and it was little better—was wasted. She herself hated the sea and had so little faith in the utility of the boat that she had even missed the youth who attended to its well-worn engines.

Mr. Marcus Stepney, who was mildly interested in motor boating, and considerably interested in any form of amusement which he could get at somebody else's expense, had so far been the sole patron of the "Jungle Queen." It was his practice to take the boat out every morning for a two hours' sail, generally alone, though sometimes he would take somebody whose acquaintance he had made, and who was destined to be a source of profit to him in the future.

Jean's talk of the cave-man method of wooing had made a big impression upon him, emphasized as it had been and still was, by the two angry red scars across the back of his hand. Things were not going well with him; the supply of rich and trusting youths had suddenly dried up. The little games in his private sitting room had dwindled to feeble proportions. He was still able to eke out a living, but his success at his private seances had been counterbalanced by heavy losses at the public tables.

It is a known fact that people who live outside the law keep to their own plane. The swindler very rarely commits acts of violence. The burglar who practices cardsharping as a side line is virtually unknown.

Mr. Stepney lived on a plausible tongue and a pair of highly dexterous hands. It had never occurred to him to go beyond his own sphere, and indeed violence was as repugnant to him as it was vulgar.

Yet the cave-man suggestion appealed to him. He had a way with women of a certain kind, and if his confidence had been rather shaken by Jean's savagery and Lydia's indifference, he had not altogether abandoned the hope that both girls in their turn might be conquered by the adoption of the right method.

The method for dealing with Jean he had at the back of his mind.

As for Lydia—Jean's suggestion was very attractive. It was after a very heavily unprofitable night spent at the Nice Casino that he took his courage in both hands and drove to the Villa Casa.

He was an early arrival, but Lydia had already finished her *petite dejourner* and she was painfully surprised to see him.

"I'm not swimming today, Mr. Stepney," she said, "and you don't look as if you were, either."

He was dressed in perfectly fitting white duck trousers, white shoes and a blue nautical coat with brass buttons; a yachtman's cap was set at an angle on his dark head.

"No, I'm going out to do a little fishing," he said, "and I was wondering whether, in your charity, you would accompany me."

She shook her head.

"I'm sorry—I have another engagement this morning," she said.

"Can't you break it?" he pleaded, "as an especial favor to me? I've made all preparations and I've got a lovely lunch on board—you said you would come fishing with me one day."

"I'd like to," she confessed, "but I really have something very important to do this morning."

She did not tell him that her important duty was to sit on the Lovers' Chair. Somehow her trip seemed just a little silly in the cold, clear light of morning.

"I could have you back in time," he begged, "Do come along Mrs. Meredith! You're going to spoil my day."

"I'm sure Lydia wouldn't be so unkind."

Jean had made her appearance as they were speaking.

"What is the scheme, Lydia?"

"Mr. Stepney wants me to go out in the yacht," said the girl, and Jean smiled.

"I'm glad you call it a 'yacht'," she said drily. "You're the second person who has so described it. The first was the agent. Take her tomorrow, Marcus."

There was a glint of amusement in her eyes and he felt that she knew what was at the back of his mind.

"All right," he said, in a tone which suggested that it was anything but all right, and added, "I saw you flying through Nice this morning with that yellow-faced chauffeur of yours, Jean."

"Were you up so early?" she asked carelessly.

"I wasn't dressed, I was looking out of the window—my room faces the Promenade d'Anglaise. I don't like that fellow."

"I shouldn't let him know," said Jean coolly. "He is very sensitive. There are so many fellows that you dislike, too."

"I don't think that you ought to allow him so much freedom," Marcus Stepney went on. He was not in an amiable frame of mind, and the knowledge that he was annoying the girl encouraged him. "If you give these French chauffeurs an inch they'll take a kilometre."

"I suppose they would," said Jean thoughtfully. "How is your poor hand, Marcus?"

He growled something under his breath and thrust his hand deep into the pocket of his reefer coat.

"It is quite well," he snapped and went back to Monaco and his solitary boat trip flaming.

"One of these days—" he muttered, as he tuned up the motor. He did not finish his sentence, but sent the nose of the "Jungle Queen" at full speed for the open sea.

Jean's talk with Morden that morning had not been wholly satisfactory. She had calmed his suspicions to an extent, but he still harped upon the letter and she had promised to give it to him that evening.

"My dear," she said, "you are too impulsive—too Gallic. I had a terrible scene with father last night. He wants me to break off the engagement; told me what my friends in London would say, and how I should be a social outcast."

"And you—you Jean?" he asked.

"I told him that such things did not trouble me," she said, and her lips drooped sadly. "I know I cannot be happy with anybody but you, Francois, and I am willing to face the sneers of London, even the hatred and scorn of my father, for your sake."

He would have seized her hand, though they were in the open road, but she drew away from him.

"Be careful, Francois," she warned him. "Remember that you have a very little time to wait."

"I cannot believe my good fortune," he babbled as he brought the car up the gentle incline into Monte Carlo. He dodged an early morning tram, missing an unsuspecting passenger who had come round the back of the tram-car, by inches and sent the big Italia up the palm avenue into the town.

"It is incredible, and yet I always thought some great thing would happen to me, and Jean, I have risked so much for you. I would have killed madame in London if she had not been dragged out of the way by that old man, and did I not watch for you when the man Meredith—"

"Hush," she said in a low voice. "Let us talk about something else."

"Shall I see your father? I am sorry for what I did last night," he said, when they were nearing the villa.

"Father has taken his motor-bicycle and gone for a trip into Italy," she said. "No, I do not think I should speak to him even if he were here. He may come round in time, Francois. You can understand that it is terribly distressing; he hoped I would make a great marriage. You must allow for father's disappointment."

He nodded. He did not drive her to the house, but stopped outside the garage.

"Remember at half-past ten you will take Madame Meredith to the Lovers' Chair—you know the place?"

"I know it very well," he said. "It is a difficult place to turn—I must take her almost into San Remo. Why does she want to go to the Lovers' Chair? I thought only the cheap people went there—"

"You must not tell her that," she said sharply. "Besides, I myself have been there."

"And who did you think of, Jean?" he asked suddenly. She lowered her eyes.

"I will not tell you—now," she said, and ran into the house.

Francois stood gazing after her until she had disappeared and then like a man waking from a trance he turned to the mundane business of filling his tank.

CHAPTER XXXV

Lydia was dressing for her journey when Mrs. Cole-Mortimer came into the saloon where Jean was writing.

"There's a telephone call from Monte Carlo," she said. "Somebody wants to speak to Lydia."

Jean jumped up.

"I'll answer it," she said.

The voice at the other end of the wire was harsh and unfamiliar to her.

"I want to speak to Mrs. Meredith."

"Who is it?" asked Jean.

"It is a friend of hers," said the voice. "Will you tell her? The business is rather urgent."

"I'm sorry," said Jean, "but she's just gone out."

She heard an exclamation of annoyance.

"Do you know where she's gone?" asked the voice.

"I think she's gone into Monte Carlo," said Jean.

"If I miss her will you tell her not to go out again until I come to the house?"

"Certainly," said Jean politely, and hung up the telephone.

"Was that a call for me?"

It was Lydia's voice from the head of the stairs.

"Yes, dear. I think it was Marcus Stepney who wanted to speak to you. I told him you'd gone out," said Jean. "You didn't wish to speak to him?"

"Good heavens, no," said Lydia. "You're sure you won't come with me?"

"I'd rather stay here," said Jean truthfully.

The car was at the door, and Morden looking unusually spruce in his white dust coat, stood by the open door.

"How long shall I be away?" asked Lydia.

"About two hours, dear, you'll be very hungry when you come back," said Jean, kissing her. "Now, mind you think of the right man," she warned her in mockery.

"I wonder if I shall," said Lydia quietly.

Jean watched the car out of sight, then went back to the saloon. She was hardly seated before the telephone rang again, and she anticipated Mrs. Cole-Mortimer and answered it.

"Mrs. Meredith has not gone into Monte Carlo," said the voice. "Her car has not been seen on the road."

"Is that Mr. Jaggs?" asked Jean sweetly.

"Yes, Miss," was the reply.

"Mrs. Meredith has come back now. I'm dreadfully sorry, I thought she had gone into Monte Carlo. She's in her room with a bad headache. Will you come and see her?"

There was an interval of silence.

"Yes, I will come," said Jaggs.

Twenty minutes later a taxi-cab set down the old man at the door, and a maid admitted him and brought him into the saloon.

Jean rose to meet him. She looked at the bowed figure of old Jaggs, took him all in, from his iron-gray hair to his dusty shoes, and then she pointed to a chair.

"Sit down," she said, and old Jaggs obeyed. "You've something very important to tell Mrs. Meredith, I suppose."

"I'll tell her that myself, Miss," said the old man gruffly.

"Well, before you tell her anything, I want to make a confession," she smiled down on old Jaggs, and pulled up a chair so that she faced him.

He was sitting with his back to the light, holding his battered hat on his knees.

"I've really brought you up under false pretences," she said, "because Mrs. Meredith isn't here at all."

"Not here?" he said, half rising.

"No, she's gone for a ride with our chauffeur. But I wanted to see you, Mr. Jaggs, because—" she paused. "I realize that you're a dear friend of hers and have her best interests at heart. I don't know who you are," she said, shaking her head, "but I know, of course, that Mr. John Glover has employed you."

"What's all this about?" he asked gruffly. "What have you to tell me?"

"I don't know how to begin," she said, biting her lips. "It is such a delicate matter that I hate talking about it at all. But the attitude of Mrs. Meredith to our chauffeur Morden is distressing, and I think Mr. Glover should be told."

He did not speak and she went on.

"These things do happen, I know," she said, "but I am happy to say that nothing of that sort has come into my experience, and, of course, Morden is a good-looking man and she is young—"

"What are you talking about?" His tone was dictatorial and commanding.

"I mean," she said, "that I fear poor Lydia is in love with Morden."

He sprang to his feet.

"It's a damned lie!" he said and she stared at him. "Now tell me what has happened to Lydia Meredith," he went on, "and let me tell you this, Jean Briggerland, that if one hair of that girl's head is harmed, I will finish the work I began out there," he pointed to the garden, "and strangle you with my own hands."

She lifted her eyes to his and dropped them again, and began to tremble, then turning suddenly on her heel, she fled to her room, locked the door and stood against it, white and shaking. For the second time in her life Jean Briggerland was afraid.

She heard his quick footsteps in the passage outside and there came a tap on her door.

"Let me in," growled the man, and for a second she almost lost control of herself. She looked wildly round the room for some way of escape, and then as a thought struck her, she ran quickly into the bathroom, which opened from her room. A large sponge was set to dry by an open window, and this she seized; on a shelf by the side of the bath was a big bottle of ammonia, and averting her face, she poured its contents upon the sponge until it was sodden, then with the dripping sponge in her hand, she crept back, turned the key and opened the door.

The old man burst in, then, before he realized what was happening, the sponge was pressed against his face. The pungent drug almost blinded him, its paralyzing fumes brought him on to his knees. He gripped her wrist and tried to press away her hand, but now her arm was round his neck and he could not get the purchase.

With a groan of agony he collapsed on the floor. In that instant she was on him like a cat, her knee between his shoulders.

Half unconscious he felt his hands drawn to his back, and felt something lashing them together. She was using the silk girdle which had been about her waist, and her work was effective.

Presently she turned him over on his back. The ammonia was still in his eyes and he could not open them. The agony was terrible, almost un-endurable. With her hand under his arm he struggled to his feet. He felt her lead him somewhere and suddenly he was pushed into a chair. She left him alone for a little while, but presently came back and began to tie his feet together. It was a most amazing single-handed capture—even Jean could never have imagined the ease with which she could gain her victory.

"I'm sorry to hurt an old man." There was a sneer in her voice which he had not heard before. "But if you promise not to shout, I will not gag you."

He heard the sound of running water, and presently with a wet cloth she began wiping his eyes gently.

"You will be able to see in a minute," said Jean's cool voice. "In the meantime you'll stay here until I send for the police."

For all his pain he was forced to chuckle.

"Until you send for the police, eh? You know me?"

"I only know you're a wicked old man who broke into this house whilst I was alone and the servants were out," she said.

"You know why I've come?" he insisted. "I've come to tell Mrs. Meredith that a hundred thousand pounds have been taken from her bank on a forged signature."

"How absurd," said Jean. She was sitting on the edge of the bath looking at the bedraggled figure. "How could anybody draw money from Mrs. Meredith's bank whilst her dear friend and guardian, Jack Glover, is in London to see that she is not robbed."

Old Jaggs glared up at her from his inflamed eyes.

"You know very well," he said distinctly, "that I am Jack Glover, and that I have not left Monte Carlo since Lydia Meredith arrived."

CHAPTER XXXVI

Mr. Briggerland did not enthuse over any form of sport or exercise. His hobbies were confined to the handsome motorcycle, which not only provided him with recreation, but had, on occasion, been of assistance in the carrying out of important plans, formulated by his daughter.

He stopped at Mentone for breakfast and climbed the hill to Grimaldi after passing the frontier station at Pont St. Louis. He had all the morning before him, and there was no great hurry. At Ventimille he had a second breakfast, for the morning was keen and his appetite was good. He loafed through the little town, with a cigar between his teeth, bought some curios at a shop and continued his leisurely journey.

His objective was San Remo. There was a train at one o'clock which would bring him and his machine back to Monte Carlo, where it was his intention to spend the remainder of the afternoon. At Pont St. Louis he had had a talk with the customs officer.

"No, M'sieur, there are very few travellers on the road in the morning," said the official. "It is not until late in the afternoon that the traffic begins. Times have changed on the Riviera, and so many people go to Cannes. The old road is almost now deserted."

At eleven o'clock Mr. Briggerland came to a certain part of the road and found a hiding place for his motorcycle—a small plantation of olive trees on the hillside. Incidentally it was an admirable resting place, for from here he commanded an extensive view of the western road.

Lydia's journey had been no less enjoyable. She, too, had stopped at Mentone to explore the town, and had left Pont St. Louis an hour after Mr. Briggerland had passed.

The road to San Remo runs under the shadow of steep hills through a bleak stretch of country from which even the industrious peasantry of northern Italy cannot win a livelihood. Save for isolated patches of cultivated land, the hills are bare and menacing.

With these gaunt plateaux on one side and the rock-strewn seashore on the other, there was little to hold the eye save an occasional glimpse of the Italian town in the far distance. There was a wild uncouthness about the scenery which awed the girl. Sometimes the car would be running so near the sea level that the spray of the waves hit the windows; sometimes it would climb over an out-jutting headland and she would look down upon a bouldered beach a hundred feet below.

It was on the crest of a headland that the car stopped.

Here the road ran out in a semicircle so that from where she sat she could not see its continuation either before or behind. Ahead it slipped round the shoulder of a high and overhanging mass of rock, through which the road must have been cut. Behind, it dipped down to a cove, hidden from sight.

"There is the Lovers' Chair, Mademoiselle," said Morden. Half a dozen feet beneath the road level was a broad shelf of rock. A few stone steps led down and she followed them. The Lovers' Chair was carved in the face of the rock and she sat down to view the beauty of the scene. The solitude, the stillness, which only the lazy waves broke, the majesty of the setting, brought a strange peace to her. Beyond the edge of the ledge, the cliff fell sheer to the water, and she shivered as she stepped back from her inspection.

Morden did not see her go. He sat on the running board of his car, his pale face between his hands, a prey to his own gloomy thoughts. There must be a development, he told himself. He was beginning to get uneasy, and for the first time he doubted the sincerity of the woman who had been to him as a goddess.

He did not hear Mr. Briggerland, for the dark man was light of foot, when he came round the shoulder of the hill. Morden's back was toward him. Suddenly the chauffeur looked round.

"M'sieur," he stammered, and would have risen, but Briggerland laid his hand on his shoulder.

"Do not rise, Francois," he said pleasantly, "I am afraid I was hasty last night."

"M'sieur, it was I who was hasty," said Morden huskily, "it was unpardonable—"

"Nonsense," Briggerland patted the man's shoulder. "What is that boat out there—a man o' war, Francois?"

Francois Morden turned his head toward the sea, and Briggerland pointed the ivory handled pistol he had held behind his back and shot him dead.

The report of the revolver thrown down by the rocks came to Lydia like a clap of thunder. At first she thought it was a tire burst and hurried up the steps to see.

Mr. Briggerland was standing with his back to the car. At his feet was the tumbled body of Morden.

"Mr.—Brig—!" she gasped, and saw the revolver in his hand. With a cry she almost flung herself down the steps as the revolver exploded. The bullet ripped her hat from her head, and she flung up her hands, thinking she had been struck.

Then the dark face showed over the parapet and again the revolver was presented. She stared for a second into his benevolent eyes, and then something hit her violently and she staggered back and dropped over the edge of the shelf down, straight down into the sea below.

CHAPTER XXXVII

Probably Jean Briggerland never gave a more perfect representation of shocked surprise than when old Jaggs announced that he was Jack Glover.

"Mr. Glover," she said incredulously.

"If you'll be kind enough to release my hands," said Jack savagely, "I will convince you."

Jean, all meekness, obeyed and presently he stood up with a groan.

"You've nearly blinded me," he said, turning to the glass.

"If I'd known it was you—"

"Don't make me laugh!" he snapped, "Of course you knew who it was!" He took off the wig and peeled the beard from his face.

"Was that very painful?" she asked sympathetically, and Jack snorted.

"How was I to know that it was you?" she demanded virtuously indignant, "I thought you were a wicked old man—"

"You thought nothing of the sort, Miss Briggerland," said Jack. "You knew who I was, and you guessed why I had taken on this disguise. I was not many yards from you when it suddenly dawned upon you that I could not sleep at Lydia Meredith's flat unless I went there in the guise of an old man."

"Why should you want to sleep at her flat at all?" she asked innocently. "It doesn't seem to me to be a very proper ambition."

"That is an unnecessary question and I'm wasting my time when I answer you," said Jack sternly. "I went there to save her life, to protect her against your murderous plots!"

"My murderous plots?" she repeated aghast. "You surely don't know what you're saying."

"I know this," and his face was not pleasant to see. "I have sufficient evidence to secure the arrest of your father, and possibly yourself. For months I have been working on that first providential accident of yours—the rich Australian who died with such remarkable suddenness. I may not get you in the Meredith case and I may not be able to jail you for your attacks on Mrs. Meredith, but I have enough evidence to hang your father for the earlier crime."

Her face was blank—expressionless. Never before had she been brought up short with such a threat as the man was uttering, nor had she ever been in danger of detection. And all the time she was eyeing him so steadily, not a muscle of her face moving, her mind was groping back into the past, examining every detail of the crime he had mentioned, seeking for some flaw in the carefully prepared plan which had brought a good man to a violent and untimely end.

"That kind of bluff doesn't impress me," she said at last. "You're in a poor way when you have to invent crimes to attach to me."

"We'll go into that later. Where is Lydia?" he said shortly.

"I tell you I don't know, except that she has gone out for a drive. I expect her back very soon."

"Is your father with her?"

She shook her head.

"No, father went out early. I don't know who gave you authority to cross-examine me. Why, Jack Glover, you have all the importance of a French examining magistrate," she smiled.

"You may learn how important they are soon," he said significantly. "Where is your chauffeur, Morden?"

"He is gone, too—in fact, he is driving Lydia. Why?" she asked with a little tightening of heart. She had only just been in time, she thought. So they had associated Morden with the forgery!

His first words confirmed this suspicion.

"There is a warrant for Morden which will be executed as soon as he returns," said Jack. "We have been able to trace him in London and also the woman who presented the check. We know his movements from the time he left Nice by aeroplane for Paris to the time he returned to Nice. The people who changed the money for him will swear to his identity."

If he expected to startle her he was disappointed. She raised her eyebrows.

"I can't believe it is possible. Morden was such an honest man," she said. "We trusted him implicitly and never once did he betray our trust. Now, Mr. Glover," she said coolly, "might I suggest that an interview with a gentleman in my bedroom is not calculated to increase my servants' respect for me? Will you go downstairs and wait until I come?"

"You'll not attempt to leave this house?" he said and she laughed.

"Really, you're going on like one of those infallible detectives one reads about in the popular magazines," she said a little contemptuously. "You have no authority whatever to keep me from leaving this house and nobody knows that better than you. But you needn't be afraid. Sit on the stairs if you like until I come down."

When he had gone she rang the bell for her maid and handed her an envelope.

"I shall be in the saloon, talking to Mr. Glover," she said in a low voice. "I want you to bring this in and say that you found it in the hall."

"Yes, Miss," said the woman.

Jean proceeded leisurely to her toilet. In the struggle her dress had been torn, and she changed it for a pale green silk gown, and Jack, pacing in the hall below, was on the point of coming up to discover if she had made her escape when she sailed serenely down the stairs.

"I should like to know one thing, Mr. Glover," she said as she went into the saloon. "What do you intend doing? What is your immediate plan? Are you going to spirit Lydia away from us? Of course, I know you're in love with her and all that sort of thing."

His face went pink.

"I am not in love with Mrs. Meredith," he lied.

"Don't be silly," she said practically, "of course you're in love with her."

"My first job is to get that money back, and you're going to help me," he said.

"Of course I'm going to help you," she agreed. "If Morden has been such a scoundrel, he must suffer the consequence. I'm sure that you are too clever to have made any mistake. Poor Morden! I wonder what made him do it, because he is such a good friend of Lydia's, and seriously, Mr. Glover, I do think Lydia is being indiscreet."

"You made that remark before," he said quietly. "Now perhaps you'll explain what you mean."

She shrugged her shoulders.

"They are always about together. I saw them strolling on the lawn last night till quite a late hour, and I was so scared lest Mrs. Cole-Mortimer noticed it, too—"

"Which means that Mrs. Cole-Mortimer did not notice it. You're clever, Jean! Even as you invent you make preparations to refute any evidence that the other side can produce. I don't believe a word you say."

There was a knock at the door and the maid entered bearing a letter on a salver.

"This was addressed to you, Miss," she said. "It was on the hall table—didn't you see it?"

"No!" said Jean in surprise. She took the letter, looked down at the address and opened it.

He saw a look of amazement and horror come to her face.

"Good God!" gasped Jean.

"What is it?" he said, springing up.

She stared at the letter again and from the letter to him. "Read it," she said in a hollow voice.

> "*Dear Mademoiselle*: I have returned from London and have confessed to Madame Meredith that I have forged her name and have drawn £100,000 from her bank. And now I have learned that Madame Meredith loves me! There is only one end to this—that which you see—"

Jack read the letter twice.

"It is in his writing, too," he muttered, "It's impossible! I tell you I've had Mrs. Meredith under my eyes all the time she has been here—is there a letter from her?" he asked suddenly. "But no, it is impossible, impossible!"

"I haven't been into her room. Will you come up with me?"

He followed her up the stairs and into Lydia's big bedroom and the first thing that caught his eye was a sealed letter on a table near the bed. He picked it up. It was addressed to him, in Lydia's handwriting, and feverishly he tore it open.

His face, when he had finished reading, was as white as hers had been.

"Where have they gone?" he asked.

"They went to San Remo."

"By car?"

"Of course."

Without a word he turned and ran down the stairs out of the house.

The taxi that had brought him in the role of Jaggs had gone, but down the road, a dozen yards away, was the car he had hired on the day he came to Monte Carlo. He gave instructions to the driver and jumped in. The car sped through Mentone, stopped only the briefest while at the customs harrier whilst Jack pursued his inquiries.

Yes, a lady had passed, but she had not returned.

How long ago?

Perhaps an hour; perhaps less.

At top speed the big car thundered along the sea road, twisting and turning, diving into valleys and climbing steep headlands, and then rounding a corner, Jack saw the car and a little crowd about it. His heart turned to stone as he leaped to the road.

He saw the backs of two Italian gendarmes, and pushing aside the little knot of idlers, he came into the center of the group and stopped. Morden lay on his face in a pool of blood and one of the policemen was holding an ivory handled revolver.

"It was with this that the crime was committed," he said in florid Italian. "Three of the chambers are empty. Now at whom were the other two discharged?"

Jack reeled and gripped the mudguard of the car for support, then his eyes strayed to the opening in the wall which ran on the seaward side of the road.

He walked to the parapet and looked over and the first thing he saw was a torn hat and veil, and he knew it was Lydia's.

CHAPTER XXXVIII

Mr. Briggerland, killing time on the quay at Monaco saw the "Jungle Queen" come into harbor and watched Marcus land, carrying his lines in his hand.

As Marcus came abreast of him he called and Mr. Stepney looked round with a start.

"Hello, Briggerland," he said swallowing something.

"Well, have you been fishing?" asked Mr. Briggerland in his most paternal manner.

"Yes," admitted Marcus.

"Did you catch anything?"

Stepney nodded.

"Only one," he said.

"Hard luck," said Mr. Briggerland, with a smile, "but where is Mrs. Meredith—I understood she was going out with you today?"

"She went to San Remo," said Stepney shortly and the other nodded.

"To be sure," he said. "I had forgotten that."

Later he bought a copy of the *Nicoise* and learned of the tragedy on the San Remo road. It brought him back to the house, a visibly agitated man.

"This is shocking news, my dear," he panted into the saloon and stood stock-still at the sight of Mr. Jack Glover.

"Come in Briggerland," said Jack without ceremony. There was a man with him, a tall, keen Frenchman whom Briggerland recognized as the chief detective of the Prefecture. "We want you to give an account of your actions."

"My actions?" said Mr. Briggerland indignantly, "Do you associate me with this dreadful tragedy? A tragedy," he said, "which has stricken me almost dumb with horror and remorse. Why did I ever allow that villain even to speak to poor Lydia?"

"Nevertheless, M'sieur," said the tall man, quietly, "you must tell us where you have been."

"That is easily explained, I went to San Remo."

"By road?"

"Yes, by road," said Mr. Briggerland, "on my motor bicycle."

"What time did you arrive in San Remo?"

"At midday, or it may have been a quarter of an hour before."

"You know that the murder must have been committed at half-past eleven?" said Jack.

"So the newspapers tell me."

"Where did you go in San Remo?" asked the detective.

"I went to a cafe and had a glass of wine, then I strolled about the town and lunched at the Victoria. I caught the one o'clock train to Monte Carlo."

"Did you hear nothing of the murder?"

"Not a word," said Mr. Briggerland, "not a word."

"Did you see the car?"

Mr. Briggerland shook his head.

"I left some time before poor Lydia," he said softly.

"Did you know of any attachment between the chauffeur and your guest?"

"I had no idea such a thing existed. If I had," said Mr. Briggerland virtuously, "I should have taken immediate steps to have brought poor Lydia to her senses."

"Your daughter says that they were frequently together. Did you notice this?"

"Yes, I did notice it, but my daughter and I are very democratic. We have made a friend of Morden, and I suppose what would have seemed familiar to you would pass unnoticed with us. Yes, I certainly do remember my poor friend and Morden walking together in the garden."

"Is this yours?" The detective took from behind a curtain an old British rifle.

"Yes, that is mine," admitted Briggerland without a moment's hesitation. "It is one I bought in Amiens, a souvenir of our gallant soldiers—"

"I know, I quite understand your patriotic motive in purchasing it," said the detective drily, "but will you tell us how this passed from your possession?"

"I haven't the slightest notion," said Mr. Briggerland in surprise. "I had no idea it was lost—I'd lost sight of it for some weeks. Can it be that Morden—but no, I must not think so evilly of him."

"What were you going to suggest?" asked Jack. "That Morden fired at Mrs. Meredith when she was on the swimming raft? If you are, I can save you the trouble of telling that lie. It was you who fired, and it was I who knocked you out."

Mr. Briggerland's face was a study.

"I can't understand why you make such a wild and unfounded charge," he said gently. "Perhaps, my dear, you could elucidate this mystery."

Jean had not spoken since he entered. She sat bolt upright on a chair, her hands folded in her lap, her sad eyes fixed now upon Jack, now upon the detective. She shook her head.

"I know nothing about the rifle, and did not even know you possessed one," she said. "But please answer all their questions, father. I am as anxious as you are to get to the bottom of this dreadful tragedy. Have you told my father about the letters which were discovered?"

The detective shook his head.

"I have not seen your father until he arrived this moment," he said.

"Letters?" Mr. Briggerland looked at his daughter. "Did poor Lydia leave a letter?"

She nodded.

"I think Mr. Glover will tell you, father," she said. "Poor Lydia had an attachment for Morden. It is very clear what happened. They went out today, never intending to return—"

"Mrs. Meredith had no intention of going to the Lovers' Chair until you suggested the trip to her," said Jack quietly. "Mrs. Cole-Mortimer is very emphatic on that point."

"Has the body been found?" asked Mr. Briggerland.

"Nothing has been found but the chauffeur," said the detective.

After a few more questions he took Jack outside.

"It looks very much to me as though it were one of those crimes of passion which are so frequent in this country," he said. "Morden was a Frenchman and I have been able to identify him by tattoo marks on his arm as a man who has been in the hands of the police many times."

"You think there is no hope?"

The detective shrugged his shoulders.

"We are dragging the pool. There is very deep water under the rock, but the chances are that the body has been washed out to sea. There is clearly no evidence against these people, except yours. The letters might, of course, have been forged, but you say you are certain that the writing is Mrs. Meredith's."

Jack nodded.

They were walking down the road towards the officer's waiting car, when Jack asked:

"May I see that letter again?"

The detective took it from his pocketbook and Jack stopped and scanned it.

"Yes, it is her writing," he said and then uttered an exclamation.

"Do you see that?"

He pointed eagerly to two little marks before the words, "Dear Friend."

"Quotation marks," said the detective puzzled. "Why did she write that?"

"I've got it," said Jack, "The story! Mademoiselle Briggerland told me she was writing a story, and I remember she said she had writers' cramp. Suppose she dictated a portion of the story to Mrs. Meredith, and suppose in that story there occurred this letter: Lydia would have put the quotation marks mechanically."

The detective took the letter from his hand.

"It is possible," he said. "The writing is very even—it shows no sign of agitation, and of course the character's initials might be 'L. M.' It is an ingenious hypothesis, and not wholly improbable, but if this were a part of the story, there would be other sheets. Would you like me to search the house?"

Jack shook his head.

"She's much too clever to have them in the house," he said. "More likely she's put them in the fire."

"What fire?" asked the detective drily. "These houses have no fires, they're centrally heated—unless she went to the kitchen."

"Which she wouldn't do," said Jack thoughtfully. "No, she'd burn them in the garden."

The detective nodded and they returned to the house.

Jean, deep in conversation with her father, saw them reappear and watched them as they walked slowly across the lawn toward the trees, their eyes fixed on the ground.

"What are they looking for?" she asked with a frown.

"I'll go and see," said Briggerland, but she caught his arm.

"Do you think they'll tell you?" she asked sarcastically.

She ran up to her own room and watched them from behind a curtain. Presently they passed out of sight to the other side of the house and she went into Lydia's room and overlooked them from there. Suddenly she saw the detective stoop and pick up something from the ground and her teeth set.

"The burned story," she said, "I never dreamed they'd look for that."

It was only a scrap they found, but it was in Lydia's writing, and the pencil mark was clearly visible on the charred ashes.

"'Laura Martin'," read the detective. "L. M., and there are the words 'tragic' and 'remorse'."

From the remainder of the charred fragments they collected nothing of importance. Jean watched them disappear along the avenue and went down to her father.

"I had a fright," she said.

"You look as if you've still got it," he said. He eyed her keenly.

She shook her head.

"Father, you must understand that this adventure may end disastrously. There are ninety-nine chances against the truth being known, but it is the extra chance that is worrying me. We ought to have settled Lydia more quietly, more naturally. There was too much melodrama and shooting; but I don't see how we could have done anything else—Morden was very tiresome."

"Where did Glover come from?" asked Mr. Briggerland.

"He's been here all the time," said the girl.

"What?"

She nodded.

"He was old Jaggs. I had an idea he was, but I was certain when I remembered that he had stayed at Lydia's flat."

He put down his tea cup and wiped his lips with a silk handkerchief.

"I wish this business was over," he said fretfully. "It looks as if we shall have trouble."

"Of course we shall," she said coldly. "You didn't expect to get a fortune of six hundred thousand pounds without trouble, did you? I dare say we shall be suspected. But it takes a lot of suspicion to worry me. We'll be in calm water soon for the rest of our lives."

"I hope so," he said, without any great conviction.

Mrs. Cole-Mortimer was prostrate and in bed, and Jean had no patience to see her.

She herself ordered the dinner and they had finished when a visitor in the shape of Mr. Marcus Stepney came in.

It was unusual of Marcus to appear at the dinner hour, except in evening dress, and she remarked the fact wonderingly.

"Can I have a word with you, Jean?" he asked.

"What is it, what is it?" asked Mr. Briggerland testily. "Haven't we had enough mysteries?"

Marcus eyed him without favor.

"We'll have another one if you don't mind," he said unpleasantly, and the girl, whose every sense was alert, picked up a wrap and walked into the garden with Marcus following on her heels.

Ten minutes passed and they did not return, a quarter of an hour went by and Mr. Briggerland grew uneasy. He got up from his chair, put down his book and was halfway across the room when the door opened and Jack Glover came in followed by the detective.

It was the Frenchman who spoke.

"M'sieur Briggerland, I have a warrant from the Prefect of the Alps Maritimes for your arrest."

"My arrest?" spluttered the dark man, his teeth chattering. "What—what is the charge?"

"The willful murder of Francois Morden," said the officer.

"You lie—you lie," screamed Briggerland. "I have no knowledge of any—" his words sank into a throaty gurgle and he stared past the detective. Lydia Meredith was standing in the doorway.

CHAPTER XXXIX

The morning for Mr. Stepney had been doubly disappointing; again and again he drew up an empty line, and at last he flung the tackle into the well of the launch.

"Even the dam fish won't bite," he said, and the humor of his remark cheered him. He was ten miles from the shore, and the blue coast was a dim, ragged line on the horizon. He pulled out a big luncheon basket from the cabin and eyed it with disfavor. It had cost him two hundred francs. He opened the basket, and at the sight of its contents was inclined to reconsider his earlier view that he had wasted his money, the more so since the *maitre d'hotel* had thoughtfully included two quart bottles of champagne.

Mr. Marcus Stepney made a hearty meal and by the time he had dropped an empty bottle into the sea, he was inclined to take a more cheerful view of life. He threw over the debris of the lunch, pushed the basket under one of the seats of the cabin, pulled up his anchor and started the engines running.

The sky was a brighter blue and the sea held a finer sparkle, and he was inclined to take a view of even Jean Briggerland more generous than any he had held.

"Little devil," he smiled reminiscently, as he murmured the words.

He opened the second bottle of champagne in her honor—Mr. Marcus Stepney was usually an abstemious man—and drank solemnly, if not soberly, her health and happiness. As the sun grew warmer he began to feel an unaccountable sleepiness. He was sober enough to know that to fall asleep in the middle of the ocean was to ask for trouble, and he set the bow of the "Jungle Queen" for the nearest beach, hoping to find a landing place.

He found something better as he skirted the shore. The sea and the weather had scooped out a big hollow under a high cliff, a hollow just big enough to take the "Jungle Queen" and deep and still enough to ensure her a safe anchorage. A rock barrier interposed between the breakers and this deep pool which the waves had hollowed in the stony floor of the ocean. As he dropped his anchor he disturbed a school of fish, and his angling instincts re-awoke. He let down his line over the side, seated himself comfortably in one of the two big basket chairs, and was dozing comfortably—

It was the sound of a shot that woke him. It was followed by another, and a third. Almost immediately something dropped from the cliff, and fell with a mighty splash into the water.

Marcus was wide awake now, and almost sobered. He peered down into the clear depths and saw a figure of a woman turning over and over. Then as it floated upwards it came on its back and he saw the face. Without a moment's hesitation he dived into the water.

He would have been wiser if he had waited until she floated to the surface, for now he found a difficulty in regaining the boat. After a great deal of trouble, he managed to reach into the launch and pull out a rope, which he fastened round the girl's waist and drew tight to a small stanchion. Then he climbed into the boat himself, and pulled her after him.

He thought at first she was dead, but listening intently he heard the beating of her heart, and searched the luncheon basket for a small flask of liqueurs, which Alphonse, the head waiter, had packed. He put the bottle to her lips and poured a small quantity into her mouth. She choked convulsively and presently opened her eyes.

"You're amongst friends," said Marcus unnecessarily.

She sat up and covered her face with her hands. It all came back to her in a flash, and the horror of it froze her blood.

"What has happened to you?" asked Marcus.

"I don't know exactly," she said faintly. And then: "Oh, it was dreadful, dreadful!"

Marcus Stepney offered her the flask of liqueurs, and when she shook her head, he helped himself liberally.

Lydia was conscious of a pain in her left shoulder. The sleeve was torn and across the thick of the arm there was an ugly raw weal.

"It looks like a bullet mark to me," said Marcus Stepney, suddenly grave. "I heard a shot. Did somebody shoot at you?"

She nodded.

"Who?"

She tried to frame the word, but no sound came and then she burst into a fit of weeping.

"Not Jean?" he asked hoarsely.

She shook her head.

"Briggerland?"

She nodded.

"Briggerland!" Mr. Stepney whistled, and as he whistled he shivered. "Let's get out of here," he said. "We shall catch our death of cold. The sun will warm us up."

He started the engines going, and safely navigated the narrow passage to the open sea. He had to get a long way out before he could catch a glimpse of the road, then he saw the car, and a cycling policeman dismounting and bending over something. He put away his telescope and turned to the girl.

"This is bad, Mrs. Meredith," he said. "Thank God I wasn't in it!"

"Where are you taking me?" she asked.

"I'm taking you out to sea," said Marcus with a smile. "Don't get scared, Mrs. Meredith. I want to hear that story of yours, and if it is anything like what I fear, then it would be better for you that Briggerland thinks you are dead."

She told the story as far as she knew it, and he listened, not interrupting, until she had finished.

"Morden dead, eh? That's bad. But how on earth are they going to explain it? I suppose," he said with a smile, "you didn't write a letter saying that you were going to run away with the chauffeur?"

She sat up at this.

"I did write a letter," she said slowly. "It wasn't a real letter; it was a story in which Jean was dictating."

She closed her eyes.

"How awful," she said. "I can't believe it even now."

"Tell me about the story," said the man quickly.

"It was a story she was writing for a London magazine, and her wrist hurt and I wrote it down as she dictated. Only about three pages, but one of the pages was a letter supposed to have been written by the heroine saying that she was going away, as she loved somebody who was beneath her socially."

"Good God!" said Marcus, genuinely shocked. "Did Jean do that?"

He seemed absolutely crushed by the realization of Jean Briggerland's deed, and he did not speak again for a long time.

"I'm glad I know," he said at last.

"Do you really think that all this time she has been trying to kill me?" He nodded.

"She has used everybody, even me," he said bitterly. "I don't want you to think badly of me, Mrs. Meredith, but I'm going to tell you the truth. I'd provisioned this little yacht today for a twelve-hundred-mile trip, and you were to be my companion."

"I?" she said incredulously.

"It was Jean's idea, really, though I think she must have altered her view, or thought I had forgotten all she suggested. I intended taking you out to sea and keeping you out there until you agreed—" he shook his head. "I don't think I could have done it really," he said speaking half to himself. "I'm not really built for a conspirator. None of that rough stuff ever appealed to me. Well, I didn't try, anyway."

"No, Mr. Stepney," she said quietly, "and I don't think, if you had, you would have succeeded."

He was in his frankest mood, and startled her later when he told her of his profession, without attempting to excuse or minimize the method by which he earned his livelihood.

"I was in a pretty bad way, and I thought there was easy money coming, and that rather tempted me," he said. "I know you will think that I am a despicable cad, but you can't think too badly of me, really."

He surveyed the shore. Ahead of them the green tongue of Cap Martin jotted out into the sea.

"I think I'll take you to Nice," he said. "We'll attract less attention there, and probably I'll be able to get into touch with your old Mr. Jaggs. You've no idea where I can find him? At any rate, I can go to the Villa Casa and discover what sort of a yarn is being told."

"And probably I can get my clothes dry," she said with a little grimace. "I wonder if you know how uncomfortable I am?"

"Pretty well," he said calmly. "Every time I move a new stream of water runs down my back."

It was half-past three in the afternoon when they reached Nice, and Marcus saw the girl safely to an hotel, changed himself and brought the yacht back to Monaco, where Briggerland had seen him.

For two hours Marcus Stepney wrestled with his love for a girl who was plainly a murderess and in the end love won. When darkness fell he provisioned the "Jungle Queen," loaded her with petrol, and heading her out to sea made the swimming cove of Cap Martin. It was to the boat that Jean flew.

"What about my father?" she asked as she stepped aboard.

"I think they've caught him," said Marcus.

"He'll hate prison," said the girl complacently. "Hurry, Marcus, I'd hate it too!"

CHAPTER XL

Lydia took up her quarters in a quiet hotel in Nice and Mrs. Cole-Mortimer agreed to stay on and chaperon her. Though she had felt no effects from her terrifying experience on the first day, she found herself a nervous wreck when she woke in the morning, and wisely decided to stay in bed.

Jack, who had expected the relapse, called in a doctor, but Lydia refused to see him. The next day she received the lawyer.

She had only briefly outlined the part which Marcus Stepney had played in her rescue, but she had said enough to make Jack call at Stepney's hotel to thank him in person. Mr. Stepney, however, was not at home—he had not been home all night, but this information his discreet informant did not volunteer. Nor was the disappearance of the "Jungle Queen" noticed for two days. It was Mrs. Cole-Mortimer, in settling up her accounts with Jack, who mentioned the "yacht."

"The 'Jungle Queen,'" said Jack; "that's the motor-launch, isn't it? I've seen her lying in the harbor. I thought she was Stepney's property."

His suspicions aroused, he called again at Stepney's hotel, and this time his inquiry was backed by the presence of a detective. Then it was made known that Mr. Stepney had not been seen since the night of Briggerland's arrest.

"That is where they've gone. Stepney was very keen on the girl, I think," said Jack.

The detective was annoyed.

"If I'd known before we could have intercepted them. We have several destroyers in the harbor at Villafrance. Now I am afraid it is too late."

"Where would they make for?" asked Jack.

The officer shrugged his shoulders.

"God knows," he said. "They could get into Italy or into Spain, possibly Barcelona. I will telegraph the Chief of the Police there."

But the Barcelona police had no information to give. The "Jungle Queen" had not been sighted. The weather was calm, the sea smooth and everything favorable for the escape.

Inquiries elicited the fact that Mr. Stepney had bought large quantities of petrol a few days before his departure, and had augmented his supply the evening he had left. Also, he had bought provisions in considerable quantities.

The murder was a week old, and Mr. Briggerland had undergone his preliminary examination when a wire came through from the Spanish police that a motor-boat answering the description of the "Jungle Queen" had called at Malaga, had provisioned, refilled and put out to sea again before the police authorities, who had a description of the pair, had time to investigate.

"You'll think I have a diseased mind," said Lydia, "but I hope she gets away."

Jack laughed.

"If you had been with her much longer, Lydia, she would have turned you into a first-class criminal," he said. "I hope you do not forget that she has exactly a hundred thousand pounds of yours—in other words, a sixth of your fortune."

Lydia shook her head.

"That is almost a comforting thought," she said. "I know she is what she is, Jack, but her greatest crime is that she was born six hundred years too late. If she had lived in the days of the Italian Renaissance she would have made history."

"Your sympathy is immoral," said Jack. "By the way, Briggerland has been handed over to the Italian authorities. The crime was committed on Italian soil and that saves his head from falling into the basket."

She shuddered.

"What will they do to him?"

"He'll be imprisoned for life," was the reply, "and I rather think that's a little worse than the guillotine. You say you worry for Jean—I'm rather sorry for old man Briggerland. If he hadn't tried to live up to his daughter, he might have been a most respectable member of society."

They were strolling through the quaint narrow streets of Grasse, and Jack who knew and loved the town, was showing her sights which made her forget that the Perfumerie Factory, the mecca of the average tourist, had any existence.

"I suppose I'll have to settle down now," she said, with an expression of distaste.

"I suppose you will," said Jack, "and you'll have to settle up too; your legal expenses are something fierce."

"Why do you say that?" she asked, stopping in her walk and looking at him gravely.

"I am speaking as your mercenary lawyer," said Jack.

"You are trying to put your service on another level," she corrected. "I owe everything I have to you. My fortune is the least of these. I owe you my life three times over."

"Four," he corrected, "and to Marcus Stepney once."

"Why have you done so much for me? Were you interested?" she asked, after a pause.

"Very," he replied. "I was interested in you from the moment I saw you step out of Mr. Morden's taxi into the mud, but I was especially interested in you—"

"When?" she asked.

"When I sat outside your door night after night and discovered you didn't snore," he said shamelessly, and she went red.

"I hope you'll never refer to your old Jaggs adventures. It was very—"

"What?"

"I was going to say horrid, but I shouldn't be telling the truth," she admitted frankly. "I liked having you there. Poor Mrs. Morgan will be disconsolate when she discovers that we've lost our lodger."

They walked into the cool of the ancient cathedral and sat down.

"There's something very soothing about a church, isn't there?" he whispered. "Look at that gorgeous window. If I were ever rich enough to marry the woman I loved, I should be married in a cathedral like this, full of old tombs and statues and stained glass."

"How rich would you have to be?" she asked.

"As rich as she is."

She bent over toward him, her lips against his ear.

"Tell me how much money you have," she whispered, "and I'll give away all I have in excess of that amount."

He caught her hand and held it fast, and they sat there before the altar of St. Catherine until the sun went down and the disapproving old woman, who acted as the cathedral's caretaker, tapped them on the shoulder.

CHAPTER XLI

"That is Gibraltar," said Marcus Stepney, pointing ahead to a gray shape that loomed up from the sea.

He was unshaven, for he had forgotten to bring his razor, and he was pinched with the cold. His overcoat was turned up to his ears, in spite of which he shivered.

Jean did not seem to be affected by the sudden change of temperature. She sat on the top of the cabin, her chin in the palm of her hand, her elbow on her crossed knee.

"You are not going into Gibraltar?" she asked.

He shook his head.

"I think not," he said, "nor to Algeciras. Did you see that fellow on the quay yelling for the craft to come back after we left Malaga? That was a bad sign. I expect the police have instructions to detain this boat, and most of the ports must have been notified."

"How long can we run?"

"We've got enough gas and grub to reach Dacca," he said. "That's roughly an eight days' journey."

"On the African coast?"

He nodded, although she could not see him.

"Where could we get a ship to take us to South America?" she asked, turning round.

"Lisbon," he said thoughtfully. "Yes, we could reach Lisbon, but there are too many steamers about and we're certain to be sighted. We might run across to Los Palmas, most of the South American boats call there, but if I were you I should stick to Europe. Come and take this helm, Jean."

She obeyed without question, and he continued the work which had been interrupted by a late meal, the painting of the boat's hull, a difficult business, involving acrobatics, since it was necessary for him to lean over the side. He had bought the gray paint at Malaga, and happily there was not much surface that required attention. The stumpy mast of the "Jungle Queen" had already gone overboard—he had sawed it off with great labor the day after they had left Cap Martin.

She watched him with a speculative eye as he worked, and thought he had never looked quite so unattractive as he did with an eight days' growth of beard, his shirt stained with paint and petrol. His hands were grimy and nobody would have recognized in this scarecrow the elegant *habitue* of those fashionable resorts which smart society frequents.

Yet she had reason to be grateful to him. His conduct toward her had been irreproachable. Not one word of love had been spoken, nor, until now, had their future plans, for it affected them both, been discussed.

"Suppose we reach South America safely?" she asked. "What happens then, Marcus?"

He looked round from his work in surprise.

"We'll get married," he said quietly, and she laughed.

"And what happens to the present Mrs. Stepney?"

"She has divorced me," said Stepney unexpectedly. "I got the papers the day we left."

"I see," said Jean softly. "We'll get married—" then stopped.

He looked at her and frowned.

"Isn't that your idea, too?" he asked.

"Married? Yes, that's my idea, too. It seems a queer uninteresting way of finishing things, doesn't it, and yet I suppose it isn't."

He had resumed his work and was leaning far over the bow intent upon his labor. Suddenly she spun the wheel round and the launch heeled over to starboard. For a second it seemed that Marcus Stepney could not maintain his balance against that unexpected impetus, but by a super-human effort he kicked himself back to safety and stared at her with a blanched face.

"Why did you do that?" he asked hoarsely. "You nearly had me overboard."

"There was a porpoise lying on the surface of the sea asleep I think," she said quietly. "I'm very sorry, Marcus, but I didn't know that it would throw you off your balance."

He looked round for the sleeping fish, but it had disappeared.

"You told me to avoid them, you know," she said apologetically. "Did I really put you in any danger?"

He licked his dry lips, picked up the paint pot and threw it into the sea.

"We'll leave this," he said, "until we are beached. You gave me a scare, Jean."

"I'm dreadfully sorry. Come here and sit by me."

She moved to allow him room and he sat down by her, taking the wheel from her hand.

On the horizon the high lands of northern Africa were showing their saw-edge outlines.

"That is Morocco," he pointed out to her. "I propose giving Gibraltar a wide berth and following the coast line to Tangier."

"Tangier wouldn't be a bad place to land if there weren't two of us," he went on. "It is our being together in this yacht that is likely to cause suspicion. You could easily pretend that you'd come over from Gibraltar, and the port authorities there are pretty slack."

"Or we could land on the coast," he suggested. "There's a good landing, and we could follow the beach down and turn up in Tangier in the morning—all sorts of oddments turn up in Tangier without exciting suspicion."

She was looking out over the sea with a queer expression in her face.

"Morocco!" she said softly. "Morocco—I hadn't thought of that!"

They had a fright soon after. A gray shape came racing out of the darkening east and Stepney put his helm over as the destroyer smashed past on her way to Gibraltar.

He watched the stern light disappearing, then it suddenly turned and presented its side to them.

"They're looking for us," said Marcus.

The darkness had come down and he headed straight for the east.

There was no question that the destroyer was on an errand of discovery. A white beam of light shot out from her decks and began to feel along the sea. And then, when they thought it had missed them, it dropped on the boat and held. A second later it missed them and began a search. Presently it lit the little boat and it did something more—it revealed a thickening of the atmosphere. They were running into a sea fog, one of those thin white fogs that came down in the Mediterranean on windless days. The blinding glare of the searchlight blurred—

"Bang!"

"That's the gun to signal us to stop," said Marcus, between his teeth.

He turned the nose of the boat southward, a hazardous proceeding, for he ran into clear water and had only just got back into the shelter of the providential fog bank when the white beam came stealthily along the edge of the mist. Presently it died out and they saw it no more.

"They're looking for us," said Marcus again.

"You said that before," said the girl calmly.

"They've probably warned them at Tangier. We dare not take the boat into the bay," said Stepney, whose nerves were now on edge.

He turned again westward, edging toward the rocky coast of northern Africa. They saw little clusters of lights on the shore, and he tried to remember what towns they were.

"I think that big one is Cutra, the Spanish convict station," he said.

He slowed down the boat and they felt their way gingerly along the coast line, until the flick and flash of a lighthouse gave them an idea of their position.

"Cape Spartel," he identified the light. "We can land very soon. I was in Morocco for three months and if I remember rightly the beach is good walking as far as Tangier."

She went into the cabin and changed and as the nose of the "Jungle Queen" slid gently up the sandy beach she was ready.

He carried her ashore and set her down, then he pushed off the nose of the boat and manoeuvred it so that the stern was against the beach, resting in three feet of water. He jumped on board, lashed the helm and started the engines going, then wading back to the shore he stood staring into the gloom as the little "Jungle Queen" put out to sea.

"That's that," he said grimly. "Now, my dear, we've got a ten-mile walk before us."

But he had made a slight miscalculation. The distance between himself and Tangier was twenty-five miles, and involved several detours inland into country which was wholly uninhabited, save at that moment it held the camp of Muley Hafiz, who was engaged in negotiation with the Spanish Government for one of those "permanent peaces" which frequently last for years.

Muley Hafiz sat drinking his coffee at midnight listening to the strains of an ornate gramophone, which stood in a corner of his square tent.

A voice outside the silken folds of his tent greeted him and he stopped the machine.

"What is it?" he asked.

"Lord, we have captured a man and a woman walking along by the sea."

"They are Riffi people—let them go," said Muley in Arabic. "We are making peace, my man, not war."

"Lord, these are infidels; I think they are English."

Muley Hafiz twiddled his trim little beard.

"Bring them," he said.

So they were brought to his presence, a dishevelled man and a girl at the sight of whose face he gasped.

"My little friend of the Riviera," he said wonderingly, and the smile she gave him was like a ray of sunshine to his heart.

He stood up, a magnificent figure of a man and she eyed him admiringly.

"I am sorry if my men have frightened you," he said. "You have nothing to fear, Madame. I will send my soldiers to escort you to Tangier."

And then he frowned.

"Where did you come from?"

She could not lie under the steady glance of those liquid eyes.

"We landed on the shore from a boat. We lost our way," she said.

He nodded.

"You must be she they are seeking," he said. "One of my spies came to me from Tangier tonight and told me that the Spanish and the French police were waiting to arrest a lady who had committed some crime in France. I cannot believe it is you—or if it is, then I should say the crime was pardonable."

He glanced at Marcus.

"Or perhaps," he said slowly, "it is your companion they desire."

Jean shook her head.

"No, they do not want him," she said, "it is I they want."

He pointed to a cushion.

"Sit down," he said, and followed her example.

Marcus alone remained standing, wondering how this strange situation would develop.

"What will you do? If you go into Tangier I fear I could not protect you, but there is a city in the hills," he waved his hand, "many miles from here, a city where the hills are green, Mademoiselle, and where beautiful springs gush out of the ground and there I am lord."

She drew a long breath.

"I will go to the city of the hills," she said softly, "and this man," she shrugged her shoulders, "I do not care what happens to him," she said, with a smile of amusement at the pallid Marcus.

"Then he shall go to Tangier alone."

But Marcus Stepney did not go alone. For the last two miles of the journey he had carried a bag containing the greater part of five million francs that the girl had brought from the boat. Jean did not remember this until she was on her way to the city of the hills, and by that time money did not interest her.

THE END

Kate Plus 10

By Edgar Wallace

CHAPTER I
EIGHTY-THREE PEARLS ON A STRING

The Earl of Flanborough pressed a bell push by the side of his study table and, after an interval of exactly three seconds, pressed it again, though the footman's lobby could not have been far short of fifty yards from the library and the serving man was never born who could sprint that distance in three seconds.

Yet, in such awe was his lordship held that morning by his man-servants, his maid-servants and everything within his gates, that Sibble, the first footman, made the distance in five.

"Why the dickens don't you answer my bell when I ring?" snapped the Earl and glared at his red-faced servant.

Sibble did not reply, knowing by experience that, even as silence was insolence, speech could be nothing less than impertinence.

Lord Flanborough was slightly over middle age, thin, bald and dyspeptic. His face was mean and insignificant and if you looked for any resemblance to the somewhat pleasant faces of the Feltons and Flanboroughs of past generations which stared mildly or fiercely, or (as in the case of the first Baron Felton and Flanborough, a poet and contemporary of Lovelace) with gentle melancholy from their massive frames in the long hall, you looked in vain. For George Percy Allington Felton, Earl of Flanborough, Baron Felton and Baron Sedgely of Waybrook, was only remotely related to the illustrious line of Feltons and had inherited the title and the heavily mortgaged estates of his great-uncle by sheer bad luck. This was the uncharitable view of truer Feltons who stood, however, more remotely in the line of succession.

Lord Flanborough had been Mr. George Felton of Felton, Heinrich and Somes, a firm which controlled extensive mining properties in various parts of the world, and the one bright spot in his succession to the peerage lay in the fact that he brought some two millions sterling to the task of freeing the estates of their encumbrances.

He was a shrewd man and an unpleasant man, but he had never been so objectionably unpleasant until he assumed the style and title of Flanborough and never so completely and impossibly unpleasant in the period of his lordship as he had been that morning.

"Now, what did I want you for?" asked Lord Flanborough in vexation. "I rang for something —if you had only answered at once instead of dawdling about, I should—ah, yes—tell Lady Moya that I wish to see her.”

Sibble made his escape thankfully.

Lord Flanborough pulled at his weedy moustache and looked at the virgin sheet of paper before him. Then he took up his pen and wrote:

“Lost or Stolen: Valuable pearl chain consisting of eighty-three graduated pearls. Any person giving information which will lead to their recovery will receive a reward of two hundred pounds.”

He paused; scratched out “two hundred pounds” and substituted “one hundred pounds.” This did not satisfy him and he altered the sum to “fifty pounds.” He sat considering even this modest figure and eventually struck out that amount and wrote, “will be suitably rewarded.”

He heard the door click and looked up.

“Ah—Moya. I am just tinkering away at an advertisement,” he said with a smile.

The Lady Moya Felton was twenty-two and pretty. She re-collected in her admirable person many of the traditional family graces which had so malignantly avoided her parent. Well-shaped and of a gracious carriage, though no more than medium in height, the face with its delicacy of moulding was wholly Felton. If the stubborn chin, the firm mouth and the china-blue eyes had come from the dead and gone Sedgelys, the hair of bronze gold was peculiarly Feltonesque.

When she spoke, however, the carping critic might complain that her voice lacked the rich quality upon which the family prided itself, for the Feltons were orators in those days when a parliamentary speech read like something out of a book. Moya’s voice was a trifle hard and without body; it was also just a little unsympathetic. Lord Flanborough boasted with good cause that his daughter was a “practical little woman” and at least one man beside her father could testify to this quality.

“Dear, don’t you think it is a little absurd—advertising?” asked the girl.

She seated herself at the other side of the desk and, reaching out her hand, opened a silver box and helped herself to one of her father’s cigarettes.

“Why absurd, darling?” asked Lord Flanborough testily; “lost property has been found before now, by means of advertising. I remember years ago when I was in the city, there was a fellow named Goldberg—”

“Please forget all about the city for a moment,” she smiled, lighting her cigarette, “and review all the circumstances. Firstly, I had the pearls when I was at Lady Machinstones’ house. I danced with quiet, respectable people—Sir Ralph Sapson, Sir George Felixburn, Lord Fethington, Major

Aitkens, and that awfully nice boy of Machinstones. They didn't steal them. I had the pearls when I left, because I saw them as I was fastening my fur cloak. I had them in the car because I touched them just before we reached the house. I don't remember taking them off—but then I was dead tired and hardly remember going to bed. Obviously, Martin is the thief. She is the only person who has access to my room; she helped me undress; it is as plain as a pikestaff."

Lord Flanborough tapped his large teeth with his penholder, a practice of his which annoyed his daughter beyond words, though at the moment she deemed it expedient to overlook the fault. The loss had frightened her, for the pearls were worth three thousand pounds and she was one of those people whose standard of values had a currency basis.

"I have asked Scotland Yard to send their very best man," said Lord Flanborough importantly. "Where is Martin?"

"Locked in her room—I have told Fellows to sit outside her door," said the girl, and then, interestedly, "When will the detective arrive?"

Lord Flanborough picked up an open telegraph form from the table.

"'Sending Inspector Pretherston'—by Jove!"

He blinked across the desk at his daughter.

"Pretherston," she repeated thoughtfully; "isn't it strange?"

"Pretherston—hum," said her father and looked at her again.

If he expected to see any confusion, any heightening of color, even so much as a faltering of glance, he was relieved, for she met his gaze steadfastly, save that there was a far-away look in her eyes and a certain speculative narrowing of lids.

The romance was five years old, and if she cherished the memory of it, it was the charity which she might show to a favored piece in her china cupboard; it was something to be taken out and dusted at intervals. Michael Pretherston was a bad match from every point of view, though his invalid cousin was a peer of the realm and Michael would one day be Pretherston of Pretherston. He was hideously poor, he was casual, he had no respect for wealth, he held the most outrageous views on the church, society and the state; he was, in fact, something as nearly approaching an anarchist as Lord Flanborough ever expected or feared to meet.

His wooing had been brief but tempestuous. The girl had been overwhelmed and had given her promise. Recovering her reason in the morning and realizing (as she said) that love was not "everything," she had written him a letter of fourteen pages in which she had categorically set forth the essential conditions to their union. These called for the abandonment of all his principles, the re-establishment of all his shattered beliefs and an estimate of the cost of placing Pretherston Court in a state of repair suitable for the reception of the Lady Moya Pretherston (*née* Felton).

To her fourteen pages, he had returned a thirty-two page letter which was at once an affront and a justification for anarchy. It was not a love-letter; rather was it something between a pamphlet by Henry George and a treatise by Jean Jacques Rousseau, interspersed with passionate appeals to her womanhood and offensive references to her "huckster-souled" father.

"He was always a wild sort of chap," said Lord Flanborough, shaking his head darkly. "I understood that he had gone abroad."

"I suppose there are other Pretherstons," said the girl; "still it *is* strange, isn't it?"

"Do you ever feel ...?" began her father awkwardly.

She smiled and laid down her cigarette on the crystal ash-tray.

"He was wholly impossible," she agreed. There came a gentle tap at the door and a girl entered.

She was dressed neatly in black, and her prettiness was of a different type to that of her employer (for Lady Moya indulged in the luxury of a secretary). It was a beautiful face with a hint of tragedy in the down-turned lips and, it seemed, a history of wild sorrow in her big grey eyes. Yet of sorrow she knew nothing, and such tragedy as she had met had left her unmoved. Her abundant hair was of a rich brown; the hand that clasped a note-book to her bosom was small and artistic. She was an inch taller than Lady Moya, but because she did not show the same erectness of carriage she seemed shorter.

"Father, you asked me to let you have Miss Tenby this morning," said Lady Moya with a nod for the girl. "I don't know whether you will still want her?"

"I am *so* sorry this dreadful thing has happened, Lord Flanborough," said the girl in a low voice; "it must be terrible to feel that there is a thief in the house."

Lord Flanborough smiled good-humoredly.

"We shall recover the pearls, I am certain," he said; "don't let it worry you, Miss Tenby—I hope you are comfortable?"

"Very, Lord Flanborough," said the girl gratefully.

"And the work is not too hard, eh?"

The girl smiled slightly.

"It is nothing—I feel awfully ashamed of myself sometimes. I have been with you a month and have hardly earned my salt."

"That's all right," replied his lordship with great condescension; "you have already been of the greatest assistance to me and we shall find you plenty of other work. I was glad to see you in church on Sunday. The vicar tells me that you are a regular attendant."

The girl inclined her head, but said nothing. For a while she waited and then at a word of polite dismissal, she left the library.

"Deuced nice girl, that," said his lordship approvingly.

"She works well and quickly, and she can read French beautifully—I was very fortunate," said Moya carelessly. "What were we talking about when she came in? Oh, yes—Michael Pretherston. I wonder now—"

The door opened and a footman announced, "Inspector Pretherston, m'lord."

"Inspector Michael Pretherston, you silly ass," corrected the annoyed young man in the doorway.

It was Michael, then!

A little older, a little better-looking, a little more decisive—but Michael, as impetuous and irresponsible as ever.

"He spoilt my entrance, Moya," he laughed, as he came with rapid strides toward the girl; "how are you after all these years—as pretty as ever, confound you. Ah, Lord Flanborough, you're wearing well—I read your speech in the House of Lords on the Shipping Bill—a fine speech; did you make it up yourself?"

Moya laughed softly and saved what might have been a most embarrassing situation—for his lordship was framing a dignified protest against the suggestion that he had shared the honours of authorship.

"You are not changed, Michael," she said, looking at him with undisguised, but none the less, detached admiration; "but what on earth are you doing in the police force?"

"Extraordinary," murmured Lord Flanborough, and added humorously, "and an anarchist, too."

"It is a long story," said Michael. "I really received my promotion in the Special Branch—the Foreign Office Branch—and was transferred to the C. I. D. after we caught the Callam crowd, the Continental confidence tricksters. It is disgraceful that I should be an inspector, isn't it? But merit tells!" He chuckled again, then of a sudden grew serious. "I'm forgetting I've a job to do—what's the trouble?"

Lord Flanborough explained the object of his urgent call, and a look of disappointment appeared upon Michael Pretherston's face.

"A miserable little larceny," he said reproachfully. "I thought at least Moya had been kidnapped. Now, tell me all that happened on the night you lost the pearls."

Step by step the girl related her movements and the periods at which she had evidence that the pearls were still with her.

"And then you reached your bedroom," said Michael, "and what happened there? First of all, you took your fur wrap off."

"Yes," nodded the girl.

"Were you in a cheerful frame of mind or were you rather cross?"

"Does that matter?" she asked in surprise.

"Everything matters to the patient and systematic officer of the law. Temperamental clues are as interesting and material as any other."

"Well, if the truth were told," she confessed, "I was rather cross and very tired."

"Did you take your cloak off, or did your woman?"

"I took it off myself," she said after a pause, "and hung it up."

He asked her a few more questions.

"Now, we will see the sorrowful Martin," he said, "and let me tell you this, Moya, that if this girl is innocent she has grounds for action against you for false imprisonment."

"What do you mean?" demanded Lord Flanborough with asperity. "I have a perfect right to detain anybody I think is guilty of theft."

"You have no more right to lock a woman in a room," said the other calmly, "than I have to stand you on your head. But that is beside the point. Lead me to the prisoner."

The prisoner was very pale and very tearful; a middle-aged woman who felt her position acutely and between sobs and wails made an incoherent protest of her innocence.

"I suppose you have searched everywhere?" asked Michael, turning to the girl.

"Everywhere," she replied emphatically. "I have had every box and every corner of the room examined."

"Suppose the string of the pearls broke, would they all fall off?"

"No, they would still remain on, because each pearl was secured. Father gave them to me as a birthday present and he was very particular on that point."

"I would like to bet," said Michael suddenly, "that those pearls are not out of this room. Show me your wardrobe."

The girl's wardrobe occupied the whole of one wall of her dressing-room, and the tearful Martin opened the rosewood doors for his inspection.

"This is your fur cloak, I presume? Did you examine this after the loss?"

"Examine the cloak," said Lady Moya in surprise, "of course not.

What has the cloak to do with the loss? There are no pockets in it."

"But if I know anything about the fur cloaks that are fashionable this season," said Michael, wisely, "I should say that there is a possibility that this luxurious garment had a great deal to do with the loss. In fact, my dear Moya," he said, "your mysterious loss has been duplicated and triplicated this year. In two cases the police were called in, and in the other case the owner had the intelligence to find her lost trinket without assistance."

He lifted the cloak down very carefully and opened it to show the silk lining and there, caught in one of the long flat hooks, dangled the pearls. The girl uttered an exclamation of delight and slipped them from its fastening.

"Wonderful, isn't it?" said Michael dryly.

"That is what has happened, not three times but half-a-dozen times since these flat hooks have been introduced. You take the cloak off in a bad temper, the hook catches the chain, breaks it, you bundle the cloak in your wardrobe and there you have the beginning of a great jewel mystery."

"I can't tell you how delighted I am," said the girl. "Michael, you're wonderful!"

Michael did not reply. He turned to the frightened waiting-woman with a kindly smile.

"I am so sorry you have been worried about this, Mrs. Martin," he said, "but when people lose very valuable property they are also inclined to lose their very valuable heads. I am sure Lady Moya is sorry and will make you due compensation for any inconvenience you have been put to."

The girl stared at him resentfully.

"Of course, I am awfully sorry, Martin," she said, coldly.

"Oh, my lady," said the woman eagerly, "I am only too pleased that you have recovered your chain. The worry of it has made me quite ill."

"You can have a week's holiday," said Lord Flanborough, magnificently. "I will get you a free railway ticket to Seahampton," he added.

"So you see, Mrs. Martin," said Michael with that bland air of his which scarcely veiled the sarcasm so irritating to his lordship, "your generous employers will leave no stone unturned to minister to your comfort, regardless of expense. And when you are at Seahampton, Mrs. Martin, (I trust you will not lose the return half of your free ticket) you will be allowed to walk up and down the promenade on equal terms with the aristocracy and breathe the ozone which, ordinarily, is created for your betters. You may sit on the free seats and watch the pageant of life step past you and, reflecting upon the generosity of your betters, you may appreciate the good fortune which brought you into hourly contact with the aristocracy of England. And on Sundays, Mrs. Martin, you may go to church where quite a number of the seats are also free and may even share a hymn-book with a Gracious Person who is so vastly above you in social standing that he will never recognize you again, and there, I trust, you will pray with a new fervence that the deliberations of the House of Lords may receive divine inspiration."

"Oh, indeed I will, sir," said Mrs. Martin almost stunned by his eloquence.

He left the woman, overwhelmed, and returned with a very ruffled Lord Flanborough and an indignant Moya to the library.

"What utter nonsense you talk, Michael," said the girl angrily. "I don't think it was kind of you to attempt to set my servants against me."

"Beastly bad taste," said Lord Flanborough, "and really, Pretherston, you came here as an officer of the law and not as an old acquaintance and I think that you exceed your duties, if you don't mind my saying so."

"Old acquaintances," said Michael, picking up his hat and his coat from a chair where he had put them before the interview, "are especially made to be forgotten, a peculiarity of which one is reminded in that Bacchanalian anthem which is sung at all public dinners where sobriety is bad form. I was merely endeavouring to inculcate into the mind of your slave a few moral principles, beneficial to you, and to society."

"Don't tell me that," growled Lord Flanborough, "as though I didn't recognize your sarcasm."

"Children and the lower orders never recognize sarcasm," said Michael with a broad smile.

He held out his hand and somewhat reluctantly his lordship extended his own flabby paw.

"Before I go," he said, "I suppose I had better take a full account of this case. You haven't a secretary or anybody to whom you can dictate the circumstances? You see I have to make a report to my cold-blooded superiors."

Moya had reached the stage where whatever remains there was in her friendship with Michael Pretherston had not only died but had been cremated in the fires of her smothered anger and she was as anxious to see the end of this interview as was her father.

"Perhaps you will ring for Miss Tenby," she said after a pause.

Her father pressed the bell and the waiting Sibble answered it.

"Send Miss Tenby," said his lordship.

"And I do hope, Michael," said the girl severely, "that when Miss

Tenby is here you will not make such extravagant comments as you did before Martin."

"Miss Tenby," interposed Lord Flanborough, "will not welcome such talk. She is a young girl with—er—"

"I know, I know," said Michael solemnly, "she is genteel. She does forty words a minute on the typewriter and goes to church, filling in her odd moments with needlework and accompanying you on the piano."

"It must be a wonderful thing to be a detective," said Moya, sarcastically; "as a matter of fact Miss Tenby is one of the fastest typists in the world."

Michael swung round on her with an odd look on his face.

"Fastest typists in the world," he repeated with all the humor gone out of his tone; "does she sing?"

It was the girl's turn to be astonished.

"Yes, she does, and very beautifully."

"Does she prefer Italian opera?" he asked.

At this, the girl laughed aloud.

"Somebody has been telling you all about her and you are trying to be mysterious," she accused.

Further conversation was cut short by the arrival of the girl, who walked in, closed the door and came straight to the desk. She stopped dead at sight of Michael. Moya saw the meeting, saw the girl stiffen and her sorrowful eyes fixed upon the detective's face.

"Why, Kate!" said Michael Pretherston softly. "'Well, well, well! and to think that we meet again under such noble auspices."

Miss Tenby said nothing.

"And what is the great game?" asked Michael, banteringly. "What beautiful impulse brought you to this sheltered home and how is the Colonel and friend Gregori and all those dear boys? By-the-way, the Colonel must be out by now, Kate. What did he get, three years?"

Still Miss Tenby made no reply.

"What is the meaning of this?" demanded Lord Flanborough, feeling that the moment had arrived to assert himself. "Do you know this lady?"

"Do I *know* her," said Michael, ecstatically; "why, I am one of her greatest admirers, aren't I, Kate?"

The girl's sad face softened to a smile which showed the regular lines of her white teeth. She spoke and her voice was gentle and appealing.

"It is perfectly true, Lord Flanborough," she said quietly, "Mr. Pretherston knows me. He also knows that my uncle, Colonel Westhanger, has been mixed up in a very serious scandal which brought him within the reach of the law. It is perfectly true that when I was a little girl I was known as Kate. It is just as true that I am trying now to live down my association with lawbreakers and am trying to rehabilitate myself in the world."

"H'm," murmured Lord Flanborough, a little taken back, "very creditable."

Moya turned to Michael indignantly.

"I suppose that you think you are rendering a great service to the world in trying to drag this poor girl down to the gutter, in exposing her to her employers and in obtaining her dismissal from honest employment."

"I do," said Michael shamelessly.

"I think it is a barbarous thing to do!" said Moya angrily.

She had not yet decided in her own mind as to what steps she would take in face of this revelation. In view of her own character, it is possible that "Miss Tenby" would have a very short shift at her hands. But for the moment the opportunity for the display of benevolence and Christian charity was not to be passed over. She saw the girl's appealing eyes and clasped hands and, for a moment, she felt a sincere thrill of pity for a brave sister struggling to escape the octopus tentacles of law and crime; for a moment she felt a genuinely unselfish desire to help another.

If she expected Inspector the Hon. Michael Pretherston—for such was his incongruous title—to wilt under her reproaches, she was disappointed. Michael had not taken his eyes from the secretary, nor had the twinkle in those eyes abated. He nodded to "Miss Tenby."

"Kate," he said, "you are really a wonder, and to think that you have never yet come into the clutches of the law until now."

"Until now," said the girl quickly, raising her voice.

He nodded.

"The Prevention of Crimes Act," murmured Michael. "I *can* take you,"—he emphasized the "can"—"on a charge of obtaining employment with forged letters of recommendation, also with being a Suspected Person."

The girl dropped her attitude of humility, threw back her head and laughed, showing her even white teeth.

"Oh, you Mike!" she railed him. "Oh, you busy fellow!"

Her amusement did not last long for instantly her face was set again and the grey eyes blazed with rage.

"One of these days you will be too clever," she said bitterly. "I have seen better men than you and cleverer men than you go out, Michael Pretherston. You and your Prevention of Crimes Act! You can't put that bluff over me. The Act does not come into operation until you have a conviction against my name, and that you will never get, you brute!"

"Kate, Kate!" murmured Michael. "There's a lady present."

She nodded.

"I guess I'll get my kit together," she said; "it hasn't been exactly a holiday trip."

"My sympathies are entirely with you," said Michael; "it must have been awfully dull after the gay orgies of Crime Street."

"There is one thing I have always wanted to know," said the girl, pinching her lip thoughtfully.

She walked to the desk, and Lord Flanborough was too much taken back to arrest her progress. Without a word she opened the silver box on the table and took out a cigarette.

"I have always wanted to know what kind of dope this dear old gentleman smoked."

She looked at the cigarette critically and with an exclamation of disgust threw it back on the desk.

"Gold Flavours!" she said scornfully; "can you beat it, Mike? And he has a hundred thousand a year!"

"You must make allowances for the decadence of the governing classes," said the soothing Michael.

He turned and nodded farewell to the girl and with Miss Tenby's arm in his he passed out of the room, and Lord Flanborough and his daughter looked at one another in speechless amazement.

CHAPTER II
MIKE SAID NOTHING—THERE WAS NOTHING TO SAY

"You might do worse than lunch with me," said Michael Pretherston.

He stood outside Felton House with the girl whose belongings in one small Gladstone bag had been deposited on the curb, pending the arrival of a taxi-cab.

"Why should I lunch with you?" she asked insolently. "I thought you were going to pinch me."

"Your vulgarity is appalling!" said Michael, shaking his head in reproof. "I cannot pinch you in the vulgar sense. I have no desire to perform that operation in the corporeal sense. You had better compromise and lunch with me."

The girl hesitated.

"Think of my reputation," she said.

"Thoughts of your reputation keep me awake at night," answered Michael lightly and called a taxi.

They found a little restaurant in Soho and in an underground cellar where the bad ventilation was compensated for by a blaze of light, they ate their simple meal.

"Now, Kate, I want to ask you what your little game is," said Michael; "and I need the information because I know it isn't a little game."

"I was scared sick over those pearls," said the girl, ignoring the question. "It would have been horrible bad luck to have been taken for a job I had nothing to do with and such a paltry job, too!"

"You owe me something," said Michael.

"I owe you more than I can ever repay you," said the girl significantly.

"I suppose one of these days," suggested the detective after an interval of thought, "you will instruct some of your hired pals, Gregori or the Colonel or little Stockmar, to inflict on me a painful injury."

"You!" said the girl scornfully. "If there were not men like you in the police we should have been destroyed years ago! You are a sort of an insurance scheme and it pays us to keep you alive and well. Why, Crime Street would go into mourning the day you were buried."

"You are not trying to be rude to me, are you?" he asked.

She looked at him slyly from under her long lashes and her eyes were dancing with fun.

"Why do you think I went to Lord Flanborough?" she asked.

He shook his head.

"I'm blessed if I know," he confessed. "Of course, I knew it was you the moment I heard of the rapid typewriting and the Italian songs. Now listen: I am not trying to speak to you for your good...."

"Don't!" she said laconically.

"But I have often wondered why a well-educated girl and a nice girl, as far as I know to the contrary, should prefer the life of a crook to...."

"To earning £2 or £3 a week and working all day to earn it," she finished for him; "to living my life in one little room on a top floor in Bloomsbury, waiting my turn every morning for my bath. To being made love to by the assistant manager and sacrificing my immortal soul for a half-a-crown dinner and a bottle of red wine! It is funny, isn't it! I have had the experience for professional purposes and I don't like it a bit, Mike."

She looked at him straight in the eyes. She had dropped her air of flippancy, her slang; the voice that spoke was not to be distinguished from that of any other gentlewoman.

"You see, a woman is differently circumstanced to a man. She wants nice things and her attitude toward life, and indeed the whole of her conduct, depends entirely upon the degree of niceness she requires. Men don't do things for women for nothing. They lend to their men friends all the money in the world and are grateful if they get it back. They expect nothing more than their money and are surprised when they get it. But if I were a typist in a city office and I borrowed £2 from the assistant manager or from the chief bookkeeper or a fiver from one of the partners, why, Mike, I should be booked for supper on Wednesday. Men want more from women than a *quid pro quo*; they want two *quid pro quo*. In return for the £2 I borrowed, I should pay interest well outside the range of the multiplication table. Suppose a man lent you £2 and asked you in exchange, not only to repay the money, but to renounce all your dearest principles for the sake of the loan; if he asked you to betray your friends, where you had been loyal to them, and lie, where you had been truthful; break your word where you had been faithful, be a thief where you had been honest? Would you surrender every reticence, every honourable instinct, every precious faith?"

Mike said nothing. For there was nothing to say. He paid the bill and escorted the girl to a cab.

"I am not going to be sorry for you," he said; "you are having The Life. One of these days I shall come along and take you; but I shall hate it. Hop in, Kate!"

Kate literally hopped into the waiting taxi, waved her hand in farewell and was gone.

Michael Pretherston stood for fully five minutes on the edge of the pavement, meditating upon what the girl had said. She had struck a responsive note in his soul, for she spoke no more than was the truth, as he knew.

He went, a little sadly, back to headquarters, remembering en route that he had forgotten to write the report. Should he go back to the Yard and compose it from memory or should he return to the unsympathetic atmosphere of Felton House? He decided upon the latter and surprised Lord Flanborough in the act of taking an afternoon nap. Michael was full of apologies and was so unusually respectful that his lordship forgot to be annoyed.

"Moya's out," he explained.

"I will endeavour to bear up," replied Michael, seating himself at his lordship's desk and preparing to take a note of the circumstances which had led to his lordship's call for assistance. He finished the report, blotted and folded it and placed the document in his pocket.

"I only want to ask you one or two questions and they concern Kate—or Miss Tenby, as you call her. I'm afraid I gave you a shock this morning."

"It was certainly a surprise," admitted Lord Flanborough cautiously; "who is this Kate? We have made a very careful search of the house but nothing is missing so far as we can tell."

Michael laughed.

"You needn't worry about that. Kate is not a pilferer. Her real name is Katharine Westhanger; they call her Kate and she is the Colonel's niece. Her age is eighteen or nineteen, and from a child she has been brought up to regard the world as her oyster. Her mother was a wholesome parson's wife, her father was a rascal who was kicked out of the army in '89 for an offence against the Law of Property. Her maternal grandfather was General Sir Shaun Masserfield, the greatest strategist the British army has ever held—Kate inherits his genius but has not learnt his code. Her father died when she was a child and her uncle, who is a greater scoundrel than her father was—the family on the Westhanger side has a criminal history which goes back at intervals for two hundred years—completed her education. Kate has been brought up to be a thief, but a big thief. She is, I believe, the brains of the biggest criminal organisation in the world. Every member of the gang has been taken, but no evidence has ever been offered against Kate. She plans the big swindles and each one is bigger than the last—but never once have we traced the offence to her door."

"Why is it that the police—?" began Lord Flanborough.

"The police, my dear Flanborough," said Michael wearily, "are human beings who have to deal with human beings. They are not angels, nor thought readers, nor are they clairvoyant. The laws of this country are so framed that the criminal has six chances to every one possessed by his enemy. We know Kate was concerned in that big bank smashing exploit which took two million crowns from the treasury of the Bank of Holland. It was Kate who organised the raid upon the London jewellers in June of last year. Kate is the mother of Crime Street. You don't know that thoroughfare, but one of these days I'll introduce you to it, if you are curious—but I warn you that if you expect to steep your soul in sordidness, you will be disappointed—it is the most respectable street in London. Her ingenuity is remarkable, her patience beyond praise, and that is partly why I have come back: I want to know why she was here and what she was doing?"

"As I say ..." began Lord Flanborough again.

"For Heaven's sake," interrupted Michael, "don't tell me that you haven't missed things! I tell you Kate would not touch a pin in your house. In the first place she is a well-off woman. Why in Heaven's name should she bother her head about your belongings? I don't suppose, if she had the full run of your house, she could find £100 worth of realisable property! No, that is not why Kate came to you. How long has she been here?"

"Nearly a month," said Lord Flanborough, a little annoyed that the result of his own private investigations had so utterly failed to impress a representative of Scotland Yard.

"What work has she been doing?"

"Ordinary secretarial work for Moya. She came with excellent letters of recommendation."

"You can forget those," interrupted Michael testily; "the gentleman who wrote them lives at No. 9, Crime Street and his name is Millet."

"She was a wonderful typist," began his lordship, who was seeking about in his own mind for some excuse which would explain why he had been deceived.

"That I also know. She is, as you say, one of the fastest typists in the world. In fact, no aspect of her education has been neglected. She speaks five languages and read French fluently when she was nine. What work has she done for you?"

Lord Flanborough considered for a while.

"She has copied a few letters and reports."

"What kind of reports?"

"Reports from our South African companies. You see, Michael, I still retain the direction of most of my old interests."

"'Were they very important—the reports, I mean?"

"Yes and no," replied Lord Flanborough slowly; "they were merely records of output, cost of production and projected shipments."

"On what other work was she employed?"

"Let me think," said Lord Flanborough.

"I *am* letting you!" replied Michael tartly. "You used to have a very private code-book if I remember rightly."

"That is true," said Lord Flanborough, "but of course, she did not see that."

"Where did you keep it?"

"In my desk," said Lord Flanborough.

"Is it possible that she could have seen it?"

"It is possible, but wholly impossible that she could have copied it."

"For how long a time together was she left alone?"

"Five minutes was the longest period she was left in the library alone," said his lordship after consideration.

Michael fingered his chin.

"Did you ever come into the library and find her in a semi-fainting condition?" he asked.

Lord Flanborough looked at him with open-mouthed amazement.

"Did she tell you?"

Michael shook his head.

"No, she has told me nothing. I gather from your question that there was such an occurrence?"

"It is remarkable that you should ask the question," said his lordship. "I *did* come in one morning to find the poor girl—er, the wretched girl, in a semi-fainting condition."

"And you went out and got her a glass of water and sent for your housekeeper, I suppose," said Michael, his lip curling.

"Yes, I did," admitted his lordship.

"Which means, in plain language," smiled Michael, "that you surprised her in the act of examining some of your private documents and that whilst you were getting the water and calling assistance, she was replacing whatever she was looking at where she had found it. Did she on any other occasion draw your attention, on your entering the room, to some peculiar circumstance, such as one of the pictures not hanging straight or a broken vase?"

Again Lord Flanborough looked astounded.

"Yes, once she pointed to the china cupboard and asked me who cracked the glass. As a matter of fact, the glass was not cracked at all," he explained.

"But you went over and examined it?"

"Naturally," said his lordship.

"That was exactly the same trick," said Michael; "whilst you were making your inspection she was able to replace any documents she had been examining and close the drawer—if they were in a drawer. Now, I wonder what her game is?"

"You don't suggest," began his lordship in alarm, "that she is scheming to rob me?"

"I hope not," said Michael gravely; "from the idea of your being robbed, the imagination reels."

"I wish you wouldn't be so sarcastic. I am afraid you have never quite forgiven Moya—"

"I bless Moya every time I think of her," said Michael quickly; "she rendered me the greatest service that one human being can render to another, when she refused me. I hope to do better than Moya. As Moya's father, you utter a pained protest. I know, I know," said Michael, and he waved his hand cheerfully from the door.

CHAPTER III
OTHER EYES WATCHED MICHAEL

Michael Pretherston was back at the Yard in time to catch his chief before he departed for the day.

Commissioner T. B. Smith, to whose recommendation this young scion of the aristocracy owed his promotion, was not helpful.

"If we took Kate on any charge it would not prevent the swindle going forward," he said; "you may be sure she has mobilized all her resources and her little army is ready to the last button of the last gaiter. There is supposed to be a fellow watching her all the time, but he seems to have missed her rather cleverly. Anyway, I don't think there is much to be gained from shadowing her, because she knows she is under observation and acts accordingly. But I have a word of advice to you, my young Hibernian friend, and that is to keep a sharp eye on your own precious life. Kate is afraid of you."

"She didn't give me that impression this afternoon," said Michael sadly.

"Kate is a bluff; you mustn't take any notice of what she says. You accept a friend's advice and go very carefully to work. I am not so sure that you didn't behave indiscreetly this afternoon."

"That is impossible!" said Michael stoutly, and T. B. Smith laughed.

"The thing to have done was not to have recognized her and to have kept her under observation, pursuing your enquiries in the usual way."

"If you can suggest any method by which I could have prevented her from recognizing me and recognizing the fact that I recognized her I will admit that I was wrong," and T. B. Smith agreed.

"You may be right," he said; "anyway, look after yourself."

Michael promptly forgot his chief's advice and spent his evening making a solitary reconnaissance of Crime Street. Crime Street does not appear upon any plan of London, but if you will look at any large survey of the Hampstead district, you will find in a somewhat irregular tangle of buildings within a stone's throw of the Heath, a curious oval which is conspicuous on the plan, not only by its own symmetry but by the graceful lines of the thoroughfares which radiate therefrom.

This is Amberscombe Gardens. The centre of the oval is occupied by four houses, Numbers Two, Four, Six and Eight; the northern side of the gardens by five houses, Numbers One, Three, Five, Seven and Nine.

Into Amberscombe Gardens from the north run three roads, the first of which (opening into the oval between Numbers One and Three) being called The Approach; the second, dividing Numbers Five and Seven, called Bethburn Avenue; the third between Numbers Seven and Nine, Coleburn Avenue. On the south side of the oval the arrangement of the streets is very similar. Originally, the central space had been occupied by nine houses but these had been pulled down by the proprietors of the remaining four and a private garden, common to all four houses, had been laid out by the owners of these properties. So that on the southern side of the central oval, there were no buildings, but a wall bisected at regular intervals by plain garden doors which form such a common feature of London suburban residences.

In reality, the roadway to the north and south of the plot is all Amberscombe Gardens, but the oval which curves round to the north was, at the period this story covers, known to the police as "Crime Street," and in this description the nine houses on both sides of the northern curve were involved.

Number One, the most modest of all the buildings, was in the occupation of Dr. Philip Garon, an American practitioner who made frequent visits across the Atlantic and invariably returned to deposit a very handsome surplus in the local branch of the London and Western Counties Bank. Dr. Garon was successful as a result of the sublime assurance of all ocean-going passengers, that the notice, conspicuously displayed in the smoking-room warning passengers not to play cards with strangers, did not apply to them.

Number Three, a pretty house smothered in clematis in the proper season of the year, with its white window sashes and its sober red front, was the town house of Mr. Cunningham, who, apparently, had no initial and no Christian name. He was known to his intimate friends as Mush, the derivation of which is a little obscure. Mr. Cunningham described himself as independent, which meant no more than that he was independent of the ordinary necessities of making an honest living. In a sense, he was by far the best known of the Colony, for Mush had served two terms of penal servitude, one in an English and one in a French prison. He had the reputation of being able to cut holes in steel safes with a greater rapidity than any other gentleman in his profession, and it is said, probably with truth, that he had improved upon the oxy-hydrogen jet and had introduced a new element which shortened the work by half.

The tenant of Number Five was a gentleman, benign of countenance and very good to the poor. He was called the Bishop by friends and foes alike. His real name was Brown and he had been concerned in more bank swindles than any of the other colonists, though he had only one conviction to his discredit and that a comparative flea-bite of nine months' hard labour.

The owner of Number Seven was described as "Mr. Colling Jacques, Civil Engineer," in the local directories. The official police "Who's Who" noted that he was a wonderful pistol shot, and recorded, in parenthesis, that on the occasion of his arrest in connection with the smashing of the Bank of Holland, no weapon was found upon him. It was also added that there was no conviction against him in England, though he, too, had seen the inside of a French prison.

Number Nine was pointed out to sightseers, with a certain amount of local pride by the guide, as the home of Millet the forger, who had received on one occasion a fifteen years' sentence, but had been released after serving two years, an act of grace on the part of the authorities which earned for him a certain unpopularity with his peers and was held to be not unconnected with the subsequent arrest of a few of his former associates, the suggestion being that Mr. Millet had turned King's evidence.

At Number Two, on the "oval" side of the street, lived H. Mulberry, a respectable and methodical man, who went to his little office in Chancery Lane every morning of his life by the 9.15 and returned to his home at exactly 5.30 P.M. year in and year out. Mulberry was a begging letter writer on a magnificent scale. He had a wonderful literary style which seldom failed to extract the necessary emolument which he sought.

Number Four, a much larger house, indeed the second largest in Crime Street, was the habitat of "Senor Gregori, a teacher of languages." Unfortunately for him, he had in the course of his thrilling career taught other things than the liquid tongue of Spain. For example, he had taught the Bank of Chili that their "unforgeable" notes which, it was boasted, defied photographic reproduction could be turned out by the tens of thousands and that the six tints in which a gold bond was printed offered no insuperable difficulty to a clever craftsman with an artist's eye and a sense of colour.

In Number Eight lived the two brothers Thomas and Francis Stockmar of Austrian extraction, who were described as political refugees but were undoubtedly criminals of a peculiarly dangerous type. The Stockmars were dour, white-faced men with short bristling hair and were certainly the least presentable of all the colonists.

Number Six has been left to the last, for this was the most important house in Crime Street. It was a story higher than any other, built squarely, with no attempt at beauty. It is said that the third floor consisted of one room and that from its many windows it was possible to command, not only all the approaches to the northern side of the gardens, but those to the south; it has even been suggested that it was so planned, that, in case of necessity, the house could be converted into a fortress, from the third floor of which a last desperate stand might be made. This then was Number Six, the abiding place of Colonel Westhanger and his brilliant niece.

Michael Pretherston was no stranger to Crime Street. He had made many visits to this locality, and it had been at his initiative that the roadway of Amberscombe Gardens had been dug up one fine morning by a gang of road-breakers and there had been revealed that remarkable subterranean passage which connected the one side of the street with the other. The passageway led from the summer house in the gardens of the oval to a stable in Number Three.

The Colonists, however, swore stoutly that they knew nothing whatever of the existence of this passage and that it must have existed years before they came to the street. The civil engineer, Colling Jacques, pointed out to the district surveyor that the very character of the passage suggested that this was some storm water drain which had been laid down and forgotten by the contractor. Or else it had been laid down in error and the contractor had been either too lazy or too rushed to break it up. There were many other explanations, none of which was wholly acceptable.

Michael, swinging his stick, passed that portion of the road in which the passage had run and wondered with a reminiscent smile where the new tunnel was, for that there was a new one, he did not doubt.

Night was falling, and Dr. Philip Garon's dining-room windows blazed with light. Mr. Mulberry's, on the right, was more modestly illuminated. Mr. Cunningham's house was in darkness, as also was "The Bishop's." There were lights in the bedroom at Number Seven but Number Six was black as also was Number Eight.

He saw Millet standing at his garden gate, smoking, and crossed the road toward him, realizing that the keen-eyed gentleman had already observed his presence. Millet, a florid man with a genial, almost fulsome, manner met him with a friendly nod.

"Good evening, Mr. Pretherston," he said. "I hope you are not looking for trouble."

Michael leant on the top bar of the gate and shook his head.

"I shouldn't come here for trouble," he said; "this is the most law-abiding spot in London."

Mr. Millet sighed and murmured something about misfortunes which overtake mankind and added a pious expression of his desire to forget the past and to end his days in that security and peace which sin denies its votaries.

"Very pretty," said Michael blandly, "and how are all our good neighbours? I was thinking of taking a house here myself. By-the-way," he added innocently, "I suppose you don't know any that are to be let?"

Mr. Millet shook his head.

"I am all alone here," he said, "if you were really serious about wishing to live in this neighbourhood, I should be honoured to act as your host, Mr. Pretherston."

"And how is Kate?" demanded Michael, ignoring the invitation.

"Kate?" asked the puzzled Mr. Millet; "oh, you mean, Miss Westhanger. I haven't seen her for several days—I think it was last Tuesday afternoon I saw her last."

"Yes, at 2:30 in the afternoon," mocked Michael, "she was wearing a blue dress with white spots and a green hat with an ostrich feather. You remember her distinctly because she dropped her bag and you crossed to pick it up. You needn't start the alibi factory working, Millet; I have nothing against Kate for the moment."

Mr. Millet laughed softly.

"You will have your joke," he said.

"I will," said Michael with grim emphasis, "but it is going to be a long time developing. I haven't seen the Stockmars lately either."

"I never see them at all," Mr. Millet hastened to state. "I have very little in common with foreigners. Whatever there is against me, Mr. Pretherston, I am a patriot through and through. I am proud to be English and I don't take kindly to foreign gentlemen and never will."

"Your patriotism does you credit, Millet," said the detective dryly as he prepared to move on. "I wish you would be patriotic enough to give me a tip as to what game is on," he lowered his voice. "You know all that is happening here and you might do yourself a little bit of good."

"If I knew anything," said the other earnestly, "I would tell you in a moment, Mr. Pretherston, but here I am, out of the world, so to speak. Nobody ever consults me and I am glad they don't. I want to be left alone to forget the past—"

"Cut all that Little Eva stuff out, Uncle Tom," said Michael coarsely.

Other eyes had watched Michael, from behind blinds, through unsuspected peep-holes, a dozen pairs of eyes had followed him as he took his slow promenade along Crime Street.

Colonel Westhanger, a tall, grey man, stood in that big room on the third floor of his house, his hands folded behind him, his chin upon his breast, following every movement of the detective. Gregori, handsome and lithe, stood at his elbow, shading the glow of his cigarette in the palm of his hand.

"Colonel *mio*," he said softly, "I would give much for an opportunity of meeting that gentleman in a nice dark passage, in one of those old Harrison Ainsworth houses which were providentially built over a river."

"You will have your wish one of these days," said the Colonel gruffly; "I don't like that fellow. He is not one of the ordinary run of policemen. They are bad enough, but this fellow knows too much."

He nibbled his white moustache, shook his head and turned away from the window as Michael took his farewell of the forger.

"Watch him on the other side," he said, "and send one of the boys out to follow him."

He descended the thickly carpeted stairs to the first floor, which was the living suite. The drawing-room in which he turned was a beautifully furnished apartment, and the girl who had been sitting at the piano, her nimble hands running over the keys, looked up as he entered.

CHAPTER IV
"THE IDEAL CRIMINAL IS A STRATEGIST"

"Where did he go?" she asked.

"He went to Millet," said the Colonel, throwing himself down to a divan and biting off the end of a fresh cigar. "I wonder what the dickens he wants?" he mused.

Kate Westhanger made a little grimace.

"You can never tell whether a policeman finds his duty a pleasure or his pleasure a duty," she said. "I suppose he is just renewing acquaintance with Crime Street."

"Don't use that phrase," snapped her uncle.

"I shall use whatever phrase I wish," she said calmly. "You are getting nervous. Why?"

"I'm not nervous," he protested loudly; "I am getting old I suppose, and the job is such a big one. It is almost too big for me and if I occupied the position I had a few years ago, Kate, I would drop it. After all, we have made a good deal of money and we might as well all of us live to enjoy it."

She was back at the piano again and was playing with the soft pedal down.

"Can't you find anything more cheerful than the 'Death of Asa'?" growled her relative.

"It is nerves, of course; I am awfully sorry."

She got up and closed the piano with a bang which made him jump.

"I don't know what to do about Mike," she mused.

"Gregori has a solution," said the Colonel.

"To cut his throat, I suppose," said the girl coolly. "Gregori is so elemental and so horrific! I can't imagine that he ever has cut a throat in his life, but I suppose he feels that it is in keeping with his sunny southern nature to talk like that. No, Colonel *mio*," she mimicked, "we have stopped short of murder so far and I think we will remain on the safe side. My theory coincides with Mike's. I was reading an article of his in a Socialistic paper the other day and it was all about the Right to Live. I don't believe in killing people. I believe in bleeding those who have grown apoplectic with their money and I don't even know whether I believe in that."

"What do you mean?" the Colonel looked up at her under his shaggy brows.

She shrugged her shoulders.

"I mean," she said slowly, "I never know whether my views are my own views or whether they are just your views which I reflect like a mirror. You see, dear," she said, "I am very young but I have a logical mind and my logical mind tells me that no girl can have any very definite views at nineteen, not of her own, I mean. Perhaps when I am twenty-five I shall look upon you as a terrible person, and all this," she spread her hands out, "as something to think of with a shudder."

"In the meantime," said her uncle practically, "you are Miss Ali Baba, chief strategist of our little army and a very exigent young lady—by-the-way, Gregori is kicking."

She looked at him with a contemptuous little twist of her lips.

"There is a great centre forward lost in Gregori," she said. "What has moved that dago's feet?"

"Hush, hush, my child," cautioned her uncle, "our admirable friend is upstairs and, anyway, it doesn't do to speak disrespectfully of one's criminal associates. There is a certain punctilio in our profession which you may have noticed."

"How queer it sounds!" she said, leaning forward and clasping her knee. "Do you know, uncle, I cannot think straight. Ever since I was so high," she stretched her hand out before her, "I have never known a desire to secure anything I wanted, save by taking it from somebody else. At the school in Lausanne I seemed to be amongst the queerest people and, honestly, although you had warned me, I thought they were all mad. All their fathers made money in business, which seems to be a slow method of stealing which is allowed by the law. Think of the horrible monotony of working steadily day after day without any holidays, with no excitement, no adventures, save the artificial thrill of a theatre and the adventures that meet you on your way home."

"I didn't even know there were those kind of adventures," said the Colonel, fingering his trim moustache and enjoying with closed eyes the fragrance of his cigar.

"Oh, yes," nodded the girl, "you meet all sorts of men who raise their hats and say, 'Good-evening, Miss,' or 'Haven't we met before?' I don't think they have ever said anything else," she reflected thoughtfully,—"they all belong to the 'Good-evening' or the 'Met you before' school, and they all want to know if you are 'going their way.'"

"What happens then?" asked the amused Colonel, carefully removing his cigar in order that he might laugh without detriment to the accumulating ash.

"I have only had one experience," said Kate. "It was with a young man with a horribly weak chin. He had studied in both schools, for his 'Good-evening' was followed by a request for information upon my immediate plans and I let him walk with me. I expected something very dreadful but he talked mostly about his mother and the difficulties he had about getting a latchkey. He wanted to take my arm but I told him it wasn't done and then he suggested that I should meet him on Sunday. By this time I had learnt all about his family, his mother and the girl he was prepared to sacrifice to retain a continuation of our intimacy. I also discovered his name was Ernest and that he was the cleverest man in his office."

"He wanted to kiss you, I'll be bound," said the Colonel.

"I think he did," admitted the girl, "but he didn't say so. All he said was that he hoped it didn't rain and asked if he might write to me. I told him he might, but, unfortunately, he forgot to ask me my address—" she broke off suddenly, "what is Gregori kicking about?"

"That Madrid affair didn't go off as well as it might," said the Colonel, avoiding her eye.

She nodded.

"I know; and Gregori blames me, I presume."

"Gregori never blames you," said the Colonel, "I think Gregori would knife anybody who said a word against you."

"No," she said, nodding her head, her eyes fixed on the opposite wall, "the Madrid affair went badly, in spite of the fact that there were forty-two sheets of manuscript in Spanish and English giving the most elaborate directions. It was a month's work for me and it was all wasted and the greater part of a hundred thousand pesetas because Gregori's trusted Señor Rahboulla thought he could improve upon my instructions and joined the train at Cordova in a light grey suit when I told him to wear the conventional black of the *madrilleno* and when I insisted upon his making his entrance to Madrid from Toledo. I knew that Cordova was watched by the French and Spanish police and I knew too that they would be looking for a stranger. Rahboulla advertised himself, was arrested and the chain, which I had carefully pieced together, was broken. By the time he had shaken off the police and arrived in Madrid the closing hour of the Prado had been advanced from six to five and the consequence is, that the Velasquez is still in the picture gallery and we are a hundred thousand pesetas the poorer."

The Colonel shook his head.

"You are a wonderful girl and I will admit you are right. Heavens! the patience required to work out these details!"

"The ideal criminal is a strategist," said the girl. "He foresees every move of the enemy and forestalls him. He makes a diversion at one point and his real attack at another. He prepares the way for retreat at the same time as he is preparing his advance. It took me six months to obtain all the information I wanted and it took six minutes for Rahboulla to upset our plans."

She laughed.

"If things go wrong, you blame the general," she said. "Three years ago, Gregori the Kicker introduced an Italian into one of our schemes— the business of the Nottingham Post Office. That went wrong, too."

"There I admit you were right," the Colonel hurried to say; "Tolmini made a mess of it."*

"And tried to drag us all into it when he was caught," said the girl; "he went to prison under the impression that I had led him into a trap— though the fool was told the mail bags were not to be touched until the night shift came on duty."

"Why do you mention him now with such emphasis?" asked the Colonel curiously.

"Because he's out of prison—and he'll be kicking, too," she replied, "just as Gregori kicks!"

"'Let the dead past bury the dead,'" quoted the Colonel. "And how is the new scheme?"

---

*See Rex *v.* Tolmini (Notts. Assizes). This was evidently the big mail robbery which failed, owing to the precipitancy of one of the criminals.—EDITOR.

"Much farther advanced than you think. There are still one or two roads to be made smooth, one or two outposts to be rushed, some barbed wire to be cut."

"By Gad!" cried the Colonel admiringly. "You ought to have been a soldier, Kate."

She leant back in the chair with her hands clasped behind her head and looked at him searchingly.

"You were once a gentleman, uncle," she said in that direct way of hers and Colonel Westhanger flushed and frowned.

"Well, my dear uncle," she expostulated, "you are not a gentleman by the ordinary code now are you?"

"I have certain instincts," protested the Colonel gruffly; "hang it all, Kate, you don't let a fellow down very lightly."

"I suppose you are still something of a gentleman," said the girl reflectively; "the mere fact that you are annoyed at the suggestion that you are not proves that. But what I mean to say is this; there was a time when you obeyed another code, when you thought stealing was a disgraceful thing and robbery under arms a crime. You must have associated with men on whose word you could rely and who would never commit a dishonest or a mean action—men who were prepared in battle to give their lives for you. And you must have commanded men who had the same views and have punished soldiers who stepped aside from the straight path and committed little crimes which, compared with yours, were as pin-heads to the dome of St. Paul's."

"I can't see why you want to talk about the past," said the Colonel irritably. He was still a fine figure of a man, grey-moustached, broad of shoulder, tall and straight of back and had about him that indefinable something which men who have commanded men never entirely lose.

"I am merely comparing you with me," she said; "you have the advantage of having seen both sides. Tell me, which is the better?"

"Which do you think?" he demanded suspiciously.

She tossed her cigarette into the grate.

"I think this is the better," she said frankly; "it is very pleasant and very exciting. And all the good people I have met have been very dull. I think that is because all good people are dull."

"There are some good people," said the Colonel, virtuously, "who are very interesting."

"Not because of their goodness," rejoined the girl quickly; "if you meet a very popular good man it is because there is something about him which is not absolutely good. If you hear a man speak of a parson as a good fellow you will generally discover that he goes to the National

Sporting Club and sees boxing or rides to hounds or does something which is quite unassociated with his professional duties or the exercise of his innocent qualities. But you have not answered me. Which is better?"

"If I had my life to live over again—" began the Colonel with a wry face.

"That's silly," said the girl calmly. "You won't have your life to live over again, so why speculate upon the possibility? Anyway, if you could live your life over again, you could not possibly benefit by your present experience, because you would not remember it. You have lived two lives, which is the better?"

"You are in a queer mood, to-night," said Colonel Westhanger, rising and stalking past her to the fire-place. "Have you got religion, or something?"

"Which is the better?" she asked again. "To be a free thief or to be in the dull bondage of honesty?"

"For your peace of mind the honest life is the better," said the Colonel. "You have no sleepless nights, no agony of mind which you have to conceal with whatever skill you possess at every knock at the door, no fear of the police, no wondering what the next day is going to bring forth."

"Really!" she looked up at him quizzically. "Do honest men never have any of those experiences? Do honest men get into debt, for example, and dread the coming of the collector? Does an honest man who is getting grey feel a little sickening sensation in his heart every time his employer looks at him thoughtfully?"

The Colonel turned round and snarled over his shoulder.

"As you seem to have all your answers ready-made, I don't know why you trouble to ask me," he snapped; "there are advantages and disadvantages on both sides of the picture."

The girl was in a restless mood and presently she sprang up, walked to the window, opened the little square of shutter and looked out into the darkening street. Then she crossed to her little desk at one side of the fireplace. She sat down and wrote for a while, then, as suddenly, she dropped her pen and got up again.

"You are going to ask another question," warned the Colonel.

"Only one," she pleaded.

"Well, fire away," he grumbled ungraciously.

"What would induce you to forsake your career and apply your undoubted talents, as the assize judge said to poor dear Mr. Mulberry, to better purpose?"

"Wealth," said the Colonel promptly,—"enough stuff put aside to bring me in a nice little income. And here again, let me say, Kate, that you and I could well afford to knock off—"

She interrupted him.

"That is a purely material inducement," she said. "What other—spiritual or ethical?"

"Oh, rot!" he snapped. "Why do you ask these fool questions?"

"Because I am wondering," she said, "what influence could be brought to bear upon me. The opinion of my fellow creatures? No, I don't care what they think. I know they are mostly fools and so why should they influence me? Wealth? No, if I were rich as Croesus I should go on, for the sport of it. Punishment? No, I should use my spare time in correcting the faults in me which had resulted in my detection. I am afraid I am incorrigible, uncle, for there is something about this life which appeals to me no end—and now I am going to dress," she said, making for the door.

"Going out?" asked the Colonel in surprise.

She nodded.

"But Gregori—"

"Gregori can wait," said Kate, "and Gregori bores me. He is always trying to make love."

"Is that remarkable?" suggested the Colonel archly.

"It is remarkably annoying," said the girl. She flung open the door and stepped back. Gregori, politest of cavaliers, stood deferentially in the entrance and she surveyed him coolly.

"Were you listening?" she asked.

"Señorita!" he said, shocked.

She laughed and passed out. Gregori watched her as she mounted the stairs till she turned out of sight, then he closed the door and came across to the Colonel.

"Our little friend is hard on me," he said with no hint of malice in his voice.

"She is a queer girl, Gregori," replied the Colonel, shaking his head.

"She is a queer girl," repeated Gregori; "queer indeed, yes."

He stroked his little black moustache.

"She doesn't like me."

"Who does she like?" snapped the older man.

"You, I trust," smiled the Spaniard.

The Colonel tossed his head despairingly.

"I hardly know," he said. "What a reversal of positions!"

The Spaniard took the seat the girl had vacated.

"I know what you are thinking about," he nodded; "a few years ago she was the obedient child absorbing our code—to-day she is the tyrannical mistress of the situation."

He deftly unrolled and rolled a Spanish cigarette, licked its edges and fumbled for a match in his waistcoat pocket.

"She is all brain, our Kate," he said admiringly, "but her heart—pouf!" he puffed out a cloud of smoke to emphasize the word.

"There is no end to her energy," he went on; "sometimes I think she is dangerous and then when I come to consider all things it is impossible to say that she can be. After all, hers is only the plan. The responsibility for the bungling is with us—the plan is so perfect that you can hardly pick a hole in it. She works out to the last minute detail the chronology of a coup, she dresses it, rehearses it. She never fails. Yes, it was Rahboulla," he agreed, "and I was wrong to kick. What was it she called me, a 'centre forward' and a 'dago'," he laughed softly.

"She is very young," said the Colonel apologetically, "and a little impetuous of speech—she talks too much, I think."

"A pretty woman can never talk too much," said the gallant Gregori; "she can think too much and talk too little. A person who talks is like a lighted house with all the blinds up and the doors open, you know where you are. Now, Colonel *mio*, how far have we got with this new scheme?"

The Colonel brought a chair in one hand and a light table in the other to where the Spaniard sat, produced from his inside-pocket a bunch of memoranda and in a few minutes the men were deep in the discussion of the most remarkable, the most startling and the most daring enterprise that Crime Street had ever undertaken.

CHAPTER V
A CHORUS GIRL AT SEBO'S

Sebo's Club was crowded, for it was the dinner hour and Sebo's is the most extensively patronized of the dining clubs. Here, all that was beautiful, all that was smart, all that was famous and brilliant in the world of society, letters and the drama met on common ground—the inherent and universal desire which humanity has for careless comfort. A Cabinet Minister and his party sat at the next table to that presided over by a great revue actress; the owner of a Derby winner sat back to back against a famous Radical satirist. The editor of a great London daily could look across his table and without shifting his eyes could count in his field of vision the pretty dancer from the Empiredrome, a royal physician, a peer of the realm and a ragtime singer.

The big dining hall blazed with lights, the little tables were crowded together so as to leave scarcely room for the waiters who, by some mysterious dispensation of Providence, seemed able to thread their ways through impossible spaces. The noisy coon band kept up its rhythmic pandemonium in one corner of the room, but did not drown the rippling laughter and the buzz of light-hearted talk.

In the little vestibule a young man, very tall and very thin, paced the tesselated floor with that evidence of resignation which tells so eloquently the story of the Unpunctual Guest. He was very fair and very pink. His countenance was vacant and the vacancy was by no means relieved when he screwed a gold-rimmed monocle into his right eye.

Presently the glass doors swung and a girl came hurriedly toward him, holding out her gloved hand.

"I am awfully sorry I am late, Reggie," she said with easy familiarity.

"If you were an hour late or five hours late or a day late," said the young man with gentle ecstasy, "I should be content to wait, Miss Flemming."

She flashed a dazzling smile at him.

"I shouldn't be horribly shocked if you called me Vera," she said.

The young man went pinker than ever, coughed, stuttered, ran his gloved finger inside the high upstanding collar about his thin throat, dropped his eye-glass, retrieved it and did all this in the space of four seconds, thereby betraying his perturbation and his gratitude.

"You have a table, I suppose?" said the girl when she had returned from depositing her coat.

"Rather!" said the young man, and added after a second's thought, "Rather!"

He fussily shepherded her through the mass of tables where his own attenuation enabled him to emulate the deeds of the agile serving man and brought her to a corner table which was smothered with rare flowers. Heads were turned, sharp eyes focussed the couple, some smiled, though for the girl the glances held nothing but admiration or cold-blooded appraisement, according to the sex of the observer.

"Reggie Boltover!" said one young man.

"Who is Reggie Boltover?" asked his companion.

"A human being loosely attached to a million," was the laconic description.

The girl was radiant, the smile hardly left her face and the eyes which glanced shyly up to her tall companion were full of wonder and delight.

"So this is Sebo's," she said. "Isn't it a dreadfully wicked place?"

Reggie Boltover's face creased alarmingly—he, too, was smiling.

"My dear Miss—my dear Vera," he said boldly, "should I bring you to a wicked place, now I ask you; should I bring you to a wicked place, should I?"

His conversational powers were not brilliant but his heart was pure. He was not really a wicked young man about town and his chief wickedness lay in his implicit belief that he was. He had met the girl one night by accident. A more daring friend of his, and nearer approaching Reggie's own ideal of doggishness, had induced him (he protesting feebly) to call at a stage-door where he was meeting a charming friend to take her to supper. The charming friend in the generous large-hearted way of chorus girls had introduced her friend, Vera Flemming, a newcomer to the ranks of the chorus, and they had all supped together and Vera had been very charming to Mr. Reggie Boltover and he had asked her to go with him up the river and had serious thoughts, because of her evident refinement, of introducing her to his mother, which shows that Reggie had reached the most dangerous stage of infatuation. There was really nothing wrong about Reggie Boltover and nothing remarkably terrible about this strangely initiated friendship.

Chorus girls are merely shop-girls with a taste for caviare and peaches. They are no more sinful than their sisters in the same social strata and the only difference between them is that, whilst they are exposed to similar temptations, the chorus girl has a larger field to pick from and the candidates are much more presentable. A shop-girl accepts the hospitality of a tea-shop, the chorus-girl goes to the Ritz. Both have one consuming passion, a desire for good food, for which they do not have to pay.

Reggie Boltover, who, to do him justice, knew everybody, entertained the girl for half-an-hour by pointing out the various celebrities in the room and Vera Flemming was interested without being enthusiastically so.

"I would rather you talked about yourself," she said, "you are ever so much more interesting than these people."

"Oh, no," said Reggie, with a little giggle; "oh, no!"

"You are, indeed, you are," she said earnestly.

"Oh, come," said Reggie; "oh, come! no! I am not interesting; oh, dear no!"

His life he admitted frankly was very ordinary. All that he did was to sign a few cheques, liquidate a few debts, see a few "fellows" about "things" and "there you are," said Reggie.

"It must be wonderful to be in a position of power," said the girl musingly. "Of course, I come from a very poor family. We only think in shillings where you think in thousands of pounds. And it is awfully hard to realize what it feels like to order people to do things instead of being ordered."

Reggie Boltover, who had never ordered anybody to do anything in his life and would not have dared to dispute the judgment of the innumerable managers and directors whom his sainted father had appointed in his life-time, wondered himself what it felt like. He had often meditated, with a shudder, upon the necessity which might one day arise, for his taking the initiative in the conduct of his business. He dimly realized that, in time, all his managers and directors would die and he had dimly speculated upon the question as to who would replace them. He had a feeling that perhaps one might go to Whiteleys and order some new ones, but it had never occurred to him that at his automatic word managers and people of that description could be made out of mud, or that an order affecting the business which he was supposed to control would be acted upon if he were to give that order.

"Well, you know," he said, "I never really tell people to do anything. You see, I never see them except very occasionally. Of course, they make reports and all that sort of thing and I have a man who reads them so everything is all right and I just sign cheques and see a few fellows and there you are."

Under the genial influence of her sympathetic interest he expanded a little and proved that he was not as wholly incompetent as he pretended to be. For instance, he knew that the iron works and ship-building yard which still bore his father's name, and incidentally his own, made "a deuced lot of money" every year and that certain other properties made no money.

There was one property of which he spoke with great bitterness but only because his father, in his life-time, had also spoken of that matter with similar violence and asperity. Apparently, the one redeeming feature about Boltover's Cement Works lay in the fact that it had no manager and therefore produced no reports. It was in fact a deserted shell of a building so infamously unprofitable that Boltover senior (now in Heaven) had directed almost with his last breath, if you believed Reggie, that his name should be erased from the official designation of the company.

"You see it was bad cement; you know how cement is made, don't you?"

"I should love to," said the girl, her eyes shining, "I have often wondered."

"Well," said Reggie looking round the table for something to illustrate the object lesson, "you dig in the river and you take out a lot of stuff and you chuck it in a cart and then you chuck it into a fire and you pull it out and do something to it and there you are! That's cement. Only our cement wasn't cement, if you understand. That is what made the beastly thing so awkward."

"How wonderful!" said the girl. "I shall always remember that."

"Of course, we've got our eyes open," said Reggie now fairly launched upon the story of his life, "and one of these days we shall catch a mug."

"Catch a—?" asked the girl, puzzled.

Reggie went very pink, but he was excited and grateful at this demonstration of the girl's refinement.

"Forgive the vulgarity, Miss—Vera; I mean we shall find a purchaser. I once nearly sold the beastly thing for £10,000 and the day the deed was to be signed, they took the poor chap away to a lunatic asylum, poor old bird, not right in his head, you know. That is why he wanted to buy our cement works. Comic, isn't it?

"D'you know," said Mr. Boltover, suddenly, "when I came round to the stage door that night I never expected to meet you?"

She looked at him in innocent surprise.

"Didn't you really?" she said incredulously as though the idea had occurred to her for the first time, and then, thoughtfully, "I suppose you didn't."

"I didn't expect to meet you," repeated Mr. Boltover, who, when he had got hold of one complete sentence, held tight to it until his groping mentality had reached out and securely grasped another. "No, I didn't expect to meet you, but I'm awfully glad. I feel I owe that young lady more than I can ever repay."

He said this with an unusual display of sentimentality.

"That young lady" was his companion's chorus girl friend, who at that moment was retailing to her youthful companion at the far side of the room such details of Vera's life as she had been able to secure in a seven-day acquaintance.

"Vera's not in our show now, of course," she said; "I don't think she had ever been on the stage before. She's an awfully fresh kid. Came late to rehearsals and all that sort of thing, but I like her immensely."

She smiled and bowed to Vera who, at that moment, had caught her eye.

"She's very pretty," said her companion.

"Yes; isn't she?" agreed the girl, her interest in her friend suddenly evaporating.

But there was one in that crowded dining-room whose every disengaged moment was employed in watching the girl and her companion. It involved his getting into the way of other waiters and called down upon his head execrations in Neapolitan, Sicilian and the choicest slang of the Montmartre. He was a man who had prayed for two years for such a moment as this, and his soul rejoiced in savage exaltation that so Heaven-sent an opportunity had come.

As the night wore on his plan took a definite shape. For the consequence he cared nothing. Here was his opportunity, here was his enemy. He seized a moment, slipped through the service door and passed down a flight of stone steps to the crowded kitchen filled at that moment with a babble of sound as the orders were repeated across the streaming brass pots and the blistering hot plates. He passed through the kitchen to the larder department, and found what he sought in the big cool vault where the butchers worked. It was a long thin knife. He waited until the butcher's back was turned and slipped it up his sleeve, passed rapidly through the kitchen, ignoring the chef's demand as to his business, and reached the warm, bright restaurant again. He had no time to waste.

The butcher might at any moment detect the theft and the thief hauled into the service room to explain his conduct. He made his way across the room to where Mr. Reginald Boltover and his fair companion sat.

Reggie thought the man had a message, but Vera, looking up, saw the man's evil face—and knew. She half twisted, half flung herself against Reginald Boltover as the waiter's hand came up to strike. She saw the knife glitter for a space of a second and closed her eyes, then there was the sound of a struggle and she opened them in time to see the vengeful man flung backward to the floor and an immaculate Michael Pretherston standing over him examining the knife with some interest.

She met the inspector's eye and smiled, though the smile was forced, for even as he bowed, she heard the mockery of his surprise.

"Why, Kate!" he murmured. "I'm always meeting you."

CHAPTER VI
KATE CAME TO THE FLAT

"At 9:40 on the night of the 15th instant I was present at Sebo's Club. The room was full of diners and amongst them was Mr. Reginald Boltover and a girl giving the name of Miss Vera Flemming, who was in reality Kate Westhanger. At 9:52 an Italian named Emil Tolmini, employed as a waiter at Sebo's Club, attempted to stab Kate Westhanger but was prevented and taken into custody. In the course of the struggle in which he was disarmed he sustained a slight scalp wound and permission was given for him to be taken to the kitchen to have the wound dressed. I regret to state that he succeeded in making his escape. He is a convict on license (record No. P.C.A./C.C.C. 85943). He is an old associate of the Crime Street gang and was obviously attempting to avenge himself upon the girl for some injury, real or imaginary, which he had suffered.

"I made no attempt to warn Mr. Boltover as to the character of his companion, but subsequently calling at his flat in Piccadilly on the pretence that I wished to get information about the attempted murder, I discovered that he had been introduced to the girl at a theatre where she was posing as a chorus girl. She had evidently laid a deep plan to meet him, for what reason it is not clear. He is a very wealthy man and it may be necessary at a later stage to warn him, but at present I have taken upon myself the responsibility of refraining from that act."

Michael Pretherston ended off the report with his neat signature, folded it and inserted it into an official envelope which he addressed to his chief. By good fortune he met that brilliant man coming into Scotland House as Michael was going out.

"I think you did right," said T. B., after he had heard the story; "I wonder what her game is? I have a good mind to detail a man to take the whole case up."

"Let me do it," said Michael, eagerly.

T. B. Smith pursed his lips.

"You are rather a big man for a job like that, Michael," he said, "it may turn out to be nothing more than a common or garden chorus girl's romance."

"Kate isn't the chorus girl type," said Michael, "if it is big enough for her to be in it, it is quite big enough for me."

The chief thought for a moment.

"Very well then," he said at length, "you can take on the job. Do it by yourself if you possibly can, I haven't any men to spare. But keep in touch with me. Blowing a whistle won't be of any service to you if these people mean business and get after you."

He hesitated again.

"Confound Kate!" he said. "I suppose you have circulated a description of the ice-cream merchant?"

All Latin criminals came under this generic description with T. B. Michael nodded.

"Well, good luck," said the chief, "but be careful!"

When the young man had gone T. B. beckoned to an officer who was passing.

"You're the very man, Barr," he said; "pick up Mr. Pretherston and don't lose him—you may choose your own opposite number."

The sergeant saluted and hurried out after his charge.

Michael went back to his rooms with a light heart. It was the kind of job that he liked better than any other. He had not told the chief all his suspicions. Kate's game was a big one. High-flyer as she was, she was out for a height record—that he realised. There was some association between her month with Lord Flanborough and the careful cultivation of Reggie Boltover's acquaintance. When he came to think of it she must have met Boltover while she was still with Flanborough. He had taken it for granted that the girl was a resident secretary but possibly he had arrived at this conclusion in error. So it proved next morning when he called Lord Flanborough's house on the telephone and had a private conversation with the butler. The young lady, during the time she had been at Felton House, had left every afternoon at four o'clock.

A little talk with the stage manager at the theatre showed that the girl had never attended any of the morning rehearsals and had missed one of the matinées. Michael saw this part of the scheme plainly enough. Kate, through her spies, had discovered that Boltover had an acquaintance who had a friend at the theatre. She had come to the stage with no other object than making a friend of the girl who all unwittingly was the instrument by which she was to meet Reggie.

The detective knew that this was no chance acquaintance. He followed the manoeuvres of Kate through all their devious paths. He took the opportunity in the afternoon to call upon Reggie at his office which was something between a board room and a boudoir.

Reggie's theoretical interests were multifarious. He was the nominal head of a dozen different corporations which his industrious father had created for his profit. In practice he knew very little about any of them and nothing about some.

"I hope your lady was not alarmed," said Michael, with spurious anxiety.

"Oh, no, the lady was not alarmed; oh, no," said Reggie, shaking his head violently. "Oh, dear no. She was not alarmed. Of course, it would have been different if she had been alone, but being with me, naturally she—er she—er was not alone."

"Naturally," agreed Michael.

"No, she was not alarmed," said Mr. Boltover, "in fact, she was very cool, remarkably cool. I have never seen anybody so cool."

"I hope when you see her again," said Michael, "you will tell her I asked."

"Certainly," said Mr. Boltover heartily; "certainly I shall tell her you asked." And he added after a moment, "When I meet her again."

"She seemed, if you will forgive the impertinence, so interested in everything," encouraged Michael.

"You are quite right," said Reggie eagerly, "you are perfectly right. That just describes her. She is interested in everything."

"It is nice to meet people who are interested in one's business," Michael went on artlessly. "I never mind people being interested in my business, do you?"

"Oh, dear no," replied Mr. Boltover in alarm, as though the very thought that anybody should be discouraged from an interest in his affairs, caused him acute mental unhappiness; "oh, dear no. Certainly not. Not at all."

"Of course," smiled Michael, "she could not very well understand all the complexities of your business, Mr. Boltover—it is such an enormous one."

"Well," hesitated the other, "I don't know. I am not so sure. She is a very intelligent young lady. I was talking to her about my business when this dreadful affair happened and she was so calm that she just went on talking about it, don't you know. My business, I mean. I thought it was a most remarkable instance of coolness. I was telling one of our directors today about it, and he thought it was a remarkable instance of coolness. Yes, even when I was taking her home she told me a lot about herself and—things. Her grandfather is a very wealthy man, a financier. I didn't know that."

Michael might have said that he too was unaware of the fact, but he knew just the moment when a tactless interpolation might dry up the fount of Mr. Boltover's eloquence.

"Very intelligent lady indeed," wandered Mr. Boltover, "oh, yes, I was talking about her grandfather—he is a very rich man. She thought that he might be able to take one of our properties off our hands. I was awfully surprised. Naturally, I did not think she had any money being in the chorus and all that—I hope I haven't been indiscreet?" he asked anxiously. "You possibly did not know that she was on the stage."

"Oh, yes, I did," said Michael with a smile; "you have betrayed nothing, Mr. Boltover."

"I am awfully glad," replied the other, relieved; "what was I saying, about her grandfather, yes. I think I might sell him that property. I hate parting with properties—we have refused quite a number of good offers—sheer sentiment, don't you know?"

"But perhaps this is not a paying property."

"Oh, no, not at all," said Mr. Boltover; "by no manner of means whatever. Still we don't like parting with them. Of course, I talk a lot of rot about people wanting to buy the works and I always tell that great joke about a lunatic—ha, ha—but really it isn't true. No, not really true, oh, no."

Michael had never heard the great joke about the lunatic. What he was anxious to hear were details of Kate's projected purchase but in this he was foiled. There was precious little of the business man about Mr. Reggie Boltover but one lesson he had learnt, and learnt thoroughly, and that was the art of silence. His revered father was wont to say, "If you never open your mouth, Reggie, nobody will know what an ass you are," and in business, at any rate, Reggie most religiously lived up to this injunction.

What was the girl's object?

Michael was puzzled. Strangely enough the obvious never occurred to him, or if it did he dismissed it without a second consideration. He did not look upon Kate as the type that would find any amusement, whatever the profit might be, in the inveigling of a young fool to the altar. Kate wanted the excitement, not the money. That was her history. He had first met her when he was in the Special Department and it had been over a little matter of a King's messenger's despatch bag which on a cross-channel journey had mysteriously disappeared, though it was practically handcuffed to the owner's wrist, that he had first become acquainted with the girl. He was interested in her, but only mildly so, because, at the time, he arrived at a somewhat hasty judgment. It was later, when the strong-room of the "Muranic" was forced and twenty-five packets of diamonds vanished in mid-ocean and when he had been in charge of the investigations which had resulted in the imprisonment of Colonel Westhanger, that he had first formed a true estimate of the girl's character—an estimate which he had had cause to modify, but never to change.

Michael lived in a big block of flats near Baker Street, where he maintained a somewhat elaborate establishment for an inspector of police. He had, however, a private income of his own which he had inherited from his maternal grandmother and as he was a man of simple tastes and very few extravagant needs, he was able to live very comfortably indeed. He reached his home a little before 8 o'clock and was astonished as he came through the lobby of the flat to meet Beston, his man-servant, clad in fine raiment and going forth.

"Hello, Beston, where are you off to?" he asked in surprise.

The man touched his hat cheerfully.

"I am going to the theatre, sir, and thank you very much for the tickets," he said. "Cook went ten minutes ago and I stayed behind to tidy things up."

"Oh, cook went ten minutes ago, did she?" said Michael. "That's good. When did the tickets arrive?"

"About an hour ago, sir, by a district messenger. It was very kind of you to wire to us that you were sending them."

Michael laughed softly.

"Your surprise at my consideration hurts me, Beston," he said. "I always do things like that. By the way, did they spell your name correctly in the telegram?"

"I think so, sir," said the man in surprise, fumbled in his pocket and produced the orange slip.

"I am sending you two tickets for the theatre tonight. May not be home until tomorrow. Pretherston."

Thus read the wire, which had been handed in at the Strand Office. Beston sensed some difficulty.

"I hope it's all right, sir," he asked anxiously.

"Quite all right," replied Michael with a cheerful nod. "Don't wait for me now, I shall not be in very long."

He mounted the carpeted stairs, opened the door of his flat and closed it carefully behind him.

He went straight to his study, pulled down the blinds and drew the thick curtains across the windows, then he turned on the light, took up the telephone and gave a Treasury number.

"Is that Sergeant Pears?" he asked. "Is there a telegram waiting at the Yard for me?"

"Yes, sir," said the sergeant's voice.

Michael winked at the wall.

"Do you mind opening and reading it?"

There was a little pause and then the sergeant repeated into the receiver:

"To Inspector Michael Pretherston, Scotland House. Come up by the earliest train. Am staying at Adelphi. T. B."

"Handed in at Manchester, I suppose?"

"Yes, sir," said the sergeant, "at three-fifteen."

"Is the chief in Manchester?"

"Yes, sir; he went by the morning train."

"Excellent," said Michael, "thank you very much, sergeant."

He hung up the receiver.

This was Kate's work—the beautiful detail of it, the knowledge she possessed of T. B. Smith's movement. She had probably sent a man up on the same train with the chief and had given him the telegram in advance, with exact instructions as to the minute it was to be handed in. Yes, it was Kate. Yet (he became uncomfortable at the thought) it was not like her to leave things to chance. How came she to miss him at the Yard? He returned to the telephone and again called up his assistant.

"What time did the telegram arrive?" he asked.

The sergeant's voice was apologetic.

"I am very sorry, sir, I am afraid it arrived while you were here, this afternoon. It was given to a messenger to take in to you and in some extraordinary way the constable forgot it. I have reprimanded him."

"That's all right," said Michael, relieved.

His relief, curiously founded, he might have found it difficult to explain. It was the relief which the matador feels when he sees the bull, which steps so proudly into the ring, will put up a good fight. It was the relief of the huntsman when a strong fox breaks from covert. He wanted Kate and that extraordinary organization, which he had set himself to conquer, to be at its best that his victory might be the more satisfactory.

He looked at his watch. It was five minutes past eight. He knew that his visitor would give the servants an hour and he must employ that hour profitably. He began to write rapidly on a pad of scribbling paper, tearing off the sheets as fast as he had filled them. He had been working for an hour when he heard a bell tinkle. Some one was at the front door. He switched out the light, walked into the passage (he had already removed his shoes) and listened. Whoever was coming had sent an agent in advance to discover whether the flat was empty. Again the bell rang. Michael made no sign. It rang a third and last time. The detective made his way stealthily to the window and slipped behind the curtains. He had left his study door open, so that he could hear every sound. He had ten minutes to wait before the faint click of the lock told him that the door had been opened. He knew that the visitor would come to the study last, and he proved to be right. Three minutes passed—as near as he could judge—before he caught the flash of a lamp which was directed cautiously to the curtained window. The light passed slowly along the floor until it reached the skirting, travelled round until it found the lower edge of the drawn curtain. Through the slit he had cut in the heavy velvet hangings Michael witnessed the search. Presently the light went out after focussing itself upon the electric switch. There was a click and the room was illuminated.

The girl who stood by the desk was soberly dressed and was apparently in no hurry. She pulled her gloves off slowly, whilst she allowed her eyes to rove over the littered table. Half a dozen sheets of writing attracted her attention and when her gloves were removed she picked the papers up, pulled the big writing chair to the table and sat down to read. She read the notes through carefully and once she smiled. When she had finished she put them down, leaned back in the chair and looked around the room, then, "Come out, Mike," she said.

Michael stepped forth without embarrassment.

"I was nearly deceived," she said, "with your precious account of the happening at Sebo's and then I realized that this could not have been written more than five minutes before. You forgot to blot the last sheet and the ink is still damp."

She rubbed her fingers over to prove the fact.

"Why aren't you in Manchester?" she asked.

The staggering question nearly took his breath away.

"Well, if you aren't the real Kate!" he said admiringly.

"I'm in your chair I'm afraid," she said.

"Not a bit."

He dropped into a deep settee.

"Now tell me all the news. But before we go any farther," he said with mock concern, "wouldn't you like a chaperone?"

"Don't worry," she replied, "I have a chaperone."

"Not in my flat I hope," he said in a tone of alarm. "You, I can trust, Kate, but the idea of your low thieving friends being up against all my movable goods gives me a little pain."

She fished in her bag and produced a little gold case. She opened it and took out a cigarette. "You won't have one, of course?"

"Not one of yours, Kate," he said reproachfully. "No, I'll have one of my own if you don't mind."

"I think you are very rude," she said with a lift of her brows.

"It's better to be rudely awake than politely asleep," he said meaningly. "When one has to deal with clever criminals one has to take all sorts of precautions."

She laughed and looked at him curiously. "I wonder what made you a policeman?"

"Nature," he said promptly.

She was puzzled.

"I don't quite get your humor," she said.

"Nature provides all things with some form of protection. It gives the oyster its shell and the tiger its stripes. It gives the squid his ink-sack and the shark his teeth. Nature always produces antidotes. When criminals are stupid they have stupid policemen to deal with them. When criminals are extraordinarily clever, Nature provides the police force with an officer of unusual intelligence. I came to the police in blind obedience to the laws of Nature."

She laughed softly in his face.

"It's so nice to be able to discuss things with a man of sensibility," she said. "Of course, some of my friends are awfully clever and uncle is very philosophical, but then they all take a very one-sided view of things, and I think it's so much better to hear the other side of every question. You can get two views on all subjects except crime," she went on. "If you believe in Darwin's theory you can meet hosts of clever people who bitterly oppose it. If you are a Christian Scientist you can meet hosts of Theosophists. Even if you are a firm believer in monogamy you can generally hire a Mormon to argue on the other side. It is only when we come down to crime that you meet the truly insular view, held by people who know nothing whatever about its finesse, or the genius necessary to break the laws without leaving a big hole to show where you went in and another to show where you came out. That is why I like you, Mike," she said frankly.

"Any appreciation is very gratifying to me," said Michael, "but that which is so enthusiastic that it leads my admirer to break into my flat to ravish my secret thoughts, is a little overwhelming."

"I wanted to know what you were saying about me," she said, "though I ought to have known that you would not leave things about for me to read—still," she justified herself, "to do myself justice, I did not expect to find your confidential reports on your desk."

There was a big safe in one corner of the room.

"I was going to open that."

She nodded toward the strong-box.

"You saw me the other night," she turned the conversation suddenly.

"At Sebo's—yes," he said, "I saw you."

"What did you think?" she asked quietly.

"I thought you were with the loquacious Mr. Boltover for a special reason of your own," he said slowly.

"He *is* an orator—isn't he?" she agreed,—"but he's quite a nice boy, really. God didn't give him brains and it's not fair to make fun of a man's deficiencies."

"What did you want of Reggie?" asked Michael.

"I just wanted to know all about him," she said, "that kind of people are always interesting to me."

"What did you want of Reggie?" he asked again.

"How insistent you are!" she laughed.

She got up and began strolling about the room, taking down books from the big bookshelf and examining their titles.

"What catholic tastes you have, Mike—and Tennyson, too. How depraved!"

"You will find a Browning somewhere," he said carelessly.

"That's more encouraging," she smiled. "It's an awfully comfortable room. Quite like the room I thought you would have."

She looked at a book plate on the cover of one volume.

"You were at Winchester, I see. So was uncle."

"The poison and the antidote!"

"You are not fair with uncle. He's a mental degenerate, too. Crime is a disease with him."

"And with you?" said Michael quickly.

"It's a hobby. It's a tremendous excitement."

She put the book down and turned to him.

"You don't know what it's like. To work things out and make them happen, to cover a couple of sheets of paper with writing and then see all sorts of things move in obedience to those instructions, to see thousands and tens of thousands of pounds change hands, to know that men are going long journeys, that special trains are being run, that telegraph wires are humming all over the Continent, that a dozen brilliant thief-catchers are working and worrying in a vain attempt to undo all that twenty or thirty lines of writing have done."

"This will be used in evidence against you," warned Michael flippantly.

The girl was not posing. Of that he was convinced. Her big grey eyes were brighter, her whole face was alight with the excitement of the thought, her voice had a new thrill. She was exalted, transfigured at the thought of the power which her shrewd brain gave to her.

"What did you want of Reggie?" he asked again.

The light faded out of her eyes and she was her normal self again.

"Oh, I wanted to pick his pocket," she said mockingly; "or, no, I know something better—I wanted to marry him. He's worth two millions."

"I don't think you will ever marry for money," said Michael.

"What makes you say that?" she asked quickly.

He shrugged his shoulders.

"That is the estimate I have formed of you. I may be wrong."

"I shall never marry," she said with decision. "I'm not of the marrying kind. I hate men in some ways. I hate them so much, that it gives me a real joy to take away the one thing in the world that they really love. You know the Claude Duval tradition—I mean the idealized Claude Duval of tradition, not the sneak-thief valet of actuality—of robbing the rich and never robbing the poor—well, I rob men, and I never rob women."

"In fact you rob the people who have the money," said Michael. "That isn't clever."

"No, but it sounds awfully good. I'm thinking of including it in the great speech I shall deliver one of these days at the Old Bailey."

"What did you want from Reggie?" he asked.

"You are almost monotonous," she laughed. "Well, I wanted information."

She turned and again he saw that bright light in her eye and that eager look in her face.

"I will tell you, Michael Pretherston," she said, pointing a white finger toward him. "We will play fair. I am going to do a big thing. I am going to make the most wonderful steal that the world has ever known. That is why I found Reggie. That is why I made a martyr of myself and endured the boredom of Lord Flanborough's society."

She clapped her hands like a child.

"It's a big thing, Michael, but it's full of complications, wonderfully full of strategy, and I am going to do it all with your assistance."

He jumped up and flung out his hand.

"Put it there, Kate," he said.

"This is going to be the big thing for both of us and I am going to be the victor. If you win you have whatever you're after. If I win, you have me," she said with a little laugh.

He looked at her in silence.

"I can almost see you gripping my arm and pushing me into the steel pen," she said. "I can see you sitting in court in a brown—no, a blue—overcoat, with your hat nicely balanced on your knees, looking up at me in the dock and wondering how I am going to take it."

A cloud passed over his face.

"You're a pessimistic little devil," he growled. "No, I wasn't thinking about that."

"What were you thinking about?" she asked, her eyes wide open in surprise.

"I was thinking I'd marry you," he said.

She looked at him in amusement.

"You're mad, aren't you?"

"Yes," he said; "didn't you know?"

"Marry you!" she said scornfully. "Great Heavens!"

"You might do worse," he said with his cheerful smile.

"Can you name anything I could do that would be more hopelessly degrading than marry a policeman?"

"Yes," he said, "you might be an old maid and keep cats. You take it for granted, of course," he went on, "that I am letting you go now."

"Naturally," she replied, "I have given you something to live for."

"You may be right," he said quietly and opened the door for her.

They walked down the felt covered passage to the front door.

"I owe you something," she said as they stood in the doorway. "The young man from the South nearly put an end to my promising career."

"A little thing like that is hardly worth mentioning. Good night, Kate, are you sure it is safe for you to be out alone so late?"

She made a little face at him and went tripping down the stairs. She turned into the street, but had not gone two paces when a hand caught her arm.

"Excuse me," said a voice.

By the light of a street lamp she recognized her captor as a detective sergeant from Scotland Yard.

Before she could protest a voice spoke from the darkness of the balcony above and it was the voice of Michael.

"All right, sergeant," he said.

She shook herself free of the man and looked wrathfully up at the dim figure.

"I forgot you'd have your nurse handy, Michael," she jeered.

"Good night, dear," said the voice from the balcony and to her intense annoyance she felt an extraordinary sensation wholly new to her, but which with her quick woman's wit she correctly diagnosed, as she hurried angrily along the street.

For Kate Westhanger had blushed for the first time in her life.

CHAPTER VII
THE PRINCESS BACHEFFSKI—BEAUTIFULLY DRESSED

Lord Flanborough gave a dinner party. He was a methodical man and invariably made his arrangements a long time in advance, and he was not unnaturally annoyed, when, at the eleventh hour, his daughter suggested a change in the plans.

"My dear Moya," he said testily, "don't be absurd. Surely after what has passed—after his extraordinary attitude—"

"Oh, daddy, what nonsense!" said the girl. "Michael is really a good sort and he will be amusing. I really cannot sit out a dinner with all those boring people, and if you don't invite him, I shall have a headache."

"But, my dear," protested her father, "Sir Ralph will be quite entertainment enough, surely?"

"Sir Ralph is the biggest bore of all," she said calmly. "Please let me have my way."

So to his surprise and amusement Michael received an invitation to dinner, couched in such gracious terms that he formed the wholly incorrect impression that some other guest had failed Moya and that he was being called in to relieve her of the responsibility for thirteen people sitting at table.

It was even a more dreary dinner-party than Moya had imagined.

Sir Ralph Sapson was amusing in his own way, but his own way was not Moya's way. He was a stout, handsome, young man on the right side of thirty, immensely wealthy and, according to her father, immensely capable. Though there had been no definite arrangement it was understood, mainly by Lord Flanborough, that Sir Ralph desired a closer association with the Flanborough family than his directorships gave him.

The remainder of the guests were even less entertaining than Sir Ralph. There were three other members of the peerage. Old Lord Katstock who was a political lord who had once occupied a position as under-secretary in some forgotten administration, the Marquis of Cheddar who was a sporting lord and had theories on the Bruce Low system of breeding, Lord Dumburton who was a soldier lord, very poor and very wicked, unless rumour lied, and an assortment of directors which included Mr. Reginald Boltover who recognized Michael with a guilty start and took no interest whatever in his dinner but waited with bated breath for Michael to reveal his guilty secret. There were two or three ladies who gave Michael the impression that they had been dipped in diamonds by their herculean maids, there was a thin, dowdily dressed lady with a hooked nose.

("Has the Duchess borrowed anything, Moya?" said Michael under his breath.

"Not from me," said the girl significantly, "but father is rather susceptible. She's an awfully good sort really, but I do wish she wouldn't take snuff.")

Michael knew, or was known to, them all.

"It's a rum idea of yours, going into the police, Pretherston," said Sir Ralph with that air of patronage which he reserved for people poorer than himself.

"It's just as rum an idea as your going into trade and keeping shops," said Michael.

Sir Ralph smiled indulgently.

"We have to do something to make an honest living," he said. "I suppose the reference to the shops is my association with the Colonial Retail Stores. That makes a hundred thousand a year, Pretherston."

"Then you have a hundred thousand reasons for selling bad jam," said Michael; "I've given up buying things at your shops."

"That is a tragedy," said Sir Ralph with heavy humor. "Try us again and we will endeavour to merit your patronage."

"I have another bone to pick with you," said Michael.

He did not like Sir Ralph Sapson.

"I came up the other day from Seahampton, the railway carriage was beastly, hadn't been cleaned for a month, and the train was fifty minutes late. The London and Seahampton is another of your profitable ventures isn't it?"

"I am told that I have an interest in it," said Sir Ralph, with a smile at the girl, "but, really, my dear Pretherston, when you find a railway so badly conducted you ought to complain to the police."

This amused him so much that he laughed without restraint and was, as a result, compelled to explain his joke to fourteen people who were anxious to share it.

Michael had to leave early.

"I should dearly love to stay and play bridge with you," he said.

"Michael, you are a little horrid, aren't you?" asked the girl.

"Horrid?" he asked, puzzled.

"You are so practical, you weren't always like that."

"And you weren't always unpractical," he laughed.

She had hoped—she did not know exactly what she had hoped, but the new Michael was so unlike the old that she could almost have cried with vexation. Gone was the old recklessness, the old extravagance (save in directions annoying to her guests) and the old adoration which shone in his eyes. There was an unpleasant feeling that he was laughing at her all the time and that did not add to her happiness.

"I don't think you're nice, anyway," she said; "won't you come more often to see us?"

"When you lose a pearl necklace, or find the hired lady surreptitiously carrying off your provisions, drop a line to Inspector Michael Pretherston, Room 26, Scotland House and I will be with you in a jiffy."

"By which I understand you don't want to see us at all," she said petulantly; "I am sorry I asked you to-night."

"I, for my part, am very glad," he said.

Later, when Michael had left, Sir Ralph was to find her a very unamusing companion, though why she should be annoyed with her sometime suitor only a woman can understand. She did not love him. In some ways she rather disliked him, and possibly the underlying reason for her inviting him at all, was in order to confirm and seal her indifference. If Michael had been in the least way attentive, had shown the slightest desire to recover the lost ground and to resume the old romance, she would have found an intense satisfaction in checking him and would have gone to bed that night happy in the knowledge that she had permanently attached to her one for whom she had not the slightest tenderness.

This is the way of women who, when offered a dish, a dress, a colour, a material or a man, invariably say, "I would like to see something else."

Her abstraction was so marked that Sir Ralph thought she was ill, which instantly produced that headache which it is every woman's privilege to adopt at a moment's notice.

"You ought to take care of Moya, Flanborough," he said to his host at parting, "she's not at all well."

"I have noticed it," said the dutiful parent who had noticed nothing of the kind and had inwardly remarked that Moya was sulking about something. "You have an extraordinary eye for things of that kind, Sir Ralph."

"I understand human beings," admitted Sir Ralph, "it has been my one engrossing study in life. It is almost a vice with me. When a man comes into my office I can generally sum up his character, his business and his capabilities before he has opened his mouth."

"It's a great gift," said Lord Flanborough solemnly.

Sir Ralph Sapson was in a particularly cheerful mood that night. In the brief interview which he had had with his future father-in-law he had not only secured a tacit agreement of his right to be admitted to the family and an expression of Lord Flanborough's approval, but he had clinched a very excellent business arrangement which had been hanging fire for twelve months—an arrangement which may be briefly summarized:

Lord Flanborough was the chairman of the Austral-African Steamship Company which carried merchandise and passengers between Cape Town and Plymouth. Sir Ralph was the chairman of the London and Seahampton Railway and was also chairman and a large shareholder in the Seahampton Dock Improvement Company. The docks had improved much more rapidly than had the trade which could justify their existence and the deal which was really a side-line to the more romantic business of a matrimonial alliance, was that the ships of the A-A line should shamelessly abandon Plymouth and Liverpool and should have their headquarters at Seahampton, an arrangement which offered advantages on both sides, since Lord Flanborough was not without interest in the Seahampton docks.

The night was chilly, a full moon rode serenely in the skies; there was a touch of frost in the air and more than a suspicion of frost on the sidewalk. Sir Ralph Sapson's car was waiting, but he ordered the chauffeur to drive home, saying that he would prefer to walk. Sir Ralph lived in Park Lane so that he had nearly a mile to cover, but he was in that mood which made light of so unusual an exercise. He reached the door of his imposing residence and his hand was on the bell when he heard his name called. He had noticed as he walked up to his door that a little distance along the road was a big motor car, its head lamps gleaming and a chauffeur busy tinkering with the engine.

"I am afraid you don't know me," said a sweet voice.

Sir Ralph raised his hat.

The girl who stood on the sidewalk was obviously a lady. She was as obviously beautifully dressed, and Sir Ralph who had an appraising eye valued the ermine cloak she wore at something not far short of a thousand pounds. A single broad collar of diamonds about her slender throat was all the jewellery she wore.

"I am afraid I don't," he said.

"I only met you once," said the girl timidly, "in Paris. You were introduced to me in the foyer of—"

"Oh, yes, at the Opera, of course," said Sir Ralph who, amongst other things, was a patron of the Arts.

She nodded and seemed pleased that he had remembered her, a compliment which Sir Ralph did not fail to observe.

"My car has broken down," she said, "and I was wondering if I could beg your hospitality. It is so horribly shivery here."

She drew her cloak tighter around her.

"With all the pleasure in life," said Sir Ralph heartily, "but I have only a bachelor's establishment, you know," he laughed.

He rang the bell and the door was opened instantly.

"Put some lights in the drawing room," he said to the servant. "Is there a fire there?"

"Yes, Sir Ralph," said the man.

"Can I get you some coffee or a little wine?"

She had pulled a big chair up before the blaze and was resting her little white slippers upon the silver fender. Her shapely hands were outspread to the fire and Sir Ralph noted that on her fingers there was no sign of the plain gold circle of bondage.

"You will think it awfully rude in me, but I cannot recall your name," he said, when the servant had gone.

"I don't suppose you do, my name is rather a barbarous one," she laughed. "I am the Princess Bacheffski."

"Why, of course!" said Sir Ralph heartily, "I remember distinctly now."

To do him justice, Russian princesses are not unusual phenomena in Paris and he had a very bad memory for foreign names.

"I suppose I am being very unconventional," she said with a little grimace, and for the first time he noticed that she spoke with the slightest accent, "but needs must when the devil drives, and I had either to sit in that cold car or grasp the good fortune which fate threw in my way. And you, Sir Ralph, are looking just the same as when I saw you last. You are one of the big business men in London, aren't you?"

"I have a few interests," admitted Sir Ralph modestly.

They talked of Paris which Sir Ralph knew, and of Russia through which he had travelled on one occasion, and of London, and then the coffee came and a few minutes later, her chauffeur, to tell her that the repairs had been effected.

"Before I go I want to ask you one favour, Sir Ralph," she said.

She was a little embarrassed and nervously twisted a ring on her finger. Sir Ralph saw this and wondered.

"You have only to ask anything, Princess, and it is granted," he said gallantly.

She hesitated a moment and bit her lip in thought.

"I am going to take you into my confidence, and I know as a man of honour" (Sir Ralph bowed) "you will not betray me. I am in London, but I am not supposed to be in London."

She looked at him anxiously as she made this confession.

"I understand," said Sir Ralph, which was not true.

"You have probably noticed—you were so quick at seeing those things—that I am not wearing my wedding ring. Well," she hesitated, "Dimitri and I have quarrelled, and I do not want him to find me. I haven't been to the Embassy or to call on any of my old friends."

"You may be sure," said Sir Ralph, "that your secret is safe. I may say," he added, "that this is not the first time I have been entrusted with a confidence as delicate."

"I know I can trust you," she said, warmly gripping his hand. "I am staying in a little furnished flat which I have taken in Half Moon Street. I have a duenna with me for the sake of the proprieties—Dimitri is so funny about those things—so if a busy man can spare the time, I am always in between four and five—"

"It will give me the greatest happiness to renew the acquaintance," said Sir Ralph and raised her hand to his lips.

Sir Ralph retired to rest that night more pleased with himself than ever.

CHAPTER VIII
AN ARTIST MAKES AN EXHIBITION OF HIMSELF

No man has ever understood a woman, for the simple reason that woman is unintelligible even to her own kind. If she were not, and if she were susceptible to explanation by her own sisters, be sure that her own sisters would lose no time in telling the first man she met all about her.

Lady Moya Felton possessed that rare combination of talents, beauty and acumen. She dressed well, she spoke well, and she looked well. She was a product of Newnham, an institution which, more often than not, gives the world a being which is something less than a woman and something more than a babu. This being is crammed with erudition and for many years fights life with a textbook. Sometimes she continues to the end, very self-assured, very confident of the facts she has culled from the printed page and very determined that she will never surrender her mechanical facts or her machine-made values. Sometimes, she succumbs to the humanising influences which daily contact with the verities of life bring to her and develops into a useful and charming member of society.

Moya had absorbed just as much of life as she thought was necessary to her comfort. She stopped short of the supreme lesson which finds expression in cheerful sacrifice but she was an eminently pleasing person and never discussed biological justice or gave forth as her own the shoddy philosophies she had acquired in hall. Therefore, she was bearable. Moreover, by realising—here her instinct served her—that Newnham had turned her out fit for nothing better than a church-going school ma'am, she conveyed an impression of her education rather than declaimed the fact.

Practical as she was, she had a guilty secret, not only a very dear one, to be hugged tight to her heart, but one which evoked the unusual emotion of profound disapproval in the more ordered compartments of her mind. Moya was a dreamer, a cold-blooded romanticist who had wonderful adventures with wonderful people whenever she walked or rode abroad. In the privacy of her big limousine, she would be absorbed in events of her own creation, wholly monopolised by men and women who bore no likeness to and had no relation with any person in her somewhat extensive list of acquaintances. She would often find herself in situations so absurdly impossible that even the penny novelette reader would have rejected them with the scorn which their crudity deserved. She did not dream of living people, the mere mental suggestion—for the roving mind has a trick of taking charge at times—that any of her visionary heroes had his prototype in flesh and blood ensured the ejection of the offending dream-man and the substitution of another, more wildly improbable but at the same time more unlikely to challenge relationship with anybody in the material world.

She could dream and yet accept the cold practicality of a Ralph Sapson and calmly consider a marriage so hopelessly prosaic.

That was inexplicable.

For an engaged lover Ralph had been singularly remiss. He had called once since his unemotional declaration of love. To do him justice he had skipped the tender demonstrations which usually accompany even the most formal engagements and had got down to the question of settlement in the shortest space of time. This was as Moya could wish, for she also was embarrassed at the thought that a human being might possibly approach—suffering in comparison—the extravagance, wordless and intangible as it was, of her shadowy friends.

It is a remarkable circumstance that romance in concrete form did not come to Moya, until the very week she engaged herself to marry Sir Ralph Sapson. It came in a curious way. She had driven to Leicester Square to see an exhibition of pictures. It was one of those collections which dawn upon London, bringing in its wake a name which has never been heard before, save in a very select circle and is never heard again outside of that circle; an orbit which swings beyond the ken of ordinary mortals.

She went into the gallery and found it a veritable desert. Save for a young man and a small, pinched and preoccupied girl, wearing a large pendant in which was inserted the photograph of her uninteresting fiancé, the place was empty. The girl with the pendant carried her excuse in her hand, in the shape of a bunch of catalogues. There was less excuse for the young man for he was healthy in appearance and it was not raining.

Moya began a conscientious inspection of the pictures, chiefly remarkable for their colouring and for the atmosphere which the artist had managed to secure. Indeed, the pictures were all atmosphere. The girl made a slow progress along the wall, comparing each framed atrocity with her catalogue and striving to sense, dimly, something of the artist's honourable intentions.

She looked around once to discover what effect the pictures had upon her fellow sightseer. He was standing before a long panel representing, if the catalogue had been rightly compiled, "A Blue Wind on a Green Hill." His face bore an expression of the deepest gloom, his hat was tilted to the back of his head and his hands were thrust deeply into his trousers pockets. The longer he looked at the "Blue Wind on the Green Hill" the more morose and unhappy did he appear.

This then was the attitude which the new colourist school demanded, one of fierce but approving antagonism if the paradox be permitted.

She moved up till she was almost by his side, never thinking that in the presence of the girl with the programmes and the photographic miniature, he would dare address her. Yet he did.

"What do you think of that one?" he asked without turning his head.

She was taken aback and was prepared to be chilly and non-committal. She looked at his face and the nearer view was a pleasing one. He was very fair, very good-looking and had the bluest eyes she had ever seen in a man. He was also unshaven and his collar was not clean, but he was well dressed enough and his tone was wholly Oxford—and Balliol at that.

"I think it is rather weird," she said.

"So do I," he nodded vigorously. "I think it is—'weird' is the word. As a work of art how does it strike you?"

She hesitated. She had a full range of studio jargon which she had acquired in the course of her after-education and could speak glibly on atmosphere, tone and light. She knew that it was possible to refer to a still-life study of a bunch of bananas as being "full of movement" without being guilty of an absurdity. In fact, she knew enough about art to have occupied a position on any average newspaper as a critic.

"As a work of art," she said, "it is original and a little eccentric."

"Frankly?" he demanded fiercely.

All the time he spoke he was glaring at the picture and had not turned his head toward her.

"Frankly," she replied, "I think these are monstrosities."

He nodded again.

"I agree with you," he said, "and I know better than anybody else how monstrous they are—I painted 'em!"

Moya gasped.

"I am awfully sorry," she began.

"I am sorry, too—that I painted them," he replied. "I am not sorry that I exhibited them, because all my friends told me that they were wonderful and naturally I get some satisfaction from proving that my friends are mentally deficient.”

He turned round and looked at her and was in turn surprised.

“Hello,” he said, staring at her with his blue eyes wide open, “I thought you were much older.”

She laughed.

“The fact is I didn’t look at you,” he confessed; “how can anybody look at anything with these beastly things staring one in the face—Hi! Emma!”

Fortunately the programme girl was looking his way and realised that he was speaking to her. “Your name is Emma, I suppose.”

“No, sir,” said the girl impressively, “my name is Evangeline.”

He turned to the girl.

“Here is an Evangeline whom I thought was an Emma; and here are my Emmas that I thought were Evangelines,” he said despairingly. “What made you come to this exhibition?”

“I saw a criticism of the pictures in yesterday’s papers.”

“In the *Megaphone*,” he said accusingly.

“Yes—it was a very flattering criticism, I thought,” said the girl.

He nodded.

“I wrote it myself,” he said without shame. He turned to the programme girl.

“Tell your master to shut up the gallery, have the pictures packed away and sent home.”

“But,” said Moya in alarm, “I hope my stupid views won’t influence you.”

“It isn’t your stupid view,” he said, “it is my original stupid view. You see, I can’t paint really. I know not the slightest thing about art, I have never had an artistic education or served under any master. I am a genius. These works are works of a genius. The frames cost a lot of money and the amount of paint I have used is prodigious. There is everything there,” he waved his hand to the covered walls, “except the know-how.”

She murmured a conventional expression of sympathy, but he did not invite sympathy, he invited condemnation and seemed to find a comfort in his own misfortune and was obviously all the happier, that he had reached a decision on his own merits.

They walked out of the gallery together and Moya wondered at herself. That she had in so brief a space of time entered into the aspirations and disappointments of a perfect stranger so that she felt something of his chagrin was truly amazing.

"I know you," he said, breaking off in the midst of a sardonic dissertation on art, "you are Lady Moya Melton or Pelton."

"Felton," she suggested, amused.

"Oh, yes, Felton," he nodded. "I saw your portrait in the academy, a very bad portrait too."

"People thought it was rather good," she demurred.

"Idealised, but Lord, what do I know about art? This char-a-banc de luxe is yours, I presume," he pointed to the big limousine.

"It does happen to be mine," she said; "my father gave it to me on my twenty-first birthday."

He inspected it critically.

"I wonder if I know as much about motorcars as I know about painting," he said. "I used to think I knew something about both, but here, at any rate, is something real, it is a very nice car."

He opened the door for her and she offered her hand.

"I am so sorry about the pictures," she said.

"Don't worry," he replied cheerfully.

She thought for a moment.

"Can I drop you anywhere?"

He fingered his unshaven chin.

"If you know of a nice deep pond where a man may drown himself without interference I should be obliged," he said gravely, then, seeing the look of alarm in her eyes he laughed. "You probably don't know my name," he said.

As a matter of fact she did not and had been trying throughout the interview to take a surreptitious look at the catalogue. She knew it was something like Brixel.

"Fonso Blaxton—" he said shortly. "Fonso stands for Alphonso, a perfectly rotten name, isn't it? It would be quite all right for an artist. If there's any need to send flowers, my address is Oxford Chambers."

He shook hands abruptly, handed her into the car and closed the door. He waited only the briefest spell and had lifted his hat and vanished before the car had started.

Moya drove back with so much to occupy her thoughts that she forgot to dream. So preoccupied was she, that she passed Sir Ralph Sapson and his chic companion turning into the park before she was aware that he was bowing to her or had time to note anything more about the lady than that she was very beautifully gowned and that her sunshade was tilted at such an angle that it was impossible to see her face.

"Who is your friend?"

Sir Ralph turned with a smirk.

"That, Princess." he said, "is Lady Moya Felton."

"Oh, your fiancée," said the girl, "isn't it a bore being in London incognito; I should so much like to have met her."

"Perhaps some day," said Ralph.

"I should dearly love to," murmured the girl; "but please go on, you interest me so much. I am beginning to realise why you English are so successful. You seem to know every detail of your business."

"Oh, dear no," protested Sir Ralph good-humoredly. "I am rather a dunce if the truth be told, but one must know something of the details."

"Something!" said the girl, raising her eyebrows. "I think you are very modest. Why, you seem to know the workings of your railway system from beginning to end."

Sir Ralph stroked his moustache thoughtfully.

"One has to go into things," he said vaguely, "and of course one takes a lot of credit for things which one is not entitled to take credit for. But the gold train was my idea altogether."

"I never thought there was so much romance in business," said the Princess, then suddenly, "do you mind telling the driver to turn about, I am tired of the park now."

He leaned forward and instructed the chauffeur and the big car circled round.

"I am glad you suggested that," he said.

"Why?" she asked.

"Did you notice a man in a grey felt hat talking to a lady in a victoria?"

She shook her head.

"He's a weird bird," said Sir Ralph; "he is a policeman, Michael Pretherston, Lord Pretherston's brother. I don't want to meet him, apart from the fact that he might recognize you, even through that veil of yours which would deny him so much happiness," he added gallantly.

"Tell me some more about the gold train," she said.

Nothing loath Sir Ralph explained. He told the story of the Seahampton Docks and the big liners which would be coming in and the new services he had inaugurated to meet the increased traffic.

"We shall carry practically the whole of the gold which comes from the Rand mines," he said impressively. "Naturally we have to be very careful although there is not much danger in England. The gold train is really two big safes on wheels. To outward appearance, they are just like ordinary closed railway trucks. In reality they are steel boxes, burglar proof and fire proof. Of course, nothing can go wrong and even if we had a smash the cars would be uninjured. But I have the best men on the system to run the train."

"How very fascinating," she said intensely interested. "I suppose you have a most elaborate time-table?"

"I have worked out every detail myself," he said.

He took a note-book from his pocket.

"I will show you, Princess," he said impressively.

He turned the gilt-edged leaves until he came to two pages covered with his fine writing.

"You will get some idea of the work involved in the running of a special train," he said; "here are the times. There is the driver's name, the fireman's name, the assistant fireman's name, the names of the two guards."

She looked at the book.

"I cannot read your writing very well," she laughed; "you must not forget that my family was very old fashioned and my dear father never allowed us to learn the Roman alphabet until we were quite grown up. But I can see what a very difficult business it is."

She handed the book back to him with a little sigh.

"I am afraid I am very stupid," she said; "figures always bother me and I can see that you revel in them. I hate writing, but by the way your book is filled, it seems that you revel in it! I cannot understand people who like to write. It is always an agony for me to compose an ordinary letter. My thoughts come so much faster than my poor hand can move."

She took a pad and pencil from the silver mounted stationery case in front of her.

"I will show you something," she said.

She wrote rapidly, resting the pad on her knee and he watched her in astonishment as she proceeded to fill the sheet.

"There," she said triumphantly, "that is what I can do best."

"It looks like shorthand," he said.

"It is something like Russian shorthand," said the girl, "and I am such a lazy person that I always use it whenever I want to write a note. My secretary, who is the only person in the world who understands it, transcribes it. I do it because I hate writing."

"So you are clever, after all, Princess."

She reached out her little hand and patted his arm.

"You don't know how clever I am," she said and they both laughed together.

CHAPTER IX
THE SHAREHOLDERS AND AN INTERRUPTION

Colonel Westhanger looked at his watch.

"She's twenty minutes late already," he said.

Gregori rolled another cigarette and looked enquiringly at Dr. Philip Garon who was fingering his trim beard and talking with some animation to the middle-aged pallid man, who was known to the world as Mr. Cunningham and to the police as an expert safe breaker.

All Crime Street, with the exception of the admirable Mr. Millet, was present. The Bishop with his large placid face was playing bezique with Francis Stockmar. Colling Jacques, who had the appearance of a prosperous butler who had settled down to the management of his own private hotel, was reading the newspaper. Mr. Mulberry, that respectable man with his grey side-whiskers and his sad dog-like eyes, was discussing Renaissance architecture with the other Stockmar and the Colonel, pacing the room impatiently, stopped now and again to fling a word to one or the other.

Presently there was a slight sound in the hall below and the Colonel went to the door of the room.

"She is here," he said and passed out to the landing to meet Kate.

She was wearing a dark coat-dress and a big black fox wrap which she loosened and flung off as she came into the room. It was notable that the Colonel, who had every right to complain of her unpunctuality, did not attempt to criticize her for her late arrival, other than to make mild reference to the fact that he had expected her earlier.

She looked around the room.

"Where is Millet?" she asked.

"Millet is working on the telegrams," he said and she nodded, satisfied.

"Everything is ready now," she said. "Did you see Boltover, Mr. Mulberry?"

He rose and came toward her with that noiseless step of his.

"A most amiable young man," he said in his unctuous sing-song voice, "such a pleasant young man! We had a very long talk together."

"And?"

"We arranged everything."

He took a long envelope from his pocket, pulled out a stiff parchment and handed it to her with the gravity and deference of an ambassador delivering a treaty to his sovereign lady. She ran her eyes quickly over the document, turned its crinkling page and read rapidly to the last flourishing signatures.

"That's all right," she said and returned the document.

The long table had been placed in the middle of the room and to this, without instructions, the whole of the company had drawn. Colonel Westhanger sat at one end and Kate at the other. From her bag she took a thick roll of manuscript, cut the strings that fastened it and smoothed the sheets out before her. One by one she called their names at the same time handing them, in some cases one, in other cases two or three sheets covered with writing.

"You have a week to master all this," she said, "and in a week's time we will meet again and I will see that everybody understands."

She caught Jacques' eye.

"About men?" she said. "How many have you arranged for?"

"Sixty," he said; "I have been bringing them into England for the past month."

"Will sixty be enough?" she asked dubiously. "How many did we use for the Bank of Edinburgh?"

"That was a different job," said Jacques; "we had to cut through thirty feet of concrete. I used two hundred and twenty in relays of thirty."

"Sixty will be quite enough," she said after a moment's thought. "You will see that I have allowed only for fifty, but if they are the right kind of people—"

"They are all good men, most of them from Italy, a few of them from France and one Portuguese. They are the pick of my men and represent years of organisation."

"You have full details there, Cunningham," she said, turning to that dour man. "I took a shorthand note about the gold train, the driver and the officials who will be on the train and I have all their addresses except one. You will find a cross against that; I think the address is Berne Street, Seahampton, but I had no time to verify it."

"This will be easy," said Cunningham, reading his instructions; "these times won't be altered, I suppose?"

"If they are, I shall know all about it," said the girl. "Everyone must make a note of those instructions in your own code and you must do it pretty quickly."

"What's the hurry?" asked Westhanger, who, alone of the men about the table, had received no paper.

"I want to see every sheet burnt before we leave the room," she said.

The Colonel frowned.

"But—" he began.

"I want all the papers burnt before we leave the room," she said again emphatically.

Her uncle growled but the others knew her well enough to realize that she had an excellent reason. Each man in his own way, some in note-books, some on the back of loose sheets of paper faithfully transcribed the instructions, using their own pet abbreviations, their own particular symbols and one by one, as fast as they completed their copies, the girl collected the papers, heard the instructions read over, corrected one, amended another and finally gathering all the sheets in her hand, she walked to the fireplace, deposited them in the grate and set a lighted match to them.

She watched them burn until they were black ash and put her foot upon them crushing the embers to dust.

"Are you nervous?" asked the Colonel sarcastically.

"Are you?" she asked coolly.

"Well it does seem a little—"

From the corner of the room came a soft but insistent purr.

The men jumped to their feet.

"Put away the tables quickly," said the girl under her breath.

They separated the table into three parts. With an agility remarkable in one of his years the Colonel flung a cloth over each, lifted a pot of flowers on to one, arranged a photograph on another and left the third to the bezique players. The girl seated herself at the piano, opened it and began a soft movement from "Rigoletto."

"Sing," she said under her breath.

The obedient Mr. Mulberry shuffled up to her side. He had a pleasing voice and the girl picked up the strain....

"I am sorry to disturb the harmony," said Michael Pretherston from the doorway.

"May I ask what is the meaning of this intrusion?" demanded Colonel Westhanger haughtily as half-a-dozen Scotland Yard men crowded into the room behind their chief.

"It is what is vulgarly known as a raid," said Michael. "Everybody will remain where he is while I run a foot rule over him. Parsons, you will take these gentlemen one by one into an adjoining room and search him most thoroughly. Mrs. Gray," he called to the door and a stout middle-aged woman with a pleasant face appeared, "you will perform the same kind office for Miss Westhanger."

"Why not 'Kate'?" asked the girl scornfully. "You are getting polite in your old age, Mike."

"Miss Westhanger," he repeated suavely.

"Suppose I refuse to be searched?"

"Then I shall convey you to a vulgar police station," said Michael, "and the process of search will be carried out in uncongenial surroundings."

"I take it that you have a warrant?" demanded Colonel Westhanger.

"My dear Colonel!" said Michael. "Do you imagine I should come without having gone through that little formality?"

He produced the document.

"Signed by two stipendary magistrates to be absolutely sure," he said flippantly; "impound all documents you find, Parsons."

"Yes, sir," said the man and led away the first of his victims which happened to be the docile Mr. Mulberry.

"It is an unpleasant business," sighed Michael as he watched the girl pass from the room followed by her searcher, "but then, you will understand, Colonel, that our profession is full of heartrending moments. You are still on ticket of leave, I understand?"

"Expired," growled Colonel Westhanger.

"Pardon me," said Michael. "I have been misinformed. I would like a word with you."

He led the other to the corner of the room out of earshot and the good humor died out of his voice as he confronted the older man.

"Westhanger," he said, "who was the tutor of this girl?"

"I don't quite get you?" said the other insolently.

"Who taught Kate to be a thief—is that plain enough for you?"

"If she is a thief it is a matter of aptitude. I deny that she is a thief or that she is a party to any illegal act of which my unfortunate friends may have been guilty—nobody taught her."

"You are a queer fellow," said Michael. "I suppose you are just unmoral."

"My personal character—" began the other.

"By unmoral, I mean you have no sense of *meum* and *teum*. In other words, you are a born thief. You forgive me, but subtlety seems to be wasted on you. I ask you again, who educated Kate?"

The Colonel smiled.

"Kate has much to thank me for," he said smugly. "I have been a father and more than a father to that child and I assure you, Mr. Pretherston, that you are altogether wrong when you think that she is a thief. Why do you ask?" he demanded, suddenly breaking off.

"Because," said Michael looking him steadily in the eye, "I believe that you have deliberately set yourself to exploit the genius of a clever child for your own profit. I believe that you, and you only, have so distorted her viewpoint that you have destroyed her soul. I am not sure yet," he admitted, "but when I am—"

"When you are," sneered the Colonel.

"On one charge or another, I shall put you into prison," said Michael simply, "and I shall keep you in prison until you are dead. I will set myself the agreeable task of ensuring your end in a prison infirmary—which, I understand, is not a very cheerful place."

The Colonel shuddered. There was something fateful, there was something malignant, a scarcely suppressed expression of hate in the police officer's tone. For a second the older man wilted and shrunk back beneath the fierce intensity in Michael's voice and then, like the weakling that he was, he burst into a torrent of abuse which was founded in fear and energised by rage.

"Damn you," he hissed; "threaten me! ... I will have your coat off your back, you damned policeman! ... You sneaking slop! ... Kate's what she is. She will beat you and all your flat-footed pals! If she's bad, you can't make her anything else. I made her, yes, I made her! She is going to beat you, do you hear, and you will never catch her or me. I made her! You can't scare me ...!"

His shrill voice trembled with anger, he was shaking from head to foot and the bony fist which shivered in Michael's face was so tightly clenched that the knuckles stood out whitely.

"She is not the kind you can cure with psalms, Mr. Policeman! You can't pray over her because she has nothing to pray to, do you hear that? You caught me. You sent me to that hell at Wandsworth and I am going to get back on you, you and all people like you. Kate's the biggest thing you have handled and she is going to break you, break you!"

"Uncle!"

He turned round to meet the white face of the girl.

"Are you mad?" she asked quietly.

He dropped his eyes before hers.

"He got me rattled," he muttered.

Michael looked at the searcher and the woman shook her head.

With a nod he dismissed her.

"Not guilty!" he said flippantly.

He looked at the trembling man in front of him with a calm intensity.

"I shall remember a lot of what you said, Westhanger, and you will hear from me one of these days."

He walked over to the fireplace, for out of the tail of his eye he had seen the burnt paper. He thrust a finger gently through the ash.

"Still warm," he said. "I gather we were a little late."

He scooped out a handful of the ash and carried it to the light. A word or two of the burnt instructions was still faintly visible but there was nothing to assist him. Nevertheless he had the whole of the ashes carefully deposited in a box and carried away—he himself being the last of the police to leave.

He stood in the centre of the room carefully smoothing the nap of his felt hat and Crime Street waited for the inevitable warning. In this they were disappointed, for Michael addressed himself solely to Kate.

"I will give you a chance, Miss Westhanger," he said and they wondered why he did not employ the more familiar style of address. "You are about to commit a crime which will render every one of you liable to long terms of penal servitude. What that crime is, I don't know, but I am certain it is what Stockmar would call 'kolossal.' It would not matter to me if everyone of you rotted in prison for the rest of your lives."

"Tank you," said Mr. Stockmar, "dat is fery goot of you!"

"When I say everyone of you," said Michael, "I exclude Kate. She is a young girl and if there is one of you who has any pretensions to manhood, you will get her out of this gang before you go any farther. If there is one of you who has a mother or a sister or any woman in the world for whom he has the slightest respect, he will try to save that child from herself. That is all."

The meek Mr. Mulberry stood by the piano, his plump fingers ranged across the keys producing a melancholy symphony.

"We will now sing Hymn 847," he said, in his melancholy oily voice and it was in the burst of laughter that this sally provoked, that Michael Pretherston took his leave, followed at a respectful distance down the stairs by Colonel Westhanger, who did not breathe freely until the front door had clanged behind his unwelcome visitor and until the oiled bolts shot home in their sockets.

"Where's Kate?" he asked on his return.

"Such nonsense," growled the elder Stockmar, "she has to the highroom gone to make scare mit Predderston."

Michael, at the far end of Crime Street, was taking leave of his assistants when there cut into the quiet night a sound almost terrifying in its unexpectedness.

It could only be described as a hollow shriek which rose and fell from a wailing scream to a throaty sob. It lasted no more than ten seconds and stopped as unexpectedly as it began.

"What's that?" asked the startled sergeant.

Michael scratched his chin.

"The Colonel in hysterics," he suggested callously. Nevertheless, the noise puzzled him.

CHAPTER X
SIR RALPH LOST A PRINCESS AND FOUND A POLICEMAN

Michael took the card from the uniformed constable and raised his eyebrows in surprise.

"Sir Ralph Sapson," he said, "what the dickens does he want?"

The constable made no reply, for he was neither thought-reader nor inquisitive.

"Show him in," said Michael.

Sir Ralph Sapson had never before called at Scotland House or showed the slightest desire to improve his acquaintance with Michael and the visit was therefore a little puzzling. Ralph bustled in, less important than usual and probably somewhat overawed by the difficulty he had experienced in reaching his objective.

"I daresay you wonder why I have called," he said.

"As long as it isn't to take me out to lunch, I don't care," said Michael with a laugh. "Sit down, Ralph, and tell me all your troubles. By the way," he said as the thought occurred to him, "I suppose you are not in any kind of trouble, are you?"

"That's just it, Michael," said the other depositing his silk hat carefully on the ground; "I am really worried over two matters and knowing what a good chap you are and how very nice you have been to me—"

"Don't be silly," said Michael kindly, "I have not been nice to you and I am not a good chap. Have you lost something?"

"I want to see you on two matters," said Sir Ralph, who was given to preambles; "they are altogether different and one, of course, is not a police matter at all—I merely want your advice as a friend. Do you know the Princess Bacheffski?"

"I don't know Her Royal Highness, Her Serene Highness, or Her Nibs as the case may be."

"She is neither," said the other, "she is the wife of Prince Dimitri Bacheffski, who is a large landowner in Poland."

Michael shook his head.

"The world is filled with the wives of princes who are large land-owners in Poland," he said.

"I met her in Paris," explained Sir Ralph.

"When I said the world," said Michael, "I meant Paris. What has she done, stolen your watch?"

"Please don't be an ass," said the other testily; "I tell you she is a princess and enormously wealthy. She had a row with her husband and came to London and I have seen a great deal of her. Yesterday, when I called to take her driving, I found that she had gone away, left without a word, paid her bill at the furnished flat she had taken and vanished—"

"Gone back to her husband, I suppose," said Michael; "I have heard of such things happening. You will not hear from her until a suit is filed for divorce and then the newspapers will be filled with grisly details, about your directorships, your early life and your hobbies; also the Sunday papers will publish your portrait."

Sir Ralph wagged his head in despair.

"If I thought you would have taken this kind of view I would not have come," he said severely; "there is nothing of that kind in this business. She is just a lady whom I had helped very slightly and who had been kind enough to give me her confidence."

"Do you want me to find her?" said the other in surprise.

"No, that isn't it," said Sir Ralph. "The story has a curious sequel. This morning I was in the city and I met a friend who asked me to lunch with him. I had a lot of business to get through and it was not until ten to one that I was able to get away. My car was not in the city but I thought I should have no difficulty in getting a taxi. When I got into the street, however, it was pouring with rain and not a taxi could be had for love or money. It was only a few steps to the Bank station and I decided to go by tube."

"Sensation!" said the admiring Michael.

"Well, to cut a long story short," said Sir Ralph, "I travelled to Oxford Circus and changed into a train which took me to the Thames Embankment. Here comes the extraordinary part of the story," he said impressively; "as I came up the escalator on the one side, the Princess passed down on the other."

"Yes?" said Michael unimpressed.

"She was plainly, even poorly dressed," said Ralph. "I raised my hat to her but she stared at me as though she had never seen me before in her life."

"You made a mistake probably," said the other.

"I will swear it was she," said Sir Ralph emphatically. "There was no mistaking her. She has a very tiny mole just below the right ear, which I had seen—"

"Eh?"

Michael was all attention now.

"A tiny mole beneath the right ear," he repeated, and went on, "dark grey eyes, large, well marked eye-brows, very delicate mouth and rounded chin?"

"That is she. Good Lord!" cried Sir Ralph in amazement. "Do you know her?"

"Oh, yes, I know her," said Michael grimly; "now let me hear the story of this Princess all over again. How did you come to meet her?"

"I met her in Paris. She was introduced to me after the opera," said Sir Ralph patiently; "as a matter of fact, I forgot all about it until she reminded me of the fact."

"Ah, this is where the story begins," said Michael; "when did she remind you of the fact?"

Sir Ralph detailed briefly the unconventional character of the meeting.

"I see," said Michael, "her car had broken down providentially just outside your house. Beautiful and most gorgeously arrayed, how could you resist her pathetic appeal? And so that is how you met her, is it? Oh, Kate, Kate!" he shook his head.

"Kate!" asked the bewildered magnate. "What on earth are you talking about?"

Michael took no notice of the question.

"I must ask you to give me a more detailed account of your meetings. Of course, you met her afterwards."

"Yes, I met her. And she was very charming," said Sir Ralph.

"And particularly interested in business?" asked Michael.

"No, she did not know much about business. There you are wrong. You are trying to prove that she is an adventuress. She knew nothing whatever about business," said Sir Ralph triumphantly; "in fact, I had to explain things over and over again."

Michael leant over and patted his arm as he might have done to a distraught child.

"What things did you explain, little man?" he asked.

Here, however, he lost the trail for, either because he could not or would not remember, Sir Ralph was very vague at this point. Michael sat at his desk, his head between his hands thinking rapidly.

First Flanborough, then Boltover, and now Ralph Sapson,—what was the association?

"Have you any business dealings with Flanborough?" he asked.

"What do you mean?" asked Ralph cautiously.

"Is there any connection between your companies?"

"My dear chap, what a question to ask," said Sir Ralph. "You know, as well as I, that all business people, who operate on a big scale, are associated in some way or other. I run railways and quarries and things, and Flanborough runs ships and gold mines. I am interested in his things and he has shares in mine."

Being a business man he did not tell Michael of the arrangement which he had entered into for the benefit of the unthriving port of Seahampton, because it is the way of business men to be mysterious and uninforming about the commonplaces of commercial intercourse.

"Well, that's that," said Ralph after waiting in vain for some illuminating observation from his friend.

"And what is the other matter?"

Here Sir Ralph found it more difficult to make a beginning.

"It is rather a delicate subject, Michael," he said, "for it touches my personal honour."

"Dear, dear," said Michael sympathetically, and, if the truth be told, a little mechanically, because his mind was occupied elsewhere with a greater and more important problem, than with the personal honour of the Sapsons.

"And not only that, but the honour of somebody we both admire," said Sir Ralph awkwardly. "The fact is, Michael, I am engaged to Moya. It isn't generally known, but it is so and naturally I haven't seen as much of her as I could have wished in this past week. Also I have been a very busy man."

"Naturally," said Michael sympathetically. "You have already told me about the Princess, you remember."

"Well, you are a man of the world," said Sir Ralph, going very red, "and you will understand. Anyway, I haven't seen as much of Moya as I could have wished. The fact is," he blurted out, "Moya is carrying on!"

"Carrying on," said the puzzled Michael, "carrying on what, or whom?"

"She meets him every day in the park and they go sketching together in the country," said Sir Ralph rapidly. "I haven't spoken to Flanborough about it, but it is all rather rotten."

"If by 'carrying on' you mean that Moya is indulging in a flirtation, it is not only very rotten, but it must have been very awkward for you," said Michael, "unless you could be perfectly certain of your fiancée's movements, you and your Princess were liable at any moment to run against her. It was very inconsiderate of Moya. Who is her friend?"

"A beastly artist," said Ralph savagely, "a man who had an exhibition of simply rotten pictures. I don't think he has a bob in the world, and he's a most untidy looking person. I have seen them together with my own eyes and he treats Moya outrageously. And Moya seems to like it."

"Does he beat her or anything?" asked Michael wearily.

He was growing tired of the interview and wanted to be alone to work out the new combination which had been presented to him.

"He compromises her," said Ralph with vehemence; "holds her hand and calls her 'child' in public. It is simply disgraceful!"

"You can trust Moya," said Michael, "she will do nothing which jeopardises her prospects."

"She has plenty of money of her own," interrupted Ralph.

"It is curious how your mind runs to money. I wasn't thinking of that. I was thinking of her social prospects. She is a very shrewd girl. A little romance will do her no harm, Ralph."

"But, hang it, she's got me!" said Ralph wrathfully.

"I said 'romance,'" said Michael with offensive emphasis; "you're not 'romance,' you're 'business.'"

But Sir Ralph was not satisfied.

"Perhaps if you saw her and had a few words with her," he suggested, "she might take a little notice."

"I should leave her presence a mental and physical wreck," said Michael decidedly. "No, Ralph, you must manage your own love making without calling in the—er, police." (Sir Ralph winced.) "I don't know Moya well enough to give her advice on so delicate a matter—I only proposed to her once and that has given me no right to urge your suit. One question I should like to ask you before you go," he said as Sir Ralph gathered up his hat and gloves. "Did the Princess question you about any bank with which you are associated?"

"I can answer you definitely, that she did not," replied Sir Ralph. "You have an altogether wrong impression of that lady—in my judgment."

"*Your* judgment!" said Michael scornfully, as he ushered him out of the room.

CHAPTER XI
LADY MOYA WAS CURIOUSLY UNLIKE HERSELF

There was a greater reason for Sir Ralph's perturbation than either he knew or Michael guessed. Both might have been enlightened, had they stood on Cannon Street Station one Sunday morning and seen the distress of Mr. Alphonso Blaxton as the big minute hand of the station clock grew nearer to nine. The guard was closing the doors of the carriages and the collector was preparing to shut the gate, when Moya came flying breathlessly through the barrier.

"Oh, I *am* so sorry!" she gasped; "my watch stopped."

Mr. Alphonso Blaxton bundled her into an empty first-class carriage and jumped in himself as the train moved.

"There's not another train for three hours," he said severely.

"We could have gone to church."

"What a mind!" said the young man in admiration. "I never thought of church!"

"Anyway, I didn't lose the train," she said tartly. "Have you brought everything?"

She looked round for the collapsible easel, the paint boxes and the paraphernalia which usually accompanied their sketching tours.

"I have brought nothing," he said frankly.

"But how can you sketch?"

"I am not going to sketch," he said. "I decided that it was too nice a day to waste."

She looked up at him and laughed.

"You will never be an artist," she said, suddenly severe. "To what part of the country are we going?"

"I thought we would go to Maidstone. There are some lovely drives from there. I've hired a motor car to meet us at the station and I thought we would go through Sussex and lunch at Seahampton."

"Not Seahampton," she said quickly; "my father is at Seahampton to-day."

She might have added that Sir Ralph was also at Seahampton, but, for reasons of her own, she kept that information to herself because Sir Ralph was not a subject which she had found it necessary to discuss. She looked at her companion approvingly.

"You are ever so much more presentable than I have ever seen you, before," she said, "and you have actually shaved! You are getting less and less like an artist every day."

He had a peculiarly sweet smile and a laugh which was all bubbling youth and happiness. He laughed like a girl, indeed it nearly approached a giggle. He laughed now as the train sped through the suburban stations, stretched out his feet on the cushions opposite and searched for a cigarette. She watched him with glee as he produced, not the ornate case in which the men of her acquaintance carried the expensive products of Egypt and Syria, but a gaudy yellow carton containing fifty of the cheapest cigarettes that ever brought discredit to the fair State of Virginia.

"Do you like those things?" she asked.

"These 'yellow perils'? Rather!"

"Your taste is awfully uncultivated, isn't it?" she bantered; "why don't you—" she abruptly attempted to change the subject by an incoherent reference to a cow which was gazing in a field by the side of the line.

"Why don't I smoke gold-laced Machinopolos through an amber and diamond cigarette holder?" he suggested. "Because, little Moya, I am a poor hard-working artist who has been saving up all the week for this bust."

"I am so sorry," she said; "I am awfully thoughtless. Won't you forgive me?"

"I won't forgive you," he said, "unless you keep in your mind the big fact that I am as immensely poor, as you are immensely rich."

"Why should I keep that in my mind?" she asked.

"Because," he said slowly, "until you are immensely poor or I am immensely rich we shall meet very occasionally and indulge in very infrequent busts."

"But what difference does money make?" she faltered.

She found it difficult to speak plainly or even clearly. There was a lump in her throat which made her voice sound unnaturally hoarse. She had a strange sinking feeling within her and to her amazement she found the hand that she put up to brush back a stray curl trembling. She had never experienced any such sensation before. Her heart was thumping quickly; she was breathless, hot and cold by turns.

He did not answer. She was seated by his side and she could only see his face out of the corner of her eyes, then she felt his arm slipping about her and before she knew what had happened, his lips were pressed to hers.

This happened in a first-class, railway carriage on a non-stop train. It had happened before to quite common people (as Moya had heard), but she never thought it would possibly happen to her, or that so vulgar a proceeding could be so wonderfully sweet.

Sir Ralph and Lord Flanborough had met the local authorities. There had been a lunch and speeches in which Sir Ralph had distinguished himself by likening the forthcoming arrival of the Austral-African mail ship to the return of Ulysses and the landing of the Pilgrim Fathers. A wireless message from the ship stated that she did not expect to make harbour until nine o'clock in the evening, and this explained the earlier festivities. That they were of a sober and restricted nature, was explained by the fact that the day was Sunday. Later, it was intended that the sailings of the Austral-African line from Cape Town should be timed to bring the ships to port on the Saturday, but there had been no time to alter the arrangements for the *Charter Queen* had sailed before Lord Flanborough and Sir Ralph had definitely decided the date on which the new service should be inaugurated.

A few press-men who had come down from London for the purpose, with certain directors and their wives, were shown over the docks; the new trains were admired and particularly two brand new trucks, the peculiar character of which was exhibited by Sir Ralph to a select few of his fellow directors. A safe on wheels was an excellent description for one of these. Specially strengthened under-carriages, each truck supported by two bogies, they were designed to carry a tremendous weight.

"I am sure Lord Flanborough doesn't mind my telling you," said Sir Ralph to the little party, "that this will carry twenty tons of bar gold tonight."

"What will be the value of that?" asked one of the interested audience.

"£2,867,200," said Sir Ralph impressively; "representing six months' output of the whole of Lord Flanborough's gold properties."

The directors made appropriate noises to signify their astonishment.

There were visitors to Seahampton interested in this great transportation, who were not invited to participate in the function. One of these, a dark foreign looking man, went no nearer to the docks than a little public house in the ancient High Street. He was visited by a man who was pallid of face and laconic of speech.

"It's all up!" he said under his breath.

"What is wrong?" said the other in the same tone.

"It is quite impossible to get the driver or the fireman. They are two old servants of the company, both have money saved and would no more think of accepting a bribe than Flanborough himself."

"You didn't press the matter, I hope?" asked the other quickly.

The pallid man shook his head.

"I went as far as I dared with the driver," he said. "I found out he had a son in the army in India and I told him that I had met the boy and got quite friendly with the old chap—but he is a sea-green incorruptible, Gregori."

"I will get on the 'phone to Kate," said the other. "I suppose we shall have to hold up the train somewhere—I don't want to do any shooting if it can be avoided. Are the drivers armed?"

"It is funny you should ask that," said the pallid man, sipping his beer. "The old man is armed for the first time in his life. He was full of it and quite proud of his ability to loose off a gun."

Gregori looked very serious.

"Kate must be prepared with the alternative scheme," he said. "Anyway, you will join me here with Cunningham at eight o'clock. I am perfectly prepared for almost all contingencies. Millet has given me a dozen authorities to meet almost any developments. Did you see the train?"

"I couldn't get near it," said the other. "I left just before Sapson brought his party to make their inspection."

Sir Ralph had carried his guests from the siding to the engine shed and shown them the brand new Atlantic locomotive which was to draw the train to London.

"They don't seem to have finished it yet," said one of the guests, and pointed to a workman busily drilling a hole in the front plate.

Ralph laughed.

"They omitted to put a bracket for the lamp. You see, I wanted three green lights in a line for the Gold Train—it is very necessary that it should be very accurately and easily distinguished and signalled. By some chance only two of the brackets were in place when the engine came from the works. It is all the more annoying, because I had already given definite instructions upon that point, but we shall not go wrong for a lamp," he said humorously.

It is agreed that the three hours between two and five on a Sunday afternoon are the three dullest in the hundred and sixty-eight which constitute a week. After the guests had left for London Sir Ralph and Lord Flanborough remained at the little station hotel—Ralph had already projected a more palatial establishment to meet the increased traffic—for it had been arranged that they should greet the *Charter Queen* on her arrival.

At three o'clock that afternoon Ralph burst unceremoniously into Lord Flanborough's private sitting room where his lordship sat dozing.

"Have you had a wire?" he said.

He held a pink form in his own hand.

"A wire! What about?" asked Lord Flanborough startled.

"Read this."

The telegram was signed "Michael," and read:

"Simultaneous attempt made to burgle your strong room at Austral-African office and Flanborough's safe at headquarters of mining corporation. Both unsuccessful. Both doors blown out by nitro-gelatine. Will confirm by 'phone."

Lord Flanborough looked at the other openmouthed.

"This is very serious," he said.

"I have ordered a special to take us to town. We will wait till we get the 'phone message through."

Ten minutes after they were in communication with Michael.

"Both doors have been blown out," he repeated, "and there are one or two very puzzling features about the burglaries. Nobody could have been present in either office when the explosions occurred. There was no fire and, so far as I can see, nothing has been taken away. You had better come up and examine things for yourself."

"It is rather awkward," said Sir Ralph thoughtfully as he hung up the receiver; "my 'special' driver is also the driver of the gold special."

"It doesn't require any great genius to drive a gold special," snapped Flanborough; "put another man on to work to-night's train and let us get up to town as soon as we can."

The special was waiting in the station by the time they had reached the platform. Sir Ralph stayed long enough to give a few instructions to the superintendent and then boarded the train and was soon flying northward.

That Sunday morning had been an interesting one for Michael. He had been aroused by telephone at five o'clock only to learn from an apologetic operator that the wrong number had been called. Although it was two hours before he usually rose, he had his bath and dressed and not waking his servants made himself some coffee.

It was a bright morning, such as so often precedes a day of rain, when he turned into the deserted street. He had no particular aim or destination but he was in that mood which invites exercise. He walked down the Marylebone Road and through Portland Place without meeting anybody save an occasional policeman and so came to Piccadilly Circus where he bought a Sunday newspaper from an early vendor and passed down through Waterloo Place to the Park.

The gates had only just been opened and beyond the park-keepers and a slouching tramp he met nobody. He sat on one of the garden seats by the side of the lake, pulled his overcoat about his legs for the morning was chilly and began to scan the headlines in the newspaper. There was nothing startling here, but he read the columns conscientiously.

There was nothing in life which did not interest Michael Pretherston. He might have taken for his motto *homo sum; humani nihil a me alienum puto*. It was a saying of T. B. Smith's that Michael could even write a readable volume on the psychology of dog-fights. Every little larceny, however sordid, every tiny embezzlement however paltry, every swindle whether it was carried out by the great confidence men who "worked London" or by the smaller fry in the half-crown line of business gave him food for reflection and some little scrap of information which he stored away for future use.

He was in the midst of a long account of an East End arson charge when he heard his name called softly and looked up. He jumped to his feet.

"Why, Kate," he said, "haven't you got any home?"

The girl was standing a few feet from him with an odd look on her face.

"I think it must be fate that brought me out this morning," she said; "sit down, Mike, and tell me all the news."

She showed no sign of resentment of his uncavalier treatment.

"Did you follow me here, or did I follow you?"

"I tell you it was fate," she said. "I could not sleep and I drove my Mercedes down."

"And how is the Princess Bacheffski?" he asked as she seated herself by his side.

"The Princess—?"

"Bacheffski—poor old Ralph! What a thing to put over him!"

She leant forward, her chin on her palm, her elbow on her crossed knee.

"You frighten me sometimes," she said. "I have not been able to make up my mind whether you are clever or whether you are lucky."

"I am both lucky and clever," he said. "Tell me something about your property in the Ural Mountains," he said.

"In Poland," she corrected him.

"Mines, I suppose?"

"There are no mines on my property," she said calmly; "would you be greatly surprised if I told you I had an estate in Poland?"

"Nothing you said would surprise me, unless you told me you were going to be a good girl and respect the law relating to property."

He folded his paper and dropped it into a wire receptacle provided for that purpose and she followed the operations with amusement.

"What a tidy soul you are," she said; "fancy doing things you are told and obeying even by-laws."

"We all obey by-laws. You are not so original as you think. For instance, I observe that you are wearing a little toque—is that the word?"

"That is the word," she agreed.

"Toques are fashionable at this present moment. You are obeying the by-laws. You haven't the courage to come out in a sky-blue tam-o'shanter with an ostrich feather because it is against the by-laws. Also I remark that your dress is very short and very full. You are not wearing a Roman toga or a Grecian gown, or even a hobble skirt. Why? Because it is against the by-laws. It is absurd to disobey one set and slavishly obey another."

"You are quaint!" was the only answer she gave.

"Will you tell me, Princess?"

"Don't call me 'Princess' if you please," she said quietly.

"Well, will you tell me, my land-owner, what was the game with Ralph? He described you with the greatest enthusiasm by-the-way. The night you met him you were all dolled up to kill. Did you bring down your birds?"

"I got him," she admitted.

She was not as bright as usual.

"You are over-doing it," said Michael; "you are trying to do too much. Your doctor would probably tell you that you ought not to commit more than one burglary a month."

She laughed softly.

"You are very quaint," she said again.

"You don't feel like making a full and frank confession, I suppose," he suggested; "you would not like to burst into tears and sob out your young heart on my shoulder?"

"That sob stuff never did agree with me."

He raised a disapproving hand.

"Kate," he said, "I have noticed a disposition in you to adopt the slang which is employed exclusively by American newspaper reporters, vaudeville artistes and other members of the criminal classes."

"I will tell you this," she said sitting upright and looking him fully in the face, "we are going to do a big thing. The most colossal, the most daring that has ever been done and we are going to do it to-day. You want to know why I went to Flanborough's, why I made up to that unspeakable person, Ralph Sapson? Those are my two victims. I will tell you more than this," she said after a moment's thought, "in order to ensure the success of my scheme I have arranged for those two gentlemen to be out of London on this bright Sabbath day. I can't tell you any more, Mike."

"You are like a serial story, you finish off at the most interesting place," he grumbled.

His keen grey eyes searched hers and she met them fairly.

"I wish you weren't," he said.

"Weren't what?" she asked.

"In this business," he nodded. "I wish you weren't."

"Perhaps I will be good one of these days," she said, "and then you can recommend me for a job at two-ten-per. I'd make an ideal secretary for you, Mike. I know all the underworld by name. You could cut out your finger print department and leave it to Kate. What would happen, do you think," she went on, "if I went to a Salvation Army officer and said, 'I have been very wicked but now I am going to be good. Will you please assist me. I have no money but I've a good heart—' Mike, he would put me to chopping wood for a week and then he would find me a place as under-secretary to a housemaid in a strictly religious family which gave me two evenings and one Sunday a month. You see, Mike, even at goodliness one has to start at the bottom of the ladder; you can't break in on the roof. I hate good people."

Michael nodded.

"I hate good people, too," he said, "if they advertise their goodness, but goodness is not hardness or sourness, it is just—goodness. For example," he went on, "I am good."

"And I am wicked," she said and appealed with outstretched hands to a startled duck who had waddled to the railings, "choose between us!"

He laughed but was instantly serious again.

"Your confession puts me in a dilemma. As you are a lady I cannot believe you are lying, as you are a criminal I dare not take your word. I am sufficiently acquainted with your methods to know that your presence is not essential to the committal of a crime, so I can gain nothing by pulling you in."

"Poor Mike," she said mockingly.

"Poor Kate," he said and the girl detected the note of sincerity in his voice.

"Kate, you can't get away with it," he said; "you have got to fall sooner or later. Think what it means. Think of that horrible drab life in Aylesbury, where every minute is an hour and every hour an eternity; think of the menial things they will set you to do, scrubbing floors, washing shirts and sewing sacks. Think, how you will be marshalled to church every Sunday and think how you will be stared at and jeered at by friends of the Home Secretary who come to visit the jail."

"When that happens I shall be dead," she said. "I believe you mean kindly, Michael Pretherston, and I will tell you this, that you nor any other human being can make me think or feel any different to what I think and feel. There is no power on earth that can tear out the foundations on which my life is built. I have read everything, all the philosophies, Christian and pagan, and all the arguments from the feeble evangelism of the tract writer, to the blatant nonsense of the professional atheist, and I am just where I began. You can't touch me by reason or by devotion, by faith or by prayers. I am all stone—here," she laid her white hand upon her bosom and he saw the mocking laughter in her eyes. "Poor Michael!" she said. "Why, if devotion could change me, think of the chances I have had! I could have taken Ralph Sapson and made of him a snake ring for my little finger. I nearly had Flanborough on the point of proposing to me. He is rather sentimental, did you know that?"

"All people with indigestion are sentimental between paroxysms," said Michael sagely.

He gave his hand to the girl though it was unnecessary and helped her to her feet and they walked out of the park together. Her little Mercedes was unattended and he cranked it up for her.

"Good-bye, Michael," she said.

"Au revoir," said Michael, "we shall meet at the sessions."

At two o'clock that afternoon a constable on duty in Moorgate Street heard the first of the two explosions which agitated police circles that day. Michael was on the spot half-an-hour later and his brief examination led to the view which he afterwards communicated to Ralph. It was then he discovered that what the girl had told him was true and that both Lord Flanborough and Sir Ralph Sapson were out of town. Curiously enough, though he had been impressed at the time, he had dismissed the girl's statement as a piece of bravado on a par with the badinage in which she usually indulged. He had cursed his folly in ignoring the warning, all the way from Baker Street to the city and it was a great relief to discover what was evident, that no attempt had been made to rifle either the safe in Bartholomew Close or the strong room in Moorgate Street. The outrages were similar in character; in both cases the steel doors had been burst open by the application of an infernal machine. In neither case had the thieves benefited by their crime. The constable who heard the first explosion said he had been admitted by the caretaker of the building within three minutes but in that time had managed to send another policeman, who came up, to guard the back of the premises. Nobody had either entered or left in that period.

The explosion in Bartholomew Close had blown a sky-light into the street. The safe was in a concrete cellar in which a light had been burning day and night and although this had been extinguished by the force of the explosion, it was possible for the constable who egas outside to see the safe and obtain a fairly comprehensive view of the chamber. He, too, had asserted that nobody had entered the room or left the building after the explosion.

"It is very curious," said Michael.

T. B. Smith had come at his urgent request and the chief was as puzzled as his subordinate.

"Did Flanborough say he would come up?"

"He is on his way now," replied Michael.

"Do you know what I think?" said T. B. after a moment's thought. "I think that this is a blind. That there was never any intention of rifling either the strong room or the safe. There is a big move on somewhere, Mike, call in all the reserves."

This was an order which Michael heard with pleasure, for he had already anticipated these instructions, and detectives were at that moment flocking to Scotland Yard from every point of the compass.

CHAPTER XII
A MOTOR CAR WAS MET BY A SPECIAL TRAIN

Whatever distress animated the bosoms of humanity on that fateful Sunday afternoon and evening there were two people riotously and supremely happy, though the car which Alphonso Blaxton drove was an old one and badly sprung and though every hill it met reduced the two young adventurers to breathless apprehension for the car had a trick of stopping with its goal in sight and refusing to budge any farther.

They were happy though no word of love had been spoken between them from the moment she had drawn from his arms. And their happiness was such that even a faulty cylinder and a choked carburettor were matters of little moment.

They had eaten a very bad luncheon in Maidstone without noticing the fact. They had encountered perils innumerable (the steering gear had gone wrong and temporary repairs had to be effected without the aid of a tool chest) and were yet cheerful. They had been bumped and shaken and jarred but they had had compensation. They had seen the uprising ridges of the Kentish Rag green and white and starred with flowers. They had looked through a golden haze across mysterious valleys. They had heard the songs of birds and had tasted the joys which come only to those who love youth and young things.

If the clouds were banking up in the west and an occasional puff of cold wind came to remind them of May's treachery they, for their part, saw no cloud in their sky, felt no chill winds in their rosy world.

They reached the top of a particularly trying hill and Alphonso stopped the car and got down. Before them the road dipped straightly down to a level crossing. A mile beyond the railway there was a little hill which promised no distress of mind.

"Wouldn't this be a lovely place to paint!" said the girl.

"Don't let's talk about art," he begged with a wry face, "let us talk of beautiful things—such as tea and shrimps."

She shrieked with merriment at his feeble jest. "I wonder what is going to happen," said the girl becoming grave.

"Happen, how, where?" he asked in surprise.

"About us," she said.

He took her two hands in his.

"I am going to be tremendously rich."

"Did I tell you I was engaged?" she asked timidly after a long silence.

It was nothing less than an act of heroism for her to ask this question.

"I have a dim idea you said something about it a long time ago," he said.

"Did I really?" she asked relieved. "I had a feeling—"

"If you didn't tell me I saw your ring," he said and she went red because she had removed that ring after their second meeting and had never worn it again.

"I think I have told you that I had £300 a year," he went on; "now that we are confessing our handicaps I might as well own up to mine."

"You told me you were absolutely penniless," she said severely. "£300 a year is a fortune."

"£300 a year is only a fortune to the immensely rich, to the poor it is worse than poverty."

"You can do a lot with £300 a year," she said thoughtfully, "and what shall I do with my money? I can't throw it away."

"You will do nothing with it," he said firmly; "when my £300 a year has become £10,000 a year we can do things."

She laughed happily, twisting his watch guard round her finger.

"I cannot understand myself," she said. "I have been such a selfish mercenary pig. I didn't know there was any happiness in the world."

For the second time that day he slipped his arm around her, raised her face to his and kissed her.

"Tea," he said practically, started the engine and climbed into the driver's seat, stretching out his hand to assist her to his side.

The car started with a jerk but ran smoothly down the hill.

"It is rather lucky that gate is open," he said as the machine gathered speed. "It would be rather comic if we couldn't stop the car."

A piercing shriek of an engine brought his head round.

"That must be another line," he said uneasily and put his hand on the brake; "anyway, the gate is open," he said relieved.

Again came the frenzied scream of the engine and he heard the thunder of its wheels. He was fifty yards from the crossing when he saw the gates begin to move. He pressed on the foot brake without producing any diminution of speed, gripped the hand brake, pulled it back until he felt the snap of the rotten hand as it broke. There was nothing for it but to take a risk. He pushed over the accelerator and the car leaped forward....

Car and gate and train seemed to reach the spot simultaneously.

The girl found herself flung headlong into a ditch, fortunately landing in the soft mud at the bottom. Alphonso's fall was broken by the quickset hedge which ripped his clothes to ribbons and scarred his face and hands. He picked himself up and went in search of the girl and found her as she was climbing unsteadily on to the permanent way.

The train had pulled up with a jerk amidst a chaos of smashed gate and mangled motor-car. Fortunately, it was slowing at the closed gate at the time the collision occurred, otherwise these two young people presenting a fantastic appearance might have ended their promising careers.

"Are you hurt?" were the first words she asked.

His face was scratched and his clothes were torn but though he had by far the worse experience his was not the woe-begone appearance which the girl presented. She was caked with mud, a dab of mud was on her cheek, her hat was gone and her long brown hair was flying in all directions.

The passengers of the "special" were perhaps more perturbed than its victims.

"It is an accident. We have run into a motor-car," reported the conductor.

"Is anybody killed?" asked Sir Ralph in alarm.

"No, sir, a young man and a young woman who are more frightened than hurt."

"Let us go and look at them," said Lord Flanborough and stepped down to the permanent way.

It is a truism that there is no such thing as a paternal instinct and he would have indeed been a wise father who recognized his child in such disarray.

He was speechless for a moment.

"Moya," he gasped hollowly. "Moya! Great Heavens! What were you doing here?"

He stared round at the scarecrow by her side and at sight of the young man. Sir Ralph, who had been struck dumb by the apparition, found his voice.

"I see, I see," he said bitterly.

"You have the advantage of me," said the young man, "for I have got a little piece of Hampshire in my eye."

The girl swung round to him fumbling for her handkerchief.

"It is nothing, dear," said the young man, blissfully unconscious of the identity of the well-fed gentleman who was regarding him so sternly.

"But, darling, you might be blinded," pleaded the girl; "please let me."

"Moya," said Lord Flanborough in a pained tone, "may I ask what is the meaning of this?"

"Oh, I want you to meet Mr. Blaxton," said the girl going red and white. "Fonso, this is papa."

"I should be glad to see you," said Fonso, groping wildly on the blind side of him.

"'Fonso'?" repeated the enraged Flanborough, "and who, may I ask, is Fonso?"

She fastened back her unruly hair and rubbed her mud-stained cheek with her handkerchief before she replied.

"I suppose it will come as a shock to you and a greater shock to Sir Ralph, but Fonso and I are going to be married," she said.

Alphonso Blaxton blinked at her.

"I haven't asked you yet," he said.

"That doesn't matter," she replied calmly, "you do want me, don't you?" And before her horrified father and her promised husband, Alphonso took her in his arms and hugged her.

It was an awkward journey back to town. Sir Ralph sat by himself and rejected all Lord Flanborough's attempts to discuss the matter. He was hurt in his pride and, if the truth be told, hurt in his pocket because an alliance with the family meant a considerable addition to his fortune.

It is a mistake to believe that rich people do not care for money or that a man with two millions is wholly indifferent as to whether he has two or three. Indeed, the reverse is the case. The man who thinks in thousands is indifferent to a figure or two, the man who counts his fortune in shillings seldom knows the number of shillings he has. Only your two-millionaire realizes the full value of money. The thrift of the millionaire might well serve as an example to the improvident poor.

"I shall speak to Moya when we get home," said Lord Flanborough. "I have never been so distressed at anything so much in my life. It is disgraceful, Ralph."

But Ralph did not encourage sympathy.

As a matter of fact, his lordship spoke to the girl before the special ran into London Street Station. It required some courage on his part, for it meant intruding upon the couple in the little stateroom which ordinarily served as a sleeping apartment when Sir Ralph's private coach carried him on night journeys.

He found them a picture of decorum sitting rigidly bolt upright, one on either side of the carriage, looking out of the window with fine unconcern; but this attitude was probably due to the fact that the door of the compartment made a very loud rattling noise when the handle was turned.

"I want to speak to you alone, Moya."

"Run away, Fonso," said the girl with a gaiety out of harmony with her rigidity of attitude.

Alphonso stepped out of the saloon and closed the sliding door behind him.

"Now, Moya," said his lordship with a badly simulated air of friendliness, "perhaps you will explain?"

"Why I am going to marry Fonso?" she asked; "because I love him. Why do you think that I should be marrying him?"

"This sounds very much like Michael. It is the way he would talk," said Lord Flanborough bitterly. "This shows the danger of letting your children associate with irregular people. You know very well that you are engaged to Sir Ralph."

"I know he gave me a ring and we agreed to get married," she said, "but I have changed my mind."

"But you *can't* change your mind," stormed her father; "it is impossible that my daughter should marry a wretched artist."

"He's not wretched and he is not an artist," said the girl; "we have both agreed that he is not an artist and he is going to find something useful to do."

"If you marry this man," he pointed a trembling finger at her, "I will not receive you as my daughter."

"I don't want to be received at all. You married whom you wanted to marry, didn't you?"

"I married," said Lord Flanborough virtuously, "in accordance with the wishes of my parents."

"Do you mean to say" said the girl incredulously, "that you had no voice in it? I cannot imagine it. My dear daddy, it is preposterous to suggest that a person of your strong character accepted the wife that somebody else found for him!"

"Well, I admit," said her father somewhat mollified, "that I had a say in the matter but I had the sense to choose the right person."

"That is just what I am doing," she cried in triumph, "choosing the right person! And Daddy, if you are rude to Fonso, I shall be very rude to Ralph."

"The man of course is a fortune hunter," said Lord Flanborough savagely. "He knows that you have money in your own right and that I cannot save you from the consequences of your folly."

"What is Ralph?" she asked tartly.

"Sir Ralph is a very rich man," said her father with emphasis.

"What does he get with me?" she asked again.

This was the question which Lord Flanborough did not find it convenient to answer. He knew that marriage with his daughter would bring to Sir Ralph a much greater fortune than she possessed in her own right.

"Go and ask your disinterested friend if he will take me without a *dot*, and if I were to give my own income to found a hospital for women."

"I am sure Sir Ralph would answer in the affirmative," replied Lord Flanborough.

"Ask him," she challenged.

He passed out of the compartment scowling at the offending Fonso and made his way to Sir Ralph. He had not intended putting the question, but some chance remark of the baronet's just before the train reached London gave him an opportunity of introducing the subject.

"Would you care to marry Maya without the settlement we agreed, Ralph?"

"What on earth do you mean?" asked Sir Ralph, astonished out of his sulks. Money was a subject which invariably aroused him from the deepest lethargy.

"I mean," said his future father-in-law, "suppose I say 'You love Moya and all that sort of thing. You are a very rich man, you can afford to keep her, take her without a settlement,' what would you answer?"

"Certainly not!" said Sir Ralph furiously, "certainly not! I don't understand this business at all, Flanborough, I really don't understand it. We made an arrangement and now, it seems, you want to back out of it. What is the objection to the settlement?"

"I have no objection at all," admitted Lord Flanborough uncomfortably, "but Moya thinks that money is a big factor in your choice of her."

"Of course it is," said Sir Ralph with brutal directness. "I was very fond of Moya, but the settlement was a big consideration."

"I see," said Lord Flanborough incoherently, "Moya's idea of course...."

Michael met them at the station and noticed the constraint of the party. He understood the reason when a bedraggled Moya and a young man, whose face was criss-crossed with scratches and whose clothes were in threads, made their appearance. There was no explanation possible and Michael wisely asked for none. He handed over Lord Flanborough and his friend to the care of the city detective officer in charge of the case and when they had gone he turned to Moya.

"Have you two people been fighting?" he asked.

"Father's horribly angry with me," she said, "because I am going to marry Fonso."

He stared at her in amazement.

"Do you mean to tell me that you are not going to marry Ralph?"

"I am not," she said resolutely.

"And this is Fonso?"

The girl nodded.

Michael threw back his head and filled the station with laughter.

"You don't know Fonso, do you?" she said. "He's horribly poor. Aren't you, dear?"

"Horribly," admitted the young man but did not seem unhappy.

"And you are going to marry him?" said Michael.

"Of course I am going to marry him," said the girl wrathfully. "I didn't expect that you would disapprove."

"Disapprove?" he chuckled and catching her up in his strong arms he kissed her.

"We will all go along and have some grub," he said; "dash home and make yourself respectable, Moya. I see your father has left his car for you. Meet me at Sebo's in an hour's time."

CHAPTER XIII
THE CHRONOLOGY OF A GREAT THEFT

It is necessary to tell the story of what was undoubtedly one of the strangest and most audacious crimes recorded in the annals of crime with greater detail and at greater length than is ordinarily necessary. Le Flavier of the French police, who is surely the greatest living authority on the subject of modern crime, has likened Kate Westhanger's masterpiece (he does not refer to her, by the way) to the first of the Napoleonic campaigns against Italy and has published an elaborate treatise showing the points of resemblance which are not so far fetched as some of the critics, in their hasty review of this work, are justified in saying.

Kirschner, a little quoted authority, but nevertheless a brilliant and talented philocriminologist, has said that it would be humanly possible to reduplicate such a crime and that at any rate it would be wholly impossible to excel the ingenuity which planned the strategics of the issue.

At 8.30 on the night of May 14th the *Charter Queen*, eight thousand tons, commander T. Brown, came to her moorings in E-basin, No. 3 Quay of the Seahampton Docks. She carried a hundred-and-twenty third class passengers, seventy-four second class and fifty-nine first class passengers, a general cargo and in her strong-room forty-four thousand, eight hundred pounds of bar gold. They were made up of four-hundred and forty-eight hundred-pound ingots, bearing the stamp of the Central Rand Gold Extraction Company.

The passengers were landed and despatched by special trains to London, preceded by another train carrying the mails. The mail train left at 9.27, the passenger at 9.42. By 10.17 the gold ingots had been landed, checked and conveyed to a waiting train where they were checked again under the superintendence of Inspector K. Morris of the Dock police. At 10.22 the engine backed into the train and was coupled up and the superintendent of the line being unavoidably absent (he was discovered locked in an empty house the next morning), the driver received his "right away" from Assistant-Inspector Thomas Massey, who had arrived that day from London and who spoke to the driver and fireman before the train pulled out.

"You know this road, I suppose?" he said.

"Yes, sir," replied the driver. "I have been down here several times."

The inspector was not wholly satisfied. In the first place, he resented seeing "foreign drivers" on his road, but the two men had arrived from London bearing a letter from Sir Ralph to the superintendent of the road, a letter which afterwards proved to be a forgery. The letter instructed the superintendent to give the men charge of the engine, offering, as a reason, their reliability and the fact that they were two of the best drivers at the North Central, which railway was under the control of Sir Ralph Sapson.

The train pulled out and from this onward its adventures began.

From the moment it left Seahampton Town station, the train was never out of sight for longer than ten minutes. Every signal box along the line had received special instructions to particularly note its passing and in addition to the conventional record which is kept of every train, to notify specially not only to the next box, but to London the hour of its dispatch. The road may be briefly described.

From Seahampton it ran straight to the market town of Sevilley and then over the S-shape road across to Tolbridge. It may be remarked in passing that between Sevilley and the Tolbridge was the level crossing at which Moya had met with her accident. Between Tolbridge and Pinham the road pushed straight through uneven ground passing successively under Tolbridge Hill, Beckham Beacon and Pinham Heights, under each of which it passed through tunnels, the tunnels being connected nearly all the way by deep cuttings.

It was a rainy night for the drizzle, which set in at six in the evening, had continued until there was a veritable deluge. Sevilley (East) signalbox reported the gold train as having passed at 11.7, and this fact was supported by the times given by six signalmen between Tolbridge and Sevilley. The train slowed at Tolbridge and entered Tolbridge tunnel. Between Beckham tunnel and Tolbridge tunnel is a signalbox which reported the Special at 11.32. The signalbox was situated close to the line and rather near the ground and the signalman states that he not only saw the train pass him in the pelting rain, but that he saw the tail lights disappear into Beckham tunnel which is built on a curve.

The times are interesting. At 11.32 the train entered Beckham tunnel. At 11.42 the signalman on the northern side of Pinham tunnel reported the train as having passed. It was raining but owing to the unusual character of this new service and his natural curiosity to see a £3,000,000 "special" he had his window open and saw the three green lights flash past and the red tail lights disappearing in the distance. Between Beckham signalbox and Pinham signalbox the distance is five miles, but the theory is that at this point the train slowed to thirty miles an hour, which accounted for the unusual length of time it took to traverse this short distance.

At Maidmore, Stanborn, Quexley Paddocks and Catford Bridge, on the outskirts of London, the train was reported and timed. The next station to Catford Bridge is Balham Hill and the signalman at Balham Hill stated at the subsequent enquiry that he was given and accepted the gold special at 11.53 and lowered the "distant off" and the "home" signals, at the same time warning the next northern station, which was Kennington Junction that he had accepted the ".46 up" which was the official designation of the special.

He waited for ten minutes and saw no sign of the train, whereupon he called Quexley Paddocks and asked if there had not been a mistake since the run was not more than seven minutes. Quexley Paddocks replied that the train had passed through, going at fifty miles an hour at the moment she had been signalled.

No further news was received and the Catford Bridge signalman, becoming alarmed, reported to the station-master on duty, who sent two plate-layers along the line. They walked as far as Quexley Paddocks but saw no sign of a train. The gold special had disappeared as though the earth had opened and received it.

All these times had been verified. Every signalman and station-master was interrogated without in any way shaking the veracity of the witnesses. When the plate-layers reached Quexley Paddocks and reported the disappearance of the train, London was informed. Between Quexley Paddocks and Catford Bridge the line runs through market gardens and what is very unusual so close to London, it passes over a level crossing, the gates of which are electrically controlled from Quexley Paddocks signalbox.

And here is the most remarkable of the statements that were made. The signalman, Henry George Wallis, states that after the gold special had passed and he had brought his signals back to danger, he had noticed a strange disturbance on the dial of the electrical apparatus by which the gates were opened or closed and it was discovered the next morning when he endeavoured to open the gates to allow an army traction engine to pass that the gates refused to work. That happening, however, was very thoroughly investigated on the following day.

Michael had dined and supped with Moya and Fonso Blaxton and they had had a riotous and wholly joyous evening. He had returned to his flat at half past eleven, calling en route at the Yard, for he was still very uneasy about Kate's threat and he was anxious also to find out if there had been any discovery made in connection with the outrage of the morning. The case was not in his hands since the crime had been committed within the jurisdiction of the city police and the city Criminal Investigation Department had control of the investigations.

T. B. was at the office and had no news to give. Michael went home and to bed. He was aroused at half past twelve by telephone. It was the voice of T. B. Smith.

"They've done it, Mike. Come down at once."

"What have they done?" asked Michael with a sinking heart.

"They've pinched the blooming train!" said T. B. vulgarly.

A special train had been made up for the police and Michael was on the platform of Catford Bridge station by half past one, and was reading the reports which had been transmitted by the various signalmen. To add to the mystery, a mineral train from Seahampton which had followed the gold special at half an hour's interval, but at a slower pace, had come straight through without noticing anything unusual. It had crossed the down empty at Tolbridge and that was the only other train that was met until it reached the suburbs of London where the night traffic was more general. Sir Ralph was one of the party that went down to Catford Bridge and a very distressed and worried man he was.

"I asked that fellow Flanborough to come," he wailed, "and what do you think the selfish beast said? He said it was my responsibility. Can you imagine anything more brutal?”

“Is the gold insured?”

Sir Ralph shook his head.

“Not wholly. It was fully insured as far as Seahampton,” he said grimly. “After that the responsibility is partly mine and partly Flanborough’s and partly the underwriters’. Isn’t it too awful for words?”

T. B. came into the waiting room at that moment, clad in oilskins and sou’wester.

“You had better take complete charge of this case, Mike,” he said. “Sir Ralph will give you any assistance, I’m sure.”

“Can I have a break-down train?”

“I can bring one down here in twenty minutes,” said Sir Ralph.

“Is it equipped with searchlights?”

Sir Ralph consulted an official.

“We’ve naphtha flares. Will they do?”

“They will do,” said Michael; “put a truck in front of the engine and arrange the flares so that they light up the line.”

He spent the night in an open truck, slowly passing down the line searching for some clue which would afford a solution to the mystery. Particularly thorough was his search of the three tunnels, but they yielded nothing, and he reached Seahampton as the dawn was breaking without having made any discovery which would help him.

He went back to town by the break-down train, sleeping in the guard’s caboose, and reached Quexley in time to receive from the retiring signalman the story of his eccentric gates.

Michael was interested and with the man for a guide he followed the course of the controlling wire which passed through a length of iron piping from the signal box to the gate.

“The electrician tells me that the wire has been cut somewhere,” said the man. “He has tried his instrument on it.”

“The wire cannot be cut if it is inside the iron casing,” said Michael.

“It is either cut or fused,” said the man.

The detective walked very slowly, pausing now and again to examine the black painted pipe. Presently he stopped. He had detected something and stooped to examine the pipe more closely. It was clear that it had been freshly painted. He passed his hand round it slowly and suddenly he felt an unexpected softness.

“This isn’t iron,” he said.

He took out his pocket-knife and scraped. A little hole had been burnt into the steel by a portable blow-pipe and the wires inside had been fused together by the heat.

"That explains it," said Michael. "What effect would this have on the gates?" he asked.

"Well, you couldn't open them from the box," said the man.

"Could you open them by hand?"

"Yes, sir. We've got a chap on duty now who does nothing but open and shut them," said the man. "While the current is on, they are locked. They work like ordinary gates, except you have to be very careful when you lock them."

Michael waited until a train had passed and then experimented.

The gates opened and closed easily enough.

"What do you mean when you tell me that you have to be careful with the catch?"

"Well, ordinarily, when you use it without the current," said the man, "the catch falls and cannot be lifted except by electric control."

Michael made an inspection of the "catch." It was a steel block working on a pivot and obviously operated magnetically.

"It doesn't go up or down, now," said Michael after testing it.

"It looks to me," said the man, "as though it has been forced up."

There was no doubt that what he said was true for the detective saw the unmistakable mark of a jemmy on the wooden casing about the lock.

But why on earth did they want to open the gate? If the train had been rifled on this stretch of line the need for an open gate would have been easy to explain. The train would have been stopped here and, supposing they could force the locks of the safe, the thieves could have loaded their gold and got away—but no train had been found.

Michael passed through the turnstile and examined the road for something to guide him to a solution.

It had been raining throughout the night and more than one traction engine had passed, as was evident from the wheel marks. He explored the road for a hundred yards and found nothing. Then he tried the other gate and found that there the catch had also been forced. The first twenty yards of the road was soft and the wheel tracks were indistinguishable. At the end of this patch, however, the going was harder, the crown of the road had drained off the rain and even the traction engine had left no great impression.

Michael walked a pace or two, then stopped and whistled, and well might he whistle, for there plain to be seen and not to be confused with any other track was the deep and narrow furrow and the broad impression which could have only been made by railway wheels!

He followed the track for another hundred yards where it struck the main road and a tram line and from there every trace disappeared.

Very weary and dishevelled he presented himself to T. B. Smith and made his report.

"You don't seriously suggest that they took a railway train off the line and put it on the road, do you?" asked T. B. in wonder. "It's impossible!"

"Of course it's impossible," said Michael irritably; "the whole thing is impossible. You can't steal a railway train—but they've done it!"

He found with the assistant commissioner Sir Ralph whose agitation was pathetic.

"It's pretty rough on me, old man," said the baronet with that friendliness which the superior person invariably adopts in a moment of his misfortune. "I have lost a wife and a railway train in twenty-four hours. What the dickens are you laughing at?"

"Nothing," said Michael recovering his gravity. "It was almost worth everything to see your face!"

CHAPTER XIV
THE REMARKABLE TRAIN THAT DID STRANGE TRICKS

By six o'clock that evening Michael Pretherston was back again at his work, passing down from station to station on a pilot engine, questioning and cross-examining the officials concerned. T. B. Smith picked him up at Maidmore going down by the ordinary train.

"Have you found anything?"

"I have a theory," said Michael. "I'd like you to listen to what the station-master here has to say."

"Have you questioned him?"

"Not yet," said Michael, "but I have an idea he will say exactly what the man at Stanborn said."

The inspector who had been on night duty at the time the train passed proved to be a very intelligent and observant man. He told the same story, that the rain was falling very heavily and that he had seen the distant lights of the gold special which had flown through the dark station at incredible pace.

"Is it not a fact," said Michael, "that it passed you before you realized it was gone?"

The man was surprised.

"That is so, sir. It seemed as though I had hardly seen the headlights come into the station before I saw the tail-lights going out."

"Did it whistle as it passed through?"

"Yes, sir," said the man, "a deafening whistle. I remarked to my porter at the time that it must be trying a new kind of siren. It made the most fiendish row and you could hear nothing else."

"It whistled through all the stations where there was somebody on duty," said Michael turning to T. B. Smith. "It is a curious fact that at Stanborn Halt and Merchley which are closed for the night they made no noise at all. Was the station in darkness?" he said, turning to the inspector.

"Practically so, sir," said the man; "there was one light on the down platform where I was standing, but it was a very dark night and it was impossible to distinguish anything on the other platform. All that we saw was the flash of lights and the train had passed before one had realized that it had gone."

The inspector at Pinham Heights station had a similar story to tell.

But the Tolbridge junction signalman and the Tolbridge assistant station-master did not report any whistle or any unusual happening.

T. B. and Michael spent the night at Tolbridge and resumed their journey at daybreak. It was a slow and laborious business. Once between Pinham and Beckham Beacon, Michael had stopped the train and switched it on to a sidetrack.

"Why is there a sidetrack here?" he asked.

The railway official who accompanied him and who by this time was very weary of the whole business, explained vaguely that it was partly to provide a very necessary relief for any congestion on this section, and partly to connect up a "chalk pit or something" which now, however, was no longer used.

Michael walked along the rusted rails for a quarter of a mile. They led toward a low line of hills about three miles away. Rank vegetation grew between the sleepers, for it had been many years since its private owners had taken the trouble to put this little branch line in working order.

The road ended abruptly with a big buffer made of sleepers and behind this the rail drooped limply over a great hole as though there had been a subsidence of the earth.

Michael turned back and joined T. B.

"It could not have passed over here. The rail is rusty and runs into a large-sized hole at the other end," said Michael in despair. "Well, go on, driver."

It was a day of enquiries which led nowhere and Michael returned that night to town, weary and sick at heart. Nevertheless, he had the dim beginnings of a theory which, however, he refused to communicate to his chief.

"It is rather fantastic," he excused himself, "but then, the whole thing is fantastic. It is obviously impossible to steal a railway train and carry it through the streets of London without somebody being attracted by the novelty of the spectacle."

"Will you see Sir Ralph?" asked T. B. "He has been waiting here for an hour to meet you."

"Hasn't he got a home?" asked Michael irritably.

He saw the distracted baronet but could offer him little hope.

"It is impossible they can get away with it," said Sir Ralph; "my expert tells me that it will take them two days to break through the steel walls whatever they use."

A thought struck Michael.

"Have you a large scale map of your southern railway system?" he asked.

"I will have it sent round to you to-night," said the baronet. "What chance do you think there is?" he asked anxiously.

"I think a very poor chance," said Michael frankly; "you see, Kate doesn't take any risk."

"Kate?" said the baronet.

"You call her the 'Princess Bacheffski.' Flanborough calls her 'Miss Tenby.' As 'Miss Tenby' she secured Flanborough's code and through some of her agents in the telegraph office learned about the shipment. As 'Princess Bacheffski' she wheedled the whole of your wonderful scheme for bringing gold from Seahampton and probably discovered the nature of the steel you use."

"Good heavens!"

Sir Ralph sank into a chair and turned pale. "You don't mean to tell me—?"

"That is what I mean to tell you. Didn't you realize that the whole thing was a put up job? Why should the car of the Princess break down at your front door?"

"But she was so beautifully dressed."

"Why shouldn't she be beautifully dressed?" asked Michael mercilessly; "she probably carried twenty thousand pounds' worth of diamonds. Wasn't it worth it? Didn't you give her information which she could not have bought for the money?"

"Then you mean to say that she is a common swindler?"

"She is a very *un*common swindler," said Michael. "There's only one thing that puzzles me," he said, half to himself; "what did she want of Reggie?"

Mr. Reginald Boltover was interrupted in the delicate business of dressing for dinner by a peremptory demand that an officer of Scotland Yard should be admitted. He was relieved to discover that it was nothing more formidable than Michael.

"I have come to ask you about your friend Vera."

Mr. Boltover winced.

"My dear fellow," he said, "don't mention that lady's name. It is a sore subject. Don't mention her, dear old fellow, don't."

"Don't be an ass," said Michael good-humouredly; "you must give me an idea of the questions which she asked you. What did she talk about?"

But Mr. Boltover's mind was a blank.

It was his boast that he did not know there was such a thing as yesterday.

"Did she ask you to give her any information about things you are interested in?"

"My dear fellow," said Reggie Boltover, shaking his head, "if she did I have forgotten it. All I know is that she very seriously compromised me. I have not been to Sebo's since."

"As you are such a perfectly hopeless person," said Michael, "will you give me a note to your secretary or your factotum or whatever human substitute for mentality you possess, instructing him to give me a full list of your properties?"

"With the greatest pleasure in life, with every happiness," said Reggie earnestly, "with the greatest alacrity!"

Armed with this, Michael called the next morning at the office of one who was frequently referred to by journalists as a "merchant prince," and when he came out into Threadneedle Street his step was lighter and his eye was brighter than it had been for weeks.

"Now, Kate," he said between his teeth, "this is where you finish!"

He could have had all the men he wanted but he preferred making his investigation without assistance. He went home and changed into a knickerbocker suit, took his oldest overcoat, a walking stick and a Browning pistol with two spare magazines. He did not ask for a special engine, but travelled to Pinham Heights station by ordinary train. He showed his authority to the station-master who, however, recognized him.

"I don't want anybody to know that I am down here," he said, "and I must rely upon your discretion to see that my wishes in this respect are carried out. Am I likely to meet any plate-layers or people on the line between here and Tolbridge?"

"You will meet nobody until you come to Tolbridge box, but be very careful," warned the station-master, "the down express goes through the tunnel in ten minutes. I should advise you not to leave until that has passed."

This advice Michael thought it expedient to accept and not until the rocking train had shrieked through the station and the receding red lamps were disappearing in the darkness of the tunnel did he walk down the sloping platform into the six-foot way and pass into the smoking tunnel.

He could have reached his destination by the high road which runs from Pinham round the foot of the Beacon, but for reasons of his own, he preferred to accept the discomforts of the darker way and the uneven going. He passed through the tunnel after a seemingly interminable walk and came to the switch line where his engine had been sidetracked. He followed this until he came to the buffer and the deep hole beyond.

He examined the buffer very carefully, retraced his footsteps and examined the rail. It was, as he had seen before, red with rust. Nevertheless, he went on his knees and examined the rail through a magnifying glass. Then he wetted his finger and drew it along the red surface. He looked at his finger. It was red. But it was not the red of rust.

He walked back, carefully examining every inch of the rail until he found what he sought. At one place by the side of the actual rail was a little red spot. It was no larger than a threepenny piece and it was, to all appearance, rust. But rust does not develop on a wooden sleeper and he found the counterpart of this spot, a trifle larger on the wood. Again he wetted his finger and was satisfied.

For this was not rust, but a very common form of distemper employed by builders.

He went back to the buffer and the sagging rail and climbed down the hole which was about six feet deep. He had noticed that a quantity of green stagnant water at the bottom of the hole advertised its age. Again he drew his hand along the water and examined his palm. It was green, but his strongest magnifying glass (and he had one of peculiarly high power) failed to reveal any sign of that florescence which forms on the surface of water and gives it its peculiar vivid green. Instead, he saw a number of irregular specks, which were undoubtedly crystals.

"Which means," said Michael to himself, "that Kate is an artist even if Fonso isn't."

The green scum which had deceived him at first had been artificially created. Some chemical had been dissolved and had re-crystallised on the surface. He dug into the soft earth on the other side without securing any data as to when the hole had been made, but nearer the surface and on the rim, he saw the white tendrils of growing coltsfoot, which were still humid. One tentacle had been shaved away, but the plant had not yet begun to die, nor the exposed root to blacken.

"This hole was dug on the night of the robbery," said Michael, "and the earth was artistically removed. Kate would depend upon the railway officials not having bothered to inspect this bit of line."

As matter of fact, this was so. It was on private property, and after it left the edge of the railway land it ceased to be their responsibility. The buffer was also newly erected. He found this when he had dug down to its foundation. The wood was still dry and there were blades of grass and tiny fragments of plant in the earth beneath. He walked round the little pit and reached the rails on the opposite side. They were rusted as artistically as their fellows. The line twisted and curved across level country for a mile before it turned the shoulder of a hill and disappeared into a gorge, evidently excavated in the course of the working.

Behind this was another chalk hole, and he gathered from an examination of the map, that along this further ridge ran a road. The abandoned cement works had been so built that they were not in view from the railway itself. Possibly the philanthropic purchaser had pulled down the one remaining smokestack on his occupation and the whitened buildings did not stand out against the chalky soil behind them. He had all the evidence he wanted before he had traversed one-half of the two miles which separated him from the chalk pits.

The mark of the heavy wheels was visible now. In places the weeds which grew thickly between the sleepers had been crushed by their passage. He now left the rail and began moving round in a wide semi-circle that would bring him to a low neck in the hill. His plan was to climb the hill from here and work his way back along its crest until he overlooked the works. He was now in the danger zone.

He shifted his stick to his left hand and slipped out his pistol and pulled back the cover. It took him an hour to gain the crest of the neck. He found it more difficult to climb than he had thought. Evidently chalk had been quarried here and, save in one or two places, he was faced by a sheer unscalable wall. It was hard climbing all the way and he was hot and thirsty by the time he reached the top.

From the neck he could only secure a partial view of the works. He had taken the precaution to bring a pair of prismatic glasses and with these he surveyed the ground. There was no sign of the train and for a moment his heart sank. Then he picked up the rail and followed it yard by yard and he could scarcely restrain himself from a yell of joy when he saw the rail led to a big shed, the gates of which were closed.

Originally, this may have been the mill house, but the new tenants had relaid the line so that it passed into the building. He replaced his glasses and continued his climb. He was half-way between the neck and the point which would directly overlook the works when he heard the hum of a motor car and dropped flat. He was within fifty yards of the road which was slightly above him, and looking up very cautiously he saw a car dash past and disappear over the rise.

There was no mistaking its occupant. It was the Spaniard, Gregori.

He rose cautiously and continued his progress, keeping a sharp look-out for the sentries which he knew would be posted on the road. The path he followed was a beaten track. He realized this before he had gone much farther and sought to find a way either to the left or the right, but without success.

He halted and debated with himself the question as to whether he should go back. It was madness to attempt to make the capture alone. Even now, he might have been detected, but if this was the case by the time he went back and procured assistance the whole gang would have gone and probably the gold with them. Of the two risks he decided to take the first.

Little time was given to him to regret this decision. He had taken three paces when he heard the unmistakable whirr of a lariat. He turned to face the danger, pistol in hand, but too late. The rope settled about his neck, he felt a sharp nerve-racking jar and fell heavily to the ground.

CHAPTER XV
AS SIR RALPH SAID, "BUSINESS IS BUSINESS"

T. B. Smith walked into his outer office.

"Any news of Mr. Pretherston?" he asked.

"No, sir," was the reply.

"Any news of Barr?"

"No, sir."

T. B. clicked his lips impatiently.

"Who's looking after them?"

"Detective-sergeant Grey, sir," was the reply. "You know we traced him as far as Pinham Heights. After that he seems to have been lost sight of."

"Have you notified the chief constables of Hampshire, Sussex and Surrey?" asked T. B.

"That has been done, sir," said the officer. "The local constabulary are making a search."

T. B. bit his lips.

"I can understand Mr. Pretherston going," he said, "but what has happened to Barr?"

His subordinate very wisely offered no solution.

There were other anxious enquirers. Moya Felton had called that morning. Sir Ralph had made two visits to headquarters though it was doubtful whether his anxiety was in any way associated with the well being of Michael Pretherston.

"I think Michael will find the gang," said T. B., "though he may be too late to get the gold."

"What do I want the gang for?" demanded Sir Ralph wrathfully. "Will the government give me £2,800,000 for them? The gang can go to the devil so far as I am concerned. I want the gold."

"You may get neither," said T. B.; "at any rate, it ought to be very pleasing to you, Sir Ralph, that Michael Pretherston is risking his life to recover your property."

"Isn't he paid to do it?" demanded Sir Ralph. "Isn't that the job of a policeman? By Gad! Commissioner, one would imagine that Pretherston was doing something out of the common! I take risks every day of my life."

"If you could see my mind," said T. B. Smith suavely, "you would realize that you are taking the biggest risk you have taken to-day. I advise you to go home and get into a calmer frame of mind."

"When shall I hear anything?" asked the truculent baronet.

"Whenever you are within earshot," snapped the Commissioner. "Show Sir Ralph out, constable."

Lord Flanborough did not obtrude his enquiries. He was so far reconciled to Moya that he could discuss the matter dispassionately, without reference to the *mésalliance* which threatened his family.

"I think on the whole, Moya," he said, "I had better not see Ralph. After all, business is business and friends are friends; but I disclaim all responsibility for that gold after it left the ship. It is Ralph's business entirely and I simply won't accept his suggestion that I share his responsibility to the slightest degree."

"Will he have to bear the loss?"

"Well, partially bear the loss. A portion will be borne by the underwriters. Ralph, I am afraid, is a very mean man. I hate saying anything about my friends but Ralph is really economical to a point of meanness. I advised him to insure the gold and, to save a beggarly premium, he only insured half of it. I am very sorry for him," he shook his head mournfully as a symbol of his sympathy. "I am very, very sorry for him, but I think it is better that we do not meet until this business matter is completely settled. On the whole," he added thoughtfully, "perhaps it is better that your engagement with Ralph is broken off. He has said some very unkind things about you, Moya, which aroused my anger. I do not think you have been wise but I cannot allow any person to discuss you uncharitably."

If the truth be told, Sir Ralph had said very little about the girl and very much about his lordship, whom he had accused of deliberately evading his responsibilities. This was at the one interview which they had had. It pleased Lord Flanborough to pose as a devoted father, but he did not deceive anybody but himself, for Moya had had a first hand account of the interview from Ralph who had asked her to use her influence to bring about a change in Lord Flanborough's attitude.

It was the day after the disappearance of Michael Pretherston and Sir Ralph's nerves were a little shaky. It was unfortunate in the circumstances that he had decided that afternoon to make a call upon the man who, a week before, he had fondly believed was to be his father-in-law. Lord Flanborough had not taken the precaution of warning his servants that he was not at home to Sir Ralph, so he had nobody to blame but himself when the door of his study was flung violently open that afternoon and Ralph Sapson stalked in.

"My dear Sapson," stammered his lordship, flabbergasted by the unexpectedness of the visit. "Pray, do sit down."

"I am not going to sit down. I tell you I am not going to sit down," roared, rather than said, Ralph.

"Let me close the door," said his lordship in alarm. "My dear man, please remember—"

"I remember nothing except that I am on the brink of ruin. That is what it means. I am on the brink of ruin," said Ralph, violently thumping the desk. "It is going to cost me a million and a half, and you must bear your share, Flanborough! You are responsible. If it had not been for your infernal daughter this would not have occurred."

"My daughter," said Lord Flanborough and feeling himself on perfectly safe ground he could speak with hauteur, "is not a matter for discussion and if you cannot speak respectfully of her, I beg you to leave this room."

"If it had not been for your daughter we should have remembered to send Griggs back."

"I am not in charge of the railway," said his lordship with mock humility. "I cannot order engine-drivers to return to Seahampton. Be reasonable, Sapson!"

"You have got to bear your share," said the other doggedly, "you are morally responsible. I wish I had never thought of bringing your infernal ships to Seahampton."

He was haggard and drawn of face. In two days he seemed to have shrunk so that his usually well-fitting clothes hung on him loosely.

"Everything can be discussed in a quiet business-like way," said Lord Flanborough. "I am very sorry that you have this loss. It is by no means certain that it is a loss, but business is business—you cannot expect me to shoulder your responsibilities, my dear friend."

"It is your responsibility as well as mine," stormed Ralph, jumping up from his chair and advancing upon the little man who stepped cautiously backward, "and I insist upon your accepting your share."

"Which would amount to?" suggested his lordship.

"About seven hundred thousand pounds," growled the other.

"Seven hundred thousand pounds! Impossible!" said Lord Flanborough emphatically.

Ralph turned livid.

"If you don't," he hissed, thumping his palm with his fist, "if you don't—"

At that moment help came in the shape of Moya. She nodded coolly to Sir Ralph and crossed the room to her father.

"There is no news of Michael," she said.

"Dear me," sighed his lordship.

"Michael!" sneered Ralph. "There is no news of the money! That's the important thing, Moya!"

"We are not on the 'Moya' terms any more, Sir Ralph," she said quietly.

"Rub it in," groaned the man.

"I don't want to rub it in. We all have our troubles, but some of us bear them less courageously than others. It won't ruin you if you do lose all this money. You know you are enormously rich."

"I am not going to lose," said Sir Ralph doggedly; "your father has to bear his share."

"If father is responsible he will bear his share," said the girl, "but it is not by any means certain that he is responsible, is it, papa?"

"Certainly not," said Lord Flanborough, placing a table between himself and his infuriated partner.

There was a tap at the door and Sibble came in, somewhat furtively.

He looked mysteriously at Moya and she went to him.

"What is it, Sibble?" she asked.

"There's a man to see you, miss," he said. "I think it is something very special."

"To see me? Who is he?"

"I don't know who he is, miss, but he has a very special message for you."

She went out into the hall. A respectable looking man stood hat in hand. By his thick coat she thought at first he was an omnibus driver. In a sense, she was right.

"Are you Lady Moya Felton, madame?"

"Yes," said the girl.

He handed her a card. She took it. It was a business card announcing that Messrs. Acton and Arkwright, contractors, were prepared to remove anything from machinery to furniture and that they had a "larger number of motor lorries than any other firm doing business in the south of England."

"I am afraid there is a mistake," she said. "I didn't send for you."

"No, miss, we've brought the goods."

"The goods?" she said puzzled.

He led the way to the door.

Lining one side of the street and stretching from the house to the corner of Gaspard Place were ten motor lorries.

"Here's the name."

He turned the card over.

"Lord Flanborough, Felton House, Grosvenor Avenue," said the man reading it over her shoulder.

"Have you any letter?"

"No, miss, these are all the instructions I had. I was told to bring the chemicals to his lordship and ask for you."

"Chemicals?" she said.

Her father had followed her to the door.

"What is it?" he asked.

"This man has brought some chemicals for you."

"Oh, nonsense, there is some mistake," said Lord Flanborough. "I am not a chemist."

He went down the steps with the girl to the first lorry. She looked inside and apparently it was empty.

"What is it you have brought?" she asked in surprise.

"There they are, miss, on the floor."

And then she saw a number of packages wrapped in sacking.

"They're pretty heavy," said the man, "considering their size."

She reached out her hand and tried to draw one toward her. It defied her efforts. Lord Flanborough tried and succeeded in moving it. Something in its shape startled him.

"Have you a knife?" he asked the man.

The contractor produced a big clasp knife and opened it.

"Be careful, my lord," he warned, "they're dangerous—"

But Lord Flanborough had ripped the canvas package and exposed a dull yellow ingot. He dropped the knife and stepped back.

"How many wagons are there?" he asked huskily.

"Ten, sir. They've all got the same number of packages—and are we to take them to the Docks?"

Lord Flanborough made a rapid calculation.

"Take them into the basement and put them into the coal cellar," he said and went up the steps two at a time and back into his study.

Sir Ralph was still waiting. The rudeness of his host neither increased nor decreased his irritation.

Lord Flanborough stepped up to him briskly.

"Look here, Sapson," he said. "What responsibility do you want me to bear in the matter of this gold?"

"I want you to bear half."

"I will do more than that," said his lordship. "I will assume the whole responsibility for two hundred thousand pounds."

Ralph swung round.

"You will?" he said incredulously.

"I will."

"Done," said Sir Ralph and pulled out his cheque book.

He wrote quickly and nervously but quite legibly enough and handed the slip to Lord Flanborough, what time his lordship was writing with more leisure but no less excitement on the other side of the table.

"There's your cheque," said Sir Ralph.

"And there's my note freeing you from responsibility," said his lordship.

"I am sorry I have been so unpleasant," said the baronet wiping his steaming brow, "but you will understand."

"I quite understand," said Lord Flanborough.

"Business is business," said Ralph.

"Business is business," repeated his lordship and folding the cheque slipped it into his pocket.

CHAPTER XVI
ON THE UNMORALITY OF PROFESSIONAL THIEVES

The main building of what had once been Boltover's Cement Works consisted of four high walls and a slate roof. Here had stood the wash mills and the revolving knives which had reduced the clay and mud from the nearby river into slurry. Leading therefrom was the heating chamber and the kiln house. There was no trace of mill, though the kilns still stood.

All the machinery had been removed, the concrete floor strengthened and the only engine visible was a great Atlantic locomotive which had stood with steam up day and night before the wreckage of two trucks. In each of these was a rough circular hole and the blistered paint and the drops of metal which hung upon the edge or had trickled down its blackened side, told of the terrific heat which had been employed to break through the steel walls.

Near one wall were a number of small packages neatly stitched in canvas and ready for removal, and on these sat Mr. Mulberry, the benignity of whose countenance was somewhat discounted by the fact that a loaded rifle lay across his knees. Leading from the main building was a small office approached through a steel door and in this were seated the seven guiding spirits of the great raid, Francis Stockmar, Gregori, Colonel Westhanger, Colling Jacques, Thomas Stockmar, Mr. Cunningham and Kate.

Gregori was talking. He leant across the table, his hands lightly clasped, his head on one side turned to the girl who sat opposite to him and a little to his right.

"I think, Kate, we finish here," he was saying. "Crime Street is getting a little too warm."

"I didn't expect you to lose your nerve," she said.

"I'm not losing my nerve," he said with a scowl. "I am afraid of losing my life, if you want to know the truth. We are watched all the time. They know you are out of town and are searching for you."

"They found me," said the girl coolly. "I am staying at Brighton."

"We have made a big haul and it will take us a year to get rid of it," Gregori went on, "but when we have got rid of it, we shall have enough to settle down."

"But why do you want to settle down?" she asked.

"My dear Kate," said her uncle querulously, "don't ask absurd questions. You know there is no reason in the world why we should not settle down. We have enough money."

"Exactly what do you mean by settling down?" she insisted. "I am not being sarcastic. I merely want information. You have taught me that it is the game and not the prize that is worth while. That has been my life's teaching. Why, you told me if you were a millionaire," she looked at her uncle under her bent brows, "nothing would induce you to be 'dull and honest.' Those were your words."

"My dear child," said Colonel Westhanger, "I have told you lots of things which have to be interpreted in a liberal spirit. We have had all the fun we want and now we will—"

He was at a loss in his desire to avoid a tautological repetition of a certain phrase.

"Settle down," she suggested; "be dull and honest?"

"But, surely, Kate," said Gregori impatiently, "you don't want to be a hunted beast all your life?"

"Why not?" she asked in astonishment. "It is just as much fun being hunted as hunting. You have said that a score of times. Does Michael Pretherston—"

"Oh, hang Michael Pretherston," said Gregori.

"Does Michael Pretherston," she went on, "get as much fun out of chasing me, as I get out of escaping him? Does Michael Pretherston find the same exhilaration of mind in following on my tracks as I find in keeping ahead of him?"

"Anyway," said Gregori. "I have had enough of it and I want to go out of the business and I advise you to do the same. And there is another thing, Kate—"

He looked at the Colonel for support, but Colonel Westhanger found it convenient at that moment to be staring at the skylight.

"What is the other thing?" she asked.

"Well, you know I am fond of you," he said, "and I want to—" he floundered.

"Settle down," she suggested innocently; "what is all this 'settling down' that everybody loves so much? Does it mean we shall never plan another great coup?" She leant her elbows on the table. "Honestly, I am not being wilfully dense. I know money is useful, because it helps one to prepare the way for making more money, but I have not been in this," she waved her hand, "in all these things for money. I told Michael Pretherston so and he believed me."

"What have you been telling Michael Pretherston?" asked Gregori suspiciously.

"I told him that," she said simply.

"But, my dear girl," said her uncle, "fun and excitement and all that sort of thing are well enough in their way, but you don't mean to tell me, at this hour, that you have not been working for the 'stuff'?"

"I will tell you as much at this or any other hour," she answered immediately.

"I see," said Gregori with a faint smile, "then really you are what I would call a criminal artist—art for art's sake, eh?"

"I mean that," she said again. "One must not judge one's successes by the amount of money one has made."

"That is how I joodge it," said the thick voice of Francis Stockmar; "so much mooney, so much sugsess, isn't it?"

"I tell you frankly," said Gregori. "I am in this for the money and so is your uncle. We have taken many risks, some of us have been caught and some of us," he said significantly, "have been lucky. I've got thirty years in front of me, with any luck, and so I am going to—"

"Settle down," suggested Kate ironically.

"I am going to quit."

"Come, come, be sensible, Kate," said the Colonel, patting her on the shoulder. "You have been a very good girl and we owe you almost everything we have. I am sure everyone agrees that you have been the brains of our—er—association. The only time when any of us have been caught is when we have gone out on a side line of our own. Now leave well alone."

"When hunters have caught the fox," she said, "do they leave well alone and never hunt again? In war, when a soldier comes through a battle safely, does he leave well alone and never go into action again? Does the huntsman who is nearly caught by a lion leave well, and lions, alone?"

"This is different," said her uncle doggedly.

"But I don't understand it. If what you say is right, then I am wrong and have been wrong all my life. I am wrong and the police are right."

"Of course, they're right," said Gregori; "what rubbish you are talking."

"The police are right?" she asked in open-eyed astonishment.

"Of course they are right. They must protect society. In five years' time, when I am settled on my little estate in Spain and my house is burgled do you imagine I shall not call in the police?"

"I know they are right in their way," she said, as if she were speaking her thoughts aloud, "but we are right, too."

"We cannot both be right," said Colonel Westhanger.

"I asked you some time ago," she said, turning to him, "which was the better life—the dull life or ours. They cannot both be better. The elementary conditions cannot change. That life must be the best, or ours."

"That life is best," said the Colonel decisively.

She looked at him steadily.

"Then why have you let me live this?" she asked. "You cannot change me. I cannot change. I cannot!" she said with vehemence and the men noted with amazement the emotion she displayed. "Nothing can change me!"

Gregori reached out and took her hand, but she snatched it away.

"I will tell you what can change you, little girl," he said undeterred by the rebuff, "love can change you. Give me a chance."

She looked at him and laughed in his face.

"Will you be good or bad, honest or dishonest? You will only be a half man, living two lives. Marry you! And am I to go into witness boxes to testify against your burglar? And prosecute your poachers? I am living now, what I believe to be the truth. I believe I have the right to match my wits against the world and take, by my intelligence, what the old robber barons took by brutal strength. If I pass to the other side I should be a liar, living a life in which I did not believe. I am going on."

"Then you will go on by yourself."

"Will I?" she asked softly.

"Go out and find somebody who thinks as you think if you can," sneered Gregori; "you will be obliged to live a lie, anyway. You will never meet a man who believes in stealing, who believes in fraud and who will go on so believing, until he is an old man. You will never meet a man on the other side of life who would trust you if he knew you, and he *would* know you unless you—went on lying."

He laughed.

"You are in a cleft stick, my little friend, and if you take my tip you will stick to the friends who know you."

He laughed again.

"Suppose I come down into Spain and burgle your house—" her eyes lit up—"and I would do it! Or, suppose, when you have—settled down—and when you have all deposited your symbols of success in your banks, I planned a little coup and smashed your banks? I could do it easily and I would do it," she said. "What would you do?"

Their faces were a study. The Colonel was stroking his white moustache. Francis Stockmar was scowling horribly. Mr. Cunningham was staring blankly at the opposite wall.

"Naturally you would not play such a lowdown trick upon your old friends," said the Colonel soothingly; "nobody believes you would, Kate. I mean, it would be tragic for some of us, after spending years of our lives accumulating a little nest egg to find we had become beggars in a night. Of course, speaking personally, I should consider myself exonerated from any responsibility I had in regard to our relationship and I should have to tell the police—"

"You would call the police, too, would you? Would you, Stockmar?"

"Yas," said the stolid Austrian, "of goorse. The mooney to recover, ain't it?"

"And you?"

"I don't think you would do anything so treacherous," said Mr. Cunningham; "naturally, we would not take that sort of thing lying down."

"Naturally," said Colling Jacques, "the whole matter is this, when we go back to the respectable world and obey the laws, we, as citizens, are entitled to the protection which the laws give us."

"I see. You are, so to speak, touching wood. The wood is the law."

"That is it," he said.

Kate got up and walked to the one window of the room and looked out upon the dreary yard with its tangle of twisted machinery, its rusted boilers, its chaos of rotting cement bags.

"Well, you can all do as you like," she turned on them, "but I tell you this, that if you think you are going to—settle down—at my expense, and if you think I have been planning and scheming and play-acting and lying in order that you might all become respected parish councillors, you have made a mistake. You talk about my friends, if you are my friends, God help me! There is one man in the world who is worth the whole crowd of you."

She was interrupted by a crash as though a heavy body had been thrown against a door. Somebody fumbled with the lock and Gregori jumped up and threw it open. They half carried, half pushed a gagged and bound man through the doorway. Behind him peered the saturnine, malignant face of his captor, Doctor Garon.

"Got him," he said triumphantly.

"Who is it?" asked Gregori, staring at the half conscious man.

The girl did not ask. She went suddenly cold, for she knew it was Michael Pretherston.

CHAPTER XVII
THE INDEPENDENT STRATEGY OF SEÑOR GREGORI

It is a fact worth remarking upon, that in all her career, though she had been associated with the most desperate of criminals, and though she had been surrounded on all sides by men who would stop at nothing to gain their ends, Kate had never witnessed an act of violence. Such arrests of members of the confederation as she had seen had been very humdrum affairs. The arrival of two strangers, a consultation carried on in a low tone by a pleasant detective officer, an urgent call to somebody to "get my hat" and the disappearance, very often for a long time, of the member affected. She had never seen a fellow creature man-handled nor did she believe that there was in her confederates the tigerish malignity which was now displayed. She looked from face to face in amazement and horror as they crowded round the handcuffed figure and flung him into a chair.

Michael had been choked to insensibility at the first attack. With the loosening of the rope, he had recovered consciousness and put up a fight, and had been hammered back to insensibility by the three men who had watched him from the moment he had crossed the open ground to the east of the railway, and had lain in wait for him. They had manacled him with his own handcuffs. This he realized, as he came back to consciousness, with his head throbbing and every bone in his body aching.

He leant his elbows on the table and buried his face in his hands, striving to collect his thoughts. It was the cold steel of the handcuff against his nose which was the starting point from whence he unravelled the situation. The blow which had felled him had fortunately been broken by his soft felt hat and he raised his hand and gingerly felt the bump which Dr. Garon's loaded cane had raised.

"Now then, wake up," said Gregori's voice roughly, "let's have a look at you."

Michael raised his head and looked at the speaker.

"Hello, Gregori," he said dully. He looked round the room and caught the girl's eyes and for a moment held them.

"You seem to have tumbled into it, my young friend," said Colonel Westhanger.

Michael slowly shifted his eyes to the speaker and smiled.

"We all seem to have tumbled into it, you worse than anybody. This means a life sentence for you, Colonel."

The old man's face went white.

"It is only bluff," said Garon; "he is here by himself. I have been watching him for an hour. You tried to pull off the job on your lonely!"

"Alone," said the Colonel and the girl watching him saw his face go hard. "Alone! Are you sure?"

"Absolutely sure," said the doctor.

He sat straddle-legged on a chair leaning on the back and puffing the cigar he had just lighted.

"It would be rather a serious business if you had made a mistake, wouldn't it?" drawled Michael. He was recovering his scattered senses and something of his good spirits. "You fellows had better make the best of a bad job."

"What is your idea of the best of a bad job," sneered Gregori,—"to take the handcuffs off you and put them on me and the Colonel? If it means a 'lifer' for the Colonel! what does it mean for me? You don't suppose I am going back to Dartmoor to build walls for the moor farmers, do you?"

"What is the alternative?" asked Michael.

"I'll tell you what is the alternative," hissed the other thrusting his face into the detective's, "it is the only alternative that will give me any satisfaction—and it is to put you out."

"Dot is id," nodded Stockman

The girl's heart almost stopped beating and for a moment she closed her eyes and gripped tight to the edge of the table. She felt physically sick and her knees were trembling under her. Fortunately their attention was fully occupied with Michael and nobody noticed that she had grown of a sudden peaked and grey. She bit her lips and by sheer effort of will regained control of herself. She looked at Michael: that little smile of his still played about the corners of his mouth and the eyes that were lifted to Colling Jacques were full of good humor.

"It is you or us, Pretherston," the engineer was saying; "you don't suppose we have been working for this stuff and taken all the risk, only to see ourselves standing in the dock of the Old Bailey?"

"Winchester," corrected the detective, "it is a very pretty assize court—the vaulted ceiling will appeal to you, Jacques. It is in the Gothic style."

"One moment," said the Colonel suddenly.

With a nod he called the men to a corner of the room and for five minutes there was a whispered consultation. The girl and Michael were left alone and obeying some impulse which she could not define, she suddenly turned her back upon him and walked to the window, a proceeding which Gregori noticed out of the corner of his eye. Presently the little conference broke up and the Colonel came back with the others.

"Look here, Pretherston, I am going to make a proposition to you. You are not a rich man, I take it."

"My private affairs don't concern you," said Michael calmly, "and I certainly am not prepared to discuss them with you."

"This job is worth two and a half millions and there are ten of us in it. Help us to make a getaway and there is not far short of a quarter of a million for you."

The girl swung round and looked at Michael. How would he take this offer? She knew how great was the appeal which money made to men, especially money easily earnt. She waited in breathless, almost painful, suspense.

"Two hundred and fifty thousand pounds," said Michael—"that is a lot of money. But, why do you put such a proposition to me?"

"It is a lot of money," repeated the Colonel significantly.

Michael laughed.

"I suppose there was a time in your life," he drawled, "when if somebody had offered you money to do a dishonest act, you would have knocked him down? But perhaps there never was such a time," he said, searching the other's face.

"I no more want to discuss my affairs, than you want to discuss yours," said the Colonel gruffly; "here is the proposition," he thumped the table, "do you take it?"

Michael shook his head.

"I won't be rude to you," he said, "because you are an older man and because you are going to end your life rather miserably in a very short time."

He saw the man wince.

"I am not saying that with the object of offending you," Michael continued. "I am just telling you what is the truth. Suppose you get away from here, how are you going to make your escape from England? By this time every port is closed to you."

"I will tell you how we are going to get out of England," said Gregori, "we are going to leave by the only route possible, by ship from London."

"By ship from London?" it was the surprised voice of the girl.

"We have done a little planning on our own, Kate," said Gregori with a grin; "this is our last job. We didn't tell you because we didn't think it was worth while upsetting you. Everything was arranged last week."

"Without my knowledge," she said.

He nodded.

"What do you say, Pretherston? It is your last chance."

"It isn't my last chance," said the other cheerfully.

"What do you mean?"

"That you will find out," said Michael with a sudden sternness. "I warn you that your time is very short."

"Your time will be shorter," said Gregori with a sinister smile.

"We will give him half-an-hour to think over it," suggested Jacques; "put him in the engine room."

The engine room was the uncomfortable little shed which had been built on to the mixing shop to accommodate a dynamo. It was now empty save for a truckle bed on which one of the gang had slept. Pad-locked iron doors led to the mixing room and to the outer world, but to make doubly sure, Garon volunteered to stand outside the building and keep guard. Michael was thrust into the little room and the door slammed upon him.

"Now," said Gregori when they were back again in the office, "we have to decide and decide quickly. If we can be sure that this fellow is alone he has got to be killed."

"Killed?" said Kate. "Oh, no, no!"

He turned on her with a snarl.

"This is our job. You keep out of this, Kate," he said. "I tell you it must be done, for all our sakes."

"The first thing," said the Colonel, "is to get the gold away."

"It will be loaded on to the trucks to-morrow morning," said Gregori, "and we had better keep this fellow alive until it is gone."

"Are we using our own trucks?"

Gregori shook his head.

"Oh, no," he said, "that would be too dangerous. I have hired ten, from a man in Eastbourne who is used to handling machinery. He has no idea what sort of factory this is and I have told him it is a prepara-tion of lead we are shipping to the docks. Young Stockmar will meet the convoy in London. Our own men are on board the ship and will load the stuff."

"It is a bit risky," said Colling Jacques shaking his head, "sending all that money through London without a guard."

"It would be more risky to guard it," said the other calmly, "our only chance lies in not rousing the suspicion of the contractor who has promised to come down himself to superintend the carriage to the docks. His people won't be allowed to handle any of it and I have told him especially that it is dangerous to touch the packages—now, Kate, you must be sensible about this business of Pretherston."

She shrugged her shoulders and leant back against the window-sill, her hands behind her.

"I suppose it is necessary," she said in her cool even tone and the Colonel heaved a sigh of relief.

"Gad, that's the way to look at it, my girl," he said admiringly. "I knew you wouldn't fail us."

She said nothing.

"You said there were ten shares," she asked presently, "do you count me—as one who is sharing?"

"You stand in with me, my dear," said the Colonel, patting her on the shoulder, "don't you be afraid. I have never denied you anything, have I?"

She shook her head.

"I have never been aware that you denied me anything," she said absently.

"When is this—" she could not find words to complete the sentence.

"Pretherston," said Gregori,—"oh, we can't do anything yet. I think you will agree, Colonel. We must make absolutely sure that he is not being followed and that he has not half the Metropolitan police force within call. I shall do nothing at all till to-morrow night."

She inclined her head.

"I see," she said simply and then, "I think I will go to my room."

They had made her comfortable quarters in what had been once the foreman's office. She passed through the great sheds slowly and stopped for a moment to look at the powerful engine which stood near the closed doors, a tiny feather of steam at its safety valve, then she went into her room.

CHAPTER XVIII
THE COLONEL WAS A GENTLEMAN AT THE LAST

It was ten o'clock the following morning before any of the gang saw the girl. She had spent a sleepless night revising her philosophies and arranging the future as she saw it.

Mulberry who had put away his rifle and was appearing in the capacity of an urbane general-manager greeted Kate with a nod.

He was superintending the transference of the ingots to the waiting trolleys which stood on the road at the top of the chalk pit and were approached by a zig-zag path which had been cut in the face of the bluff by the original owner of the property.

Later Mr. Mulberry climbed up the path to interview the stout contractor.

"I will pay you in advance," said Mr. Mulberry beaming benevolently and producing a wad of notes from his pocket book. "You have full instructions as to where these packages are to go?"

"Yes, sir," said the man. "To the Thames Docks and I am to hand them over to the gentleman who engaged me the day before yesterday."

"Mr. Stockmar," said Mulberry.

"That is the name, sir. Are these things valuable?"

Mulberry shook his head.

"Scientifically they are of the greatest value, commercially they are of no value. You have probably heard of dioxide of lead, the heaviest metal that the earth holds?"

"I can't say that I have, sir," said the contractor frankly. "I am not much of a scientist."

"It is a very useful element," lied Mr. Mulberry glibly, "in the creation of paper. It is highly inflammable but not explosive so long as it is handled by experts like my men here," he waved his hand to the procession of swarthy labourers who were coming up the hill, each bearing a package on his shoulder.

"They are Italians, aren't they, sir?"

Mr. Mulberry nodded.

"They are the only people who can handle this chemical," he explained.

"I see, sir," said the master carman wisely, "some of these foreigners are wonderful chaps with chemicals."

He looked down into the hollow.

"Mighty nice young lady that, sir," he said respectfully, not knowing whether Kate, who had just emerged from the building and was wandering aimlessly across the yard, was an employee or a friend.

"Oh, yes, that is my confidential secretary," said Mr. Mulberry.

"Mighty nice, if I may be allowed to say so, very lady-like."

"Yes, yes," said Mr. Mulberry.

He lingered long enough to see the last packages laid on the floor of the last truck, shook hands with the contractor with great affability and strode nonchalantly down the slope and none to see him would have imagined that he had just entrusted nearly three million pounds' worth of gold, to the tender mercies of a chance carman.

He was half way down the first of the slopes when he met Kate coming up.

"Kate," he said in a low voice, "if you are going up to the top and that fellow asks you who you are, you must tell him you are my confidential secretary. I hope you don't mind, I had to explain you."

She nodded and continued her slow walk until she came to the road. The cars were now buzzing preparatory to making a start. The contractor, whom she had met before, gave her a cheery nod.

"Have you a piece of paper?" she asked.

"I've a card, miss," he said.

"That will do," she said; "lend me your pencil."

She wrote a few lines and handed them to the man.

"I am the managing director's confidential secretary," she said.

"I know, miss," replied the man.

He looked at the card with a frown.

"You are to take the trucks first of all to this address and see the gentleman whose name I have written."

"But I was told to go straight to the docks."

She smiled and nodded.

"I know," she said, "but my chief thinks you had better go here. His lordship will either accompany you to their destination or he may store your chemicals for the night."

He looked at the address.

"The Earl of Flanborough," he read; "suppose he isn't there, miss?"

This was a contingency which she had overlooked.

"Ask for Lady Moya Felton—that is his daughter," she said; "you had best see her first in any circumstances."

"I see, miss," said the man a little impressed. "I know his lordship. I have often seen him at Seahampton."

"Now I think you had better go," said Kate, "before you receive any fresh instructions."

The man chuckled, swung himself into the seat of the second car beside the driver and first one and then the other of the great lorries, moved slowly down the white road. She watched them until the last one had passed the crest of the hill, then she slowly descended the zig-zag path.

She met Gregori in the doorway.

"Where have you been, Kate?" he demanded.

"I have been to see the loot off," she said flippantly.

"The less you are seen, the better," he grumbled. "I told that ass, Mulberry, not to let the man catch a glimpse of you. Don't go in, I want to talk to you."

He was ill at ease and evidently found it difficult to make a beginning.

"You know, Kate, I am very fond of you," he said.

"You have every reason to be."

"I still have," he said.

"I am not so sure of that," she interrupted, "but go on."

"What do you mean by that?" he asked suspiciously.

"Go on," she demanded; "where does your fondness lead?"

"It leads to your marrying me," he said; "your uncle does not object and we will be married as soon as we reach South America."

"South America!" she stared at him. "So that is our destination, is it?" she said slowly. "And I am to marry you when we arrive, by arrangement with my uncle?"

"That's about the size of it," replied Gregori.

"And suppose I make other arrangements?"

"There are no other arrangements you can make," he said with easy confidence; "the fact is, Kate, that you have to drop these high and mighty manners of yours. We stood them very well because it paid us to stand them, I suppose. But we are all in the same boat—and shall be literally." He laughed aloud at the sally. "You hold some queer views, you know, and we can't afford to let you run loose."

She jerked up her head and turned abruptly away and would have left him but he caught her by the arm and pulled her back.

"When I say you must marry me," he said, "I mean just what I say."

"Have I a voice in this arrangement?" she asked, slowly disengaging her arm.

"You have a voice in it if you agree. You have no voice if you cut up rough."

"I see," she said. "I will think about it. This is not a decision which I can arrive at in a minute."

She went to her room and locked the door.

At five o'clock that evening her uncle came for her.

"Have you been to sleep?" he asked.

It was curious, she thought, how the manner and even the tone of these men had changed in the past few hours. She was so used to an attitude of deference, almost sycophantic, which they ordinarily displayed, that the change had come in the nature of a shock. And there was a change. Even her uncle had dropped his mask of good-nature and now treated her as a child, and a child that needed to be disciplined.

"I have been thinking," she said.

He grunted something and walked back with her to the office.

"This fellow, Michael Pretherston, has to be settled with. Do you understand that?"

"Yes," she replied.

"The cars will be on the road in half an hour and you and I will be the first to leave."

"Do you think so?"

"What do you mean?" he asked sharply. "I warn you, Kate, that I am not going to stand any monkey tricks from you."

To this she made no answer but pushed at the iron door that led to the meeting place and entered. To her surprise, Michael was present. In addition to his handcuffs his arms had been drawn back by the insertion of a short stick and secured with ropes. Gregori was sitting on the table and made no attempt to stand up, which was another piece of evidence that the hold she thought she had over these men had gone, if it had ever existed.

"Kate, you can use your persuasion on this fellow," said Gregori wearily; "it is his last chance. He has had a night to think it over and he's still obstinate."

The girl walked up to the detective.

"Michael," she said softly, "would nothing induce you to become—one of us?"

"Nothing," he said.

"Nothing that we could give you—that I could give you?"

He looked at her steadily.

"Nothing that I would take from you at that price," he said quietly.

"Don't you love your life?"

"'As dearly as any alive,'" quoted Michael.

"Don't you love anything in the world? Isn't there a girl?" she asked with a little break in her voice.

He nodded.

"There is a girl," he said and looked past her.

It seemed as though an icy hand had gripped her heart and for a while she could not frame the next question.

"Isn't she worth it?" she said, recovering her balance at last.

"She is worth many things," said Michael, "but not that."

She looked down at the floor.

"Poor girl," she said.

"Having tried sentiment," sneered Gregori, "we will now try a little practical argument—Pretherston you have got about an hour to live."

"I shall die in very bad company," said Michael with a wry face. "I had hoped at the least that I might die at the hands of a lawful hangman, as you will die. To be butchered by a cheap cutthroat half-breed is not a pleasant prospect."

"Damn you," said Gregori with passion and struck him in the face.

He would have repeated the blow but the girl slipped between them.

"Michael, you shall die in good company," she said in so matter of fact a tone that none of them realized immediately what she was saying; "that is, if you think I am good company."

"What do you mean?" gasped the Colonel.

"Why, I think you will kill me, too," she said with a serenity which to Michael was wonderful, "because I have betrayed you all."

Garon came flinging through the door.

"They haven't turned up," he screamed, "the wagons have gone."

"Gone," said Gregori huskily, "gone where?"

"I have just been on the 'phone," gasped the doctor; "they went to Lord Flanborough's. He has got the stuff."

There was a dead silence broken by the girl.

"They went to Lord Flanborough's," she repeated nodding her head. "I know that. I sent them there."

The tension was dreadful, no man spoke, then suddenly Gregori swung round on the girl and his face was the face of a devil.

"You!" he grated and leaped at her throat.

In that one moment all the scattered atoms of race, of pride, of kinship united in the distorted brain of Colonel Westhanger. His lean arms shot out and Gregori fell headlong to the floor.

"Back, you dog!" roared the old man.

It was the last word he uttered. There was a stinging report from the floor and Colonel Westhanger fell limply across the table with a bullet through his heart.

The girl who was half fainting with terror shrank back against the wall as Gregori rose, his still smoking pistol in his hand.

"You are a prophet," he said harshly; "you said you would die with Michael Pretherston and by God! you spoke the truth. Put them together," he said, "I want to think things out."

CHAPTER XIX
MICHAEL DEVELOPED A FONDNESS
FOR THE CRIMINAL CLASSES

The girl rose up from the chair where she had been sitting and crossed to where Michael lay on the floor where they had thrown him.

He looked up and smiled.

"Why, Kate," he said faintly, "always ... meeting ... you."

She sat down at his side and lifting his head laid it upon her lap.

"That's nice," he murmured.

"Why is it nice?" she asked curiously, "because I make a softer pillow than the stone?"

"That and something more," he answered.

"What more?" she insisted.

"Oh—because it is you, I suppose," he said vaguely.

Her lips twitched in amusement.

"But it would be just the same if it were any other person," she said, "wouldn't it, Mike?"

He looked up at her.

"Put your hand on my forehead," he said.

"Like this?"

She laid her soft palm against his throbbing head.

"What does that do?" she asked after a long interval of silence.

"It just makes my head better—don't ask a lot of questions."

Her fingers stole down his face and she gently pinched his nose.

"Oh, Kate," he murmured sleepily, "I was just going to sleep."

"Then don't," she said, "what is the use of dozing—you'll be dead soon and so will I."

She said this very calmly, in the same matter-of-fact tone in which she might have announced that there would be a roast chicken for dinner.

"I hope they kill you first," she said thoughtfully.

"You're a bloodthirsty little beggar," said Michael indignantly; "why do you wish that?"

She shrugged her shoulders and went on pressing back the hair from his forehead, never taking her eyes from his face.

"I don't know," she said at last, "only I want to make sure that you're gone and nobody else can have you—and then I shan't care."

He did not move; for a second she saw his eyelids quiver, but he lay still staring past her to the dingy roof of the engine house.

"Say that again," he whispered.

"Say what again? That I want you to be killed first?" she asked innocently.

"Mike," she said suddenly, "who was the girl?"

"Which girl?"

"You know," she said, "the girl you—care about."

"Why, you of course," he said in surprise.

Her hands slipped down from his forehead covering his eyes.

"Say that again," she mimicked.

"You," he repeated. "You see I am more obliging than you were."

"And you would not come in with us, not even for me?"

"Not even for you."

She did not speak for some time.

"How did you know we were here?" she asked.

"I knew you could be nowhere else," he said.

"You are an awfully arrogant young man, aren't you? Do you know how it was all done?"

He nodded.

"The train ran into the tunnel where you had a long motor-car mounted with flanged wheels and having three green lamps on the front and two red tail lamps behind. That was the 'train' which the signalman saw dashing through the rain and you had a horrible siren."

She laughed softly.

"It was terrible, wasn't it?" she admitted. "Do you remember that day you were in Crime Street? You heard it."

He recalled the uncanny sound which had then excited his curiosity.

"When you got to the level crossing gates, the car was lifted off the rail and went on to the road. It followed the tram lines for some distance where it turned into a convenient garage, which I suppose you had already arranged for?"

"That's right," she nodded.

"The train went no farther than the tunnel. It then backed on to a side track. Gregori had his Italian workmen ready and fixed up the buffer which had been dropped—you know the rest. The hole behind the buffer and the green scum—that was your idea, I suppose."

"It was cunning, wasn't it, and did you see the rust I made?"

"It is a fortunate thing you are dying young, Kate," he said; "you have a criminal mind."

"But I haven't a criminal mind," she protested; "it is a game, a sort of highly complicated jigsaw puzzle. Do you ever read detective stories?"

"Very seldom."

"But you have read them?" she persisted.

"I have read one or two," he confessed.

"Did the men who wrote those have criminal minds? It was a game to them. It was a game to me. I know it is all wrong, horribly wrong, but I never thought I should realize that much. I thought nothing would turn me."

"And what has turned you?" he asked.

She hesitated.

"I don't know what it is," she said shaking her head. "It is a curious feeling that I get when I meet one man in the world. A feeling that makes my heart turn to ice and makes me tremble. That is all it is, Mike—how do you think they are going to do it?"

Her thoughts had gone back to the approaching end.

"Heaven knows," said Michael. "I haven't any time to think of it. I am thinking of something else. Why do they keep the steam up in that engine?" he asked.

"It was Gregori's idea," she said; "he had the hole filled in to-day and the buffer taken down. He thought it might be useful to let the engine run on to the main line and block it. That is, if we had word that they were sending a lot of police down to search this part of the country."

"Here they are," said Michael; "help me to sit up."

She raised him to a sitting position as the door opened and a dim figure appeared silhouetted against the dusk. It struck a match and lit a candle and Dr. Garon was revealed. He placed the candle carefully upon the floor just behind the half-closed door and passed slowly over to where Michael lay.

"Well, my young sleuth," he said pleasantly, "the best of friends must part."

"Fortunately," said Michael, "I do not fall into the category of your friends."

The doctor hummed a little tune as he took a small leather case from his pocket.

"You have seen a hypodermic syringe before, I suppose?" he held up the tiny instrument. "I am going to give you a slight dope, which won't hurt you."

"One moment," said Michael, "do I understand that this dope is—final?"

The doctor bowed. From his heightened colour and his unsteady hand Michael guessed he had been drinking, either to give himself nerve for his task or to drown the memory of his misfortune.

"Very good," said Michael. He looked up at the girl and raised his face and Kate stooped and kissed him on the lips.

"That is it, is it?" said the doctor unpleasantly. "Gregori will be pleased."

He caught the manacled wrists of the prisoner and pulled back his sleeve and the girl's heart almost ceased to beat.

It was at that moment that the light went out.

"Who is there?" said the doctor releasing his grip on Michael's arm and turning quickly.

He took a groping step forward through the darkness.

"Who's there?" he said again and they heard a soft thud followed by the sound that a body might make, when it struck the ground.

Michael caught his breath. Suddenly a beam of light danced in the room and focused upon the prostrate figure of Dr. Garon.

"Got him," said a well-satisfied voice.

"Barr," whispered Michael, "where did you spring from?"

"I came through the door," said the voice. "Did you see it open. That is what knocked the candle over."

He flashed the light on his superior.

"They have got the bracelets on you, sir," he chuckled softly, took a key from his pocket and with a few deft turns released the other. His pocket knife finished the work.

Michael stretched his cramped limbs.

"I tried to get in last night but they had too many sentries—I couldn't come here or get back to a telephone. I have been lying on that hillside all last night and all to-day," said Detective-Sergeant Barr. "I dared not move until it was dark. I tell you, sir, I had a bit of a fright. I thought they would get away."

"Have you a revolver?" asked his chief.

The man slipped a weapon into his hand. They made their way softly back through the room where the engine was still smoking, through the little steel door of the office. It was empty save for a shrouded figure which lay beneath the table. There was a second door in the room. Michael tried this. It was locked. He heard voices and tapped at the door.

"Who is there?" said Gregori.

"Open the door," said Michael.

"Who is there?" demanded Gregori again.

"Open, in the name of the law," said Michael.

He heard a shuffle of feet and an oath and stood waiting, his pistol extended but the door did not open. A sudden silence came.

"Is there any way out of here?"

"There is a door leading into the shed where the engine is," said the girl. She was white and trembling ... that shrouded figure under the table had been the last straw.

Michael dashed out into the shed but it was too late.

As his feet crossed the foothold a bullet struck the steel door and ricochetted to the roof. In the dim light offered by an oil flare he saw Mulberry and Stockmar hoisting the inanimate figure of Dr. Garon to the cab of the engine. He fired twice and Cunningham stumbled but was dragged into the cab. Then with a mighty "schuff!" which reverberated through the building the engine began to move toward the closed door. It gathered speed in the dozen yards or so it had to traverse and then with a crash it struck the gate, splintering and sending it flying.

Michael flew the length of the shed and arrived at the outer gates in time to see the engine disappearing round the edge of the bluff. Barr was at his side and the two men stood helpless, as their enemies gradually receded into the grey dusk.

"There is a telephone here," said Michael quickly, "but it is probably laid for their own purpose."

"I left my motor-bike on the top of the hill somewhere, sir," said Barr.

"Get on to it," said Michael.

He stood listening to the sound of the locomotive going faster and faster. A hand touched his timidly.

"Did they get away?"

He slipped his arm round the girl.

"I am afraid they have," he said.

He was turning back to the shed when the roar of an explosion set the building trembling.

"What was that?" whispered the girl.

They walked back to the end of the bluff. There was no need for him to speculate as to the direction from whence the explosion had come, for a bright red glow two miles away illuminated the whole countryside.

"Something has happened to the engine," he said.

He did not know till an hour later that running at full speed the Atlantic had dashed into a down goods train and that the blaze he witnessed was the blaze of a burning petroleum tank which the wrecked Atlantic had crushed in its death flurry.

"We have not been able to recognize any of them," said T. B. "Do you think Kate Westhanger was with them?"

"Kate Westhanger is no more," said Michael gravely, and he spoke the truth for Kate Pretherston was at that moment on her way to France, where her husband intended joining her just as soon as his resignation was accepted.

"But why give up the work, Michael?" said T. B.

"I found, sir," said Michael, "that it was sapping my moral qualities."

"Your moral qualities?" said his puzzled chief. "I didn't know that you had any. What particular form did the sapping take?"

"I found, sir," said Michael, "that I was developing a fondness for the criminal classes."

THE END

THE FILMING OF KATE
By Ed Hulse

Kate Plus Ten was one of the earliest Edgar Wallace crime novels issued in hard covers by an American publisher, its 1917 printing by Boston-based Small Maynard & Company predating the British first edition by two years. Arguably the first of its kind—a thrilling "caper" story featuring an attractive young woman as criminal mastermind—*Kate* also enjoys the distinction of the first Wallace yarn captured on celluloid by an American motion-picture firm.

In early 1920, when screen rights to *Kate Plus Ten* were purchased by Carl Laemmle's Universal Film Manufacturing Company, Wallace had already seen four of his novels brought to the screen—rather poorly, if contemporary reviews are to be believed—by British producers. Likely he was delighted to have one of his thrillers made by America's most prolific film factory.

Producer-director Stuart Paton, an old Universal standby best known for his 1916 production *Twenty Thousand Leagues Under the Sea* (the first major motion picture to employ underwater cinematography), commissioned a scenario from Wallace Clifton, who had scripted some 80 short subjects and feature films over the last eight years. The story's locale was changed from London and surrounding villages to an unnamed American city and its suburbs. Much of the film was lensed at Universal City, Laemmle's 260-acre facility in the San Fernando Valley just over the historical Cahuenga Pass. Cinematographer Harold Janes was much praised for his camerawork, especially superb night photography lit for maximum atmosphere.

Production began in mid-August, with the picture's working title listed in movie-industry trade journals as *Kate Plus Ten*. By mid-September the footage was being welded into a five-reel feature film now titled *Wanted at Headquarters*. The final cut ran to some 4,560 feet mounted on five reels, for a running time of 60 to 70 minutes depending on the speed of projection (which varied considerably in those days, with many operators still manning hand-cranked projectors).

Although *Wanted at Headquarters*, like nearly 90 percent of American silent movies, is a lost film, we know it was generally faithful to Edgar Wallace's novel by the synopsis printed in Universal's house organ, *The Moving Picture Weekly*:

Michael Pretherson (Leonard C. Shumway), independently rich and of social position, has a natural aptitude for criminology and his exploits as an amateur detective arouse the wonder of his friends. He is engaged to Moya (Agnes Emerson), daughter of capitalist George Flanbaugh (William Marion).

Only 20 years of age, brainy and beautiful Kate Westhanger (Eva Novak) is the leader of a criminal organization in which her uncle, Colonel Westhanger (Harry Carter), is one of the guiding spirits. She has the organizing genius of a Napoleon and is planning the most sensational haul ever—that of holding up a special, burglar-proof train carrying 20,000 pounds in gold ingots in which George Flanbaugh is interested. To carry out her purpose, she acts as Flanbaugh's secretary, and her identity would have been kept secret had not Pretherson seen her there and disclosed it. To set him off guard Kate goes to his rooms later and tells him she has reformed. She is seen there by Moya and the first breach between Moya and Pretherson starts.

The big robbery is pulled off in a daring night-time attack on the train. It is a success and Kate is elated, but her elation turns to anger when her uncle tells her that he and the gang have had "enough" and intend beating it with the gold to South America to live in luxury. As a bit of revenge, Kate changes the message given to the truckmen currently holding the stolen ingots, which are returned to Flanbaugh. She herself is anxious to continue the operations of the gang just for thrills, and her uncle's decision has infuriated her.

Pretherson, seeking to trace the robbers, is caught by the gang. When the crooks discover Kate's treachery they prepare to kill her with him. However, the police, who have been shadowing Pretherson, interrupt the attempted murders and kill most of the gang during the ensuing fight.

Kate realizes now that she loves Pretherson, and her former desire for a criminal life evaporates. She wants to go straight. Moya releases the detective from his promise to marry her, and Pretherson then asks Kate to marry him. She accepts readily, but their new-found happiness is threatened by the sudden reappearance of Tommy Carter (George Chesebro), the only gang member to have escaped. He has always had designs on Kate himself and now, with hatred in his heart, plans to kill her rather than lose her to another man. Pretherson intervenes at the critical moment and overcomes Carter, whose better nature asserts itself after he calms down. Kate and her husband are delighted when they hear of his reformation.

The plot of *Kate Plus Ten* was generally adhered to, although the book's principal heavy, Gregori, was omitted, with some of his narrative function assigned to Tommy Carter. The main plot device, the ingenious hi-jacking of the gold train, reached the screen virtually unchanged and was favorably mentioned by industry reviewers who otherwise were not overly impressed with Stuart Paton's effort.

Wid Gunning of the popular *Wid's Daily* had this to say: "Director Paton has done this end of his work with much skill. The hold-up of the gold train and the subsequent blowing-up of the two engines are exciting sequences. . . .On the other hand, the story is just about as inconsistent as a story could be. And running it a close second in this respect are the various important characters. Characterization is not looked for in a melodrama, to be sure, but when a character at certain points turns completely about face and starts working contrary to its previous course without any explanation whatsoever, the entire action is likely to falter as it does here. Consistency is the least that can be expected of melodramatic puppets."

Motion Picture News critic Lawrence Reid also commented favorably on the artistically illuminated scenes of the nighttime train robbery while finding fault with plotting, motivation, and characterization. "The action presents a good deal of a puzzle," he wrote, "and the motive of the heroine, the master mind of the group, is never explained. Nor the reason why she should be double-crossed. The picture is based upon the formula of a girl destined to go straight because of sentimental feeling and the fact that she hasn't been trusted by her cohorts. The director has failed to catch the psychology of the characterization."

Moving Picture World's Robert C. McElravy said the film "is like a serial in certain respects," going on to explain that "the characters are represented by an agreeable cast, but after the first introductions they seem to lack individuality." McElravy was the only trade-paper reviewer to make notice by Eva Novak. "[She] is pleasant to look at and moves with assurance, but there is nothing about this story that draws out her best work. The action of the piece is largely to blame for this, as it at first tends to the narrative style and later even the melodramatic events are sketched in too lightly to make any great impression."

Venerable show-business journal *Variety* delivered the *coup de grace* without mincing words: "A reviewer on this paper in a resumé of a Universal production some time ago declared after looking it over it was an utter waste of time. . . .The same conclusion is arrived at after observing *Wanted at Headquarters*. There is nothing at all instructive in the picture. At best it is a poor type of melodrama . . . translating to the screen a story which offers a climax with a gang of thieves holding up a steel-constructed, gold-filled train. The supposedly big punch follows when the heroine, an accomplice of the gang [who is] double-crossed, turns the tables and is rescued in the nick of time by the ever momentous arrival of the police."

Its poor critical reception notwithstanding, the first screen version of *Kate Plus Ten* found favor with undiscriminating picture patrons, especially those in small towns and working-class neighborhoods in big cities, who enjoyed crude melodramas as long as they offered a sufficiency of action and thrills. (This was the same market for pulp magazines, which by this time were printing Wallace's yarns as fast as they could obtain them.) The average Universal five-reeler of this period was made for $35,000 or less, and although Carl Laemmle's company didn't have its own national theater chain, it sold product to so many independently owned picture houses that most Universal films were assured of turning a profit.

Eva Novak never became a big star, but she worked consistently in such film fare and was frequently teamed with such larger-than-life celluloid daredevils as Tom Mix, Buck Jones, William Russell, and Richard Talmadge. Lost in the shuffle during the transition from silents to talkies, she made just a handful of appearances in the Thirties before returning to the screen in the post–World War II years as a bit player. Novak toiled in movies and TV shows through the mid-Sixties. Her *Wanted at Headquarters* co-star, Leonard C. Shumway, subsequently essayed a dozen or so leading roles before sliding into supporting-player status; during the sound era he was known as Lee Shumway but rarely won featured billing. Nonetheless, he appeared in over 200 talkies before retiring in 1953.

Kate Plus Ten reached movie screens again in 1938, this time under its original title and in its country of origin. British moviegoers loved thrillers involving trains, as demonstrated by the successes of *The Wrecker* (1928) and its remake, *Seven Sinners* (1936); Alfred Hitchcock's *Number Seventeen* (1932) and *The Lady Vanishes* (1938); and multiple film adaptations of Arthur Ripley's popular play, *The Ghost Train*. Independent producer Richard Wainwright dusted off Wallace's novel and assigned it to playwright and scriptwriter Jeffrey Dell, who updated the property and gave it a patina of sophistication.

New York-born Genevieve Tobin, a former child actress who debuted in films as Little Eva in a 1910 production of *Uncle Tom's Cabin*, was nearly 40 when she accepted the role of Kate Westhanger in Wainwright's remake. Having played stylish socialites in most of her Thirties films, Tobin was not only too old but entirely too polished for the part. Her leading man, Cambridge-educated stage star Jack Hulbert, had been Britain's top male box-office draw as recently as 1934 and still enjoyed tremendous popularity. Noel Madison, another American actor temporarily working in British movies, played Gregori, a Wallace-created heavy anglicized in *Wanted at Headquarters*.

Interiors were staged and shot at the Shepperton Studios in Surrey. Train sequences dominating the film's final third were taken along the main rail line between Bath and Westbury, and on a branch line through Limpley Stoke and Camerton, with the Monkton Coombe station in Somerset used for the scene in which a locomotive crashed through wooden shed doors.

Genevieve Tobin's Kate was less the ingénue and more the female Napoleon of crime imagined by Edgar Wallace, her obvious worldliness being an asset in that respect. Her exchanges with Hulbert's Michael Pemberton (changed from Pretherson) bristled with snappy dialogue, much of it written by the male star himself. The supporting players— including Francis L. Sullivan as Lord Flamborough, Arthur Wontner (an excellent Sherlock Holmes in British movies of the Thirties) as Colonel Westhanger, Leo Genn as Doctor Gurdon, and Googie Withers as Lady Moya—were uniformly well cast and extremely effective. Director Reginald Denham eschewed heavy-footed melodrama in favor of a breezy, lighthearted tone. His handling of the actors suggested nobody was taking the business at hand very seriously. Even deep-dyed villain Noel Madison seemed less menacing than usual.

Coming in at a crisp 81 minutes, *Kate Plus Ten* was distributed by General Film and released throughout the U.K. on August 1, 1938. It fared considerably better with homegrown critics than *Wanted at Headquarters*. Retitled *Queen of Crime* and released in America in February 1941, the film was not as enthusiastically received. *Motion Picture Daily*'s critic called it "an improbable melodrama which concerns Miss Tobin, as a gang leader directing a big gold robbery, and a Scotland Yard detective, Jack Hulbert, who strives to be funny on every occasion, but without marked success. Moreover, many of his speeches are not carried clearly enough, resulting in what sounds like a British version of Broadway double talk." That was a typical notice. Considered the U.K. equivalent of a "B" picture—of which there were a surfeit in 1941—*Queen of Crime* got relatively few bookings stateside and was promptly forgotten.

However, movie producers weren't done with Edgar Wallace's old thriller. *Kate Plus Ten* was pulled off the shelf one more time, in 1966, and updated beyond recognition as *The Trygon Factor*, a Britain-West

Germany co-production filmed in Shepperton Studios and starring Stewart Granger, Susan Hamshire, and Robert Morley. Practically the only plot element to survive from the original source material was the female head of a crime ring. But the "Kate" character became an elderly matron played by British actress Cathleen Nesbitt, at that time familiar to American audiences for her regular guest-star appearances in Hollywood-filmed TV series. A modest hit in West Germany, where a whole string of Wallace adaptations had been produced in recent years, *Trygon Factor* failed to achieve much success in the United States, where it was distributed by Warner Bros.-Seven Arts. *Variety* called it "a complicated Scotland Yard whodunit which the spectator will find it taxing to follow," adding: "Script is pocketed with story loopholes and attempts to confuse, plus certain motivations and bits of business impossible to fathom."

To date more than 200 feature films, TV shows, and cliffhanger serials have been adapted from the works of Edgar Wallace, the first of them more than a hundred years ago and the most recent—a French-made version of *The Daffodil Mystery*—in 2014. Few modern authors have demonstrated such cinematic staying power. Though the vast majority of his output remains unavailable to today's readers (a situation Stark Press is attempting to redress, one volume at a time), Edgar Wallace still lingers in the fringes of popular culture. Let's hope his influence continues to be felt, one way or another.

—October 2016
Morris Plains, NJ

EDGAR WALLACE BIBLIOGRAPHY

Series

Four Just Men

The Four Just Men (1905)

The Council of Justice (1908)

The Just Men of Cordova (1917)

The Law of the Four Just Men (1921; aka US as Again the Three Just Men)

The Three Just Men (1926)

Again the Three Just Men (1929; aka Again the Three & US as The Law of the Three Just Men)

Commissioner Sanders

Sanders of the River (1911; stories)

The People of the River (1912; stories)

The River of Stars (1913; novel)

Bosambo of the River (1914; stories)

The Keepers of the King's Peace (1917; stories)

Sandi the Kingmaker (1922; stories)

Sanders (1926; aka US as Mr. Commissioner Sanders; stories)

Again Sanders (1928; stories)

Lieutenant Bones

Bones (1915; stories)

Lieutenant Bones (1918; stories)

Bones in London (1921; stories)

Bones of the River (1923; stories)

J. G. Reeder

Room 13 (1924)

The Mind of Mr J. G. Reeder (1925; aka US as The Murder Book of J.G. Reeder)

Terror Keep (1927)

Red Aces (1929)

The Guv'nor and Other Stories (1932; aka US as Mr. Reeder Returns)

Sergeant Elk

The Nine Bears (1910; aka The Cheaters & The Other Man; revised as Silinski—Master Criminal, 1930)

The Fellowship of the Frog (1925)

The Joker (1926; aka The Park Lane Mystery & US as The Colossus, 1932)

The Twister (1928)

The India-Rubber Men (1929; aka The Pool)

White Face (1930)

Educated Evans

Educated Evans (1924; stories)

More Educated Evans (1926; stories)

Good Evans (1927; stories)

Ringer

The Gaunt Stranger (1925; aka Police Work, US as The Ringer)

Again The Ringer (1929; aka US as The Ringer Returns; stories)

Smithy & Nobby
Smithy (1905)
Smithy Abroad (1909)
Smithy and the Hun (1915)
Nobby (1916)

Supt. Minter
Big Foot (1927)
The Lone House Mystery (1929;
    aka The Lone House)

Tam of the Scouts
Tam o' the Scoots (1918)
The Fighting Scouts (1919)

Novels
Angel Esquire (1908)
The Duke in the Suburbs (1909)
Captain Tatham of Tatham
    Island (1909; also published as
    Eve's Island; revised as The
    Island Of Galloping Gold
    1916)
Private Selby (1912)
The Fourth Plague (1913; aka
    The Red Hand)
Grey Timothy (1913; aka Pallard
    the Punter)
The Man Who Bought London
    (1915)
The Melody of Death (1915)
1925—The Story of a Fatal Peace
    (1915)
A Debt Discharged (1916)
Tomb of T'Sin (1916)
The Secret House (1917)
The Clue of the Twisted Candle
    (1918)
Down-Under Donovan (1918)
The Strange Lapses of Larry
    Loman (1918; serialized only)

Those Folk of Bulboro (1918)
The Adventures of Heine (1919)
The Green Rust (1919)
Kate Plus 10 (1919)
The Man Who Knew (1919)
The Daffodil Mystery (1920; aka
    The Daffodil Murder)
Jack o' Judgment (1920)
The Book of All Power (1921)
The Day of Uniting (1921)
The Angel of Terror (1922; aka
    The Destroying Angel)
The Crimson Circle (1922)
Flying Fifty-five (1922)
Mr. Justice Maxwell (1922; aka
    Take-a-Chance Anderson)
The Valley of Ghosts (1922)
Captains of Souls (1922)
The Clue of the New Pin (1923)
The Green Archer (1923)
The Missing Million (1923)
The Dark Eyes of London (1924;
    aka The Croakers)
Double Dan (1924; US as Diana
    of Kara-Kara)
The Face in the Night (1924; aka
    The Diamond Men & The
    Ragged Princess)
The Sinister Man (1924)
The Three Oak Mystery (1924)
The Blue Hand (1925; aka
    Beyond Recall)
The Daughters of the Night
    (1925)
King by Night (1925)
The Strange Countess (1925)
The Avenger (1926; aka The
    Hairy Arm)
Barbara on Her Own (1926)
The Black Abbot (1926)
A Debt Discharged (1926)

The Door with Seven Locks (1926)

The Man from Morocco (1926; aka Soul in Shadows & US as The Black)

The Million Dollar Story (1926)

The Northing Tramp (1926; aka The Tramp)

Penelope of the "Polyantha" (1926)

The Square Emerald (1926; aka The Woman)

The Terrible People (1926; aka The Gallows' Hand)

We Shall See! (1926; US as The Gaol-Breakers)

The Yellow Snake (1926; aka The Black Tenth)

Flat 2 (1927)

The Feathered Serpent (1927; aka Inspector Wade & Inspector Wade and the Feathered Serpent)

The Forger (1927; aka The Counterfeiter)

Hand of Power (1927; aka The Proud Sons of Ragusa)

The Man Who Was Nobody (1927)

The Mixer (1927)

Mr Justice Maxwell (1927)

Number Six (1927; novella)

The Squeaker (1927; aka The Sign of the Leopard & US as The Squealer)

The Traitor's Gate (1927)

The Brigand (1928)

The Double (1928)

The Flying Squad (1928)

The Gunner (1928; aka Gunman's Bluff)

A King by Night (1928)

Four Square Jane (1929; aka The Fourth Square)

The Golden Hades (1929; aka Stamped in Gold & The Sinister Yellow Sign)

The Green Ribbon (1929)

The Iron Grip (1929)

Planetoid 127 (1929)

The Calendar (1930)

The Clue of the Silver Key (1930; aka The Silver Key)

The Day of Uniting (1930)

Down Under Donovan (1930)

The Feathered Serpent (1930)

The Hand of Power (1930)

John Flack (1930)

The Lady of Ascot (1930)

The Thief in the Night (1930)

The Coat of Arms (1931; aka The Arranways Mystery)

The Devil Man (1931; aka Sinister Street, Silver Steel & The Life and Death of Charles Peace)

The Man at the Carlton (1931; aka The Mystery of Mary Grier)

On the Spot: Violence and Murder in Chicago (1931)

The Frightened Lady (1932; aka The Mystery of the Frightened Lady)

When the Gangs Came to London (1932; aka Scotland Yard's Yankee Dick & The Gangsters Come to London)

The Green Pack (1933; play novelization by Robert George Curtis)

The Man Who Changed His
  Name (1935; play novelization
  by Robert George Curtis)
The Mouthpiece (1935;
  screenplay novelization by
  Robert George Curtis)
Sanctuary Island (1936;
  screenplay novelization by
  Robert George Curtis)
Smoky Cell (1936; play
  novelization by Robert George
  Curtis)
The Table (1936; screenplay
  novelization by Robert George
  Curtis)
The Road to London (1986)

Story Collections
Admirable Carfew (1914)
Adventures of Heine (1919)
The Books of Bart (1923)
Chick (1923)
The Black Avons (1925)
The Brigand (1927)
The Mixer (1927)
Elegant Edward (1928)
The Orator (1928)
Thief in the Night (1928)
The Big Four (1929; aka Crooks
  of Society)
The Black (1929; aka
  Blackmailers I Have Foiled)
The Cat Burglar (1929)
Circumstantial Evidence (1929)
Fighting Snub Reilly (1929)
For Information Received (1929)
The Ghost of Down Hill & The
  Queen of Sheba's Belt (1929)
The Governor of Chi-Foo (1929)
The Iron Grip (1929)
The Lady of Little Hell (1929)

The Little Green Man (1929)
The Lone House Mystery (1929)
The Prison-Breakers (1929)
The Reporter (1929)
The Terror (1929)
Killer Kay (1930)
The Lady Called Nita (1930)
Mrs William Jones and Bill
  (1930)
The Stretelli Case and Other
  Mystery Stories (1930)
Sergeant Sir Peter (1932; aka
  Sergeant Dunn, C.I.D.)
The Steward (1932)
The Last Adventure (1934)
Nig-nog and Other Humorous
  Stories (1934)
Woman from the East (1934)
The Edgar Wallace Reader of
  Mystery and Adventure (1943)
The Undisclosed Client (1963)
The Man Who Married His
  Cook (1976)
The Sooper and Others (1984)
The Death Room: Strange and
  Startling Stories (1986)
Winning Colors: The Racing
  Stories of Edgar Wallace (1991)

Omnibus Editions
The New Mammoth Mystery
  Book (1920)
Four Complete Novels (1925)
Three Complete Novels by Edgar
  Wallace (1925)
Fourty-Eight Short Stories (1929)
The Scotland Yard Book of
  Edgar Wallace (1932)
Edgar Wallace Foursome (1933)
The Edgar Wallace Reader of
  Mystery and Adventure (1943)

The Edgar Wallace Souvenir Book: Four Complete Novels (1950)
Selected Novels (1985)

Plays and Screenplays
African Millionaire (1904; play, pub 1972)
Forest of Happy Dreams (1910; play, pub 1935)
Dolly Cutting Herself (1911; play, unpublished)
The Manager's Dream (1914; musical play)
Nurse and Martyr (1915; play, filmed same year)
The Four Just Men (1921; filmed screenplay)
M'Lady (1921; play, unpublished)
Double Dan (1926; play, unpublished)
The Mystery of Room 45 (1926; play, unpublished)
A Perfect Gentleman (1927; play, unpublished)
The Terror (1927; play, filmed 1928)
The Traitor's Gate (1927; play, filmed as The Yellow Mask, 1930)
The Man Who Changed His Name (1928; play, screenplay 1934)
The Mark of the Frog (1928; filmed screenplay)
The Ringer (1928; filmed screenplay 1928 & 1931; play, 1929)
The Squeaker (1928; play, filmed screenplay, 1930)

The Valley of the Ghosts (1928; filmed screenplay)
Persons Unknown (1929; play, novelized as White Face, filmed 1932)
Prince Gabby (1929; filmed screenplay)
Red Aces (1929; filmed screenplay)
The Calendar (1929; play, pub 1932)
Criminal at Large (1930; filmed screenplay, pub 1934)
The Mouthpiece (1930: play, novelized by Robert George Curtis, 1935)
Should a Doctor Tell? (1930; filmed screenplay)
Smoky Cell (1930; play, novelized by Robert George Curtis, 1936)
To Oblige a Lady (1930; play, filmed 1931)
The Case of the Frightened Lady (1931; play, pub 1932)
The Old Man (1931; play, filmed screenplay)
The Green Pack (1932; play, filmed 1934)
Hound of the Baskervilles (1932; filmed screenplay)
King Kong (1932; filmed screenplay, though only parts of it were used; novelization by Delos W. Lovelace, 1932)
The Lad (1932; play, filmed 1935)
Sanctuary Island (date unknown; screenplay novelized by Robert George Curtis, 1936)

The Table (date unknown;
   screenplay novelized by Robert
   George Curtis, 1936)

Poetry
The Mission That Failed (1898)
War and Other Poems (1900)
Writ in Barracks (1900)

Non fiction
Unofficial Despatches (1901)
Famous Scottish Regiments
   (1914)
Field Marshall Sir John French
   and His Campaigns (1914)
Heroes All: Gallant Deeds of the
   War (1914)
The Standard History of the War
   4 Vols. (1914-1916)
The War of the Nations (1914;
   with William le Queux)

Kitchener's Army and the
   Territorial Forces: The Full
   Story of a Great Achievement
   (1915)
Famous Men and Battles of the
   British Empire (1917)
Real Shell-Man: The Story of
   Chetwynd of Chilwell (1919)
This England (1927; stories)
People: Autobiography (1926)
The Trial of Patrick Herbert
   Mahon (1928)
Great Stories of Real Life (1930;
   with William le Queux)
The Trial of the Seddons and
   Other True Tales of Suspense
   (1930)
My Hollywood Diary (1932)

9 781944 520151